The Unforgotten

～

Ava Bradley

Pink Pixel Publishing

Other books by Ava Bradley

Stories with a hint of magic
One Snowy Night Before Christmas
Once Upon a Christmas Carol
Kiss Me Before Dawn
Valentine Bride

Historical Romance
Once Upon a Midnight Sea
Lord of Darkness
Lady Outlaw

Romantic Suspense
August Unknown
The Lost Finder
Edge of Midnight
Last Rights

Deadly Sight Series
Deadly Vengeance
Her Darkest Fear
Her Dangerous Desires
Her Deepest Secret
Her Dying Breath

The Unforgotten

Jessica Harding didn't think her life could get any worse.

And then it did.

Late to her senior prom because her falling-down-drunk mother knocked out a tooth, Jess finally arrives at the school gymnasium to find it eerily empty. Her best friend and the only person on earth who cares about her has disappeared, and Jess is about to lose her mind. A few other stragglers show up late, but at first, none of them believe her when Jess insists something bad has happened. In the same breath, they're too scared to venture back into the school to find a phone, and the only one courageous enough to go inside with her is quiet and nerdy Will Taylor.

It's both a curse and a blessing when Will arrives late to the prom to discover all his friends have vanished; all of them except for his life-long crush Jessica Harding. At first, Will and the four other students who arrive late believe there's a logical explanation, but when FBI helicopters descend on their sleepy town within twenty minutes, they realize something is terribly wrong. Nevertheless, even after hours of questioning by grim and disapproving authorities, when Jess wants to sneak into the gymnasium to look for clues, Will is all-in. After all, life in a federal prison is a small price to pay for a night of sleuthing with brave and gorgeous Jess, who's finally noticed he exists.

PART ONE

Ten Years Earlier

Jessica Harding ignored her mother's bellowing and leaned closer to the small mirror on her dressing table, carefully applying mascara. She didn't usually wear makeup, but Shreya had insisted she do her hair and makeup to complement the fantastic prom dress they'd spent the last two months sewing.

The hard truth was she couldn't afford to buy a prom dress. It was either make one herself, or wear an old black cocktail dress that had been her mother's uniform at Harrah's.

Shreya knew the truth—Jess's second-hand clothes made it obvious to the naked eye—but Shreya never brought up her friend's pathetic financial state. She knew, her teachers knew, her schoolmates knew—hell, *everybody* knew Jess's mom was on welfare. If they didn't, the rusting mobile home in Kileyville's eyesore of a trailer park told her pitiful story.

"Hey," June barked from the doorway.

Jessica caught her mother's frown in the mirror as she gave Jess a hard once-over. Obviously, she'd forgotten it was prom night.

"I need you to go to the Cask 'N Flask and get me some cigarettes."

"I can't."

"You can if you want to drive my car tonight."

Jessica paused over a long heartbeat. "I don't."

"Oh, that's right," June snarled. "Your rich friend sprung for a limo for you and the other mooches."

Jess closed her mascara tube and gave herself another dusting of blush if only to continue ignoring her mother. In truth, she had too much on already. But ignoring her mother was Jess's favorite guilty pleasure and a much more effective way of annoying her than taking the bait for another shouting match, which June seemed to love.

"You want to go out tonight? Then go get me some cigarettes. You got time if you go now."

Like I need your permission. "Why don't you go?"

June shoved off the doorframe and pointed her finger. "They don't let me in no more on account of you told them not to sell me booze."

She swiveled on her chair and faced her mother. The cool white gown slid over her skin like water. Jess was tempted to ask if the real reason she was banned from the store was the tantrum she'd thrown for being refused alcohol, knocking over a potato chip rack at the register and stomping on the bags.

"Where'd you get the vodka, then?" Jess asked instead.

Tonight was not the night to start a fight. Tonight was prom, which marked the first day of the rest of her life. Her eighteenth birthday had been two weeks ago, and she'd essentially graduated and had nothing more to do than show up at the ceremony.

She and her friends had been planning this night for months.

Jess had been planning her departure from Kileyville even longer.

"You know, I don't have to let you live here," June said, as if reading her mind. "You're eighteen."

Jess swiveled back toward the mirror. "Okay."

June uncrossed her arms and planted her fists on her hips, as if buying cigarettes was the ticket to staying in this sorry excuse for a home. Tonight's ticket, anyway. Every day, some new order or demand carried the heavy threat.

Do the dishes or get out. Drive me to the store or don't come back. Buy me booze or pay the rent.

Jess wondered why she continued to try manipulating her this way when it never worked. After so long, her mother's desire to always fight was nothing but exhausting.

"So when are you leaving?"

"When would you like me to?" She dabbed on her Broadway Lights frost pink lipstick, the one luxury she had allowed Shreya to buy her for her birthday. *Because I love these lips so much,* Shreya had told her.

"Don't think I don't know you been packing your shit. Are you gonna go live with your *special* friend?"

Jess sighed inwardly. "What do you care where I go?"

Is the alcoholic parolee embarrassed that her sober daughter is friends with a lesbian, or is it because Shreya is from India?

2

June turned and stalked down the narrow hallway, muttering something derogatory under her breath. The moment Jess had learned that it irritated her mother more than anything to be ignored, she'd become an expert in vague, dismissive answers.

Her mother loved a hot, knock-down, drag-out fight, but she hated Jess's disinterest.

A brawl was not happening tonight. Besides, Jess didn't want to be the main topic of gossip in their trailer park—*again.* The mobile home was like an aluminum can. Neighbors could hear each other fart.

A crash kabonged from the other room, followed by a loud thud. Her mother shrieked and then let out an unholy wail. Jess sighed and capped her lipstick. She stared at her reflection in the mirror. *Not tonight. Not tonight. Not tonight.*

"Ah God, Jessie..."

She stood and shimmied the wrinkly material down her hips. The Wonder bra she'd borrowed from Molly made it look like she actually had a bosom, which maybe wasn't the best idea—Brendan already had the wrong idea about tonight. She wished she hadn't agreed to be his date. But Cliff Barnes, stacked water polo captain and overall blond dreamboat, had already asked Sara Mailer, and Jess didn't want to be the only one without a date.

She found June face down, wedged between their outdated TV and the bookcase. She flailed like a tipped cow that couldn't get a leg under itself to stand up.

"What did you do?"

"Go'thamit, help me!"

"But you look so funny like that."

"You're a real comedian."

"How did you even get in there?"

"I was tryin' to open the window, and I slipped."

Jess looked at the pint of vodka on the coffee table. It was two-thirds dead, and no orange juice in sight. *Slipped, nothing.*

"Help me, dammit."

Still wearing flip-flops, Jess inched in and grasped her mother's hand. When she pulled her mother out of the narrow slot, Jess gasped.

"Oh my God." Blood curtained down her mother's chin and a dark gap

3

loomed in the front of her mouth. June had really done it this time. *Of course.*

She hauled her mother to her feet. June swayed and almost went down again. She touched her mouth.

"I knocked my fuckin' tooth out." At *fucking tooth,* blood sprayed from her upper lip.

All over the front of Jess's dress.

She jerked her hand free and stared down at the beautiful creation that had taken so many weeks to make, without a pattern, into an exact replica of a red-carpet gown Jess had seen on the cover of a magazine. No, an even prettier version with its sweetheart neckline and two Goodwill-found rhinestone embellishments glinting at the gathered straps.

"Jess, I—"

Jessica slapped her.

Her mother blinked three times. She brought a hand to her cheek and stared back with complete shock, mouth hanging open, that bloody gap right in the middle of her mouth. She gawped like a fish, but Jess leaned in and pointed a threatening finger.

"You couldn't let me have just one night where your drinking isn't my disaster."

She stalked back to her room and threw the flimsy hollow-core door shut. The slam wasn't anywhere near satisfying. Jess dropped into the chair at her tiny vanity and stared at the damage. They were small droplets, mostly a mist, but they turned the white gown into a murder scene.

Outside, her mother slumped against the door.

"Jess." Thump. "I'm sorry."

Two more slow thumps, which Jessica recognized as her drunken knock.

"Jess, please. I'll make it up to you. I promise."

Now comes the feeble apology stage, Jess thought. *Shortly followed by the sorrowful "I love you," stage, and immediately after, the furious "You never loved me back," stage.*

"My tooth. Jessie!"

God, she hated being called Jessie.

She sighed at her reflection. The urge to cry rose and then vanished in a split second. She felt no anger, no resentment. Just disappointment. She had expected something to ruin tonight; if not this, then something else. She was just...sick and tired of it all.

This is the last straw. I really am leaving this time.

"Pleathe, Jessie. It hurths."

She pushed from the chair and pulled open the door, stalking past her mother without a word. She picked up the tattered notebook on the kitchen counter and flipped through for Dr. Patterson's number. At this time on Friday, his office was definitely closed, but Jess knew there was an answering service for emergencies. She glanced at the small clock on top of the TV. Seven-twenty-five. Shreya and Brendan would be here any minute.

"Exchange."

"Um, hi. This is Jessica Harding. Would you be able to page Dr. Patterson for me? My mother's knocked out a tooth, and it's really bad."

June slinked into the living room and sat on the couch, crying silently. Tears streamed down her face and snot bubbled at her nose.

"Thank you," she mouthed. She picked up the pint bottle and swigged the remaining vodka in a single mouthful.

Her mother was already three sheets to the wind. Jess would drive her there, but June was walking home.

Nothing is going to interrupt this night.

Outside, a shrill of brakes and a low, throaty rumble announced the limo. She saw it pull to a stop through the kitchen window, black and magical, as out of place in the ratty trailer park as a show poodle in a pig pen.

Dr. Patterson came on the line. Like most people in town, he didn't like her mother but seemed to like Jess well enough. She assumed a good amount of it was pity. He agreed to meet her at his office to see if the tooth could be saved.

"Put it in a cup of milk," he told her.

"We'll see you in fifteen minutes." Jess hung up and went to the door. "Stay right there. Don't get into any more trouble."

Outside, she trotted to the limo.

The rear window powered down. Concern filled Shreya's pretty face. The deep cranberry dress that had probably cost more than Jess's trailer looked gorgeous against her mocha skin. Her glittering necklace was made of real diamonds, a fact Shreya's mother had announced as if it were necessary to explain to someone like Jess that *they* did not wear *rhinestones*.

"What's wrong? Oh my God, Jess, your dress!"

"My mom knocked out her tooth. I have to take her to the dentist." She didn't mention it was Dr. Patterson, who mostly treated Medicaid patients.

"What—*now*?" Shreya glanced at the trailer. "What about the dance?"

The roof slid open and Brendan stood up through it. "Heya, gorgeous. You coming, or what?"

"I'll meet you guys there."

"No, Jess! We'll wait for you."

"I don't mind waiting," Molly offered. "Better fashionably late than on time."

"Don't you dare." Jess leaned closer to the window. Inside the mobile home, June was bellowing for her again. She hoped her friends couldn't hear the drunkenness in her voice. "It'll just take a few minutes. I'm going to leave her there and come right home and change. I'll just ditch the car at school, and then we'll go out afterward like we planned."

Shreya's mother had hired the limo for the whole night. After the dance, they were going to get a late dinner at Chance's Steakhouse, and then drive to Ethan's house in the hills. His father was out of town on business, and Ethan had the six-bedroom house to himself.

"You worked so hard on this dress." Shreya fingered the cap sleeve. "That lipstick looks gorgeous on you. Come here." She cupped Jess's face and pulled her in the window, planting a delicate kiss on her lips.

"Watch out, Brendan," Ethan teased. "Or she'll run off with your date."

"Hey, let me get in on some of that action." Brendan leaned over the roof and reached comically for Jess.

"Let us drive you," Shreya said.

"No way. She is not tainting this night any more than she already has. It'll take ten minutes, fifteen, tops. I'm just dumping her and coming right back."

"You better."

"You think I'm going to miss my first ever ride in a limo? I'm right behind you guys. I promise."

❧

Jess pulled the ruined dress over her head. There would be no saving the snowy white material, but she filled a small bucket with cold water and submerged it anyhow. She'd become an expert in blood cleanup after Shelley Jones, a kindly old lady who'd lived in the trailer next door for a time, had taught her that if she didn't let it dry, there was a chance it would come out. Jess then pulled on shorts and a t-shirt and stalked into the kitchen.

"Let's go."

June lifted the bottle and tried to shake out invisible drops of vodka.

"Now!" Jess shouted. "Or you can walk your ass there."

She snatched the keys from the counter and flip-flopped outside. June stumbled after her, moping.

"I'm sorry, Jessie," she mumbled through her hang-dog expression. She sounded genuinely sorry, but she wouldn't remember this humility later. She never did.

Jess attempted to start the old Civic. It chugged without turning over.

"Now what?" she said, even though she really knew. June's license had been suspended since her second DUI, but that didn't stop her from driving. So, Jess had loosened an alternator cable, and that did.

"Shoulda had your friends drive us." June's S sounded like *th* as she spoke through the gap in her teeth. "I wouldn't mind a ride in a limo."

Jess hopped out and opened the hood. She moved her hand around, wriggling this and that before tightening the cable, in case June was peeking through the tiny gap. As far as her mother was concerned, the car was a broken-down heap.

She hopped back in and cranked it over again. The car started right up. June was slumped against the passenger door, too drunk to have noticed the fix. Jess reached over and secured her seatbelt.

"I'm dropping you there. It's only a few blocks. You can walk home."

"Hm-kmph."

She pulled out of the trailer park and turned onto the two-lane expressway toward town. It had a raised sidewalk that was separated from the road with a big aluminum rail mounted to a concrete break-wall. She'd be safe enough walking home.

"Come inside with me, Jessie," June managed over a moan. "That doctor doesn't like me."

Jess turned on the headlights. The sun still sat above the mountains, but fluffy clouds had brought twilight early tonight. "Be nice to him. He's coming in after-hours for you."

"Coming in for *you*," she muttered. "You know that old perv just wants into your pants. All men think poor girls are easy targets. 'Specially one pretty as you."

Jess rolled her eyes.

Dr. Patterson was unlocking the door as they pulled into his small lot. A young woman Jess recognized as one of his assistants climbed out of her car in her regular clothes.

Great, one more person whose Friday night was ruined by June.

"She fell and knocked out a tooth," Jess explained as they walked inside. It wasn't worth mentioning that June was drunk as a skunk. If they couldn't tell by the way she was weaving, they would smell the telltale sourness wafting off her.

Dr. Patterson smiled. "It happens."

To *five-year-olds*, Jess thought. She handed him the plastic cup of water containing the tooth. "We didn't have any milk."

"Come on, hon. Let's get you inside." The hygienist gave Jess a pitying smile as she helped June inside. Jess hated the pity card, but she'd play it when she had nothing else in her hand.

"I'll do what I can, but I'll be honest. She's got considerable bone loss." Dr. Patterson was kind not to say it was because of her drug and alcohol use.

"Don't give her any meds. She's drunk already."

"That's probably why she's bleeding so profusely. Alcohol thins the blood."

Then she must have water flowing through her veins.

"I'm not coming in with her. She can walk home, it's not far." She swallowed, and then hated herself for the guilt-motivated urge to explain. "It's my prom tonight."

She might sound like a selfish teen, but her entire childhood had been a series of setbacks and disappointments, and Jess didn't like looking like the villain for no longer picking up the pieces after a lifelong drunk.

"I understand. Have a wonderful time, dear."

"Thank you, Dr. Patterson. Really, I mean it. I'm so sorry to call you after hours."

He guffawed. "You did me a favor. I was going to eat a TV dinner because I was too lazy to go out for Sonny's Friday night special—chicken fried steak. You got me off the couch."

Jess grinned. "Well then, you're welcome."

She hopped back in the car and headed home. The black cocktail server's uniform would have to do. June had tossed it out when the hem had come unraveled, but Jess rescued it from the trash and fixed it. She'd been considering wearing it before deciding to sew the Vogue gown. Two safety pins were all she needed to affix the gem clusters to fancy it up a bit, and then she'd be on her way.

At Happy Hollow trailer park, Jess pulled back into an oddly empty lane. The trailer park looked creepy against the cloudy sky. A bright yellow glow slipped through a slit between the mountain and the clouds, and streetlights were on, creating an eerie juxtaposition. The air had a peculiar electricity to it. Maybe it was the excitement she felt at finally deciding to leave.

I really am going to do it.

Graduation couldn't come soon enough.

Strangely, no one was out, not even Mrs. Greenly, who always walked her miniature dachshund around this time.

Jess quickly changed into the black dress and gathered the straps into a bunch to secure the rhinestone clusters. She gave herself a quick once-over in the mirror. Not bad. The rough, polyester material was about as far as you could get from a Vogue design, but the rhinestone clips gave it a flattering sweetheart neckline. Molly's bra was still working miracles, and the frost-pink lipstick popped against the black fabric. She'd been planning on wearing black, high-heeled strappy sandals anyway, and they went well enough with the dress. At mid-thigh, the cocktail dress was shorter than she felt comfortable wearing, but at this point, it was her only option.

With one last top-to-bottom look in the mirror, Jess grabbed the car keys and hurried out the door to the end of life as she knew it.

Two

Curtis DeGroot thought the girl's dresses were getting more and more risqué every year. He hated working weekends at school functions, but this was prom, which meant summer vacation was two weeks away, and soon, his days would be spent in blissful silence.

His job was merely a front, a cover for the marijuana business that padded his secret retirement fund, but while he'd never admit it to anyone, Curtis liked working at the high school. There was an energy here, a youthful electricity he enjoyed watching.

He'd missed out on most of his youth, being bullied by a forbidding and angry father. People thought Curtis was a conspiracy theorist? They should have met his old man. He ranted day in and day out about one plot or another, and Curtis learned at an early age not to voice his own opinion. Speaking his mind only got him a backhand across the skull. Working at the high school allowed him a few vicarious hours a day of the fanciful, careless bliss of youth that had been denied him.

When his ma got sick, Pop pulled him out of school. He'd only been fourteen at the time. She hung on for three long years, just enough for him to miss out on his remaining years of high school while playing nursemaid to her, and his selfish father. He'd always wanted to leave, but didn't have the education to do more than pump gas down at the Arco. Then his old man had taken a drunken spill down the mountain and bonked his head on a rock, and Curtis had inherited the thirty acres and already well-established marijuana business, as well as the ramshackle house. It wasn't more than a hillbilly shack, but to Curtis, it was a castle in his own kingdom. And ever since, he'd lived in pure bliss, finally relieved of the torment his father had unleashed on him for twenty-eight years.

The pot operation was small by typical standards, but that kept him under the local radar and netted him about forty grand a year on top of his salary.

Inside the gymnasium, Principal Renner was giving his annual *end-of-the-year-you're-about-to embark-on-your-future* pep talk. The halls were nearly empty, just a few stragglers left, and the ticket-takers had already gone inside.

Curtis peered through the small glass windows on the double doors. The gymnasium looked like the banquet room of a hotel. Blue and white lights swirled in the school colors, and streamers hung from hundreds of helium-filled balloons bobbing against the high ceiling.

The microphone boomed, and a cheer erupted. These kids were enthusiastic, to say the least. Curtis turned back the way he'd come and headed toward the electrical cabinet. He needed to stay close. The fun would come to a quick end if a fuse blew, and when the music started up, the DJ was going to suck a lot of juice.

Two giggling kids, a girl and a boy, crossed the hall and entered the girls' bathroom together. Curtis rolled his eyes. Kids certainly seemed randier these days, too.

He'd planned to do a check of the restrooms but chose to go to the ones in the other hallway first; he didn't want to interrupt anything. Dumb kids; he hoped they used protection.

After a quick check of the power box, he headed back down the hall, giving a glance inside the gymnasium.

"To the senior class of West Ridge High!" Principal Renner boomed. Another cheer erupted.

Then, a shrill whine squealed through the microphone, cutting off the principal's speech. There was a loud pop, and then silence.

A fuse must have blown. If the darn fool would stop shouting into the darn thing, this wouldn't happen.

He quickly headed back the other way. He'd been hoping that after the music started, he could settle down in the janitor's closet and look at the latest Jugs magazine. Instead, he'd be staring at a fuse box all night.

Curtis passed the gym doors but stopped. Something was off. The hairs on the back of his neck bristled. He took two silent, careful steps backward and looked through the glass.

The inside of the gymnasium was dark, the main lights blown. The only illumination was an eerie glow from the blue and white battery-powered lanterns set around the perimeter of the gym.

There were no voices, no laughter. No Principal Renner assuring everyone the power would come back on.

No glittering rhinestones, no gleaming white tuxedo shirts.

There was no one inside.

Everyone was gone.

❧

The parking lot by the gymnasium was full as far as Jess could see, so she parked the old Civic in the fire lane. She didn't care if it got towed, it would just be another way to keep her mother from driving. The fire lane was long, stretching the length of the mezzanine that ran from the sprawling campus's main buildings down to the gym. It wasn't a fire hazard, not really.

She kicked off her flip-flops and slipped into her heels. They tapped along the pavement as she started toward the gym. Jess stopped and looked back at the car. She was going to leave it here all night, which would probably result in its getting towed sometime before Monday. Her mother couldn't legally drive, but Jess might need it for something before she left. Reconsidering her plan, she jumped back in and moved it behind a fenced utilities cage to a spot reserved for service vehicles. At least there, it probably wouldn't get towed.

The gymnasium building was dark, and she couldn't hear any music. Maybe the principal was still giving his talk. In that case, she was perfectly on time. She'd heard enough of his boring speeches to last a lifetime.

She hurried through the main doors and down the hallway to the entrance to the gymnasium. She had the right place; she'd been watching the prom committee decorate for the past two days, and a frilly table sat outside decorated with streamer bows in the school colors. A small box for the claimed tickets sat next to another box for students to place their votes for prom king and queen.

A man's strangled cry made chills roll across her arms.

"Oh, God. Oh, God, OH, GOD!"

The creepy old janitor-maintenance man backed out of the gymnasium and let the door fall shut. It slammed closed, echoing through the silent halls. Jess slowed her step as uncertainty tightened in her chest.

The bathroom door banged open, making her jump. Dean Ellison and

Jasmine Dodson came out together. They were grinning and cuddling, but when they caught sight of Mr. DeGroot, they froze.

He backed away with his hands against his head, pulling the too-long strands of his thinning hair through his fingers. He turned away from Jess and ran, letting out a shriek that made a pit form in her stomach. Dean and Jasmine watched him go with wide eyes.

"They're gone! They're all gone!"

He nearly crashed into Will Taylor. Will jumped aside and watched the crazy old man go.

"What the hell is his problem?" Luke Findley asked, not yet aware of the eerie sense of unrealness. He and Katherine Cummings were behind Jess, arm in arm. Katherine wore a corsage of purple orchids that complemented the pretty knee-length lavender dress Jess had seen in Mathilda's, an upscale boutique in town. Jess knew the dress cost over three hundred dollars, and wasn't surprised to see the wealthy girl wearing it.

She swallowed. "I don't know."

"That guy is *so* weird," Katherine said.

"Uh, guys?" Dean pulled a wary Jasmine closer. He leaned over to peer through the narrow glass windows near the center of the double doors. "Where is everybody?"

Will stopped and looked at Jess. "What's going on?"

"I don't know," she repeated.

For a moment, nobody moved. She gestured with a hand. Still, no one moved. Jess took a deep breath and stepped up to the push-bar on the door. Not to be outbraved by a girl, Luke stepped up to the other door. She pushed open one, and Luke opened the other. A streamer fluttered slowly to the floor, and a suction of air from pulled a wave of confetti swirling out around their feet.

No one made a move to go inside.

"Is this the right place?" Katherine asked.

Jess would have been annoyed by the stupid question if fear wasn't making her heart stutter.

Nobody moved. An eerie sense of *wrongness* settled in Jess's gut. Her brain kept trying to convince her it was nothing; the dance was somewhere else, it must have been. But the decorations, the stage, the tables...

"This is the right place," she confirmed in a whisper.

There had to be a rational explanation.

A loud slam made them all jump.

"Help! It's happened!" the janitor screamed as he ran toward them. "It's finally happened! They're all gone!"

They all tensed, frozen in place, before he veered toward the outer doors and ran outside.

Jess eased backward, and the others moved with her. She and Luke let the doors fall shut.

"What is he talking about?" Katherine asked in a shaky voice.

"That dude's nuts." Luke scowled. "Don't listen to him."

"Yeah, but where is everyone?" Dean's voice cracked. Jess knew him as a loud and arrogant jock, but now he seemed unnerved and hesitant.

Jasmine grabbed his hand in both of hers and tugged him away. "Dean, I don't like this. I want to leave."

"Maybe there was a fire evacuation. Or something." Will looked at her, the only one who didn't have wide, scared eyes, but his bobbing Adam's apple as he swallowed betrayed his outward calm.

She didn't know Will very well, had only talked with him sophomore year on a group science project, but she'd found him nice enough. He didn't appear to have a date tonight. If he'd been meeting someone here, he didn't have a corsage for her. And seriously, what girl would tolerate her date showing up to prom in jeans and a tacky tuxedo-printed t-shirt? It was obvious that he hadn't wanted to come. His mother was one of the school administrators, bubbly and outgoing whereas Will was quiet and shy. She'd probably insisted he attend.

"But where would they go?" Luke asked. "The muster points are in the parking lot."

"Not all of them," Dean said. "Let's check the dais."

In silent agreement, they turned and walked to the other doors. Their shoes made eerie clicking sounds that echoed through the empty hall. At the rear of the building, two of the six sets of doors opened to a lawn area with a dais built around a massive oak where the graduation ceremonies took place.

"I don't like this," Jasmine persisted. "I want to leave. Please, Dean."

"Prom hasn't been cancelled. There's probably just a gas leak or something."

Katherine rolled her eyes. "Oh, great."

Luke glanced at Will and grinned. "I feel like I'm in a high school slasher movie."

"How is that funny?" Katherine snapped.

"Would you feel better if I grabbed the axe out of the fire box?" Dean asked.

"They don't have one," Will pointed out. "As if they would give axes to high school kids."

"Maybe that's why so many of them bring guns," Dean said.

Katherine pulled her hand free. "You are *not* helping!"

Outside, they found only Mr. DeGroot sitting on the dais steps with his head in his hands, sobbing. Nobody seemed willing to approach him, and Jess didn't want to, either. But he was the only person there who may have seen something, and none of this was making sense. She looked at the others. Katherine scowled and opened her hands in an exaggerated "*what?*" gesture. Jess sighed and made her way over to the distraught man.

The narrow points of her heels sank into the damp grass. She tiptoed carefully on the balls of her feet. Mr. DeGroot didn't look up, even when she stood directly in front of him. Jess sat gingerly on the lowest step, pulling her too-short skirt against her thighs.

"Mr. DeGroot?"

He let go of his hair. It stood wildly on end, pointing in all directions.

"Hmm, what?" He lifted his head slowly, as if afraid to make eye contact.

Jess touched his arm. "What did you see in there?"

"I didn't do it...at least, I don't think...I didn't want to do it..."

"Do what?"

"No." He gripped his head again and violently shook his head back and forth. "No. No. No. I couldn't have! It must have been them!"

"Them who? Mr. DeGroot! Where is everybody?"

"Gone. Just...gone."

They couldn't be gone. Her thoughts flashed to Shreya, so beautiful in that burgundy gown. The idea was horrific, lancing Jess's heart with sharp pain, even as it was so outrageously ludicrous it was almost laughable.

There had to be an explanation.

"They aren't *just gone*."

"You don't understand." His eyes swam with tears. "They planned this. It's just like he said...I can't believe they finally did it!"

"What did they do, Mr. DeGroot?"

"I can't say! They'll kill me!" He finally focused on her, his eyes wide with fear. "You should leave now, before they get you too!"

"They?"

He jumped up and bolted away so suddenly Jess gave a little shriek.

She stood up and tiptoed back to the others, heedless to the mud sticking to her heels. "I'm calling the police."

"What are you going to tell them?" Dean asked.

She threw her hands up. "I don't know!" She wouldn't blame Mr. DeGroot, that was all she knew. One scrawny old man did not murder one hundred fit young students and dispose of their bodies without leaving a drop of blood behind. The old guy was obviously insane.

"Fuck, I smoked a blunt tonight. I can't see the cops."

She frowned at Luke. "I seriously don't think they care."

"And I may have taken some Ex."

"Luke!" Katherine jerked her hand out of his. "Ugh! That's it!"

"For fuck's sake!" Jess snapped. "Nobody can tell, so stop talking about it." *Just my luck, I had to get stuck with the senior class's biggest dimwits.*

Mr. DeGroot could be seen running across the football field toward the pedestrian gate that let out to the city park behind the school. She frowned. What did he know that they didn't?

There had to be a logical explanation. Shreya was not gone—she couldn't be!

"Somebody give me a phone," Jess demanded.

Luke scowled. "Where's yours?"

"It broke." Not really a lie; it had broken, but she couldn't afford to replace it. Her mother carried an outdated flip phone that had been given to her from a woman's shelter, but Jess was too embarrassed to use it.

Katherine pulled hers from her wristlet and handed it over. It was sleek and new, with a vibrant display of colorful apps. Jess dialed 9-1-1, but nothing happened. She tried a second time.

"It isn't working." She handed it back. "Does anyone else have service?"

One by one, they all tried. Will shook his head.

"Oh my God!" Jasmine wailed. "What is going on?"

"Probably the cell tower is down," Jess assured her. "Just stay calm."

"What should we do?" Luke asked. "Should we leave and find a landline?"

"There are landlines in the coaches' offices," Jess said. Nobody moved. She fisted her hands on her hips. "I guess there are no volunteers."

"Hell, I'm not afraid," Dean said, but his voice cracked.

Jasmine grabbed his arm. "No! Dean, I don't want to go back in there. I have a serious case of the heebie-jeebies."

"Okay, sweetie. Stay out here."

"No! Don't leave me out here alone!"

"Jesus." Jess rolled her eyes. "I'll do it."

"I'll go with you." Will managed a thin smile.

"Ooh, your hero, Jessica! Will's gonna go with you." Dean socked him in the arm. "What's your scrawny ass gonna do?"

"Ow." He rubbed his shoulder and frowned. "Not stand around out here, doing nothing."

"I know there's one in Coach Anderson's office," Jess said. "Let's see if it's locked."

They started inside alone, and he surprised her by grasping her hand. His were dry and warm, and his grip was light and hesitant. Even though she didn't know him very well, it was reassuring, so she held on.

Back inside the building, the halls seemed even darker and eerier now that they were alone. Jess wished Luke hadn't mouthed off about slasher movies.

"There has to be a rational explanation." Only after she'd said it did Jess realize she'd whispered the words aloud.

"Of course." Will met her gaze. In his, she saw the same hope, and doubt, she felt.

They stopped in the main hallway at the rear doors to the girls' locker room. Jess told herself it was the closest door, but in truth, she wasn't willing to enter through the gymnasium. Something about the emptiness in there seemed alive—malevolent.

The locker room door had the same push-bar release as the main doors. She activated it slowly and gently, trying to bring as little sound as possible, as though some malicious spirit might be listening. It creaked like the entrance to a haunted house when she pushed inward. Jess threw a look at Will and he laughed, but it died away quickly. They slipped inside and let the doors fall shut behind them.

The girls' coaches' office was a separate room off the main locker room. Jess tried the knob.

Locked.

"Okay. We either head to the boys' locker room..." He picked up a small metal trashcan. "Or we break the window."

"Let's try the boys'," she told him. "When all this blows over, I don't want to be holding the bill for a giant sheet of plate glass."

They left through the same creaky door and turned into the hall. At the main doors to the gymnasium, they stopped and looked through the small glass windows.

The party was still dark and dead.

Wordlessly, they both turned and continued to the boys' locker room. Jess's feet were hot, her knees like jelly. The door opened silently, and she let out a sigh of relief. Her nerves were frayed past the shredding point, and the mere flutter of a bird or the scamper of a mouse would have put her over the edge.

Shreya, you're all right. I know you are.

Will turned the knob on the coaches' office door, and it opened.

"Thank God," Jess breathed out.

They walked inside and looked at the phone.

"What are you going to say?" he asked her.

Now that she thought about it, it sounded unbelievable, even to her ears. "Only what I know. They either believe me, or they don't." She picked up the receiver and dialed 9-1-1.

"Nine-one-one emergency. Do you need fire, ambulance, or police?"

"Police, I think. Where is this, have I reached Sacramento?"

"We dispatch all counties, ma'am. What's your emergency?"

Now that she had to put it into words, her throat grew tight with impending tears. "My name is Jessica Harding. I'm a senior at West Ridge High School in Kileyville. Tonight is our senior prom and...this is going to sound really strange...I just got here to find everyone gone." She swallowed. "They're all gone."

"What do you mean gone, Jessica? Has there been an accident?"

"No. It's just empty. All the cars are in the parking lot, but inside the gymnasium, it's empty."

"Could everyone have gone somewhere else?" the dispatcher asked.

"Well, that's just it... We looked, but there was no one anywhere around."

"Who's we?"

"I'm calling you from the coaches' office with Will Taylor. Outside is Dean Ellison and Jasmine Dodson, and Katherine Cummings and Luke..."

"Findley," Will supplied.

"Luke Findley," she finished. "They were also late. We were all late getting here. And when we looked in the gymnasium, everyone was gone."

"I'm not sure what you mean by *gone*, miss. We haven't had any calls about an evacuation—"

Jess lost it. Her breath caught on a sob, and she turned away before Will could see her face scrunch up with tears.

"Why can't you understand what I'm saying? They're gone! Everyone has vanished! We need the police here *now*!"

Three

Outside, Dave Sumner and Mike Rollins had joined the others. They sat on BMX bikes wearing jeans and Motorhead t-shirts, obviously not planning to attend the dance.

Jasmine went into a near panic when she saw Jess blotting her tears. "What? What happened? What's wrong?"

"Nothing," Jess assured her. "We called them, and they're on their way. Where did you guys come from?"

"They were out in the park, toking up. They came to make fun of the prom dresses."

Jess was already over the edge. "Yeah? Well, not all of us can afford three hundred dollar dresses to wear for one night." She sliced an angry gesture at Katherine.

"What's that supposed to mean?"

"You want to make fun of my dress?" she demanded. "Prize goes to the one who can guess where it came from."

"Uh, Goodwill?" Mike quipped with sarcasm.

Dave scowled. "What's got your panties in a bunch?"

Jess held onto her anger like a lifeline; it was all that kept her panic at bay. Jasmine, Dean, Katherine, and Luke weren't her friends, not really. They were all part of the privileged crowd who wore designer clothes and received cars as sixteenth-birthday gifts. "Did any of these dumb shits bother to fill you in?"

"Hey!" Luke frowned.

She wished it was one of them who'd gone missing Instead of Shreya. Was this her fault? If she'd allowed them to take her mother to the dentist in the limo, they all would have been late, instead of who knew where.

"Yeah, they did." Dave threw his cigarette on the ground and stepped on it. "But I don't believe it. I'm going in."

"I wouldn't," Dean said.

"Yeah, well, you're a pussy." The two stoners snickered.

"A pussy who could kick your ass."

Blue and red lights reflected off the far-away fence at the edge of the parking lot. A moment later, two patrol cars pulled down the driveway.

"Hey-o, it's the 5-0," Mike said snidely.

"Don't be an asshole," Jess warned.

One car shined a spotlight over the lot and buildings. The lead unit turned toward them, and the other followed. They parked adjacent to the mezzanine, and three officers got out. Jessica recognized the pot-bellied sheriff who'd been to their trailer park so many times they were practically on a first-name basis.

"Who called it in?"

The rest of the group held back, so Jess and Will approached. "I'm Jessica Harding."

"Harding?" the sheriff barked. "That's a name I recognize."

Jess groaned inwardly. "You're thinking of my mom." She couldn't keep the defensive edge from her voice.

"Ah. Yep, I remember. I picked her up at the Cask 'N Flask on disruptive behavior."

"Quality," Mike snickered under his breath.

Sheriff Weasley turned a warning glare on Mike, and then heaved his belt up under his protruding belly. "Dispatch says everyone is gone. What does that mean, exactly?"

Jessica took a deep breath, and then another. Silver spots danced in her vision.

Will picked up on her developing panic and answered for her. "The six of us all arrived at about the same time, after the dance had started. Only when we got to the gym, there was nobody inside."

The sheriff looked them over and gestured with his pen. "The six of you? What about those two?"

"They were outside. They just showed up now."

In the distance, helicopter blades chopped the night sky.

"You two came together?" The sheriff's fat index finger flicked between her and Will.

Will looked aghast. "What? No. I don't have a date. I didn't even want to come. My mom made me."

"My date..." Jess's breath hitched as she thought of Shreya and Todd, Molly and Ethan, and Brendan, who might not have even come tonight if she hadn't accepted his invitation. "My date was already here. Like I said, I was late."

"All right, let's start with your names."

Sheriff Weasley jotted notes on a small pad. The deputies ambled slowly toward the gymnasium building, as if they, too, were hesitant to enter.

"All right, y'all stay here—"

He looked up as the helicopters hovered directly overhead. Powerful beams lit up the lot, searched the cars, and then passed over them. They stirred up a gale that pulled at her hair and made talk impossible. Both helicopters veered off and rocketed to the center of the football field where they set down.

The two deputies looked back at the sheriff. He hitched his pants again.

"Let's see what this is all about first. That do look like the eff-bee-ah."

The stadium lights were off at the field, so it was hard to see more than silhouettes of the passengers who emerged from the first helicopter, but the swarm of soldiers with rifles who spilled out of the second helicopter were unmistakable. Six battle-bots in full riot gear hurried ahead of the others, sweeping their rifles left and right as if expecting bank robbers or Colombian drug dealers. As the group behind them moved into the lights from the overhang on the main building, Jess identified three men in suits and two scientist-looking types in lab coats carrying large plastic cases.

Headlights caught her attention. The limousine angled down the main drive and turned toward them.

Shreya! Hope exploded in her chest. *Maybe they hadn't arrived yet either!*

Four

Jess ran straight for it, making the limo lurch to a stop. The driver's window powered down, and an older black man leaned his head to the side.

"What's going on? Did someone take the party too far?" he grinned.

Jess ran past him and pounded on the passenger door's glass. It didn't slide down.

No! She pulled on the handle. The door was locked.

"You're the girl from the trailer park."

"Open the door!"

The locks popped up. "Did somebody leave something?" he asked, but her mind still didn't register the defeat until she pulled the door open and saw the interior.

Empty.

She braced her hands on the edges of the opened door, willing her friends to appear inside.

"No." Jess dropped to her knees on the ground as full on, chest-heaving sobs crashed over her. "No, please." She covered her face with her hands, unable to stop the torrential agony in her heart.

They couldn't be gone. It couldn't be.

"Jessica, come on." Gentle hands pulled at her shoulders. "We'll figure this out."

"Here, let her sit down." The driver got out and helped Will urge her to her feet. They eased her onto the edge of the seat. "Have some water." The driver opened a bottle and offered it, but Jess couldn't focus.

Will brushed at the gravel stuck to her knees, but quickly pulled his hand away. His ears turned pink.

"What's happened? Did somebody get hurt?" the driver asked.

"We're not sure," Will told him. "But the cops are here, and maybe the FBI, too."

"I saw the helicopters come down and thought something big must be going on." The driver stood back to look over the rows of cars.

Will squatted down to face Jess. "Those men are going to want to talk to us."

"The way she's carrying on like that, I thought something might've happened to one of her friends," the driver said to Will.

"Something did happen to her," Jess whispered. She looked toward the field where the two sleek helicopters sat, their powered-down blades still turning lazily. "How did they know?"

"What?"

"We called like, what, fifteen, *maybe* twenty minutes ago?"

She looked into Will's eyes, saw the realization dawning there.

"How did they get here so fast?"

∽

The next few hours passed in a blur. The parking lot was sealed off to incoming traffic. Two black vans arrived, and a massive tent was set up on the grass in front of the dais. Jessica and the others were given folded chairs, but they were strategically placed far apart from one another.

She looked up as her mother's tattered cardigan draped over her shoulders. Will offered Jess her flip-flops and a sad smile.

"I thought you might be cold, so I looked in your car."

She slipped out of her heels and kicked them aside. Will knelt in front of her and held her hand. Jess tried to return his smile. She'd always thought him kind of a geek, and his sweetness touched her.

A loud cry made her jump. Mr. DeGroot had been strapped down to a gurney and was being wheeled out of a zippered-off section of the tent.

"It isn't real! I tell you, it isn't real! It's all a dream!"

Jess went cold at those words. He slipped into incoherence, and his next words were nothing but babble. She wondered what he had seen that had made him freak out so badly. *Maybe I don't want to know.*

Shreya, what's happened to you?

"Mr. Taylor, you're next." The young agent softened his command with a brief smile. "Please."

Will stood, lingering long enough to let his fingers slip slowly from hers. A twist of fear tightened in her chest as Jess watched him follow the agent through the plastic flaps into the adjoining tent. She listened absently as the others were questioned by the agents who played round robin, switching off and asking all of them the same questions again and again.

It was still before eleven, but when one parent arrived and found they weren't allowed in, the news spread across the small town like wildfire. Jess heard the angry voices of the parents through the radio blasts as the agents in the tent communicated with those at the gate, and at one point, Sheriff Weasley came in shouting about the mob at the front and demanding answers. He was an elected official, dammit, and this was his town.

"I don't give a rat's ass about jurisdiction. Now you tell me what I wanna know, or I'm gonna make sure those reporters you won't let in get the full rundown of what's going on back here."

Jess hadn't heard much more as he was ushered out by the lead agent—a severe looking, rail-thin man with unfriendly eyes. He wore a plain black suit with shiny lace-up loafers and had died his hair jet black. It looked ghastly on him, his deeply lined face and gnarly, spotted hands betraying his real age.

Wasn't there a mandatory retirement age in the FBI? Was he from some other agency? Thinking about it only made her more confused, and amped up her panic all over again.

The man spoke softly, but that only made him more frightening. Thankfully, he hadn't yet questioned her, but her stomach jittered with dread as she anticipated her turn.

Only the six of them were inside the tent with the three agents who had landed in the helicopter and four others who had come in the vans. Jess wondered where the men with the guns had gone.

The other men from the helicopters who looked like scientists had set up computers on tables and were monitoring radioactive levels—and who knew what else—with small, complicated devices. One of them had a strange, antique-looking radar graph whose sweeping arm didn't seem to detect anything. Every now and then, one of the agents would speak softly to the man operating it, and he'd answer with a shake of his head.

Dave Sumner and Mike Rollins were questioned initially, but when they said they hadn't gone inside the main building, they were released.

The first agent to question her introduced himself as Special Agent Larsen. He couldn't have been more than thirty, and was shockingly handsome. Or he would have been without the ugly suit and greased back hair. And, of course, if he wasn't a dick. He repeated the same round of questions, ignoring her growing anger.

"Name?"

"Jessica Anne Harding."

"Date of birth?"

"March fourth."

"Address?"

"318 Happy Hollow Way."

"Who do you live with?"

"My mother."

"Where does your father live?"

"You tell me."

"How long have you lived in Kileyville?"

"Six years."

"Where did you live before that?"

"Reno."

"Where did you go to school there?"

"Billinghurst Elementary."

"Why did you move to Kileyville?"

"My mother inherited a luxurious mobile home in an exclusive, upscale neighborhood."

None of the other agents had reacted to her sarcasm, but Larsen gave a snort.

"What time did you arrive at the dance tonight?"

"Around 8:15."

"Specifically? As close as you can."

"Between 8:10 and 8:20."

"Did you go inside the gymnasium?"

"No."

"Where did you go inside the main building?"

"In the halls, into the locker rooms. The coaches' office in the girls' locker room was locked. We went in the office in the boys' locker room to use the phone."

"Who went with you?"

"Just me and Will in the locker rooms."

"Which halls did you enter?"

"Me, or everyone?"

"Both."

"Will and I went in all four that surround the gymnasium. The others, only the three sides, I think."

"Which three sides?"

"All three except the one on the boys' locker room side."

"Did you see anyone else at the school?"

"Mr. DeGroot, and Dave and Mike outside."

"Did you hear any sounds coming from inside the gymnasium?"

"No."

"No shrilling, scraping, hiss of white noise, thumping, banging?"

"Nothing."

"Did you see any lights inside the gymnasium?"

"The candle lanterns on the tables."

"No strobes, flashes, or anything glowing?"

"No."

"Did you feel anything strange; static electricity, pressure on your ears, a gust of heat or cold?"

"Not that I remember."

"What did Mr. DeGroot say?"

"He said, 'They're gone.'"

"Did he say anything else?"

Jess had paused to think back to her interaction with him on the dais. No one else had been close enough to hear.

"No."

The next time she was asked the question, she did so without pause. If the first agent suspected she was lying, he didn't let on. By the time the mean, older man who introduced himself as Special Agent in Charge Roycroft took his turn questioning her, she met his eyes and answered as flatly as he questioned.

"No sounds at all, like a voice, a whisper, or crying?" he asked, completely void of emotion.

"Like what, from another dimension?" Jess was exhausted, and her irritation at his unemotional evasiveness trumped her fear of him.

He looked up from his notepad and studied her with dispassionate eyes, but Jess didn't look away.

"Where are my friends?"

He looked back at his notepad.

"Where are my friends?" she repeated louder.

"We're trying our best to figure that out, Ms. Harding."

"By asking me questions about where I went inside the building? Where I used to live? You know where they are. Tell me, please."

"Ms. Harding—"

Jess leaned forward and grasped his wrist. "Just Shreya. Please, just her. I can't bear it if she's gone."

She was crying now but hiding it from the others. She didn't sob, didn't wail, didn't scream. Her tears were silent, scalding.

"She's my best friend. I love her so much, and she's the only person in this world who loves me back. I can't lose her. You can't know how badly I need her. I can't lose her." She lowered her voice to a whisper. "Please, just her, and I won't say anything to anyone else. Please."

He surprised her by placing his hand lightly over hers where she held his wrist. "I would bring them all back if I could. I truly do not know where they've gone." He smiled, but it was the devil's smile. "I promise you, we'll do everything in our power to find them." He lifted her hand from his wrist and urged her to sit back.

She dragged in a breath. *How can I make him understand? He has to bring Shreya back. He has to!*

"You may join the others now."

Jess shivered at his unsettling choice of words.

The agent stood and gestured for her to return to the other section of the tent. "Can someone please get Ms. Harding some coffee and a donut?"

"I don't drink coffee."

She fell into the uncomfortable chair next to the others. Why wouldn't he understand? All she wanted was Shreya. Her energy was draining, and Jess felt like she was fighting the effects of a sleeping pill.

"How about some tea, then?" He gave her that creepy smile again, and Jess shuddered.

Will walked over and tossed him a threatening glare. He then knelt beside her and took her hand again, and Jess rejoiced in the touch. She felt utterly, hopelessly alone, and Will's was the one face she could look into without dread.

"How're you holding up?"

"I'm scared." She hated the meekness she heard in her own voice.

"Me too."

"What if they never find her?"

"They will. They'll find all of them. The authorities know what they're doing."

"The hell they do," Luke snapped. "They're probably behind it. This is all just a ploy to see what we know."

Special Agent Roycroft swiveled toward him. "Mr. Findley is tired. Someone get him a cup of coffee." It wasn't a suggestion as much as an order.

"As if." He snorted and shot a look at Jess and Will. "Word of advice: don't drink the Kool-Aid."

"I want to go home," Jasmine whined. "When can we go?"

He looked at his notepad. "Ms. Dodson?"

"Yeah, and my dad's a lawyer. You can't hold me against my will. You're not even supposed to be questioning me without my parents present. I'm only seventeen."

"I am well aware of *state* law, Ms. Dodson."

She eased slowly back into her chair, horrified by his clear message. *I am the Federal Law, and don't try to intimidate me, because you'll never succeed.*

He lifted a radio. "Send in Mr. and Mrs. Dodson, parents of Jasmine Dodson."

Her shoulders slumped in obvious relief.

"What about the rest of us?" Luke demanded. He looked down at Katherine, who slouched in her chair, clutching his tuxedo jacket around her shoulders and sobbing quietly. "How many times are you going to ask us the same questions before you're satisfied with the answer?"

Jess cast a warning glance at Will. She shook her head slightly. She wasn't leaving until she had news about Shreya. She'd watched enough episodes of the X-*Files* to know she was on the inside right now. Once she was on the outside, there'd be nothing but silence and secrets.

Silence, secrets, and lies.

"Mr. Findley, we have a few more questions for you." He lifted the radio to his mouth again. "Do you have a..." he consulted his notepad. "Mr.

Cummings, father of Katherine Cummings?"

The response from the agent at the gates came with a background roar of outraged parents, demanding to know why only Jasmine's parents were allowed in. "Affirmative."

"Send him in."

Katherine stood and hugged Luke. "I'm sorry." She slid his coat over his shoulders.

"It's okay, babe. I'll be all right."

Jasmine had exited the tent. Through the part in the flaps, Jess saw her run into her parents' arms. She let out a wail and her mother sobbed a loud thanks to God.

Jess dropped her face into her hands and cried silently. There was only one person in this world who would be that happy to see her, and though she'd never abandon the hope she desperately clung to, a small part of her knew Shreya was gone forever.

༄

"Ms. Harding, Mr. Taylor, is there someone who can come and get you?"

She looked up, having been in a daze. A red digital display showed 1:23. Could that possibly be the time?

Only Will and Dean remained in the tent with her. Will sat on the ground by her chair, and Dean stood nearby, shrugging back into his tuxedo jacket.

"You guys need a ride?" Dean asked them. "My parents can drop you."

"Perhaps it would be better if an agent drove you home," Special Agent Roycroft said.

A spike of adrenaline brought Jess instantly alert and then left her with a surge of nausea.

"Thanks, but no." Will climbed to his feet. "My mom takes allergy medicine. She's sound asleep, and God willing, she doesn't know any of this is even happening. I live behind the park; I'm gonna walk." Will settled a hard look on Roycroft. "If I'm allowed."

Will's tone was soft and pleasant enough, but Jess caught the snide undertone to the question. He was challenging the agent.

She shot to her feet and grabbed Will's hand. "I'll walk with Will," she said awkwardly. As tired as she was, she couldn't formulate an excuse. She caught herself before saying she lived in that direction. She'd already told them she lived in Happy Hollow trailer park. Would they know what direction that was?

She held her breath, waiting for him to stop her.

Agent Roycroft gestured to the tent's opening. "You're free to go."

"All right." Dean gave them a salute goodbye. "See you on the other side."

Jess faced Agent Roycroft. "You'll keep us updated?" Fresh tears threatened, but she swallowed them back. "Anything you find, I want to know."

He surprised her by offering a business card. "You have my guarantee we will use every resource at our disposal to find those who went missing tonight."

She tucked it into her sweater's pocket. "Thank you."

Jess's legs were noodley as she walked toward the tent's flap. She held her breath, waiting for the agent to change his mind and force her to get into a car with one of his creepy cronies.

Once outside, she breathed out a sigh of relief. The night air was crisp and cool and refreshed her with new life.

Will tossed a subtle glance back as they walked away. "You know they're not going to tell you anything."

"Yeah." Anger replaced her grief, flushing her skin with heat. "That's why I'm going in."

Five

"What?"

"Shh!"

Two armed agents stood guard at the gymnasium's doors that faced the dais. She'd only seen four disembark the helicopter, which meant the other two were at the front doors. She could only hope more hadn't come in the vans.

They didn't look in their direction as she and Will exited the tent, but she knew they were aware. She linked her arm in Will's as they walked across the grass. They didn't attempt to go up to the paved walk under the building's overhang.

The guards wore riot helmets with clear visors that held a reflective sheen, making it impossible to see their faces. Nevertheless, she saw the slight swivel of his head as one of them tracked their progress.

"You're doing a great job!" she shouted with clear sarcasm. "Keep up the good work."

Will chuckled softly. "Jesus, Jess."

Once past the building, they veered around on the gravel path that led to the athletic field. Jess glanced back to make sure they were out of sight of the guards.

"What did you mean, you're going in?" he whispered.

"I want to see what's going on for myself." As she angled toward the side of the building, Jess pulled him along, but he didn't need much convincing. At least it seemed he didn't.

"You mean into the *gym*?"

"Yes."

"Do you not *see* the *armed* guards holding AK-47s *right there*?"

"I don't think those are AK-47s," she said, trying to sound glib. "And I'll be quiet."

"You're crazy!"

Crazy, probably. She'd rather go wherever Shreya had gone—even though it was probably somewhere horrible—than exist without her best friend in the world.

Take me, too.

She stopped by a gap in the brambly hedges that separated the walkway from the side of the building. High, pebbled-glass windows were the only source of ventilation to the locker rooms, and let in milky light during the day.

"You said so yourself, they're not going to tell us anything. Look, Will, I appreciate your being so nice to me tonight. You don't have to come with me. Just go home, I'll be okay."

"What if whatever made the others disappear is still in there?"

"Then I'll know what took them."

"Yeah, but what if it takes *you?*" He grabbed her wrist, forcing her to face him. "You won't let me talk you out of this?"

She shook her head.

"Then I'm going with you."

"I can't let you do that." She felt better saying so, even though she didn't really mean it.

"You can't stop me, either. Now, how are we getting inside?"

She hesitated over two heartbeats. She didn't want him to take any risks on her account, but she was glad she wouldn't be alone. The gymnasium hidden behind the walls of the locker rooms was like an evil, hungry monster.

She looked up. "The windows hinge at the top, and the latch on this one is broken. If you give me a leg up, I can slip inside. I don't know how you'll get up, though."

Jess eased between the shrubs and reached up. She could barely reach the bottom of the sill with her fingertips. She took her flip-flops off and pushed them through the window. The glass flopped inward loosely, and her shoes disappeared inside. She gave a silent thanks that they still had not repaired this window, where last semester Duncan Petrillo had been caught peeking on the girls. *Thank goodness for budgeting restrictions.*

She hooked her fingers over the narrow edge. Once she got a grip, she lifted her foot.

"Like you're helping me get up on a horse."

"Yeah, I don't know how to do that."

"It's not rocket science."

He laced his fingers together and held them like a cup. She stepped in with one bare foot, and he hefted her up. She hadn't counted on the windowsill being so sharp. In truth, it wasn't, but it hurt to brace her weight on her hands. With the other foot, she threw her leg up like she was mounting a horse and pushed the window farther open with her knee. Will probably got an eyeful of her panties, but there was no room for modesty now.

Getting down was easier, and once inside, she turned over a metal garbage can and stood on it to hold the window open for Will.

He had to climb the wall with his feet and made a lot more noise than she did. Once inside, they both crouched down and squatted against the wall, as if making themselves smaller would help avoid detection. Jess put her finger over her lips, holding her breath. They waited an eternity.

She understood they could face federal prison for this. But the idea of never knowing Shreya's bright smile or contagious laugh again cracked her heart in half, and no risk was too great. If there was any shred of evidence in there, she had to find it.

"I think we're good," she whispered.

"I can't believe I'm doing this," Will whispered back. He glanced around. "Your locker room is so much nicer than ours."

She rolled her eyes, and Will rewarded her with a smile. It was a small gesture, but it lifted her spirits and reinforced her confidence.

They pushed upright and walked slowly toward the double doors that opened onto the gymnasium. Jess had horrific visions of a black cloud that would swallow them, or a weird bubble that looked empty, but once she passed through would transport her to another dimension where fancily dressed teenagers gyrated to Britney Spears.

When Cher's *Believe* played, she and Shreya had planned to defy convention and dance it together. *Slow.*

The night was surreal, and as Jess's heart thundered in her throat, she half expected to awaken with a jolt and find herself in her sagging bed back in the mobile home.

She cracked the door and listened.

Nothing. No voices, no shoes on wood, no music.

No laughter, no teasing, no happy friends celebrating their last school function before high school ended and they went their separate ways, off to live the rest of their lives.

She pushed the door open wider, and she and Will peered inside. The gymnasium was dark and empty, eerily void of any signs of life. The battery-operated candles still fake-flickered in the paper lanterns lining the walls, but the light was dim, sinister.

Jess took a deep breath and stepped inside.

Again, nothing.

No magical transportation to another dimension, no black cloud enveloping her, no swooping vampire descending from the rafters to snatch her away and eat her.

No shrilling, scraping, no hiss of white noise. No thumping, no banging.

No lights, no strobes, no flashes.

No static electricity, no pressure on her ears, no white noise, no gust of heat or wave of cold.

Absolutely...fucking...nothing.

She walked out into the center of the enormous gymnasium. Confetti fluttered away from her footfalls. The faint odor of perfume and cologne wisped its way over her senses. She stopped in the center of the room and turned in a circle, willing the scent to come stronger and bring the missing back with it.

Please. Please. Please!

Will waited a single step inside, holding the door open with a hand as though afraid to let it fall closed. His gaze slowly scanned every corner.

How could this be possible? Jess had the urge to run back to the FBI's tent, thinking she'd missed their return, that a bus had pulled in that had taken everyone out for ice cream.

It was just so unreal. A full gymnasium of people *did not* simply disappear.

She looked around, in low corners and at high edges, searching for something, anything, that didn't belong.

A small black object was fixed in the high corner of the room. She wouldn't have seen it if not for a streamer attached to a balloon that drifted out of the way on a silent current.

At the beginning of the year, the school had faulty speakers removed from the ceiling. They no longer worked properly and posed a danger if they were to fall. Their principal had somehow finagled the donation of a new "used" moveable sound system that could be wheeled from location to location, and she'd seen them setting it up yesterday. It still sat on the empty stage, two huge speakers and a stand-mounted microphone with no one behind it.

She walked over to Will and pointed to the corner of the ceiling. "What is that?"

He shrugged.

"There's one over there, too."

"Maybe a speaker?"

"No, they were taken down."

"A camera, then?"

"That's what it looks like, sort of. Does the school have security cameras?"

Again, he shrugged.

She tiptoed across the room. There was one of the objects in each of the four corners. Jess went to the nearest bleacher. The sixteen-foot-high retractable bleachers were fully closed, but she could easily scale the face. The ceiling was at least thirty feet, but a beam ran from side-to-side only seven feet above the top of the bleachers. If she could jump from the top of the bleacher to the beam, she could hoist herself up and easily walk along the high windowsills.

Will hurried over beside her, sneakers squeaking lightly on the hardwood floor. "What are you doing?"

"I'm going up there."

"No, Jess, it's too dangerous. You'll fall."

She wouldn't. But she didn't care if she did.

She started a free climb up the bleachers. It was easier than rock climbing, only without a safety rope. Her lightly sweaty hands achieved perfect tack on the varnished wood. *Thank goodness for old-fashioned bleachers and no money to replace them.*

"Jess!" Will hissed from below.

"I've got this," she whispered back, too softly for him to hear. He was definitely getting an eyeful up the loose skirt of her Harrah's uniform now.

Once at the top, she shook out her arms and hands. It hadn't been difficult, but her adrenaline was raging and her breath was on fire. She smoothed her sweaty palms down the front of the dress and made the leap. The edges of the solid-steel I-beam bit into her arms, but hosting herself up was a simple gymnastic move. She dragged herself to a sitting position on the beam and looked at her hands. She hadn't counted on the inch of dust that had made the beam slippery and caused her a split-second jolt of pure terror.

Jess waited thirty seconds to calm her frantic heart. The rest was easy. From the beam to the sill was a small step. Easy peasy.

As long as I don't look down.

The high windows were like the ones in the locker rooms, but these had flat sills wider than her feet. It was still a precarious walk, especially as she had to fight with herself not to look down, and transferring from one window to the next made her feel a bit like Harrold Lloyd. She kept her eye on the prize.

At the last window, Jess fixed a careful grip on the edge of the windowsill and leaned over. The device was about the size of a camera, with a shiny black area that might serve as the lens, but it didn't look like any camera she'd ever seen. The black lens looked more like the multi-faceted eye of a fly. Even from the ground, it hadn't looked like a camera, and now she could plainly see that it wasn't. She stretched her arm as far as she could and pulled it free. Only when it stopped did she realize a low hum had been coming from it, which had cut off the instant her fingers touched it.

Below, Will put his hands on his head and turned in a circle. "Holy Christmas, be careful!"

The object broke away easily, even though when she first touched it, it had felt solidly attached. It had only been tacked there with some kind of shiny blue gunk.

Jess held it in two fingers, careful not to touch the blue stuff. Still using the other hand to balance herself on the edge of the window, she carefully made her way back. Once back on the top of the bleacher wall, she held her hand out, indicating he should catch it.

"Don't touch the blue stuff."

"The what?"

She gingerly let it slip from her fingers, and Will caught it perfectly.

Climbing back down was almost harder than going up, and the slick surface burned her hands when she slipped a few inches. Still, she managed to land quietly on her bare feet and tried to make it look graceful. Will wore a panicked expression like he was about to go out of his mind.

She slipped back into her flip-flops. "I told you I could do it."

"I'm going to call you Jessica Fearless from now on."

He handed her the device, and they bent their heads over it.

"What is it?" he asked her.

"Hell if I know. Look at the blue stuff."

"Probably *Ectoplasm*."

"This thing almost looks like...some sort of puzzle box." She turned it in her hands. Strange markings peppered the back and sides, and there appeared to be no way to open it. The markings looked like the alien symbols in *Predator*'s forearm-mounted computer device. She hoped it wouldn't start counting down to a nuclear detonation.

"Do you think this had something to do with the disappearance?"

The blue stuff moved, undulating like a live jellyfish.

"What the fuck!" Will snatched his hand back, and Jess nearly dropped the device.

The gymnasium door burst open. Jess screamed.

"FBI! Get on the ground now!" Guns were pointed at their heads as the armed guards charged them. "Get on the ground! Don't move!"

Jess and Will dove for the floor. She landed hard on her chest, arms stretched out in front of her. Shiny loafers appeared in her vision, and a gnarled hand reached down and seized the device.

Six

"You're free to go, Ms. Harding."

Jess jerked awake. A muscle in her neck twanged. Dazed, she forgot about the handcuff around her right wrist and pulled against the bar in the center of the table. Her shoulder and the muscle under her breast cramped, and for a moment, the room spun.

For twenty-three hours she'd been confined to a chair and handcuffed to the table. They had not turned off the lights. All day yesterday and through the long night, the police station was noisy and raw on her senses. Her head pounded so painfully it was hard to hold her vision steady. She'd had only one bathroom break, but she hardly needed that; she'd cried away all her excess liquid and then some.

Agent Roycroft sauntered into the room, followed by a sheepish looking Agent Larsen. He unlocked the cuff at her wrist, and Jess sat upright for the first time in a day. At first, the relief was divine, but then almost immediately, muscle cramps knotted in her back.

"Agent Larsen will drive you home."

They'd given her water, but not nearly enough. She'd cried a hundred times since they'd taken control of the police station and forced her into this bleak interrogation room. Not for herself, but for Shreya. For all the lost students. For those left behind in that agonizing unknown.

She'd answered their endless questions again and again.

Why did you go into the gymnasium? They'd asked this question a hundred times.

To find Shreya, she'd answered each time.

She'd begged, cried, demanded, apologized, sobbed, and begged again. *Please, just tell me what happened to my friend.* But no one would. She didn't ask about the black device, was afraid to even mention it, and they didn't bring it up either. They would probably deny its existence. And if she asked, who knew how long they'd keep her in custody?

She hadn't eaten since yesterday, partly because of the misery she'd endured at the FBI's aggressive questioning. One of the local officers had offered her a greasy burger and some congealed French fries, but she'd declined. She'd been hungry but nauseated. Nothing would have stayed down anyway. At one point, alone in the room, she'd dry heaved.

Jess massaged her wrist then let her arm fall by her side. Her pinky finger started to tingle. Then all of her fingers did.

"Come on, Ms. Harding." Agent Larsen rounded the table. He grasped her upper arm and guided her out of the chair. Jess felt as if she were floating.

He's taking me...no! I can't get in a car with him. What can I do? Think! Ask to use the restroom again, stay on the toilet until he gets bored and goes away. All men hate girl issues. I'll ask for a tampon, that will send him running...

She exited the room to see Will coming the other way, jerking his arm out of the grip of another black-clad agent.

She ran to him and threw her arms around his neck. He caught her readily, squeezed her back, and held on tight. His grip was like an elixir, and though the protective gesture brought tears rushing forward, it also fed her with new life.

"Will," she whispered against his neck.

"It's okay." He tenderly eased her around, keeping his arms wrapped around her, and walked her past the two agents.

"My car is this way," Larsen mumbled, hooking a thumb in the other direction.

"Let them go," Roycroft said.

They exited from the side of the building, through an employee's door to the parking lot where officers parked their personal vehicles. Outside the police station the sun shined brightly. A soothing breeze danced through the trees, and birds sang merrily. *This isn't right; it should be dark and cloudy to match the turmoil in my heart. Storming. Cold.*

A crowd congregated on the street in front of the main doors. Jess heard the angry shouting, saw a news van parked at the curb, its cameraman holding a bulky camera on his shoulder pointed at the police station's front doors. In silent agreement, she and Will turned the opposite way and headed toward the small park in the center of town. The fresh air brought her vision back into focus.

People on the sidewalk stopped and stared, and Jess swallowed down a painful lump of embarrassment. *Look at those troublemaking kids, taking the walk of shame from the police station.* After all the times she'd picked up her mother here, she'd vowed it would never happen to her. Jess saw Chuck, her mailman, standing in front of his truck. He gawked at her in wide-eyed horror, and she suddenly understood why they were all staring.

Survivors. She still wore her black cocktail dress, and Will his ridiculous tuxedo-print t-shirt.

"It's okay, Jess. It's okay."

She realized she was crying.

What will I do? Where will I go? How will I live?

The thought of facing her mother, of another pitiful, pointless, alcohol-induced argument, of their shitty mobile home in that gross trailer park, made her breath cut off.

"I don't want to go home." She couldn't go back to the awful life she had, not without Shreya, her one shining light.

"I know."

She followed him blindly, not willing to give up the security of his arm around her waist. Out of the park to the end of Main Street. Right on to Palomar, left onto Crescent. The sidewalk ended for rustic street edges as the town opened to widely spaced suburbia. Meadows and wild shrubbery surrounded these neighborhoods, dry with an early summer's heat. The high-pitched buzz of insects in the grass helped the world seem real again.

Finally, left onto Waterhouse. She'd been down these quiet, rural streets with their immense properties before, but she had never known anyone who lived here. He turned up the walkway to a magnificent two-story Colonial, nice by most standards but to Jess, a literal palace.

"William!" Mrs. Taylor burst from the front door. She ran across the porch, down the steps, and across the walk toward them. She grasped his face in both hands. "Thank goodness!" Tears shined in her eyes.

She pulled them both into an embrace that was both a complete surprise to Jess, and intensely comforting. Will's mother was shorter than him, plump, and so very obviously in love with her son that it was a foreign experience to behold. She smelled wonderfully of perfume, cookies and...the absence of booze.

She leaned back and finally gave Jess a good look. "Oh, you poor dear."

When she touched Jess's cheek, all Jess could do was stand numbly, dumbfounded.

A neighbor stood at the picket fence separating their yards, staring. Jess had never seen the woman before, but as quickly as she started to take offense, she noticed silvery trails on the woman's face.

"Come inside, both of you." Mrs. Taylor took Will's hand and pulled him toward the house.

"Jess needs a place to rest," he said.

"Of course. You both look exhausted. Let me make you something to eat. Does your mother know where you are, hon?"

Jess swallowed. She only shook her head.

"I'll call her." On the porch, she paused and turned to Will. "Your father is here."

"What?" His tone went hard. "Why?"

"I was scared, Will, and I needed his help. He's the best lawyer I know. And despite all else, he's still your father."

Will clenched his jaw and exhaled sharply through his nose. Jess realized that regardless of the pretty house and the loving adoration of a protective, *sober* mother, his life might not be so perfect, either.

A rolling suitcase stood just inside the door. Mrs. Taylor led them to the kitchen, where a man in a tailored gray suit leaned against the counter. Will's father looked to be in his fifties. He was deeply tanned and wore his longish hair pulled into a ponytail, but slivers of gray at his temples revealed the dark color was a professional's work.

He pushed away from the counter and extended a hand to his son. "Will."

"Dad." Will shook his father's hand.

"Come here." He yanked Will into a hug. Will returned it, but it was brief and formal.

"Your mother's call scared the hell out of me. We've been outside the police station for hours."

"I figured." Will shrugged. "Sorry."

"They could only hold you for twenty-four hours. We were about to head back there now."

"Yeah, thanks," Will said idly. He faced Jess and took her hand. His touch was like a lifeline.

She glanced past him at Mrs. Taylor. She was always smiling, one of the friendliest administrators at the school, but now she looked miserable. Suddenly Jess felt like an intruder. Even though they were all safe, this family needed to heal, too.

"I'm sorry. I should go."

"Don't be silly." Mrs. Taylor seemed to shake herself. "Sit down, Jessica. I'll make you both a sandwich. Two is as much work as one."

New tears rushed forward. Jess grabbed a tissue from a box on a small nook under the phone. They tried not to stare as she wiped at her eyes, and an uncomfortable moment stretched for an eternity. Jess sat at the cozy table in the center of the large kitchen, prompting Will and his father to do the same, while Mrs. Taylor pulled a loaf of bread and a jar of mayonnaise from the refrigerator and started building sandwiches.

Mr. Taylor cleared his throat. "I can't imagine what you two have gone through these past two days," he offered thinly.

As awful as it had been for her, what was Shreya going through right now? Had she been swallowed into Hell? Or snatched away to some galaxies-distant planet where she was now a captive? It didn't seem possible, and yet it was. At this point, there was no assumption that was too far-fetched.

"You're both eighteen, so I couldn't demand to be present while you were questioned, and neither of you were officially charged with a crime. But you trespassed on a federal investigation—"

"It was my fault," Jess interrupted. "Will didn't want to do it." She glanced up at the sweet woman holding a freshly washed tomato, the epitome of the Disney mom, and guilt lodged in her throat. "I'm sorry, Mrs. Taylor."

"That's not true," Will said quickly. "It was your idea, but I wanted to just as much."

"I'm sorry," Jess said again. "But I had to know."

"Of course you did, and we don't blame either of you," his father said. "You're just foolish kids who didn't understand the magnitude of your actions, and nobody can fault you for wanting to know what happened to your friends."

"Or not trusting the government," Mrs. Taylor muttered. She turned back to her cutting board and began slicing the tomato with angry chops on her cutting board.

"Lucille," Mr. Taylor said.

"I'm sorry, but I do not appreciate the secrecy of those agents when they have information about the fate of *our* children. Something terrible happened right here in *our* town. They have no right to be secretive with us."

"They're just doing their jobs."

"What if Will was one of..." She stopped and pointed with the kitchen knife. "I sure hope you'd be singing a different song then."

Mr. Taylor winced, eyes darting to the blade. "I would move heaven and earth to protect either of you."

She went back to the tomato she was murdering. "Sure you would. All the way from Florida."

Mr. Taylor cleared his throat. "The sheriff gave an impromptu press conference while you were in custody. It was so brief he nearly incited a riot, so that FBI agent, Roycroft, gave a private statement to the parents only, no press. They're calling it an 'unexplained event,' but they insist they weren't behind it."

"They're lying," Jess said, suddenly never more certain of anything in her life.

Mr. Taylor's gaze shot to her. "That hasn't been established yet. We don't even know what happened, and it's too premature to lay blame." He held a finger over his lips and shook his head. *Don't say anything.*

A chicken sandwich on a real, ceramic plate appeared before Jess. Mrs. Taylor had sliced it corner to corner, with a sprinkling of potato chips and a sliver of pickle next to it. It looked as fancy as the sandwiches they served at Angelina's Tea Room, where her mother had taken her for her birthday a year ago, during a rare period of sobriety. This birthday had passed in a haze of drunkenness, their arguments alternating between accusations that Jess was planning to leave soon, and demands that she do.

"Thank you, Mrs. Taylor."

Will's mother slid into the open chair next to Jess and patted her hand. "You can call me Mrs. Taylor when we're at school, but here you call me Lucille."

A spike of fear lanced her heart. "I'm never going back to that school again."

Mr. Taylor's mobile phone rang with a shrill jingle that made her jump. He stood and moved away from the table to answer, *hmmm*-ing and *yes*-ing mysteriously.

Jess picked up the sandwich. This wasn't packaged deli meat; Will's mom had cut thick slices from a grilled chicken breast. Meaty slices of tomato and ruffly lettuce protruded from the edges. Jess took a bite and felt like Popeye eating a can of spinach. New energy coursed into her and the fuzzy edges on everything turned sharp again.

She choked over a laugh.

"Everything all right, dear?" Mrs. Taylor asked her.

"This is the most delicious sandwich I've ever had." Her face scrunched up embarrassingly, and Jess used her napkin to blot away the new rush of tears.

"I should call your mother." She pushed out of her chair.

"No, please! Not yet. I just want to close my eyes for a few minutes before I face her."

Mrs. Taylor eased back down. "All right. I understand."

"Thank you." She nibbled another small bite. "This really is so good."

"My mom makes the best sandwiches," Will said. "Eat at least half, and then I'll take you upstairs to lie down."

Jess felt a pang of good-natured envy as Mrs. Taylor beamed at her son. For as long as she could remember, everything June cooked came out of a can or a cardboard box. The sandwich was truly delicious, but by the time she got to the end of the first half, she was forcing it down through a tight throat. It seemed shameful to enjoy a delicious meal while Shreya was in agony–or worse, dead.

Mr. Taylor ended his call and strode back into the kitchen. "I have to go to the police station. I'll be working in conjunction with Hayworth-Castleberry. Larry Castleberry's daughter is one of the missing."

"My dad used to work for their firm when he lived here," Will explained. Mrs. Taylor subtly placed the box of tissues on the table.

Jess nodded. She took another tissue and blew her nose.

"They're talking gag order. That could mean settlement. Larry's case will set precedent. Until I come back, I don't want any of you talking to anyone. Jessica, you're free to choose your own representation, of course."

She snorted. She was also free to take a Caribbean cruise or fly to New York for a shopping spree. The only thing stopping her was having no money.

"I understand I might not be the most conventional choice—"

"I live in Happy Hollow," she said softly. "I can't afford any lawyer. Conventional or otherwise."

"You'll be well represented, I promise you." He placed a reassuring hand on her shoulder before grabbing his briefcase. "Lucille, don't open the door for anyone, and don't answer the phone."

Will seemed more relaxed after his father left. "I'm going to take Jess up to my room."

"Okay, sweetie. I'll be right here in case you need anything." When he stood, she snatched him into a quick, tight hug. "I love you, Willie-bear."

"I love you too, Momma-bear."

Jess almost didn't understand the exchange. Had June ever uttered a sentiment even remotely close to that?

"You're so lucky," Jess whispered as she followed him up a staircase decorated with dozens of family portraits in frames behind glass, most of them starring Will at various stages of life. It was odd that his mother would let Will take a girl upstairs to his room, but she figured normal households possessed not only love, but trust.

His room was neat but cluttered. She collapsed on his bed on her side, kicking off her flip-flops before bringing her feet up. Her body was heavy, like a sack of potatoes. Though the day was warm, her bare legs felt cold as they pressed together.

"Oh, sorry." She tried to push upright. "I didn't think—"

"No prob." He swallowed, cleared his throat. "Get comfortable."

She could see he was trying to act nonchalant, but his ears turned pink.

"Somebody likes model making," she said over a yawn. They were everywhere—planes hanging from the ceiling, sleek muscle car replicas and military vehicles on every spare surface, a Viking longship on a wall-mounted shelf, and a half-finished nineteenth-century passenger liner on his desk.

"Helps pass the time." He closed the door and sat at his desk, bringing his computer to life with a slide of the mouse. "Schoolwork isn't much of a challenge for me."

"You helped me get my first A in science ever, sophomore year."

"You remember that?"

"Of course. You were so quiet and so shy. I thought you were such a nerd."

He laughed, but when she reached out her hand, Will's expression sobered. He hesitated over two heartbeats, and then he took it and let her urge him onto the bed. He lay down next to her and Jess rolled over, pulling him in behind her on the mattress.

"Your mom doesn't mind me being in here with you?"

"She's probably downstairs rejoicing right now."

"Never brought a girl home before?"

"You're the first. I think that's what had her worried." His voice was soft, his breath warm in her hair. "She was afraid I would take after my dad. Not that she had any reason to...I mean, I'm not..."

"Did he leave her for another woman?" Jess felt herself grow heavier. She blinked to stay awake, terrified of the nightmares that might come.

It felt wrong to sleep. She needed to be working on a plan to rescue Shreya.

"My dad lives in Florida." When she stayed silent, he went on. "He left her for another man."

She looked over her shoulder. "Really?"

"You didn't notice the plucked eyebrows? The shiny fingernails? He dresses up in women's clothes. Apparently, there's a whole population of cross-dressers down there who like to impersonate female celebrities."

"I had no idea."

"Last year, I found my mom up here, crying, after she flipped my mattress and found my collection of Playboys. I thought she was upset, but it turns out she was thrilled." He let out a long breath. "That's why she made me go to the dance."

A swoop of anxiety rolled through Jess. How close he'd come to vanishing into nothingness, all because his mom wanted him to socialize with girls.

"So, you build models and collect Playboys."

He chuckled. She squeezed his hand.

"You're a ton of surprises, Will Taylor." *And you were the only one brave enough to go back inside the school with me to call for help.*

"Good ones, I hope."

She yawned and blinked the grittiness from her eyes. "You like girls."

"That's a surprise?"

"No Just stating the obvious."

"What about you, Jess?" he asked in a soft voice. "Do you like girls?"

"I like one girl." She sighed. "You heard things about me and Shreya."

"There's talk," he offered hesitantly. Then quickly, "It's no big deal, really."

Tears welled anew. Jess had thought she was all dried up. "She's very special to me."

"But you went to the dance with Brendan. You could have gone together. I heard Lisa Calloway and Rosalina Gutierrez were going together."

Two more students mysteriously gone. There had been a small amount of hullabaloo over the girls going to prom together, but it had been allowed. The principal at their small high school had probably decided that trying to stop them would be the worst of two controversies.

"We're not like them." She sighed again. "I mean, not a couple. I definitely like boys. But...I just love her so much."

"I think I get it."

She glanced back again. "You do?"

"Sure. Girls are complex and emotional."

That made her smile. Or at least feel like smiling.

"I shouldn't have said yes to Brendan. We're not even dating or anything. Just...neither of us wanted to go alone. He might not have even gone to the dance if I hadn't said agreed to be his date. Does that make me a terrible person? Now he's...*gone*, and I'm wishing I hadn't said yes to him."

"No. It doesn't make you a terrible person."

She still felt like one. Nearly the entire senior class had disappeared, and all she could think of was one single person.

"Where do you think they are?" She'd been afraid to ask the question, afraid even more to hear his answer.

He waited a long time before speaking. "I don't know."

"Why do you think we didn't...Do you believe in God?"

He paused over a heartbeat. "Before, I wasn't sure. Now, I don't."

Her throat tightened up, and Jess gulped down two deep breaths before asking the question that scared her the most.

"What if she never comes back?"

Seven

Jess's summer dragged by agonizingly slowly, and yet flew by with record speed.

Nine days after the disappearance of the West Ridge High School senior prom, the FBI presented pain-and-suffering compensation and non-disclosure agreements to all local residents within the city limits. If there was any ruckus by anyone other than the affected parents who didn't want to sign, Jess never heard it. It seemed all people could talk about was what they weren't supposed to; the hush money checks that were deposited and found not to be rubber.

A total of ninety-seven people had vanished from West Ridge High's gymnasium. Among the missing were three school administrators including Mr. Renner, the principal; two volunteer parent chaperones; and ninety-two students. The national news flashed and burned with what little information the FBI released, and the missing were nicknamed the Kileyville 97. After the first weekend when the FBI had chased off the prime-time news vans, as far as Jess knew, they had not been allowed back.

Sheriff Weasley resigned a week later, citing emotional and physical ailments not necessarily related to the job. She'd seen him twice after being released by the FBI. The already overweight, red-faced smoker had looked ten times worse than normal, wiping sweat from his neck on a seventy-degree day that carried a nice breeze.

The FBI packed up their tent and left town twelve days after prom night. Just for the heck of it, Jess tried calling the number on the business card Agent Roycroft had given her. It rang endlessly with no answer and no voicemail.

Jackass.

A group of parents set up tents in front of the police station, probably contributing to Sheriff Weasley's speedy resignation. As the weeks passed the group grew smaller, but even today, ten or so still remained.

With only five months until the election and no deputy sheriff to step in, Sheriff Weasley was replaced with an interim police captain named Sinclair on loan from Sacramento. He had not dared to try and make the parents leave. His too-cheerful nature seemed fake, his permanent smile stiff and insincere, and he made exaggerated statements about not resting until every missing person was safely home. He wasn't even from Kileyville yet he acted like the incident was a personal affront against *him*. Jess gave him a wide berth.

Graduation was canceled. The families of the ninety-two missing students were presented with diplomas in lieu of a ceremony. Jess and the other remaining seniors, now dubbed the "Lucky 13," were also given theirs in a small and very somber meeting in a banquet room at the Holiday Inn.

June had sobered up the morning after the "incident" to find the town in chaos and her daughter missing. She assumed Jess had disappeared with the other students, and it was her undoing. After signing her confidentiality agreement, she reserved herself a bed at a local rehab clinic, and Jess borrowed a neighbor's more dependable car to drive her there. After the thirty-minute drive, June grasped Jess's cheeks the way Will's mother had and told Jess she loved her, and Jess broke down in tears.

Jess was glad her mother was getting the help she needed, but a secret, greedy part of her was glad to have the distance. Her mother had always been an unstable bucket of dynamite, and Jess didn't think she could keep a handle on her own emotions with June around.

Neither Jess nor Will had set out to spend time together, but over the summer, their paths kept crossing. One day, they shared a pizza at Rudolpho's, and Jess called in sick to her job at the Dairy Queen to spend the rest of the afternoon hanging out with him at the reservoir. Employees were notified the day before that the company was closing Kileyville's location anyway. They found Katherine and Luke there, but no one mentioned prom night or the missing students. They smoked a joint and hung out in silence in the sun, but it made Jess feel emotionally funky. Katherine and Luke started making out, leaving Jess even more uncomfortable.

"I gotta go," she said simply, and got up and walked home alone.

Two days later, she went in search of Will. She passed by the comic book store, went through the arcade hall at the bowling alley, and finally found him at the library.

She leaned on the edge of the privacy desk he'd piled with books. "Sorry I got so weird on Wednesday. Pot makes me way too emotional."

To this, he laughed.

"Especially now," she added, and his smile faded.

"I don't like it either," he admitted. "It makes me feel dumb."

She smiled and nudged him on the shoulder. "That's why they call it *dope*." She nodded toward his book. "Seriously? Chemistry? Are you unaware it's your summer vacation? Or are you just trying to build back the brain cells you fried?"

He closed the book and leaned back in his chair. "It doesn't really feel like summer vacation."

There wasn't anyone else in the study room, but one of the librarians passed through and shushed them anyway.

"Can we talk outside?" she asked him.

"Sure." He closed the book. "Let me check out these books, and I'll meet you out front."

Jess sat on the concrete edge of the fountain in front of the library and watched sunlight reflecting off the water. She smiled when she saw him coming through the doors. He hefted an overstuffed backpack onto both shoulders and unlocked his bike. He wheeled it over and leaned it against the low wall of the fountain.

"You really are such a nerd."

"Sorry."

"I like it." Jess tossed a nickel into the water.

"I know what you wished for." He dug into his pocket and handed her a quarter. "Here, buy a more expensive wish."

She laughed but tossed it in anyway. She waited a few minutes to speak, hiding the fact that even now, tears threatened. She was starting to look pathetic. He must have sensed it.

"You should wear dresses more often," he offered as a sideways compliment. And then, "It softens the whole 'badass trailer park' persona."

She laughed again. Will had a knack for making her feel better even on the worst days.

"I would have thought all my bawling ended my badassery a long time ago." In truth, she felt confident and pretty in the fluttery yellow sundress, her first independent purchase that wasn't from Goodwill.

"Don't worry. You're still a badass in my eyes."

"Gosh, thanks. I think."

"No, seriously." His voice took on that nervous quaver she'd come to recognize. "Nobody's as brave as you, Jess."

She stared into the water, aware Will was looking at her. She glanced up and caught him staring. His cheeks went pink.

"I think you're pretty great. Even when you're not wearing a dress."

"Come on. I can walk with you as far as the..." She almost said school. She meant what she'd told his mother that day; she was never going back there.

Even though she had free use of the Honda now, she walked most everywhere she went. She could go through the park near his house and cut around the school on the bike path that ended at Homestead, and then go past the cemetery. That was only the slightly longer way to Happy Hollow trailer park.

He grabbed his bike and walked alongside her.

"So...you're going to New York next week," she ventured cautiously. It was almost painful to bring it up. Soon she'd be alone again. "I want to say be careful in the big city, but after what we've been through, it would take an *Independence Day* to rattle you."

"I'd prefer *Mars Attacks*," he said.

She laughed. "Yeah, I like those aliens better, too. What about *The Blob*? That'd creep you out."

"Naw, just pour salt on it. Maybe *Deep Impact*."

"I forgot about that one." This was why she liked spending time with him. Will was easy to talk to, and when a super-smart guy liked the same corny movies she did, it made her feel a little bit smarter, too. She was truly going to miss him.

"Yeah, well, don't tell anyone, but part of me is kind of nervous," he admitted. "Country bumpkin at Times Square, and all that."

She swept her arms wide in exaggeration. "How could you leave all this grandeur for New York?"

"The other part of me can't wait to get the hell out."

They walked in silence for a while. Not a single car passed them on the street. Ever since prom night, going downtown felt like walking into the

Twilight Zone.

"I never considered going to college because I didn't have any money."

"Now, you can go wherever you want," he said softly.

"That's just it; I wouldn't dream of leaving now," she responded without hesitation. "I feel like there's an invisible chain around my ankle."

"Is that why you wanted to talk? You need me to convince you you're wrong? Seriously Jess, you have no reason to feel tethered here."

"But I do." She swallowed, and brought up the subject that had been making her sore for weeks. "Actually, I wanted to talk to you about the money."

Another long silence passed, and she knew he was reading her mind. He probably felt the same way.

"Do you feel guilty about taking it?" she asked him.

"Not really. I mean, I have some survivor's guilt, but that's all it is."

"I do. I feel like we gave up on them. Like we're saying, 'it's okay you took our loved ones away, as long as you give us money as compensation.'"

"We don't know the government had anything to do with it."

"Now you sound like your dad," she said more harshly than she intended. "The fact they even offered it is a huge guilty banner: 'Yeah, we did it. But we're the government, so what you gonna do? Take the money and shut up.'"

"They didn't have to give us anything. It's not poof they're behind this." He hesitated, as if holding his breath. "Remember that blue stuff? It didn't seem like anything from this world."

"Maybe," she said. "But then why did Roycroft grab that device from me?"

He didn't respond, and Jess felt bad for the harsh edge that had found its way into her voice.

"You know, even though people aren't supposed to be talking, they are. I don't know how much they gave you..." she cast a sideways glance at him. "But they gave me a lot more than others are saying. If the rumors are true."

"Yeah, me too," he admitted softly. "Two hundred thousand."

She nodded. "Same here."

"Maybe it was just more to us six who were at the school," he deduced. "Anika Kumagi's father told my dad a hundred and twenty-five thousand isn't enough for the nervous breakdown she's going through now, and she wasn't even at the school that night. I could probably find out what the other 'thirteen' got, if I snoop through his briefcase."

"My mom got eighty," she told him. "When you consider everyone in the whole town got at least that much, it seems like a lot of money to keep people quiet if they didn't have anything to do with it."

He sighed. "I guess you're right."

"I'm not blaming you for not feeling guilty," she added. "And the money has probably saved my mom's life. I'm just saying I feel really shitty about the whole thing."

"I get it," he conceded. "I didn't lose anybody. Not like you did, or the parents did. Yeah, some of them were my friends, but...then again, they weren't. I didn't exactly fit in like you did."

She snorted. "Yeah, right. I was miss popularity." With her blah-brown hair and unremarkable features, she was the kind of girl who would only be called pretty by her mother.

"You were. Everybody loved Jess, volleyball captain and track star. Your semi-final win in the mile junior year was what took West Ridge to the regionals."

How funny it was, the perceptions of others. Here she had spent her whole summer being envious of Will's loving parents and stable home. In fact, she's spent most of her life thinking she would never be as good as everyone else because she didn't live in a pretty house and wear nice clothes that hadn't belonged to someone else first.

"I feel like I betrayed Shreya for not telling them to shove their offer. I should be looking for her, not taking hush money to forget about her."

"Nobody says you can't continue looking for her."

"I wouldn't even know where to start." She'd wracked her brain over it until she couldn't think of anything else. The other half of her guilt came from the exhaustion, from wanting all this to be over.

From not wanting to keep looking.

Jess was one hundred percent guilty, and she was tired of feeling that way. She looked sidelong at Will and got that little blossom of warmth in her chest again. She wanted to enjoy these last few days with him, even if that added to her guilt.

"I always do this, don't I?"

"Do what?"

"Make it all about me. You're going off on the adventure of a lifetime, and I haven't even asked you what you're going to study."

He looked forward, grinning slightly, turning pink. She'd come to realize that was his bashful look, and she adored it.

"Oh. you know me. Nerd to the end."

"Astrophysics?"

He laughed. "Chemistry, with a minor in literature."

"Ah. The easy degrees, then."

He stopped his bicycle in the shade of Brewed Awakening's awning and faced her. "So...um. When I get there...can I tell people I have a girlfriend?"

"Well, I don't know," she teased lightly. "You haven't even kissed me yet."

He blinked, confused.

Jess put her hands on his shoulders and eased closer. He sucked in a breath, closing his eyes at the last instant as if he couldn't believe she was really going to kiss him. Her lips met his cautiously at first, and he responded with vigor. His hands went around her back and scooped her closer, and Jess heard his bicycle crash over behind them.

Her heart felt light as a butterfly, and her guilt slipped away for the first time in months. She imagined if Shreya were here, she would squeal with delight. His kiss was sweet and inexperienced, and he smelled like freshly cut garden herbs and boy sweat.

A woman's harsh voice broke the spell. "It isn't fair!"

Lola Carson stalked toward them on the sidewalk. Her face was red, and tears filled her eyes. She pointed her finger accusingly.

"It isn't right that trailer trash like you is spared when my daughter was taken, and now you're having a summer romance like nothing happened? Shelby had everything going for her. A bright future, a college scholarship—"

"Don't talk to her like that," Will shouted back.

Mrs. Carson recoiled.

"Jess was the only person who did anything to try and find them. The FBI held us for almost *two days* because we broke into the gymnasium looking for clues. It was Jess's idea—she's the one who saw the device and climbed up to the ceiling to pull it down without any thought for her own safety. She risked *federal prison* to find *your* daughter. You owe her your gratitude, not your insults."

Mrs. Carson glanced back and forth between them. Her mouth opened once, and then twice, like a fish on dry land.

"I'm sorry." She whirled around and dashed off in the other direction.

Will picked up his bicycle and straightened his backpack straps. He took Jess's hand, and they continued walking.

Butterflies danced in her stomach. She couldn't believe quiet, shy Will had defended her like that.

"That's the sweetest thing anybody has ever done for me."

"So, that's a yes on the girlfriend thing?"

Eight

Jess changed her mind, and then changed it back a hundred times. In the end, it was the lonely, rattletrap mobile home that convinced her to go to Will as much as her blossoming feelings for him. She could almost say she loved him, if she understood what that truly meant. All she knew was that if there was one person alive who could make her feel happy, it was him.

She borrowed Mrs. Jessup's beach cruiser and pedaled the long way to the bike path that ran behind the school and through the park to Will's quiet neighborhood. She couldn't bear to see the memorial of flowers, candles, teddy bears, and school banners the townspeople had set up on the front lawn of the school. Instead, she took the road along the cemetery to come in on the other side, which was almost as bad. Cemeteries gave her the willies.

Will's neighborhood appeared to close for business at nine o'clock. There were no streetlights out here, but pretty path lights and lawn posts in the yards made it look like a postcard. Somewhere in the night, a lonely dog woofed twice and fell silent. The neighborhood was so quiet she could hear the buzz of the bicycle's fat tires on the pavement.

Her heart sped with her daring, but in her gut, this felt right.

Jess dismounted the bike and walked it through the gate of the Taylors' picket fence. She leaned it against the shrubs on the side of the house and looked for a small pebble. Bluish, flickering light in the front room downstairs probably meant his mother was awake, watching television. The lights were also on in Will's room. She tossed a pebble up, hearing the light 'tink' it made on the glass. She tossed a second, and watched his window slide up.

His face brightened. "Hey."

"Can I come up?" She kicked off her flip-flops.

"Sure, I'll open the door," he whispered back, but Jess had already climbed onto the back stoop's railing. Barefoot, she placed one foot on the porch post that supported the small overhang and hefted herself up.

Will laughed and shook his head. "You make that look so easy."

"That's because it is."

He stood back and let her climb through the window. "What's up?" He looked confused. She'd been here in the evening before, but she'd never come over this late.

"I came to say goodbye."

"I thought we were meeting for lunch at Jack's Grill tomorrow."

"Not that kind of goodbye." She grabbed his shoulders and kissed him. He kissed her back happily, but Jess pulled back quickly.

She grabbed her sundress by the skirt and pulled it over her head. Beneath she wore only panties.

Will's eyes went wide, and he glanced unabashedly down her body. She stepped close and kissed him again. His warm hands slid around her back, pulling her against him. His breathing increased, and his kiss was hungry. When she pulled his t-shirt free of his jeans, he caught his breath.

"Jess. You don't have to."

"I know I don't have to," she whispered back. She pulled his shirt over his head and urged him backward. His legs collided with the mattress, and he sat.

"I want to." Heat filled her cheeks. "Do you?"

"Yeah," he croaked. "Heck yeah."

Jess went to the door and quietly locked it. When she turned around, she stood in the center of the room, content to let him stare. She hooked her thumbs under the straps of her panties and slowly dragged them down. His Adam's apple rose and fell.

She smiled as she walked over, straddled his lap, and urged him to lie back. She kissed him lightly. He closed his eyes and returned it softly, as if afraid to wake himself from a dream.

"I'm on birth control," she told him. "June made me since I was fifteen. But..."

His eyes blinked open.

"It's my first time."

His arms slid around her back in a slow, savoring caress. "Mine too." He flipped her over and fell between her legs. Lanky, nerdy Will was stronger than she anticipated, and excitement fluttered in her chest. He made her feel feminine, and delicate.

He fumbled with the button fly on his jeans and Jess helped him nudge them down. When his naked body came against hers, fireworks exploded in her eyes.

He kissed her slowly, sliding his hands over her. She was content to let him explore, to learn every inch of her.

He rose onto his elbows and looked down at her. "You're very special to me," he told her. "This is very special."

When their bodies joined together, the emotional heartache of the past three months lifted away. She felt connected to another person in a way she never had before—an emotional bond she hadn't felt since losing Shreya. Even though he was leaving the day after tomorrow, touching him this way healed her soul. Nobody else understood her like Will did, nobody else but him had been through what she had. Now they were together in a way neither of them ever had been with anyone else.

Later she dozed in his arms with the breeze of the warm summer night caressing her bare body.

"That 'girlfriend' thing?" she whispered. "I'm not holding you to that."

"You don't have to." With his arm looped around her, he bent his wrist and traced his fingertips up and down her arm. "*I'm* holding me to it."

"There'll be a lot of girls at college. I want you to feel...untethered."

"There's only one girl. It's you, Jess. It's always been you. Longer than you know."

She'd sensed he might have been harboring a long-time crush. That was hugely flattering, but college was supposed to be fun, and a learning experience for the rest of life—both academically and personally.

"Promise me you'll go to lots of parties and drink lots of beer, and I want you to talk to at least ten girls at each one."

Will laughed. "Not gonna happen."

"Promise me, and I'll make it worth your while."

He breathed deeply in and out. "One girl. The pimply one with crooked teeth."

"Ten pretty girls, or you're in trouble when you come home." She snuggled closer and slid her hand over his hip.

"Okay. The prettiest, so-far-out-of-my-league-it'll-never-happen girl."

"Oh, ye of little faith."

"I'll talk to her about enthalpy and transuranic elements."

"You'll make lots of friends that way."

She slid on top of him and poised to take him again.

"And when you get tired of life in the big city, I'll be here waiting."

PART TWO

Present Day

A part of Jess had been hoping Will would come back to town after his mother suffered a stroke, while another part of her gnawed on the chip on her shoulder that had gradually built over the last decade to become so heavy she could barely hold it up anymore.

Before she saw him—truly looked up and acknowledged it was in fact Will Taylor watching her from the sidewalk in front of the coffee shop—she'd recognized the presence from the corner of her eye; sensed the taller, broader more powerful essence of the man who'd left town all those years ago but never truly left her thoughts.

He'd existed there in her mind, like Shreya did but differently; a growing, flourishing entity until he'd occupied a place in her heart and head almost as large her missing friend's.

He'd written letters at first, and she'd written back, but they'd become farther and farther apart until neither of them even sent Christmas cards anymore.

Just as well. Jess had never been a Christmas card kind of person.

She stopped and looked up, finally settling her gaze on him. He truly had blossomed, in height and the width of his shoulders, but mostly in the maturity in his face.

Damn, it was hard to stay irritated with a man who had turned in to a Grade-A hottie.

His lips moved. *Jessica Harding.*

She formed a little smile. *Will Taylor.*

Jess advanced on the sidewalk, watching him watching her, holding his paper cup in one hand and his other stuffed in the pocket of his jeans, leather jacket slung through the loop of his arm like a damned Ralph Lauren model.

Don't make this easy on him, her inner Devil said. *He can't just disappear for ten years and then show up again like it's no big deal.*

A tiny, angelic part of her brain argued, *You can't resent him for finding the life you were too scared to reach for. Weren't you the one who told him to go off and live it to the fullest?*

"Hey, stranger." She hated herself for glancing at his ring finger. Hated herself even more for the warm relief at seeing it bare. She'd suspected he hadn't married; his mother would have told her if he had.

The gentle smile he returned was so familiarly Will, and yet so different, it made her heart ache for all the time lost between them.

He'd matured, both in looks and in the air of self-assurance wafting off him. There was a confidence in his stance and the way he held his chin that hadn't been there before, and though his bashfulness was something she'd always loved, she couldn't deny this was just as appealing.

"Damn, Jess." His smile grew. "My mother sent me the picture of you in your uniform, but it isn't as impressive as seeing you in real life."

A flicker of surprise grew from his words. Then again, Mrs. Taylor had never stopped rooting for her; she'd said as much as over the years.

"I was going to send congratulations when you graduated the academy, but..."

She couldn't fight her own smile as the old, bashful Will showed through. "Don't worry about it," she assured him. "I'm guilty, too. What've you got now, three degrees?"

"Something like that." He gave a non-committal shrug. "You look great, Jess."

"You look good too, Will," she returned in a guarded tone. "I read all of your books. *The Longest Bridge* was my favorite. It was almost like I could hear your voice as I read."

She wanted to ask if it had been him who wrote *The Night They Vanished: The True Story of California's Kileyville 97*, and not Stan Herlinger, whose quick and mysterious departure after he refused the government's hush money was almost as conspiracy-worthy as the 97's disappearance. No one would have ever called the feed store owner a wordsmith, and the book had come from the same publisher that had released Will's four thrillers.

But that was the kind of information that could make a person disappear in this town, or at least face federal prison, so she figured if he wanted her to know, he'd volunteer it.

"Thanks." His cheeks colored. There he was, the old Will she loved and missed terribly.

Jess cleared her throat as building grief choked her. "I'm so sorry about your mom." She blinked away tears before they could form. "It seems like she's doing better, right? She's sitting up now."

He glanced away. His Adam's apple rose and fell. "Her speech is improving, but she can't walk because she can't work the crutches with her left arm. But I'm sure that's temporary. She's tackling her therapy like a gladiator."

Jess laughed. "Are you staying at the house?"

He nodded. "She told me you bought the Peabody farm. I was going to pop out and see you."

"Oh yeah?" She swallowed down a spike of hurt. *If he knew I moved there, why had his letters stopped?*

"Care to get a cup of coffee?"

"Looks like you already have one." She gave him a mouth shrug. "Besides, I still don't drink it."

"Tea, then."

"Maybe later." A part of Jess regretted the disappointment that clearly settled over his features. Another part thought he deserved it. *No, that's not true,* she told herself. *But I can't give him the wrong idea.* All these years, pebble by pebble, she'd been building a wall around her heart, and it was now ten feet high. The loneliness was almost comforting, and certainly better than being hurt again.

He nodded awkwardly, and silence stretched.

"So, how've you been? Seeing anyone?" He gave a little laugh, and his cheeks colored again.

Now she looked away. "I'm uh...yeah." She regretted the tiny lie, but in truth, she was fully committed to her job. It might as well be her lover; it occupied almost every moment and every thought.

But mostly, Will Taylor was a risk she couldn't gamble on at this point in her life. He was practically a celebrity, had built a life in New York that was so solid he hadn't been back to Pine Bluff once, not even for Christmas, in ten years.

"I'm glad." Whether he believed her or not, his tone and the settling of his body language said he got the message.

Her shoulder radio squawked. "All units, ten-ninety-eight."

She held up a finger. "Nineteen-six, I'm ten-eight, go ahead."

"Eleven-forty-four. Sheriff is on scene, requesting backup. Over."

"Nineteen-six, I'm available."

"We've got a Union Pacific dead on the tracks one mile north of Arroyo Seco Drive. Coroner is on route. Acknowledge."

"Nineteen-six, responding." She looked at Will. "I have to go."

"Raincheck on that cup of tea? Just to catch up."

"Maybe." She tossed him a smile as she turned and jogged back to her cruiser. "No promises."

Jess set the lights as she raced toward the scene, telling herself not to feel pathetic. As delicious as he looked, Will Taylor was a jar of emotional angst she couldn't open up right now.

❧

Bruce stood near the train waiting for her, thumbs hooked into his belt.

"Mildred Hedge called it in because it activated the safety arms at Arroyo Seco Drive. She said the train drifted to a stop and then just sat here."

Jess's boots crunched up the gravel slope to the tracks. Her shoulder radio warbled and she turned down the volume. She stopped and surveyed the behemoth idling before her. It rumbled like thunder that never ended. These things were enormous and daunting when you stood right next to them. Three years ago, she'd seen what one moving at moderate speed could do to a car and the occupants inside.

"I don't suppose shutting it off is as easy as turning a key in the ignition?" she surmised aloud.

"Driving this thing is about as easy as flying the space shuttle. It's all computerized and linked to the main network, but Doris says Union Pacific wasn't aware of any malfunction due to a glitch in their system."

Jess rolled her eyes. "That's fantastic." California's deteriorating railway system was a tragedy waiting to happen.

"They've closed off this track and a conductor is on his way, but Caltrans will probably get here sooner."

She looked at him. "From Sacramento?"

"From Sacramento," he confirmed grimly.

Their dying town had few resources of its own. She continued up the slope toward the locomotive, but Bruce stepped into her path, holding his hands up.

"It's grisly."

"I can handle it." He was always looking out for her, and sometimes Jess appreciated it.

Sometimes she didn't.

"This time it's different."

Now she did stop. "Different how?"

"Jess, I know what you're thinking."

She frowned. "How can you know what I'm thinking when I don't even know what I'm thinking?"

"You said it yourself; every call gives you a jolt, a spike of hope. 'Maybe this time.'"

Her heart kicked a double beat. She glanced at the train. "What's going on, Bruce?"

"It's a mutilation. But it's more than that."

She snapped her attention back to him.

"It's strange."

"Strange how?" Her voice quavered.

"They've disappeared." His lips formed a tight line.

A ball of ice dropped into her stomach. She moved past and stalked up the rising ballast, a renewed energy coursing through her heart that she hadn't felt in *years*.

Metal stairways on each side of the locomotive rose to a platform on the very front. The windows were too high to see inside from the platform. An access door stood open; Sheriff Brady had already been inside. Jess grabbed the locomotive's handrail and felt the heavy throb of its heartbeat.

Even after seven years on the force, some calls triggered a sliver of remembrance, a hint of *what if*, a shadow of *could it be*? But that was all it ever was; a hint, a sliver, a shadow of what she would never be able to forget.

Nothing she could ever prove was related, even when she knew in her gut it was.

*But this...*Bruce was right. This felt different.

The scene inside was so odd Jess switched on her flashlight and knelt down to get a clearer look. Two pairs of legs, severed neatly just below the knee, lay fallen where men had been standing. Though the flesh and muscle were bloody, the wounds weren't ragged, and there was very little blood evidence in general. The tibia on each leg was neatly severed, as was the fabric of the pants each man had been wearing. There were no saw marks or burn marks. No torn tatters of fabric or ripped shreds of skin.

"Bizarre," Jess whispered to herself. She used her personal phone to snap several pictures, and then stood and looked around the small conductor's cab. She'd never been inside a locomotive before, but everything she saw looked like legitimate train mechanics with the expected amount of rust, grease, and grime. No odd-looking items that seemed unfitting.

No mysterious blue goo.

A red button blinked red on the dash. MALFUNCTION.

Jess climbed down, noting a gathering crowd that had come through the small section of woods behind the Fill 'N Feast.

"We've got another one back here, and two more in the rear locomotive. Five in all," Sheriff Brady told her.

"All the same?"

"Exactly."

Three teens on BMX bikes lingered on the ballast about a half mile down. She saw one kid thumbing rapidly across his phone. More onlookers would be here soon. In Pine Bluff anything odd brought people out of the woodwork—afraid to look but more afraid not to.

"Let's get this thing taped off," Sheriff Brady said.

Len Potter eased the coroner's wagon around the warning arms and onto the ballast at the crossing on Arroyo Seco Drive. Even at this distance, she could hear his tires popping over the gravel as he rolled slowly toward them. He gave a toot of his horn, and the kids on bikes wheeled out of his way. Fortunately, the bells at the crossing were silent. The only indication that anything was wrong were the lowered arms and flashing red lights.

Sheriff Brady spoke into his radio, calling for deputies to block off the road in each direction to discourage gawkers. That left one deputy on patrol.

Perfect time to rob the town bank, Jess thought wryly. Hell, nowadays, anytime was the perfect time to rob the town bank.

She went to her patrol car and retrieved two rolls of crime-scene tape from the trunk. Deputy Swenson sidled over, wearing his standard green-at-the-gills face. She'd seen him throw up on duty twice; once at a drunk-driving fatality and again at Salty's when two drunk numb nuts had punched each other senseless, and one split open his forehead falling against a no-parking sign.

"You ever seen anything like this?" He swallowed, and Jess made a mental note to be on the alert for chunks. He'd gotten her shoes and the cuff of her pant leg last time, and she'd walked around all day stinking of regurgitated French toast and stomach bile.

"No," she lied. He was from Chico, and like Sheriff Brady, hadn't lived here long enough to know firsthand. All they had to go on was Herlinger's book.

Even if they wouldn't admit it, every single newcomer to Pine Bluff read the book, morbidly fascinated with the Bermuda Triangle-like history of the town formerly known as Kileyville.

The Night They Vanished had been a bestseller for years. They had no choice but to read it if they wanted to know, and they all wanted to know. The longtime residents wouldn't talk about their tragic past, especially to newcomers—not that there were many of those in Pine Bluff. Nobody wanted to risk their share of the government's hush money. Later, those who remained didn't want to relive it, and Jess was no exception. It was the dark and ugly side of their history, and people of Pine Bluff didn't want to spend each day dwelling under the heartache of that black cloud.

Jess felt that pain as sharply as anyone who had lost their child that horrible night.

In under two years the town's population dropped from eleven thousand to just over four. Many of the families of the 97 took their money and fled, glad to be given the opportunity, and the means, to start new somewhere new. She suspected those who remained did so for the same reason she did—the invisible shackle of hope in their hearts that would never allow them to leave.

"Jesus. This fucking town. What next?"

She laughed. "How long have you lived here, Mitch?"

"Yeah, I know. I read the book. You're one of the Lucky 13."

She stiffened. "Don't call me that."

Thirteen students from her senior class of the former West Ridge High had spent the last ten years hiding from that nickname. She hated it and wished that "Herlinger" had left that little tidbit out of his book.

Mitch had never come out before and said he knew about her. No one did, but Jess thought she could see the change in each person's eyes at the precise moment they learned who she was. They looked at her differently after reading *The Night They Vanished*, a new kind of emotion in their faces that could only be called a mixture of pity, curiosity, and awe.

While she had received one of the larger payouts and now lived a comfortable life here in the town officially renamed Pine Bluff, Jess wouldn't call herself lucky. Not a day went by without the pain that would always live inside her. It was a chronic sickness that she learned to live with but never overcame, an always-there uneasiness of *will it happen again?* buzzing at the base of her skull like a low current of electricity.

"Sorry. But seriously, why do you stay? If I were you, I'd have run as far away from this place as I could."

She shoved a roll of police tape at him. "Start the barricade, would you?"

Jess strode over to the sheriff. "When you reported this, what did you call it?"

Bruce looked at her knowingly. He was a smart man with a deep sense of morals. He sometimes bent the rules to do what was right, and Jess respected him with every part of herself. He was more than a father figure; he was her role model and her idol.

"Train accident."

"Did you use the word..." *Missing. Disappearance. Vanished. Unexplainable. Freak occurrence. Paranormal event.*

"11-44," he clarified. "Just like you heard it from dispatch."

The relief that washed over her was a cooling dose of hope. Could this be related? It was so strange, it had to be. It was almost too painful to think *maybe this time I can finally get some evidence.*

Jess looked down the track. "How long does it take a train like this to stop on its own?"

He turned and looked with her. "Hard to say. Depends on how fast it was moving, how heavy it is. I don't know much about running a train, how long it would accelerate on its own. It just came off a slight grade, so I can guess it was already moving fairly slowly."

"I'll be right back." She started off.

"Jess—"

She stopped and looked at him. His eyes held what she hadn't seen in a long time, only in them was more than pity. There was compassion there, too.

"I figure you've got fifteen minutes. Maybe twenty." Yes, he'd read the book, too.

She nodded, turned, and ran.

⁓

The man-made canyon cutting through the forest of towering Ponderosa pine was cast in shadows this late in the afternoon. A mile down she slowed to a walk, scanning the trees, the ballast, the tracks, even the wire fence marking the property line at Shannon's Goat Farm for anything out of the ordinary.

She found nothing unusual. Just like that night. *Nothing.* Pressure built in her chest and Jess wanted to scream.

But I did find something that night, she reminded herself, and kept walking. She asked herself again, could this possibly be related?

It has to be, if for no reason other than my own sanity.

What would sever a man's legs so neatly like that, leaving no blood spatter, no sign of struggle? Nothing that indicated one of them saw anything and attempted to escape? Was it because the train had been moving?

More importantly, where had the bodies gone?

It was different, yes, but too similar to be unrelated. *Ten fucking years later.* Today was April 23rd. Almost ten years *to the day.*

She flipped on her flashlight. A crow cawed at her loudly, making her swing the beam. It took flight from its perch in the tree and a shiny glint of black caught her eye as the branch flexed under its takeoff. She shifted the beam, but it was gone.

"No, you don't, not this time." Jess glanced back up the track. She'd gone about a quarter of a mile past the bend and down a gradual grade from the train. No one at the scene could see her.

She looked around, searching for cameras.

Whatever had happened ten years ago, and whatever had happened today, both were man-made occurrences. These events were not paranormal; Pine Bluff was not the second Bermuda Triangle.

Today's sportsman had incredible technology just for hunting: cameras were small, remotely accessed, independently powered, and painted in camo. The military and the FBI possessed technology twenty times as sleek. There could be cameras anywhere—she'd bet money there were—and she'd never see them.

She didn't give a crap.

She holstered her flashlight and looked into the clear sky, now a vivid cornflower blue as the sun dropped low in the west. No sound of chopper blades.

Yet.

Jess knew they would come. Even if they didn't know already, this would have to be reported. These precious minutes were pure gold, and she wasn't going to waste a single one.

An ordinary person wouldn't have been able to climb this tree, but after her scramble up the bleachers that fateful night, Jess had taken her rock-climbing hobby into the realm of extreme.

Somehow, she just knew she should.

She removed her blazer and set it on the ground. It would be easier barefoot, but the rough bark would cut her feet to shreds. Jess took a running leap and managed the lowest branch. She swung like a gymnast, hoisted herself up to her waist, and from there, it was easy.

Bark came away in her hands and in seconds she was sticky with pine sap. *God, I love that smell.* She climbed to the approximate point she thought she'd seen the glint and balanced on a thick branch. Her heart, already speeding from the exertion, gave a leap.

Eureka!

Jess tumbled back in time as she came face-to-face with the enigma that had haunted her dreams for years.

The device was an exact replica of the black apparatus she and Will had found that night, ten years ago.

Ten

A crowd had gathered in front of the train. As usual, Sheriff Brady was working his magical ability to calm the irate, but it was like he'd said—this time was different.

Still, Bruce was great at what he did, and people loved him. That was why he'd been re-elected twice and would probably be re-elected again next year.

Despite his white hair and beard, nobody had ever said he was too old, and most residents loved his quiet devotion to a town that was not in his roots.

"What happened to the conductors on board? Is this another disappearance?" Hank Nussbaum was shouting the loudest, and several others were egging him on.

"Now folks, everybody calm down. We are not dealing with a disappearance here. Y'all see Len Potter there." He gestured to the coroner.

"So, somebody is dead, then," Nell Thompson said. "Was it a murder?"

"At this time, all we know is there was an accident that resulted in the fatalities of several workers on the train. I can't say more until we have a better understanding of what's happened. We don't want to get the wrong information out there."

"Is it a terrorist attack?" another woman shouted. She looked at her friend. "I heard it's the railways they'll attack next, because they're so vulnerable with very little security, carrying tons of toxic material. It's like we're driving the bomb for them."

"Yeah, and I heard that's how they'll really strike fear in our hearts," the other woman said back, but loudly for the whole group. "By attacking small-town America, like us, who've already been hurt so bad. Not by attacking big cities where nobody knows their neighbors."

"Come on now, folks. Don't get yourselves all riled up. There's no reason to think this was a terrorist attack."

Jess sidled around the coroner's wagon and bypassed the scene to get to her cruiser. She stashed her jacket in the trunk and then quickly swabbed her hands with an antibacterial wipe. It cleaned most of the dirt off, but her hands were still tacky with sap.

She went back to the crowd, sliding in behind Bruce as a second measure of authority.

"Is a killer loose in our town?" a woman shouted.

"Who would want to kill a bunch of train operators?"

"Is it domestic terrorism, like that Timothy McVey guy?"

"Hold on, hold on, everybody." Bruce was becoming agitated but did a great job at keeping it under wraps. "Now, nobody said anything about a terrorist attack, domestic or otherwise. For all we know, this was purely accidental caused by an equipment malfunction. I don't know enough about trains to speculate."

"Trains don't just blow up in the faces of their conductors and then idle to a stop," Hank said.

"This train did not blow up!"

Nell jumped in. "What's really going on here, Sheriff?"

"Yeah, we've got a right to know," said the woman who'd spoken earlier. "After what we've been through, we've suffered more than most."

The muscles in Jess's back tightened. There it was, the first reference to the Kileyville 97. The first indication they suspected something strange had happened *again*. Jess recognized her as a long-time resident but didn't know her name. She wondered if the woman had lost someone that night.

Jess's phone rang. She let it go to voicemail.

"Hey!" she barked. "The sheriff's said all he can." Her tone was sharper than it should have been, but the woman clammed up. It wasn't the first time someone brought up the 97, and usually, all it would take was a word from Jess to shut them up.

Sheriff Brady held up a hand to Jess in a subtle warning. Her tension was high, and her pulse was racing after finding the device. She shouldn't even be working crowd control now, she was liable to bite someone's head off, but with only five deputies on a good day, he was already too shorthanded for a scene like this.

"How many bodies have you got there, Sheriff?" This question from Janis Rosenblum, one of the freelance writers and photographer for the *Pine*

Bluff Blotter, their town's local post and want-ads. Janis had lost her daughter that night. Maybe it was because of that, or her more pleasant tone of voice, that compelled Bruce to answer.

"Five."

"How do five men in random parts of the train get killed by the same accident?" someone else demanded.

Jess's phone rang again. She pulled it off her belt. The caller ID said W TAYLOR, and she wondered how he'd gotten her new number. She punched the decline symbol.

"Can you at least tell us if it was a toxic leak of some kind that we should be concerned about? What would kill five men who weren't even on the same car?"

"Yeah, should we evacuate the town, Sheriff?"

"At this time, I don't see any indication of a gas leak or any other reason to evacuate the town. But if you feel uncomfortable, you have to do what you feel is right for yourself."

The phone rang again while it was still in her hand. Jess answered. "I'm in a situation here, Will."

"You have to get to the old gymnasium right away." Will's breathless voice made Jess's tension ratchet into overdrive.

"What are you talking about?"

"You're not going to believe it. It's the Kileyville 97. They're back."

Eleven

Jess swallowed. Hissing rose in her ears and her legs went rubbery. She'd heard wrong over all the shouting.

Four train cars down, Len Potter leaped off the train. He went down to his hands and knees, but just as fast, he was up again and running up the ballast toward his wagon. She'd never seen the sixty-five-year-old coroner move so fast, usually he walked with a pronounced limp from arthritis in his knees.

The outspoken woman in the crowd had a cell phone to her ear. She turned and started into the woods. Jess saw her break into a run.

Dr. Potter wheeled the coroner's wagon in a fast circle and gunned it, spraying gravel on the train that pinged off its metal hide like ferocious hail. He sped up the ballast toward them, making Jess and Bruce step closer toward the crowd to avoid getting run over.

"Whoa, there, doc. Don't make yourself any extra customers today," Sheriff Brady said in a jovial tone.

A light titter sounded from the crowd, but Bruce's worry showed through as he looked at her.

"Jess?" Will's voice came tinny, from far away. "Er, Deputy Harding?"

"Will, this isn't funny." Her heart was pounding so fiercely the words didn't come out right. "If you're fucking with me, I'll arrest you myself."

"God, Jess. I would never do that to you."

She took a deep breath, held it for two seconds, and blew slowly out. "Are you sure?"

"I wouldn't believe it either if I weren't seeing it with my own eyes."

"I'll be right there." She dragged the phone down her face and somehow managed to snap it into her belt clip. "I have to go."

"Jess?" Bruce took a step toward her.

Could it be? Why today? What the hell is happening here?

Reality skipped like a record with a scratch. *Shreya is here. No, she's* been gone ten years. *Is she back? It isn't possible. But how was any of this possible?*

She ran toward her cruiser. "Mitch! Get your ass over there. That's enough tape." She jumped in and fired up the engine. Her charger roared to life.

I'm dreaming. Today never happened, this isn't real. She'd slipped into a surreal netherworld, and for a moment, her mind went completely blank.

Pounding on the passenger-side window jolted her back to reality. Janis Rosenblum stared back with sheer panic in her eyes. "Take me with you!"

Jess popped the locks. Janis jumped into the passenger seat. "You're going to the senior center?"

She nodded numbly and dropped the car into drive. Ballast gravel machine-gunned the undercarriage. Once on the pavement at Arroyo Seco Drive, she hammered the gas and sent the car into a slide around the warning arm. Janis yanked her seatbelt on.

Deputy Parks lifted both hands in question when she raced past. Noise squawked on her radio, but she couldn't make it out. The traffic signal at Peabody turned red. She turned on her lights and siren. Once safely through the intersection, she glanced over to see what the strange keening was coming from the passenger seat. Janis's lips were moving as she whispered prayers over and over.

"*Please-oh-God-please-oh-God.*"

"Stay calm. We don't know what's happening."

Janis wrapped her arms around herself and hummed, rocking in the seat.

Getting her hopes up like this is bad, Jess thought. Her own heart was sledge-hammering, and her stomach rolled like a cauldron of boiling acid. All these years of hoping, praying, and dreaming, and now she couldn't believe it.

A small part of her hoped it wasn't true. She swallowed down the laugh trying to bubble up in her throat. *How's that for irony?*

Distracted, Jess nearly missed the turn onto Alvarado. She spun the wheel, sliding around the corner on squealing tires. People on the sidewalk were already staring, now they gawked openly. She cut the siren.

She raced up the long, four lane road leading to the *Pine Bluff Senior Living Center,* what used to be West Ridge High School, and cut her speed in time to turn into the driveway. She was still driving too fast as she bypassed the senior housing to the crumbling parking lot in front of the old gymnasium building, which was now used as a rec center for youth activities and town functions.

If it is true...thank goodness for the proceeds from Stan's book that kept this old building standing.

The coroner's wagon sat unevenly in front of the main building's entrance, one tire jumped onto the curb.

Jess emerged from the car on numb legs, barely feeling herself moving toward the building. Janis left the passenger door standing open and sprinted for the main entrance.

Could it be...could it be...could it be? Tingling started in Jess's fingertips. She paused to close the cruiser's passenger door, almost afraid to go inside the rec room.

Afraid it wasn't true...or afraid it was? She wasn't sure at this point.

I can't relive this pain again.

The noise inside the rec center made her heart thunder. Voices crying, shouting, wailing.

Jess walked through the wide hallway and stopped at the main doors to the gymnasium where she had stood ten years earlier, and her heart stuttered in her chest.

Twelve

The old gymnasium was filled with people.

Young people.

Formally dressed people.

Jess moved inside, hardly able to believe what she was seeing. Fancy dresses, elegant hairstyles, gleaming tuxedos, clean-cut young men and pretty young ladies. Foreign, unrecognizable, yet...*exactly as I remember.*

Her mouth went dry. Jess stepped into the crowd. In the center of the room, Len Potter was sobbing loudly, arms wrapped around a young woman in a powder-blue prom dress. Those nearby backed away from them, as if uneasy at the sight.

A shriek, followed by wailing, called her attention to Janis Rosenblum. She sobbed "Lizzy," over and over, holding her daughter by the shoulders. *Her daughter.*

Flashes of light sparked in Jess's brain, not allowing her to believe what she was seeing. It was as if this was a movie on a screen that wouldn't properly display the picture and she couldn't make out what was happening.

She blinked several times. Principal Renner stood in the crowd wearing a confused expression, his gaze stuck on the floor. His lips moved in wordless confusion.

Jess's focus hit and locked onto a heart-wrenching sight. All sound slipped away. The room grew dark at the edges of her vision.

Shreya.

Jess moved into the room on legs commanded by someone else, watching her friend grow larger and more real with each step.

"Shreya."

Jess's world started crumbling away, like giant shards of ice shearing off a glacier. She stopped, unable to believe her best friend, her *lost* friend, was truly standing before her.

She still wore the burgundy gown and sparkling diamond necklace. Her short, curly hair was still pulled back on one side with a jeweled comb. The orchid corsage at her wrist was still alive, but slightly wilted. Jess glanced up and down, noting the high-heeled strappy sandals with rhinestones they'd bought together on a shopping trip to Sacramento. The day Shreya had insisted on buying that expensive lipstick for Jess.

She hadn't aged a day. None of them had.

Jess took two steps closer. "Shreya. My God. Shreya."

Time had dulled Jess's memory, but seeing her now brought it all back in vivid technicolor. Shreya, in all her striking beauty, those intelligent, knowing eyes. Her dazzling smile, hesitant now, glad to see Jess but quite obviously alarmed. Even her posture, the graceful movement of her arm as she lifted her hand toward Jess, was exactly as she remembered. This was absolutely, irrefutably *Shreya*. A mere hint of one dimple sent Jess rushing toward her.

"Shreya!" Tears blurred her vision. Jess grasped her by the shoulders. She even felt like Shreya, still smelled of Joy perfume.

"Jess, what's happening?"

Jess hauled her into a hug, and Shreya gladly returned it.

"My God, Shreya." She leaned back, still holding her. "Where have you been?"

Shreya shook her head. "I... What do you mean? I've been here. We were waiting for you."

Jess let out a whimper and quickly smacked a hand over her mouth. Could it be they had somehow been transported through time?

Slowly, gradually increasing in volume, sound returned as if someone had turned up an invisible volume knob in her head. There were more cries, more sobbing, more voices raised in alarm.

"I'm outta here," Tom Crawford said, stalking past. He tugged at his bowtie.

Shreya grasped Jess's arms. "Jess, I'm scared. What's happened to you?"

She jerked her attention back to Shreya, read the concern in her friend's face with confusion. Shreya reached up and brushed back a strand of hair that had fallen out of her bun.

"You look...different. You cut your bangs." Her gaze slipped down, tracing over the uniform. "Is this a costume?"

"It's all right." She grabbed Shreya's hand. "Everything is all right now.

I'm not going to let anything happen—" She whirled around, scanning the corners of the room.

There were black objects fixed to the ceiling in each corner, just like the night of the prom.

Thirteen

Fear shrilled across her flesh like a spray of icy water.

Will and another man Jess recognized as the senior center's maintenance supervisor wrangled an extending ladder through the man doors. Will's gaze met hers, and in a split-second, the ten years separating them were gone. The two men jogged to the corner of the room and righted the ladder against the wall with a bang.

"Come with me." Jess dragged Shreya through the crowd to Principal Renner. "Sir? Principal Renner?"

He dragged his gaze to her almost drunkenly. "Whu... Jessica?"

"Come with me, please. You need to address the room." She placed her hand on his shoulder and tried to maneuver him toward a low platform that now stood where the stage had been ten years ago. There was a podium, but no microphone. The rec center used this stand for Bingo on Tuesday nights.

Shreya, as smart and strong and courageous as she'd ever been, urged Principal Renner along with pressure on the other shoulder. Still, Jess did not let go of her hand.

The principal stepped onto the platform, and Jess hesitated. She didn't want to let go of Shreya. "Stay right here. Don't go anywhere."

Shreya nodded.

"Promise me!"

She nodded again, but now in her eyes was the understanding that Jess desperately needed her to say so. "Yes, I promise."

Jess stepped up beside the principal. She noted the ladder come away from the wall, and Will and the maintenance man hurry toward the other corner. Will glanced at her.

The people in the room, with more elderly parents now, noticed her and the principal on the platform but the noise continued.

"Can I have your attention, please?"

Ignored, she repeated the request louder, and the voices slowly died down. Jess scanned the room, stunned by the familiar faces of classmates she thought she'd lost. They were scared, confused, and she was sure most of them felt as numb as she did. She hated the sadness she saw in their angelic, youthful beauty.

So young, so innocent. So wronged.

Had she looked this helpless ten years ago when the FBI harassed her for twenty-three hours in a windowless interrogation room?

Now that they were all staring at her in sharp silence, she didn't know what to say. In the other corner, she saw a black box drop from the ceiling, and Will began climbing down the ladder. She let out a sigh of relief, though wouldn't truly feel better until he removed all four of whatever those evil things were.

"I'm Jessica Harding. I went...I go to school with you."

Blank faces stared back. She focused on Shreya.

"I know you're all scared and confused. I'm scared and confused too."

"Where's all our cars?" Mike Dennehy asked. There was a hesitance in his voice Jess had never heard before. He had been a popular, confident young man who could charm the habit off a nun. His tuxedo hung off him a little too large, and Jess noted many of the returned students looked too thin for their clothes. Even Shreya, whose soft curves had always been part of her beauty, looked slimmer than Jess remembered. The thin strap of her gown's belt hung like it wasn't tied properly.

Returned. Dear God, it was too big to comprehend. They were gone, and now they're back. How was that even possible? Time travel; it had to be. As impossible as it was, there was no other explanation. And given that the FBI was involved, it was slightly more believable.

Slightly. But still...unfathomable.

And if they had gone through time, why were they thinner now?

Shreya's expression had morphed into something close to terror. She understood Jess wasn't wearing a costume.

"What's going on?" Hector Reynoso demanded. A murmur rolled through the crowd.

"I don't know exactly what's happened, but I will tell you what I know. On the night of your–our–senior prom, the town of Kileyville experienced a paranormal event."

In perfect harmony, a roar of voices rose. Some even laughed.

"Listen to her!" Elizabeth Schumacher's shout cut the room to silence. She stood beside her daughter Emily, tears silently rolling down her cheeks. "She's trying to tell you what happened."

"Shortly after the dance started, ninety-two students, two chaperones, and three administrators—Principal Renner included—vanished."

Another rumble of voices rolled through the crowd. Principal Renner grasped the podium for support. He looked like he was going to collapse.

Brendan Fisher pushed through the crowd to stand beside Shreya. "What do you mean, *vanished*? Jess, you were right here with us."

"No, I was late. I had to take my mother to the dentist, remember? I wasn't here when it happened. Me, Will Taylor, Katherine Cummings, Dean Ellison, Luke Findley, and Jasmine Dodson, we were all late. There were also seven other students from the senior class who didn't go to prom. We were the only ones who didn't disappear."

"We didn't go anywhere," Hector insisted. "We've been right here. It's just the decorations that are gone."

"No." She looked down at her best friend as she said it. Shreya's expression crumbled, and Jess fought tears of her own.

"It was you who disappeared," she confirmed, and Shreya dropped her face into her hands. Her shoulders shook with silent sobs.

"It's true," Dr. Potter said in a hoarse voice. "Nobody knew where you went."

"Or if they did, they weren't saying," Mrs. Dalrymple cut in harshly.

"What did you mean, 'shortly after the dance started,'" Troy Benedict asked, looking at Dr. Potter. "It started, like, ten minutes ago. You make it sound like this isn't 2013 anymore."

"How long has it been?" Brendan demanded.

Everyone looked at Jess. At her hesitance, more voices rose, demanding the answer.

She took a deep breath and held up her hands. The noise died down, and finally, silence waited for her answer.

"It's been ten years."

Fourteen

Cries of horror and shocked disbelief rose through the rec center. Kitty Omagi fell to her knees. Many of the students hugged their prom dates, and the sound of crying filled the room like a sudden torrent of rain.

"My parents."

"Oh my God, my sister."

Shreya lifted her head and swiped at her tears with the back of her hand. Jess ached for her, and it took everything she had not to jump off the platform and run to her.

"Listen to me," Jess shouted. She raised her voice and enunciated her words. "The FBI will be here any minute. They will want to question you. Do not tell them where you have been. Do not tell them you don't know where you've been. Do not tell them *anything*. Answer every question with, 'I cannot say at this time.' This is very important."

Principal Renner finally spoke. "Did they have something to do with this?"

"Why is it important? What are they going to do?"

"Is it a conspiracy?"

Fearful rumbling rose, echoing off the high ceilings.

"Everybody!" A woman's voice brought silence again. It was Lola Carson, holding her daughter Shelby in her arms. Jess had believed the woman never forgave her for escaping the disappearance, but now she looked at Jess like a leader. "Do what she says. Jess knows what she's talking about."

"I don't have all the answers. But I do know this—" Jess raised her voice even louder. "This time, we are not going to let them get away with it!"

The older people in the crowd cheered—Jess was surprised how many of them had arrived—and Dr. Potter raised his fist in the air.

She stepped off the platform and put her arms around Shreya. "It's okay. You're all right. We're going to figure this out together. I won't leave your side for a minute."

Shreya hugged her back, and for a moment, they just stood there, cherishing each other's embrace. Finally, Jess eased back, letting Shreya wipe at her tears. "Has it really been ten years?"

Jess could only wrinkle her brow and nod, realizing too late she'd made that pitying face she herself had hated for so long. "I'm so sorry."

Will materialized next to her.

"Did you get them all?" she whispered.

He nodded. "Gus is taking them somewhere safe."

"I need a list of the 97. Can you see if the senior center's library has a copy of the book?"

Will nodded and turned, but Jess grabbed his arm. "Make a photocopy at the nurses' station. I don't think the students should see the book just yet."

"I'll take care of it." Will touched her shoulder. "Be right back, Deputy Harding."

"Deputy Harding," Shreya repeated. "Is it really true? You're a cop?"

"It's really true. God, Shreya, I almost can't believe it. You're standing here...after all this time."

"*You* almost can't believe it."

Shreya laughed, and they hugged again, and now Jess didn't bother to hide her tears.

All around them, more and more parents and family members were joining in. The old gymnasium, which was rarely used anymore, now held more people than it had in a decade. At the rear of the room, Principal Renner sat on the edge of the platform, head in his hands.

Sheriff Brady angled through the growing crowd. A rush of profound relief washed over Jess.

"Bruce, thank God."

He glanced around. "This is them?"

"This is them." Jess's breath hitched. Great, now she was going to start bawling like a fool, just in time for her boss to see.

"And I'll bet this is Shreya. After all I've heard about you, I practically feel as if I know you. This one never gave up hope on you, little lady."

She grinned and leaned closer to Jess, squeezing her shoulders. "Somehow I already knew that."

Jess lost control as the sobs overtook her. She covered her face with her hands. "I'm sorry." She quickly swiped the tears away and straightened her spine. "We need to get a roster going. Will Taylor is getting the list, but people are already leaving, we need to try and keep them here."

"Is this the best place to do it?"

As usual, her smart boss used simple words to convey a big meaning.

"We're safe, now," she responded in kind. Shreya looked back and forth between them; not understanding but trusting.

Jess looked at the door as another couple tried to leave. Jess recognized them as Mike Waterson and Hayley O'Phinney. They stopped when a humorless looking duo, a man and woman in crisp suits, entered in front of them. The woman held her hand up in a severe gesture. *Halt.*

"Great. Scully and Mulder just showed up."

Two men in matching black suits entered behind them and blocked the doorway, feet planted apart and hands crossed together. Their appearance sent a message, complete with black aviators, granite faces, severely short haircuts, and a coiled wire leading from an ear into the collar of their starched white shirts. They could have been twins if not for the fact that one had blond hair and the other black.

"Let's see if we can't grab the reins before they try to steal the horse." Bruce strode onto the platform and raised his voice. "Hiya folks. Most of you know me, but for those who don't, I'm Sheriff Brady. Now, I know you're all wondering what in the heck is happening, but I want to assure you, the most important thing right now is getting y'all reunited with your families. If you could all just sit tight for a few minutes, we want to take a roll before you leave, just to make sure everyone is accounted for."

Will squeezed between Sentry One and Sentry Two as Bruce was speaking. He held a yellow clipboard with a neatly printed roster showing the names in alphabetical order listed in two columns.

"Compliments of Stan Herlinger." He leaned close. "The internet went down right after I called you. Cell reception is down now, too."

"Probably thanks to our friends in black." From the corner of her eye, she saw the suits weaving through the crowd toward her while their two guard dogs remained at the door. Jess turned toward the stage and held the clipboard up.

"Ah, I see Jess has a roster," Sheriff Brady continued in his affable voice. "Now I know a lot of calls have already gone out, I see lots of parents here already. But for those of you whose family members aren't here, Jess and I will help you in making contact. Any of the parents here with cell phones are asked to help out with that."

"My cell phone isn't working!" someone shouted.

"Yeah, mine, too," another parent echoed.

"Can you start with this?" Jess handed the clipboard back to Will, and he silently slipped back into the crowd. If he truly was the author of *The Night They Vanished*—of which she now had little doubt—he probably knew the list by heart. And with the research he must have done, he probably knew more about the Kileyville 97 disappearance than she did.

She was certain he had just as much distrust of the FBI.

The man and woman approached Jess and opened their badge wallets. Jess tightened her grip on Shreya and realized she'd never let go of her wrist. Shreya adjusted her grip to take Jess's hand and slid closer to her, her silent message saying *I'm not letting go of you, either.*

"I'm Special Agent Crenshaw, and this is Special Agent Larsen."

Jess ignored the woman speaking. She swiveled toward the man and stared hard.

"Agent Larsen. You certainly have a knack for materializing at a moment's notice."

He set his lips in a firm line. "Jessica Harding. Nice to see you again."

She scoffed. "You're looking older."

"You two have met." Agent Crenshaw seemed taken aback. "Er, we received notice that a large group of missing people have turned up suddenly."

"Did you? How? I just heard the internet and cell reception went down." Jess shifted her gaze back to Agent Larsen. "You must have been close by to get here so quickly. *Again.*"

"We're going to need to speak to these people," Agent Crenshaw continued as if she weren't being ignored.

Larsen managed a smile. "We're thrilled at this news. These are wonderful circumstances—"

"Don't tell me what wonderful circumstances these are. You didn't lose *your* family members. You didn't suffer for ten years wondering what agony they were enduring or what horrific end they'd met. You didn't suffer nightmares and depression and heartache like these survivors—"

Jess cut herself off, realizing too late she'd showed vulnerability to this man who didn't give two shits about her emotions and would only see them as weakness. She couldn't believe she'd ever aspired to join the FBI, even if it was only for the inside information that would bring her closer to the disappeared. Thank goodness she'd never pursued it harder, or she might be just like them now.

Agent Crenshaw cleared her throat. "Deputy Harding, we'd like to gather everyone together—"

"No."

Agent Crenshaw's brows crawled upward. "I'm sorry, that wasn't a request," she said in a voice that was anything but sorry.

"No," Jess repeated firmly. "You're not going to do anything to these people."

Agent Larsen cut in. "I understand this is a very emotional time for you—"

"Cram it, Suit. You don't understand *Jack*. Don't you dare waltz in here and think you're going to turn this into a circus like you did ten years ago. These people are not going into your custody."

"Deputy, in case you don't understand we outrank—"

"What are you going to do?" Jess demanded. "Point your guns at them? Arrest them if they don't obey you?"

Crenshaw recoiled. "In case you hadn't noticed, these students haven't aged in ten years."

She glared at the woman. "Do I look stupid to you?"

"They're going to need a full physical and psychological evaluation."

"What they *need* is their families. What they *need* is reassurances. What they *need* are people they know and trust, who will genuinely try to ease their fears and not just placate them with a bunch of bullshit." She threw a pointed look at Larsen. "What they *don't* need is a bunch of stiff, unfriendly strangers locking them into an interrogation room for two days. These are my friends, my classmates. I've lived with their parents for the last ten years. I know exactly what they need, Agents. You do not."

SA Crenshaw returned her hard look. "I think we should speak with the sheriff now, deputy."

"Yeah, I'm gonna let Deputy Harding take lead on this," Bruce said behind her. "I'm busy with the train accident and all."

Jess hadn't realized he'd stepped up behind her, but she wanted to kiss him. At the same time, she cringed inwardly, wondering how much of that he'd heard. She knew she was expected to hand over any investigation to a requesting federal agent and assist in any way they needed.

But this was different. She'd turn in her badge if she had to. She'd just gotten Shreya back, and she was not letting the FBI take her anywhere.

And no way was she letting them put Shreya through the pain and fear they'd inflicted on her.

She forced the anger out of her tone. It was as hard as rolling a two-ton boulder up a steep hill. "Agent Larsen, I know this case has been sitting on your desk for ten years, but it's been my *life* for ten years."

"And I value your input, Deputy Harding. But I also remember a headstrong eighteen-year-old who sneaked into a federal crime scene. I need to know I can trust you to act in the best interests of these people and not just yourself."

Shreya gave her arm a squeeze. It was like a magic energy shot. Will passed through her line of sight, still checking names off the roster. He gave her the bashful smile she remembered so well, and her confidence soared.

She wasn't alone here like she had been ten years ago. She had allies and friends, townspeople who believed in her. People who applauded her for staying. People who would stand behind her if called.

The FBI was going to have to arrest her again if they wanted her out of their hair. She finally had Shreya back, and nothing on this earth would get her to let go of that.

"That's what you don't understand, Agent. I was never acting in my own best interest. It was always about them." When he opened his mouth to speak, she quickly continued. "I understand you are the federal government, but from where I'm standing, you look like nothing more than the responsible party. As your partner already mentioned, these kids don't appear to have aged in ten years. If they have time traveled, it's because of something *you* did, not something they did, or something I did. Not something this town did, not something some mad scientist living out in the woods did."

Both agents bristled.

"So, while I fully accept that you hold rank over state and local, understand this: you can *try* demanding your authority over local law enforcement, but you're going to find getting around in this town is a lot easier with our help. There are very few newcomers in Pine Bluff; most everyone who lives here remembers the first time you showed up. I feel safe saying they're not happy to see you again. You want to put these kids in a Petri dish? Why don't you start by rounding up the twenty or so who've already left? See how far you get on your own."

"What I think my deputy is trying to say," Bruce cut in with his jovial, laid-back country-bumpkin voice, "is we're more than happy to assist the FBI in any way we can, but we won't be bullied. And we're certainly not going to stand for our people being hurt any more than they already have been. Now, you have to take a minute to try and understand my deputy's trepidation. As I heard it, you locked her in an interrogation room for two days without letting her see her family. She may have just turned eighteen, but she was still a frightened young girl who'd just lost a hundred of her friends. That's no way to treat anyone."

Agent Larsen softened his expression. "Deputy Harding, believe it or not, I regret the way you were treated ten years ago. I don't blame you for breaking into the gymnasium that night, and I truly wish Agent Roycroft had handled things differently. You didn't deserve what he did to you. I wish I could make you understand that we're not the same agency we were back then. I know I'm going to have to prove myself with actions, not words. Let us show you that Agent Crenshaw and I want nothing more than to help the people of this town recover from the tragedy that befell them all those years ago."

Agent Crenshaw forced a stiff smile. It looked like it took a huge amount of effort and caused her a considerable amount of pain. Shreya waited in silence, her attention swiveling between them like a spectator at a tennis match.

"But at the same time, you must understand we need to figure out what happened, if only to make sure it doesn't happen again, and that these young people are healthy and safe."

Jess smiled back and then slid a knowing look to Larsen. "Agent Larsen can take a look around for himself and see how safe they are now."

He held her gaze without flinching. "We appreciate your help and look forward to working with, not against, local law enforcement. We want only to help."

Paloma Nolan had been edging closer. "Jess?"

She turned away from the agents. "Palo." There were tears in the girl's eyes, and Jess extended her arm to encourage her close. "I'm so glad to see you."

Shreya reached for her, too, and together they brought Palo into a three-way hug.

"It's okay," Shreya told her. "Jess is looking out for us."

"I'm freaking out here. I mean, oh my God, it's just so unreal. Is it really ten years later? Are you really a cop now?"

"It's true, yes. I'm sorry, hon."

Paloma started crying. "I don't know what to do. I don't know where to go. They're saying my parents moved away."

Bruce gave Jess a silent nod. He went to the center of the crowd and asked the parents to gather round. There were students who would receive worse news than that, and he should be the one to deliver it.

Jess's heart sank. Shreya was one of them.

She smiled and combed back a loose curl from Paloma's fancy updo. "They're not far. We'll contact them and they'll be here soon, I'm sure of it. In the meantime, we'll put you up somewhere comfortable. The FBI is here to help; they're going to secure rooms for you and anyone else who needs a place tonight."

She threw a smirk at Crenshaw. "You want to help? No tents tonight. No interrogation rooms. Comfortable, safe, *private* rooms."

"I can help," Roberta Ellwood said. She didn't have a child among the Kileyville 97, but she provided arts and crafts sessions to the senior center. She still wore a big round sticker on her shirt that said "Hi, I'm Bobbi," for the seniors who sometimes forgot her name. "Ellwood's has six rooms open right now, and Lila Davidson is by herself in that big farmhouse. We'll find a place for everyone who needs it."

"Thank you, Bobbi. This is Special Agent Crenshaw and Special Agent Larsen. They're going to assist with housing the students whose parents aren't local anymore." She phrased her statement carefully, dreading the bad news she had to deliver to Shreya. "I'd like you to assist them. Sheriff Brady will compile a list of everyone who needs a room. Please let me know where everyone is once they get situated." She took out her phone and asked for Bobbi's number.

"My phone isn't working," Bobbie told her.

"Neither is mine, but I can program in the number. I'm sure the agents will also help us get our communications back up." She didn't look at them as she said it.

"I'll send one of our nurses out to Lila's right now," Bobbi said after they'd both typed in each other's numbers to their contacts' list.

Will stood at the platform with Bruce, scanning the list. Bruce gave a nod as Will pointed out names. The crowd had thinned, and Jess watched as George Walker called out a goodbye to Bruce. Bruce gave him a wave, and George and Mary left with their daughter Ella.

Some of the parents were asking questions of the agents, and as they moved farther into the crowd, Jess leaned close to Bobbi.

"I want to know everything the FBI says and does."

"On them like glue," she whispered back before hurrying away.

"Cool phone," Shreya said.

Jess took a deep breath. "Shreya, your parents moved back to India a few... They still own the house here, but I want you to come home with me tonight."

Shreya took Jess's hand back into both of hers. "There's no place I'd rather be. Besides, it sounds like we've got some catching up to do." Her eyes glistened with fresh tears.

"Gavin!" The panic in the shout caught everyone's attention. "Where's Gavin?"

Fifteen

Jess wound through the crowd, pulling Shreya along with her. On the platform, Will and Sheriff Brady were also looking at the girl. Jess hadn't known her very well but remembered her name was Faye Garnette.

She stood by herself, hugging her bare arms. Her eyes were wide, pupils narrowed to pinpoints despite the dim interior.

"Gavin Swift?" Jess asked her.

Faye nodded. "He's my date. He's not here. I haven't seen him since...it all changed. He said he was getting us some punch. Now he's not here."

"All right, sweetie, we'll find him. What was he wearing tonight?"

She sniffled. "A tuxedo. Black with a silver shirt."

She looked at Will. He shook his head. He leaned close to Sheriff Brady and pointed out the name on the list.

Sheriff Brady looked around. "Okay, listen up. Has anyone seen Gavin Swift? Did he leave? Gavin Swift."

There were even fewer people in the rec room now. Nobody spoke up. Agent Crenshaw approached the platform. Will expertly extracted himself and hurried over to Jess before the agent could ask for the clipboard.

"Who are we missing?" Jess asked him. She glanced around, uncomfortable at the idea of Shreya leaving her sight. Lindsey Keyes was with her, showing her a pair of rollup slippers. Shreya examined the flexible ballet shoes and then slipped out of her heels.

"So far, we've got about sixteen people—eight couples—but I've noted here if someone saw them leaving." Thanks to his clear, tiny writing, Jess saw that only five kids were completely unaccounted for.

She pointed to an unmarked name. "I saw Tom Crawford leaving just after I got here. I don't know who he was with."

If Tom's date went with him, that left only three: Gavin and one of the parent chaperones and her daughter.

Shreya came over to see the list. "Tom Crawford? I think his date was

Aiko Masaki."

"Aiko Masaki?" Sheriff Brady called out. "Is Aiko Masaki here?"

"She left with Tom," Carrie Snodgrass answered.

"Are you sure?" Jess asked her, and Carrie nodded.

"Okay, that leaves three." Jess headed toward the platform where Principal Renner was speaking to Agent Larsen. Across the room, Bobbi was with Agent Crenshaw and a group of about twelve kids.

"Principal Renner, did you see Darlene and Steffie Gamada?"

His already shell-shocked expression went even darker. "I...I think so. I think they left right after...the room changed. I'm not sure."

"I'll send Mitch over to their house," Bruce said. "If nobody called Ronnie, he's going to be in for the shock of his life."

"That leaves Gavin Swift as the only unaccounted," she told him.

Bruce spoke into his radio. "Nineteen-one to dispatch."

"Go ahead Nineteen-one."

"I need a BOLO on a Gavin Swift. Male, approximate age: eighteen, wearing a black tuxedo. He's a Kileyville 97. Over."

"Nineteen-one, did you say Kileyville 97?"

"Affirmative, dispatch."

"Copy that. Repeat the last name."

"SAM-WILLIAM-IDA-FRANK-TOM."

Dispatch put out a call to the other deputies. "All units, report."

"Nineteen-four. I'm still at the train. Over."

"Nineteen-two. I'm on the barricade at Elm and West Everett. Over."

"All units be advised, BOLO for a missing student, Kileyville 97, Gavin Swift. Break." Sheriff Brady said into his mic. "And notify me when channel six arrives. Over and out."

Despite the FBI's efforts to shut down communications, Sheriff Brady had effectively pulled a fast one. She clamped down on the smile. Her shrewd boss was getting a home-cooked triple layer chocolate cake for Christmas.

Jess noted the only kids remaining who weren't with adults were grouped with Bobbi and Agent Crenshaw. There were still a lot of people in the rec room, but it appeared they were civilians—looky-loos, and residents of the senior housing facility who no doubt remembered the disappearance ten years ago.

She stepped onto the platform. "Can I have any students who have not seen their parents, please come over here with Roberta Ellwood and Agent Crenshaw." She pointed, and several students crossed the room with her.

Carrie Snodgrass had been quiet through much of the chaos. When Bruce approached her and said, "Come with me, hon," her expression broke, and she started crying even before he sat with her on two folding chairs at the side of the immense room.

Jess blinked away a new wave of stinging in her eyes. Carrie's parents' accident had been one of the worst roadway tragedies Kileyville had ever suffered, and one of the first traffic accidents Jess had ever worked. Speed limits were slow in town, and high-speed drunk-driving wrecks just didn't happen here.

A heavy-set man in a brown suit entered the rec room. He scanned the area and then crossed to Sheriff Brady and Carrie Snodgrass. Jess recognized him as John Hayworth, one of the partners at Hayworth-Castleberry. Jess had met him once, shortly after the accident. He'd told Sheriff Brady that Carrie's house and all her parents' assets were to be put in a trust for her if she ever came back. Jess hoped that was still the case. Still, it was little consolation to a girl who had gone to prom, and then what felt like only hours later, learned that both her parents had been dead for years.

A sudden shrilling of phones erupted all at once. The service was back on. Jess tossed a look at Agent Larsen. He was staring at her with what might be apologetic humility. She gave him a sharp nod.

She glanced back at Shreya and her heart gave a little jump. It took every ounce of will she had not to run to her and grab on again. Jess fought off a strange feeling of disorientation, a sense of disbelief she thought she might never overcome, and willed her pulse to slow back to normal.

"Jessica, is my dad okay?" Bernita Castillo held up the smartphone someone had loaned her. "Our house phone is no longer in service." As though already knowing the answer, a tear slipped down her cheek.

Jess didn't know how to say it. She hadn't set out to keep track of the families of the 97, but when someone died, there was no ignoring the fact if they were somehow related. Being one of the Lucky 13 and a sheriff's deputy had made her intimately aware of the family members still in Pine Bluff.

"Bernita, I'm so sorry."

She sniffled. "He was forty-nine when I was born. I was an accident."

She gave a teary chuckle. "I'm the baby, I have six sisters. Do you know if any of them are still...here?"

"I'm pretty sure all of them are. It sounds like the phones are working again. Let's see if we can reach them."

Bruce and Carrie had vacated the chairs, which Jess saw had been put there by the maintenance supervisor as he put out two more. A man Jess recognized from the senior center carried in another two and unfolded them. She urged Bernie over and sat with her.

"Whose phone is this?"

Bernita pointed out the man, Jason Wicht's father, who had loaned it to her.

"What's your oldest sister's name?"

"Lupe. Lupita Castillo-Alamillo." She spelled the hyphenated last name.

"Let's look her up on this phone, and I'll make the call from mine. We don't want to give her a terrible shock."

At this Bernita laughed.

"Or make her think someone is playing a cruel prank. I'm going to ask her to come right away, but let's wait until she gets here to give her the news. We don't want her distracted out on the highway."

Bernita gave another teary laugh. "That's a good idea. My sister isn't the greatest driver to begin with." She shifted to see the phone better as Jess typed in Lupita's full name. Jess chose one of the free white pages sites that popped up. If the information was still current, Lupe was living in Redding, about an hour and a half away. Before dialing, she called Bobbi over.

"Can we put Bernita in Ellwood's tonight? Her family will be coming in from out of town."

Bobbi showed her the list she'd made. "I've put these kids at Lila's place. They've all lost one or both parents since..." She hesitated and glanced at Bernita. "Sheriff Brady says he got Dr. Crabtree to agree to come over to provide counseling. These four are at the B&B, so I've got two rooms left."

"You remember Dr. Crabtree, she was the school psychologist. She went into private practice after your disappearance," Jess explained. "She's mostly retired now, but still practices for the families of the 97. I spoke to her myself for several years, she's really great. She knows a lot about what happened and how it's affected people. You can talk with her if you'd like."

Bernita sniffled. "Right now, I just want to see my sister."

"Of course. I understand." Jess dialed, and a woman picked up on the third ring.

"This is Deputy Harding from Pine Bluff Sheriff's Department in Hillsdale County."

Right away Lupe asked if it was about Bernita.

"I am calling about Bernita, yes. Are you able to drive here tonight? I have urgent information. Yes, I understand. I'm sorry I can't say more at this time, but you'll want to come tonight. Do you remember where Ellwood's Bed and Breakfast is located? Great, Bobbi Ellwood will be expecting you. Okay, please drive safe."

"Pine Bluff?" Bernita asked when she'd hung up.

"The residents voted to change the town's name about two years after your disappearance. By then, Kileyville's population was more than cut in half, and the town pretty much went bankrupt. The mayor thought it was best to change our name and put an end to the negative association, but it didn't help."

Bernita made a face. "I can imagine. What did people think?"

"Nobody knew what to think. Rumor and speculation ran wild. A lot of people left because they were scared, but many of the long-time residents stayed because they love it here, and believed things would get better. Others had to leave to find jobs when our economy tanked."

"And you? Why did you stay?"

Jess smiled. She swiveled toward Shreya on her left and took her hand, weaving their fingers together. "Well, I was waiting for you, of course."

Shreya smiled back, filling Jess's heart with sparkles.

Jess made three more phone calls to local families before noticing it was almost nine. By then, the rec room was nearly empty. Shreya and Bernita sat a few chairs down. Bernita blotted her tears with a tissue, and Shreya glanced around with wide, scared eyes as though she were afraid someone would come over and deliver her bad news as well. Jess's stomach knotted at the thought.

Jess approached Sheriff Brady. "Lauryn and Vance should be on duty now. My shift ended three hours ago—"

He held up a hand. "Go. You're dead on your feet. The FBI can handle what's left here."

"What about the train?"

"Word is there're three more agents at the train. No doubt there are units intercepting the news vans, too."

"Well lucky us," she said snarkily. A fresh surge of adrenaline hit when she remembered the device hidden in her trunk.

And no doubt a few agents combing the woods for their mysterious devices.

She swallowed. "I'm taking Shreya with me. Bobbi says she'll take Bernita and the others to Ellwood's."

"All right, kiddo. Take tomorrow for yourself. You've earned it." He spoke into his radio. "Nineteen-one, on route to Lila Davidson's on Cherry Grove."

"Nineteen-one, affirmative."

"You sure?" Jess asked him.

"I'm sure. But Six—" Bruce gave her a last look. "Keep your cell on."

Sixteen

"You must be exhausted," Jess said as they walked to the car. The cool air helped clear her head, but if she held a blink for too long, she'd probably fall asleep on her feet.

"All of this is a lot to take in. I don't know how to make sense of it."

She still held tight to Shreya's hand. Jess tingled all over, hardly able to believe she was walking with the friend who had been missing for ten years. Touching her. Hearing her sweet voice. Staring at her beautiful, unchanged face.

"I've had a little longer to get used to it than you," she said. "But now I'm turned upside down all over again." At the car, they stopped. "How do you feel? Are you in any discomfort? Anything that makes you feel different than that night?"

"I'm kind of hungry," Shreya said, and Jess laughed.

"You always did have an appetite like a lumberjack."

Shreya paused and eyed the cruiser. "Should I get in the back like a convict?"

"Get in front with me, silly girl."

"It must have been hard for you, being left behind."

Hearing those words made the world feel like it dropped two feet out from under her.

You have no idea.

She opened the door for Shreya, and then walked around the front of the car, not taking her eyes off her. Jess hadn't wished she went wherever the 97 had gone, except for that first night. Her grief had been vivid and fresh, and she'd almost felt left out.

But only that night.

Her painful life had gone on with a little less pain each day, and she'd come to treasure all the things that happened to her as the years had passed. Watching her mother get sober and stay that way. Graduating from the police academy. Working with Bruce. Buying the farmhouse. Small triumphs for a person living one day at a time, just like a recovering alcoholic.

The small, guilty part of her cherished those things she got to experience, when others did not.

"It was the not knowing that was the worst part." She leaned over to pull the seatbelt across Shreya's lap. She secured her friend into the seat and breathed in her perfume. Jess touched her face, and Shreya leaned toward her. Jess pulled her into a kiss, and Shreya responded in kind.

It was sweet and tender and finally made Jess believe it was real. She went tumbling back in time to a day when she believed her mother's drunkenness was the worst thing that could happen to her.

Jess pulled back. "I'm sorry, I shouldn't have done that."

"Why not?" Shreya whispered back, not letting go. "It's still me, Jess, and it's still you."

"I thought I'd never get the chance to do that again." Jess stayed where she was, her forehead pressed to Shreya's. "God, Shreya, I missed you so much. I...I died."

"No, you lived."

When she stayed silent, Shreya said, "And you moved on without me."

"No. Never. Not in my heart. But time went on anyway, and now..."

"If I had to guess, I'd say it was that guy."

Jess eased back.

"The one who was giving you the meaningful looks. You gave him back one or two of your own."

"Will Taylor." Jess slid back into her seat and wiped her eyes. "No. He and I...he helped me that night. We were both alone. Both so scared. But then he left. He's been gone almost as long as you."

"Then he hurt you almost as badly as I did." Shreya took her hand. "I'm sorry. I wish I could do something to ease your pain."

Jess wove her fingers into Shreya's. "Don't think like that. It wasn't your fault. You didn't do anything to hurt me. He didn't either. What I've been through these past ten years..." She turned and looked out the windshield. "I wallowed."

"My Jess isn't the wallowing type."

She sighed. "I think I needed to pay a penance. My life got better after...the disappearance, and I felt guilty about it. The government paid the townspeople to keep quiet. My mother sobered up. I went to college and bought a real house. But I didn't want any of that. I only wanted you back."

Shreya turned sideways on the seat and gave her a little smile that sent a zing of magic straight into Jess's heart. "Did you really break into a crime scene to find me?"

Jess laughed through the tears she no longer tried to contain. "Everything I ever did since then has been to find you. I joined the police force with the hope it would lead me to the FBI. I went to college for the degree required to apply. I didn't make it on my first try, and I hated myself for that. And then I didn't try again, and I hated myself even more."

Shreya cupped her cheek and wiped a tear away with her thumb. "You're the best friend I could ever hope to have, and I love you for it like you'll never know. I'm only sorry I didn't tell you that before it happened. Don't you dare hate yourself for that."

Jess took her hand and squeezed it. "Now I've got you back, and I'm never letting go."

⌇

"This is a step up from Happy Hollow," Shreya said as the farmhouse came into view at the end of its long, private drive.

"This is *ten* steps up from Happy Hollow."

They got out of the car into the noisy silence of the woods. No cars, no neighbors, but an orchestra of crickets and whip-poor-wills and beetles and owls performing a magical chorus for the moon and stars.

"It's the Peabody farm, right?"

"Not a working farm anymore, and I renamed it Anna Grove."

Shreya shot her a smile. "I love it. That's so sweet."

"Anna, for your middle name, and Grove, for the old oaks on the property. After the payout, a lot of people left even if they couldn't sell. There are farms like this standing abandoned all over Hillsdale County."

"And houses like mine, I'd assume. Did my parents keep the house because they couldn't sell, or because they thought one day I'd be back?"

Jess took her hand and they crunched across the gravel to the house. "They never gave up hope. Just like me. We'll go there tomorrow and get some of your clothes. Believe it or not, before they left, your mother told me

I could live there, but I'd already set my sights on this place. There was an auction scheduled to take place for several properties, but I made an offer to Warren Peabody, and he gladly took it. I got it for a steal."

Shreya took a deep breath. The clean, grassy scent was one of the things Jess loved most about this property. "This was what you always wanted. I know you hated that trailer park."

She retrieved a key hidden inside a ceramic frog by the front door. After unlocking it, she handed the key to Shreya.

"This is for you to keep."

Jess led her to the dining room where her laptop sat half-buried under a pile of mail on the formal table she never used for eating. She waited until Shreya was seated.

"It's the early afternoon in India. We can call your mom on video chat. I think she's going to need to see your face to believe this is real."

Shreya's smile faded, and Jess realized her mistake. She sat on the edge of the chair next to hers.

"Before we make the call, there's something I need to tell you."

"Just give it to me straight," Shreya said. Her eyes were already shiny with tears.

"I'm so sorry. I wish I didn't have to tell you this."

Her expression crumbled and she bit down on her bottom lip.

"Your father passed away about five years ago."

"No." Shreya bent her head and covered her eyes with a hand. Jess slid to her knees beside her and rubbed her back.

"I'm sorry, sweetie. I know you two were very close. He died in his sleep from a heart attack. He went peacefully."

"He never got to know that I'm okay."

"I think a part of him always knew you would be. He was the one who insisted on keeping all your things in the house."

"I can't believe it. I feel like I just saw him today. Five years?"

Jess scooted back into her chair and waited as Shreya cried, holding her hand.

"I'm okay." She wiped at her face. "I'm okay."

"Do you want a minute before we call your mom?"

"No, I need to hear her voice."

Jess nodded and swiveled the laptop around.

Shreya sniffled and used a finger under each eye to swipe away her smeared makeup. "You said she offered you our house? I hope that means she learned to be nicer toward you."

"Rent free," Jess confirmed.

"That doesn't sound like my mom." Shreya managed a smile.

"The disappearance of the 97 changed people. She was only surprised that I went into law enforcement because she thought I'd want to be an investment banker, or some other career that paid well, because of my upbringing. I told her I wanted to be a cop so I could find you. She and I still talk a couple of times a year. Mostly because I look after your house, but she always asks about my personal life."

"I'll be able to see her on this?"

"Perfectly well. Video conferencing has come a long way. And it's free, too, so stay on as long as you like."

Jess dialed up the number in India using WorldChat. It rang three times.

"Hello? Jessica, is that you?"

"Hi, Mrs. Sanvi. How are you doing?"

"I'm well, thank you. It must be the middle of the night there. Is everything all right?"

"There's no easy way to say this. There's someone here who wants to talk to you."

Jess slid the laptop to Shreya.

"Mommy?"

She heard Mrs. Sanvi gasp. "Shreya?" Her voice rose. "Is it really you?"

Jess rose and stood behind Shreya. She put her arms around her neck and pressed her cheek to Shreya's. "It's really her, Mrs. Sanvi."

She went to the kitchen to give them privacy, but it was impossible not to hear the joyful crying coming from the dining room.

Jess went to the gun safe, locked her service weapon inside, and removed her handheld radio. She busied herself cleaning up her breakfast dishes and then took a mournful look in the refrigerator. Pickles, ketchup, cheese, and a half carton of eggs. A yellowed, wilting bunch of celery. Packaged deli-slice turkey. She sniffed at a carton of milk. The sell-by date had passed, but she had only opened it two days ago, and it still smelled fine. She quickly jotted down a grocery list.

It was time to start living like a human again.

Seventeen

Shreya rubbed her cheeks as she entered the kitchen. "I feel better after talking to my mom. She's booking the first available flight out."

Jess hugged her. It was so good to feel her again. Though thinner than Jess remembered, Shreya was real and solid and sweet in her arms, and the overwhelming relief was almost too much to bear. "I'm glad. You're both welcome to stay here. I've got plenty of room. Come, sit."

She held onto her hands as they sat kitty-corner from each other at Jess's small eat-in table. "I still almost can't believe you're here. I know it feels like no time has passed for you, but for me..."

"I can't even imagine," Shreya whispered. "I'd do anything to take away the hurt. I don't know how you survived it for ten years."

Jess smiled even as her eyes filled with tears. "Now that I know you're okay, that you weren't hurt, some of that pain is gone."

She stopped there, not liking that her thoughts were headed toward anger. She had always blamed the government for the disappearance of her classmates, and now she was even more convinced. They had robbed the Kileyville 97 of a decade of their lives, but they'd robbed her, too. Those left behind were the ones who had suffered all this time. What right did the government have to do this to people?

"You're looking at me like you really don't believe. It *is* me, Jess."

"I'm sorry. I know it's you. You still look the same, you still feel the same, you even smell the same. But you have to understand, not only am I someone who lost the girl I loved, only to have her reappear ten years later without aging—"

Shreya choked out a laugh. "I'm having a hard time with that part, too."

"—but I'm a deputy now. I've got survivor's questions, and I've got police questions."

A tear slipped down Shreya's cheek, but she smiled through it. "And I know if anyone can get to the bottom of this, it's you. You always were so strong. Now I can see you've built on that."

"How are you feeling? I mean, I know this is all strange and probably feels surreal, but physically, do you feel any different?"

Shreya's brows knit as she thought about it. "I feel like I've been asleep for a long time. Like I need to get up and get moving to clear my head."

"Do you have any aches or pains? Is anything off that you can think of?"

She shook her head. "Not really. I'm hungry. And I'd kind of like to take a shower."

"Of course. I'm sorry. You skipped dinner because we were planning on going out after the dance." It felt odd to say those words, but Jess forced herself to remember that for Shreya, it was still prom night.

Jess stood washed her hands in the kitchen sink. She opened the cupboard, relieved to find a loaf of bread that didn't have any green spots growing on it.

"Remember when we..." She turned around and forced a smile. "How would you like a grilled cheese sandwich?"

"I'd love one."

Jess started butter melting in a pan and grabbed the hunk of cheese from her fridge. Then she poured a glass of milk and set it before Shreya.

"I'm glad you have this place. It's exactly what I pictured for you. Though it's strange seeing you here, cooking. You were always so awkward in the kitchen."

She laughed. "Don't be fooled. I still am. I only know how to make about three dishes, and grilled cheese is one you taught me."

Grilled cheese sandwiches had been their favorite comfort food. Because Shreya's house was so close to school, they'd often gone there during the lunch hour, when Shreya's parents were at work. It was one of her most treasured memories of their time together, and Jess remembered how she'd fantasized about the apartment in San Francisco they'd talked about sharing one day. Shreya had been accepted to the Cal-State program for architecture, and Jess was going to enroll in nursing school to become an X-ray technician.

Those memories felt like a lifetime ago.

Jess didn't often eat grilled cheese, but she quickly made two sandwiches the way they used to in high school, sprinkling cheese on the outer sides of the bread to make a crispy cheese crust on the. She flipped each sandwich and left them to melt.

"I can't get over this uniform. My Jess is a cop."

"It was the only way I could cope, and it appeals to my bossy nature."

Headlights splashed through the front windows as a car pulled to a stop on the open space in front of the house. Shreya bristled as Jess went to the window.

"It's Will." She glanced back to see Shreya relax. "The guy from the rec center."

"I was right. There is something going on there."

Jess decided against denying it, and she liked the way Shreya perked up at the idea of Jess having juicy gossip. She deserved a little fun after all she'd been through tonight.

"Mostly for him." *Especially now*, Jess thought. Her head and her heart were fully consumed with Shreya. There was no room for anything or anyone else.

She stepped into the hall and opened the front door. He brightened at the sight of her.

"You weren't lying when you said you were thinking of popping by."

"Sorry to come so late. I need to talk to you." He skipped up the front steps and strode across her porch with purpose.

"We were just about to eat. I made grilled cheese. Come on in."

He stopped in the doorway to the kitchen. He stared at Shreya like he didn't believe she was real. "I don't think we really knew each other in high school. I'm Will Taylor. I was with Jess the night...I was late, too."

"So I heard," Shreya said in a teasing voice. "One of you is going to have to tell me what happened that night." She raised her brows and shifted her gaze between them.

"Will was..." Jess took a deep breath. "I wouldn't have survived if not for him."

He blushed. Jess turned to the stove and grabbed the pan off the burner. She didn't need his adorable sex appeal distracting her from Shreya, now a hundred times more potent with ten years of sexy maturity on him.

"Then I owe you my gratitude," Shreya stood, reaching out a hand. "Anyone who looks out for my Jess is a friend of mine."

Will stepped into the kitchen and reached across the table to shake her hand. "It's nice to finally meet you. I remember when you arrived, our sophomore year." He smiled. "I kind of feel like being there with Jess that night made me one of the popular crowd."

Jess slid the sandwiches onto a cutting board and sliced them into triangles to spread them three ways, which she placed on the table on one large platter. "I tried to convince him I was never part of the *in* crowd, but he wouldn't believe me."

"You were a star athlete and the best friend of beautiful, exotic Shreya from India. Both of which made you popular, whether you liked it or not."

That made Jess laugh.

"I can see why you like him," Shreya said, and Jess's face grew hot. "Quite the flatterer."

"Will is being humble. He's actually a bona-fide celebrity. He went to New York to become a chemist, but became a bestselling author instead."

"Now look who's flattering," Will cut in.

She pulled the carton out of the fridge again. "You want milk?"

"I could use something stronger, but I know you don't have it." He gave her a weary half smile.

"A bottle of pinot is the strongest thing in this house. I could use a glass myself. Shreya? I figure you're old enough now."

Shreya shook her head. "I'll stick with milk."

Jess retrieved the bottle from the refrigerator and poured two small wine glasses. She sat down between them. Her stomach grumbled at the scent of the grilled cheese. She took a triangle and ate it in two bites.

"I remember you, too," Shreya said, chewing. "You made that atmospheric balloon for the science fair."

"Oh jeez, that seems like forever ago." He caught himself as he realized his blunder. "Sorry."

Shreya held up both hands. "Hey, don't worry. It's the two of you who spent ten years in a single day. Tell me about your books." She picked up another triangle and looked at Jess. "You've got them, right? I could read one?"

Jess put down her cheese triangle and looked at Will. Her smile softened and her heart rate kicked up. "I've got them all. There's one in particular you should read." She wiped her hands on a napkin and walked over to the small bookcase in the hallway behind the kitchen.

Jess sat down again and put the book on the table. "You might find this one interesting. Will, why don't you autograph this one for Shreya?"

"When did you figure it out?" he asked in a low voice.

"Most in town suspect as much, but I always knew because I knew you."

Shreya turned the book to read the cover. *The Night They Vanished: The True Story of California's Kileyville 97.* The cover was a picture of the front of their high school, shot at night. The image had a soft-focus quality that made it look eerie.

Will went to the counter for a pen and returned with Jess's notepad. He slid the book in front of himself and flipped the front cover open, where Shreya could see the photo of old Stan on the jacket's inner flap. He scribbled out an autograph. *To Shreya, welcome home. Stan Herlinger.* He winked and handed her the book.

Shreya looked up at Will, and then to Jess. "Okay. Should I not ask?"

Jess shifted forward in her chair. She cleared her throat and spoke loudly. "And this book was written by Stan Herlinger, the only resident in Kileyville who didn't accept the gag money. You might remember him; he used to own the feed store near Sunset Stables. It might be uncomfortable to read, but I think you need to know the whole story."

Shreya seemed to shrink in her chair. "Okay."

Will took the notepad with Jess's grocery list and flipped to the next sheet. He quickly scrawled out a message while he spoke. "He moved to Florida about three years after it happened. Or at least, that's the story."

Be careful what you say. We don't know who's listening.

Shreya's gaze rose from the note and flicked between Jess and Will. "The story?"

"Some believe he was killed because he wouldn't sign the gag order," Will explained. "But I heard he's going to release another book soon. I know his editor, and according to Mike, Stanley's alive and well."

They can't insist someone else wrote it without implicating themselves in his disappearance.

Shreya took the notepad. *They?*

Will wrote FBI? CIA? *Shadow org?* He shrugged.

Jess tore the paper off the pad with the one beneath it and folded them twice. She went to the stove and turned on the burner again and fed the paper into the flames.

"We need to talk," Will said when she returned to her seat. "Maybe someplace else would be better?" He popped another cheese triangle into his mouth and then wiped his fingers on a napkin.

"It's late."

"It's important."

Jess sighed. She rose again to turn on the clock radio on the counter. The local classic hits station played a Brittney Spears song.

She flopped back into her chair and considered swigging back the rest of her wine, but it had clashed badly with the grilled cheese. "Larsen got here in record time. Again."

His lips formed a straight line. "I noticed that."

"Who's that?" Shreya asked. "That tall FBI guy?"

Jess stayed silent.

Shreya put her palms on the table. "If you guys want some privacy, I get it. But if you're worried about me, don't be. I can handle it." When nobody moved, she leaned closer and lowered her voice. "Do you really think someone's listening?"

Jess leaned her elbows on her knees and rubbed at her forehead with the tips of her fingers. This had been the second longest day of her life.

"The night of the prom, the FBI arrived by helicopter not twenty minutes after I called 9-1-1. Today, they got there almost as fast." She shifted her gaze to Will. "It was the same guy—Agent Larsen. Now he's the special agent in charge. That can't be a coincidence."

"You said this case was probably gathering dust on his desk all these years, but you don't think that's true, do you?" Shreya asked.

"I think he knows exactly what's going on."

Will nodded. "They can't be trusted. That's what I came here to tell you. I left the rec center to meet up with Gus, the maintenance guy who helped me get them down."

Shreya looked from one to the other. "Get what down?"

"Strange devices," Jess told her. "We think they had something to do with your disappearance. There were four of them in the ceiling at the corners of the room the night you disappeared."

"And four more of them in the rec room tonight," Will supplied.

"Do you think those were the same ones?" Jess asked. "That the FBI put them back up tonight to cause the return?"

"We'll never know. Someone got to Gus before I did. His wife found him unconscious in his barn."

Shreya gasped. "Oh no." She covered her mouth with her hand.

"He didn't see who it was or even if there was more than one person. All four devices were gone."

"Is he okay?" Jess asked. "Did you call it in?"

"He's fine, but someone conked him over the head good. When I arrived, his wife was sewing three stitches into his scalp. I convinced her not to call it in, I said I would tell you in person." Will's expression became even more guarded. "I don't know your boss. I didn't know if I could trust him."

"He's the only person in this town I do trust, besides the two of you." Jess shot to her feet. "Stay here."

She snatched her keys off the hook by the door and ran for the car. Her jacket remained bundled up in the trunk the way she'd left it. She glanced around—not that she could see into the darkness surrounding her property. There were a million places someone could hide in the darkness, all of them less than fifty feet away.

She grabbed her jacket and hurried back to the house. She could feel the solid object within. Once inside, she turned the deadbolt and locked the knob.

"There was another incident tonight."

Will's eyes widened. "You mean another disappearance?"

"Worse." She moved her plate aside and set her jacket down. "I was at the scene when you phoned me. Five men disappeared off a moving train. At least, most of them."

She glanced at Shreya.

"Jess." Her tone held a warning. *Don't keep things from me.*

"Their legs were severed beneath the knee. Neatly, very little trauma. No evidence they saw it coming or tried to run. That was all that was left of them."

"Jesus." Will leaned back heavily in his chair and drove a hand through his hair. When she revealed the device inside her jacket he stiffened. "Where did you find that?"

"What is it?" Shreya started to lean closer as if to get a better look, then eased back, obviously deciding that was a bad idea.

"It's one of the objects we found that night, and again tonight. It was in

110

a tree almost two miles from where the train stopped." She shook her head. "It was a miracle I even saw it."

Will's face had gone two shades paler. "Were there others?"

"I don't know, I didn't look. I knew I didn't have time, and I was right." She looked at Shreya. "If this isn't one of the objects we found the night you disappeared, it's an identical replica." Jess lifted it from her jacket and set it on the table. She tossed her jacket on the empty chair and turned the device over to examine the strange symbols.

"It's exact," Will breathed out. "Look, it's even got that blue gunk on it."

They all leaned closer. The blue substance was sparkly and gelatinous, about the size of a half-dollar, and for a moment, Jess thought the shimmer was its surface reflecting the light as she moved closer. When it moved, they all jerked backward. Will's chair shrieked against the tile floor.

The substance slid off the device and rolled onto the table. Jess stared in confusion, wondering what had caused it to fall. Her blood turned to ice when she saw it was shifting and undulating on its own—a living, coherent entity.

And it was inching toward Shreya.

"What the hell?" Will exclaimed.

"Get it away from me!" Shreya jumped up, sending her chair toppling. She ran from the kitchen and stomped up the stairs.

Jess leaped to her feet. Will remained in the chair, frozen in wide-eyed horror as the goo continued writhing and surging toward Shreya's empty seat. It suddenly jerked back as though it were living tissue that had been burned, and Jess saw it had touched a single grain of salt on the dark wood of the table.

Will nearly fell off his chair as he awkwardly struggled to escape, but he must have seen it, too. He reached for her saltshaker and twisted the top off. He thrust the opened shaker once, and then a second time, sending waves of salt raining over the table. He staggered back and braced against the wall, arms splayed.

The goo shivered like ripples in a glass of water. It lost its opalescent turquoise hue and went still. Slowly, the color darkened and seemed to harden. In seconds, it resembled a dark blue jellyfish that had dried out on a beach.

Will dragged his gaze away to look at her, chest heaving. "Holy fried chicken!"

The sound that came out of her was half laugh, half sob. "Good thing I'm a slob."

He stared at her in disbelief, and for a minute, she thought he was going to snap at her for joking at a time like this. Then his face cracked into a smile, and he laughed, too. It was the sound of someone who'd just had the fright of their lives but then discovered it was a prank.

Only this hadn't been some prank.

Jess had learned to control her panic in police situations, but this was completely different, and her adrenaline was pumping. An awkward laugh rolled out of her as well. Will stood upright and shook his arms out, laughing more at himself than the situation.

"I remember someone who said he wasn't afraid of 'the blob.'"

That made him laugh even harder. He swiped a hand over his face. "Hell, I guess I was wrong," he deadpanned.

Jess burst out laughing with him. Then she suddenly realized– "Where's Shreya?"

She bolted for the stairs. Her panic climbed with each step she leaped.

"Shreya, where are you?"

"Here."

She was in the first guest room, sitting on the bed with her arms wrapped around her knees. A thundercloud of relief washed over Jess. She rushed inside and pulled Shreya into her arms.

"It's okay, it's okay." She repeated it again and again, convincing herself just as much.

"What was that?"

"I don't know, but it's gone. You're safe."

"Gone!" The idea seemed to frighten her more. "Where?"

"Will took care of it. He killed it. Don't be afraid. I promise, I'm going to keep you safe."

Warning bells went off in Jess's head. *Don't promise what you can't deliver.*

"I feel strange. I've never seen that stuff before, but I feel like..."

"Like what?"

Her friend's silence made Jess's terror double. Triple.

"Shreya, like what?"

"It was weird, I...I felt something inside me."

Jess leaned back. "What do you mean?"

"Like...a pull. I don't know. Jess, where was I all this time?"

Eighteen

Jess found Will at the kitchen sink washing the pan she'd used to make the grilled cheese. The plates, cutting board, and wine glasses were neatly stacked in the drainboard. He set the pan behind them and then dried his hands on a towel.

"She's in the shower," Jess said in response to his questioning gaze. "You didn't have to clean up." She glanced around but held her tongue now that he'd turned the radio off.

"I put it there." He pointed to a paper bag on the end of the counter. Jess peered inside. He'd sealed the device inside a gallon-size Ziplock storage bag.

Will opened her upper cabinet and pulled out a mason jar with the lid screwed on tight. He'd filled it about halfway with water. Jess could see the blue substance at the bottom; it looked like a thin blue potato chip.

"I did a little experiment. It didn't work."

He'd tried to revive it, whatever it was.

"I can't say I'm disappointed." She wrinkled her nose. "I'm not sure I want that in my house. But I don't think pouring it down the drain is a good idea, either."

He chuckled. "Probably not."

A long silence stretched. It wasn't a comfortable one, like those they'd shared as teenagers.

"How's she doing?"

Jess merely raised her brows and glanced away. "Who can say?"

"Actually, I should ask how you're doing."

"I think the shock is setting in." She picked up her jacket and examined the inner lining.

"I already looked, it's clean," Will supplied. "It seems it doesn't smear or leave a residue. Nothing on the table, either."

She nodded and set it down again, and then slid into her chair.

"Jess, I—"

"I meant to thank you." She finally looked up at him. "For calling me so persistently tonight. I was on the scene at the train, but...I'm glad you did."

"Yeah, of course. I figured you'd want me to. Persist, that is." He slid into the chair kitty-corner to her. "But sorry about earlier. I was too pushy."

She nodded and leaned her head forward to smooth the loose hairs back into her bun.

He cleared his throat. "I realize even though you didn't leave Kileyville— I mean Pine Bluff, you have a new life here. It wasn't just me who went off—"

"You never came back."

Her softly spoken accusation sent him to silence. His shoulders settled and he broke her gaze.

"I waited for you for five years. You didn't come back, not even once."

"I know." He finally looked at her, and Jess blinked away tears. She vowed she wouldn't cry again, at least not over him. She'd shed enough tears tonight, and they were for the girl who deserved them. Will didn't.

Upstairs, the water shut off. The old pipes rattled.

"We had Christmas in New York. My mother loved it there, and I could finally get my parents to spend it together again." He glanced up at her sheepishly. "We invited you."

He had, once. The first year. She'd turned him down. It was his family's holiday, she didn't want to intrude, and June had still been in rehab. The holidays had been especially hard for her mother, and Jess had to be there. Over the years, Lucille had invited her again, but Will never had.

"That's a shitty excuse," he admitted to her continued silence. "You're right. It was crappy, what I did to you."

She didn't intend to make him squirm, but Jess didn't know what to say. It was past midnight, and she was exhausted.

"Sorry for assuming you didn't have a boyfriend. Just wishful thinking, I guess. I'm sure you had to beat them off. I mean..."

"I know what you mean."

He sighed. "I'm sorry. I know that doesn't mean much to you, but it's true. I'm really sorry."

"No, I'm sorry. For expecting too much of you. Even though you never came back, you never gave up on the Kileyville 97, and that means a lot to me." She gestured to the hardback on the table. Salt still spilled across its cover. "It was very...*thorough*."

"Every word was written..." He took a deep breath and slowly let it out, as if carefully considering what he said next. "With the hope of your approval."

She managed a thin smile. "I give it my official stamp."

He relaxed, relieved by the thin olive branch.

"Everything in it...you took a big risk," she acknowledged. "That must have taken a lot of courage."

"That's one of the things I learned in journalism. If there's no risk, it's not worth the paper it's written on. I had to learn to put the fear aside, and never hide from the risk. That's why I'm here, Jess. I know I hurt you, and you have a boyfriend now, but I had to come back to you. You're worth the risk. I—"

The ringing of her cell phone interrupted him.

Jess rose to retrieve it from the counter as Shreya walked into the kitchen wearing the fuzzy sweats and slippers Jess had put out for her. Merely the sight of her made Jess feel warm inside.

"Hi, Bruce, what's up?"

Shreya slid into a chair and both she and Will watched her expectantly.

"Sorry to call so late," Bruce said. "Did I wake you?"

"No, we're up."

"How's Shreya doing?"

Jess glanced at her. "She's as good as can be expected. We're both still trying to wrap our heads around this."

"Yep, I understand. Listen, I thought you'd want to know, I'm headed to a call on the missing kid; Gavin Swift. He was found walking on the tracks in a daze. An ambulance has already got him on route to Trinity Med."

Nineteen

"I'll be there in twenty," Jess told her boss.

"You don't have to unless you want to talk to him. I just wanted to let you know."

"I do want to talk to him." The fact that he was found walking on the tracks was a coincidence she couldn't ignore. "What's the status on his parents?"

"Mother's down in San Francisco. I didn't contact her yet because, well..."

"Yeah. Okay. On my way." She punched off. "I have to go to a call. Will, can you stay here with Shreya?"

"Of course."

"Is it about us?" Shreya asked.

"Gavin Swift has been found. I want to know why he wasn't with the rest of you."

And why he was found near the site of another incident involving those strange alien devices.

She went to the other room and opened her safe. She didn't expect to need her gun, but she was officially going back on duty. She came back into the kitchen and picked up her jacket again. It was chilly outside, but she wasn't comfortable putting it on if some of that blue stuff had gotten on it. After examining it carefully, Jess decided Will was right and none had smeared off.

"I don't need a babysitter," Shreya said in a small voice.

"No, you don't." Jess squatted in front of her and grasped her hands. "But I need him to stay. Please, humor me. I spent too many years wondering what happened to you. I can't do that tonight, not for a single second."

Shreya must have seen the hot wave of emotion that came over Jess because she smiled and nodded.

"I'm going to ask him all sorts of probing questions."

Jess laughed and quickly dashed away a tear she hoped neither of them had noticed. "I know you will."

"And then later I'm going to compare his answers to yours."

"Uh oh. Maybe I should spend a moment with Will before I go." She touched Shreya's cheek. "I wouldn't leave if it wasn't important."

"I know." This time Shreya's voice was a whisper as her own fragile emotions showed through.

Jess cupped her face. "I'll be back as soon as I can." She leaned in and kissed her, and Shreya pulled her tight. When Jess leaned back, she saw a tear. "I promise."

She stood and faced Will. "Lock the door behind me. And don't tell her anything."

Shreya pouted. "No fair!"

⁓

Jess grabbed the paper bag from the counter. Walking to the front door was as difficult as fighting a hurricane-force wind, and Jess almost couldn't do it. She tucked the bag under her arm inside her jacket and turned to face Will through the glass panel by the door. He gave a single nod and turned the deadbolt.

Panic twisted in her chest. *You're okay. You're okay.* She walked to the barn, dragging in deep breaths of the clean, night air. Jess threw open the barn doors and strode into the dark behind her restored police-auction Charger. She swept away the straw from the loose floorboard and hid the device underneath, then covered it again.

Let them find it now.

She slid into the driver's seat. A twist of the key brought the Charger roaring to life. She raced through the doors and left them standing wide, an invitation to anyone who might want to search inside.

Go ahead and try.

She flipped on the headlights and fog lamps and hit the portable dash strobe. Gravel sprayed as she fishtailed down the narrow drive, and her tires chirped as she hit the pavement and put the pedal down.

Streetlights lit up Highway 9, so Jess stopped on the dark rural road and let the car idle. She sat there for a moment, wondering how to play this, when a food wrapper on the floor caught her eye. She threw the driver's door open and jumped out, holding the food bag with its empty French fry carton inside. She let the bag swing in her hand and looked around, trying to appear sneaky. She ran into the meadow and knelt behind an enormous oak, crushing the bag and stuffing it in her coat pocket as she did. If anyone was watching, they'd think she stashed the device out here somewhere.

She jogged back to the car and hopped in, revving the engine loudly twice before dropping it into drive and racing away. Maybe she wasn't fooling anybody, but if someone was watching, they'd have to wonder what she was up to.

Bruce's cruiser was parked at the curb in front of the hospital's main door. He paced the sidewalk, talking into his phone. Jess pulled in behind him and cut the lights.

He punched off the call. "You didn't have to come."

She fell into step beside him. "If it gives me one more iota of what happened to them, then for Shreya's sake, I have to know. For all of their sakes."

"That's what makes you my best deputy, Harding. This is more than just a job to you."

Jess groaned inwardly. He was going to hate her come morning. Leaving the department wouldn't be easy. Bruce and her coworkers were like family, but Shreya's reappearance only compounded the decision she'd been mulling for months.

"What have you got so far?"

"Joey Foster and his friends were out behind his dad's place, messing around at the bridge when Gavin came down the tracks in his tux. They tried to talk to him, but he went right on by in a daze, limping pretty bad. They went back to the house and told Oran, and he called it in."

"Oran Foster's place is twelve miles outside of town. He walked that far?"

"It looks like he did more than just walk. Apparently, he's in bad shape. He's covered in cuts and bruises, and may have a torn meniscus."

They walked into the blindingly white hallway and bypassed the check-in station for the emergency room. A doctor coming out of an exam room saw them and waited. Jess recognized him; he'd been on staff here for years, before the disappearance, and before her mother's recovery. His name was

Hanson, but in drunken delight, June had called him Dr. Handsome. Jess couldn't look at him without an embarrassed flush, even ten years later.

"He's in here," the doctor said, gesturing with a clipboard.

"Dr. Hanson, have any other patients related to the reappearance of the 97 come in tonight?" Jess asked.

Bruce cut a smile. "Do you mean did Ronnie Gamada have a heart attack seeing his wife and daughter return after ten years? Deputy McManus was able to get to their house first, broke it to him gently."

"I'm wondering if anyone else is feeling or acting strangely." Jess hoped she didn't pique either man's suspicions. "What about the FBI? Have they been here asking questions?"

Dr. Hanson stopped beside a curtain-shrouded bed. "Nobody in an official capacity, but I've got an agent here who broke his foot coming off the helicopter."

Jess hadn't heard the helicopter, but it didn't surprise her that one had flown in with reinforcements. She wondered how many black-clad, humorless-faced MIBs were running around Pine Bluff, or worse, how many soldiers in riot gear with automatic machine guns.

She sucked in a breath at the sight of the young man sitting on the examination bed. His tuxedo jacket had been removed and a nurse had rolled up the sleeve of his formal shirt to administer an IV. Like the other returned, he was thinner, but Gavin looked like he hadn't slept in days. His shirt was filthy, as was his face, and Jess detected the strong scent of pine. His hands had sticky brown spots, which still had dirt clinging to them. Bruce hadn't lied; he was covered in cuts and bruises, and one of his dress loafers had a flopping sole. He held an icepack to one knee.

"Hey, Gavin. Rough night?" They'd been friends in high school and had sat together in social economics on a four-person study group with Dave Sumner and Mike Rollins, two screw-ups who had shown up to class stoned more often than not. She'd liked Gavin, he was smart and funny and got her wry sense of humor, and because the class was easy for them, they'd spent most of the group time just talking while Dave and Mike imitated Beavis and Butthead.

Gavin swallowed, and it seemed to take great effort to focus his attention on her. "Jess?" He glanced over her uniform. "You...Jess?"

"Yeah, it's me." She leaned her hip on the side of the bed and put her hand on his shoulder. "How are you feeling?"

His vacant stare slid away, and he blinked slowly. "Not so good."

"Have you been drinking tonight?"

He glanced at Bruce.

"It's all right. We just want to help you feel better. Don't worry, you're not in any trouble."

She rubbed his shoulder while she planned her escape strategy for the vomit he looked like he was going to spew any minute.

"Yeah. Two beers. But I took some Ex. Must've been bad."

"Do you remember leaving the dance?"

He stared off again. A line formed between his brows. "Not really. Are you going to call my mom?"

"You need to stay here tonight and get this out of your system. We'll call her, and she'll be here in the morning."

"She's gonna be pissed."

"No, she won't. I promise you that." Jess gently turned one hand. He let her expose his palm. She glanced at Bruce. "Pine sap."

"Did you black out, son?"

"I think so." He looked at Jess again, this time glancing up and down. "Why are you wearing a police uniform?"

"It's...I'm in a special apprenticeship program."

"On prom night? Or is it...was prom yesterday?" He looked at Bruce again, eyes sticking to his nametag. "Where's Sheriff Weasley?"

"This is Sheriff Brady." She tossed a warning glance at the nurse. "From, uh, Redding. He heads the junior deputy program."

"He's letting you ask the questions?" Gavin huffed a weak laugh.

"It's part of my training. Do you know why you were walking along the railroad tracks?"

"No clue."

"Do you remember climbing a tree?"

"I remember falling out of one." He switched hands holding the ice pack and turned the other for her to see. His palm was scratched badly. "I think I hurt my collarbone."

"That might need a stitch or two," the nurse said, and she turned to leave. Sheriff Brady followed her out, yanking the curtain along the track in the ceiling with a shrill *whirr*.

"I twisted my knee real bad. I won't be able to play in the next game."

"They're going to fix you up just fine." Jess's promise felt empty, almost a lie.

"I don't think so." His eyes drifted shut, but he snapped himself awake, as if afraid to fall asleep. "I feel...off."

Jess's worry cranked up a notch. All this unknown left her sick with fear; for him, and for Shreya. "Do you feel like you've been away somewhere? Like you've been asleep a long time?"

"I do." He fixed his gaze on her, and Jess finally saw some clarity. "Weird, huh? I'm gonna clean up my act. No more Ex."

"That's definitely a wise choice. Can you tell me anything you remember after arriving at the dance?"

He drifted off again as he thought about it. "I remember...I got really cold. Wet cold, like walking into a meat locker. And then I just remember falling out of a tree, and wondering how I'd gotten up in it."

Jess struggled to control her frantic heart. "What did you do after that?"

"I was supposed to...I don't know. Do something in the forest."

She wanted to grab him by the shoulders and shake him, but she knew handling him gently was the only way to get answers.

"Who told you to do something in the forest? A man, or a woman?"

"Someone...I'm not sure anymore." He looked at her again and managed to smile. "I remember a voice, but I can't picture a face. Sorry, Jess."

An idea hit her. "Was it nighttime or daytime when you found yourself in the forest?" If he placed the objects that caused the train incident, that meant he was returned before the others.

"It was um, like super early in the morning. I remember the sky getting lighter, and then I was walking around in daylight, but I knew I couldn't go home until I sobered up. Damn, that must have been some bender. I don't remember any of it."

"Don't worry about it. Dr. Hanson will take good care of you."

The nurse returned. "All right, young man, let's have you lean back so we can take a look at that knee. We need to get you fixed up for the big football game."

Jess gave the nurse a grateful smile as she eased out of the way. "I'm going to come back and visit you before you leave, okay?"

"Okay, Deputy Harding." He gave her a mock salute.

She turned to leave but stopped when he called her name.

"Are you going to call my mom now? She'll want to know what happened to me."

A zing of tingles ran over her spine. She smiled. "I will. Don't you worry, Gavin. You're not in any trouble."

She met up with Bruce at the admission station near the door.

"I told her not to let him know about the missing decade. I'll come back tomorrow and talk to him when he feels better."

As usual, her astute boss was right on target. "Thank you, Bruce. He didn't seem..."

"Ready for it?"

They walked outside into the brisk night.

"What's your take on this?" he asked as they walked to their cars.

Jess dragged in a deep breath. Where could she even begin? She was thankful for Will's book, because he'd eloquently put things into words that would have left her tongue tied. Thank goodness he was here. He'd help her sort through her spinning thoughts with his logic and articulacy. Sometimes, it was how a person said a thing that made it either credible or ludicrous.

"It's one-thirty in the morning, and I'm dead on my feet, so I'll indulge in theories I probably wouldn't in the hard light of day."

She stopped and faced him. He nodded. "I'll indulge with you."

"Because they don't appear to have aged—Jesus, I can't believe I'm saying this—theory one is time travel. Because they all appear to have lost weight, theory two is cryogenic stasis. Theory three is alien abduction, but I refuse to entertain that one."

His brows rose, but Jess held up a hand. "I know, I know. You once saw a UFO in the desert, and you believe man's assertion that he's all alone in the universe not only proves his ignorance but also his arrogance."

Bruce laughed. "You know me so well. I'm touched, Harding." He sobered quickly. "At this point, I won't rule out anything, and I don't know how you could, either."

She grumbled a sigh even as she nodded. "I don't want to believe theory three because it's so frightening. Feds, I can deal with. Aliens, I can't."

"Fair enough. Truth be told, I'm leaning more toward theory one or two as well. Ditto on the FBI's involvement. Given their quick appearance in town, both this time and at the original disappearance, we can surmise they knew about it, if they aren't directly responsible."

"That much we agree on." She forced away a yawn. "I'm heading home, I'm beat—"

"What's going on with Shreya?" Bruce asked her point blank.

"What?" Fear spiked. She was too tired for another surge of adrenaline, and this one made her queasy.

"You asked Dr. Hanson if anyone else was feeling strange. Come on, Harding. I can see it in your face."

She sighed and glanced away. "If I told you why, I'd have to explain, and I'm not sure you want to know." He'd always given his deputies a loose rein to use their best judgment but preferred not to hear about detours from the straight and narrow. He was especially lenient with Jess, given her past, but at the same time, he was especially strict with her on that rule, as well.

One corner of his mouth quirked. "I think I've officially traveled past the point of plausible deniability."

She glanced past the hospital, staring at the dark woods behind the square building. A part of her still didn't want to tell him, while another bigger part wanted him as her team captain.

"You read *The Night They Disappeared*?"

He gave a curt nod. "I did."

She sighed. "Then you know those three theories are really Stan's."

Rather, Will's. Straight-laced, reasonable, educated, calm, and rational Will Taylor had come up with time travel, cryogenic stasis, and alien abduction, with a full chapter devoted to the argument for, and against, each one.

"I know he had a strong influence from special friends who went through the experience firsthand," Bruce said in a soft voice.

She looked deeply into his eyes. So, he knew the truth, then. Probably most in town suspected it.

"The night of the prom, Will and I broke into the gymnasium and found mysterious objects mounted to the ceiling at all four corners of the room."

"And you climbed up and pulled one down, and the FBI agent in charge stormed in and took it away from you."

"There were four of them in the rec room tonight. Will and Gus, the senior center's maintenance man, brought them down before you and the

FBI arrived. Gus sneaked them out, and he and Will arranged to meet up later."

He remained silent as she told him, his only reaction a slight upward twitch of his brows.

"He doesn't have them anymore," she continued, answering his unspoken question. "As Gus was hiding them in his barn, someone sneaked up behind and hit him over the head. When he came to, the objects were gone. Will arrived to find Gus's wife stitching up the back of his scalp."

"And nobody called it in. Jesus, Mary, and Joseph."

"Will thought it would be safer to tell me directly."

Bruce blasted a sigh through clenched teeth as he stared at the starry sky. "Thank God we have you on our team, or nobody in this town would trust us enough to spit on us."

"Look, you're not the only one with plausible-deniability impulses," she offered lamely. "Nobody here likes the FBI, and nobody wants to incite their wrath. Calling in something like that implicates them in wrongdoing as well. And we all know the FBI isn't very forgiving of wrongdoing."

"Yeah, yeah." He grumbled as he paced in a small circle, hands on his hips. Finally, he looked at her. "I guess you know that better than most. But you gotta be upfront with me, Harding. I already have the FBI skulking around my town, keeping secrets. I can't have you doing it, too."

"I didn't know about this until two hours ago, when Will came over to the house. Or at least about Gus getting attacked. I knew about the two of them pulling the objects down when I got to the rec center, but you have to agree, I was a little distracted." Her defensive hackles notched up. "I only just had Shreya magically reappear back in my life. There wasn't much room for anything else in my head at the time. And the choice not to report it was Will's and Gus's. Will doesn't know you like I do. He didn't know if he could trust you."

"All right, all right." He put a hand on her shoulder. "I get it. No harm, no foul, Deputy. But just promise me, moving forward, we work together on this, not against each other."

She swallowed. "Here's the upfront. Earlier today, I found one of the objects in the woods near the train."

He went silent again for two heartbeats. "Jesus. So, it *was* related." He swiped a hand over his face. "Just one?"

She nodded. "I couldn't tell you at the scene, there was a crowd. And then I got the call."

"Was it the same device?"

"Exactly the same," she returned passionately. "The same shape, the same size, the same mysterious markings. The same eerie blue gunk on the back. Only this time, we realized it almost seemed..." She stared off and shuddered, remembering how it had crawled toward Shreya.

"Seemed what?"

"You're not going to believe it. This will give credit to your alien theory."

He settled back on his heels with a haunted look on his face. "Try me."

"It seemed *alive*."

Twenty

"Where is it now?" Bruce demanded.

"Hidden. I didn't want it at my house. I stashed it in the woods between my place and Highway 9."

That should send anyone listening on a wild goose chase and lend some credibility to her performance earlier tonight. If anyone *was* listening. And if anyone had been following. She was willing to bet her next paycheck on both.

"I want to see it."

A zing of uncertainty made her heart kick but ultimately left her drained. She had chills, and the three triangles of grilled cheese sandwich weren't nearly enough fuel for this exhausting day.

"I'll bring it to you tomorrow." She turned toward her car.

"It already is tomorrow," Bruce called after her.

Jess grinned before hopping into her Charger. "Then you don't have long to wait."

She left the portable strobe off and drove slower on the way home, letting the cool night air blow through the windows. When she turned off Highway 9, she checked her mirrors. No one behind or ahead. The rural Wyandotte Way was as desolate as the moon, not even a cricket or mockingbird heard over the low hum of her purring Charger. If anyone had seen her earlier or heard her bogus explanation, they were waiting until later to search the area. If they did, she hoped they found no shortage of frustration.

Lights were still on inside the farmhouse. Jess left the old Charger parked near her cruiser and walked to the house without looking at the barn. Will waited for her on the other side of the door and turned the deadbolt when she mounted the porch steps.

"She's asleep on the futon. She wouldn't go up to the guest room."

Jess gave a weary sigh and bypassed the family room through the kitchen. She unhooked her duty belt and locked her gun back in the safe.

"First thing she asked me after you left was 'did you two do the nasty?'"

To this Jess gave a single chuckle. Shreya was ever the spitfire she used to be. She turned around and pinned Will with a penetrating stare.

He cleared his throat. "I told her she'd have to ask you for the personal details about who you're sleeping with."

"Nice try, Will." She brushed past him and noted his sleek laptop on the dining table next to her dinosaur. "You can take the spare room if you want to crash here." She didn't wait for his answer.

Instead, she yanked the laces of her boots loose and kicked them off, then laid down on the futon and wrapped her arm around Shreya.

༺

Where am I? This can't be my house.

The scent of frying bacon and freshly brewed coffee pulled her out of dark dreams. She realized she was on her futon under her fuzzy Afghan, and then she realized I *am alone.*

Jess jerked upright. A wave of dizziness rolled across her senses.

"Jess doesn't drink coffee."

The spike of relief she felt hearing Shreya's voice was almost painful. A second later, a headache throbbed to life in her skull. She ran a hand over her face that came away greasy with the previous day's stress. She threw off the Afghan and found herself still in her uniform. She probably stank like she'd slept in a Dumpster.

"Good morning!" Shreya shrieked when she dragged herself into the kitchen.

Jess leaned over her shoulder, wrapped her arms around her, and kissed her cheek. Realizing that Shreya's return wasn't a bizarre dream was like waking on Christmas morning, and she held on tight.

Shreya yelped teasingly. "You're choking me!"

Will gave her a sheepish grin. "Just in time." He slid a plate in front of Shreya and set one in the empty place across the table. "We were just discussing who this coffee dripper might belong to since we both know it isn't yours."

She narrowed her eyes as she dropped into the chair across from Shreya. Damn, if he was this unrelenting, she was going to have to come up with a fake boyfriend. She immediately forgave him when he tore open a packet of Constant Comment and dropped the teabag into a super-sized mug curling with tendrils of steam.

"Oh, bless you." She wrapped her hands around the too-hot mug and looked at her plate. A Denver omelet enticed her with its bright colors and impossibly uniform half-circle shape. A perfectly toasted English muffin glistened with strawberry preserves. Jess thought back to the summer they spent together and tried to remember if she'd confessed her love of jam.

"Seriously. Did you minor in cooking, too?" Where had he even gotten these ingredients?

He blushed. Damn, her resolve to torture him crumbled when he did that.

"One of my many talents."

"It's good!" Shreya shoveled another gigantic mouthful.

"You're such a morning person," Jess muttered. The first sip of sweet, orangey tea made a cloud move away from the sun.

"Always have been," Shreya said cheerfully.

Jess groaned.

"Maybe these will help." He set a bottle of aspirin next to her plate.

He sat at the short end between them with a plate of scrambles for himself. "I was thinking...unless, of course, you had another idea..."

Jess held her mug under her nose. It was like aroma therapy. "Out with it."

"Maybe we, as in you and Sheriff Brady, should organize a private meeting with the 97 before the FBI sticks their fingers into the pot and fouls up the soup."

Jess took a bite of the omelet and did her best to hide her pleasure as it melted in her mouth. "Good idea."

"Really?"

"I think so, too," Shreya cut in. "I could tell at the school yesterday that you don't like the FBI very much."

"Uh oh. It showed?"

Shreya laughed. "Well, I wasn't sure," she said in a teasing voice, "until you told one of them to cram it."

Jess sighed and set her fork down. "Listen, about that. I acted unprofessionally."

"You were dealing with a lot," Will said in her defense.

"And nobody can blame you after what they did to you." Shreya patted the book. "I read a couple of chapters last night after you left."

"Look, I'm sure you both know Federal law enforcement has jurisdiction over State and Local. As long as I'm with the Sheriff's Department, I have to play nice. But as soon as I resign, all bets are off."

"What are you saying?" Will asked her.

"I've been thinking about quitting. To be honest, everyone in the department knows cutbacks are on the way, so I was halfway expecting it to come whether I was ready or not. At least that way I'd get a nice severance package. Now I'm not waiting anymore." She reached across the table and covered Shreya's hand with hers. "The minute you came back, I decided."

"Jess."

"You can't," Will said.

"Sure, I can." She picked up her fork and dismissed their arguments by eating. "I've waited ten years for you to come back, Shrey. I'm not wasting a minute of our future together."

⤸

After her shower, Jess found Will at the kitchen sink for the second time in as many days. Her counters were neater and he'd scrubbed the stains out of her old ceramic sink.

"I could get used to this."

He grinned at her. "Just say the word."

"You don't give up easily, do you?"

"Not where you're concerned, Jessica Fearless." He dried his hands on a towel and gave her a direct look up and down. "You look good in your civvies."

Shreya shut off the television in the next room and joined them. "I could use some civvies of my own."

"I'm taking you to your house this morning." She pulled out a chair. "First, I'd like to talk more about this meetup Will suggested."

The two of them joined her at the table.

"Where should we have it," Jess asked, "and how do we notify everyone in such a way the FBI doesn't catch wind of it?"

Will leaned his elbows on the table, flexing arm muscles she hadn't noticed before. Today he wore a clingy gray shirt that made the blue of his eyes gleam like sapphires. "That's a good question. I don't suppose anyone wants to go back to the senior center any time soon."

Shreya made a face. "Not me."

"Me either," Jess agreed. As it was, she was going to spend the rest of her life searching every room she entered for mysterious black objects. Their former high school gymnasium was a place she'd *never* feel comfortable again.

"Facebook and Twitter are still down, not that anything electronic would be an option."

Jess agreed. "I don't think phones are even safe. I hate to say it, but we'll probably have to rely on face-to-face communication."

"That'll be tough," Will said. "That's a lot of people."

"You could cut the number in half at least if you start with one half of the prom couples," Shreya suggested. "Ask them to contact their date."

"Good idea." She looked at Will. "Do you still have that list? I can check for addresses in the police computer."

"Assuming that's still up and running," Will cut in wryly. "Who knows how much they're interfering with Pine Bluff's services."

"We'll just have to assume that's a go until we find it isn't." Jess thought for a minute. "How about Ellwood's B&B? They can host weddings for up to two hundred guests in the yard behind the house."

Will shook his head. "Too open, and nothing to stop the FBI from wandering in. Even if they stayed out of sight, they could easily use an L-R-L-D to listen in."

"Also, with the parents included, this will be more than two hundred people," Shreya reminded them.

"What about the Elks Lodge?" he suggested. "They have a room that can easily fit three hundred, and I could see if they'll give it to us gratis."

"Bad idea," Jess said immediately. "The parking lot faces Main Street. A hundred cars suddenly filling its lot would raise suspicion. The agents are probably staying at the Pine Brook Lodge, right down the street." The MIBs would have to be blind not to notice.

"I know you said a lot of things have changed in town," Shreya ventured. "Is the old movie theater still there?"

Jess formed a slow smile. "It is."

Twenty-One

Every time Sara looked at her dad now, she got a jolt from seeing him with all white hair. He stood in the doorway of her bedroom with that odd look on his face again, like he was scared or worried. When he saw her looking, he smiled and blinked his eyes a bunch of times.

"Hi, Pumpkin."

She set down her magazine. "Hi."

Sara loved him dearly, but his constant hovering was starting to annoy her. She understood what everyone was saying—that yammering busybody Mrs. Buenez from next door wouldn't leave her alone when Sara just wanted to sunbathe in peace—but she truly couldn't believe she'd been gone ten years. Not really, anyway. She felt like she'd been asleep for a long time, like when she was eleven and had pneumonia and was out of it for a while, but it felt like she was here just yesterday, getting dressed for prom. All her makeup was still in the decorative box on her pretty dressing table, all her favorite photos were still stuck in her mirror by their corners, all her clothes were still in the closet. Except for the layer of dust on everything, her room was exactly as she'd left it.

"Can you pack up some clothes? We're going to visit your Aunt Loretta."

"What, now?" Summer break was not even three weeks away, and she'd planned on going to cheer camp. "I've got school."

"No, you don't, sweetie." His face had aged so much it was hard to look at him without feeling weird. He formed that pitying frown again, which was starting to infuriate her. Everyone was treating her differently, when they were the ones who were different.

"I have plans with Ella," she snapped.

He pinched his mouth tight. "You can reschedule."

"No, I can't—"

"Just pack your damn clothes, Sara!"

She shoved off her bed. "I don't want to go visit Aunt Loretta. This is my last summer vacation before college. You said we didn't have to go there this summer. You said this could be *my* summer to choose."

He visibly struggled past his anger, his nostrils flaring. "Your aunt hasn't seen you in ten years."

"You keep saying that! I don't care. I hate Phoenix in the summer. It's so hot you can't go outside. All she does is sit around watching daytime soap operas. Why can't she come here?"

He stepped into the room and took her by the arms. "Listen to me—you have to trust me on this. There's something wrong with this town. We're leaving, and we're not coming back."

"What? No!" She shrugged free and stepped back.

"No arguments!" He sliced a hand through the air, his famous way of saying his was the final word, and she had no say in the matter. "Now pack what's important to you. Anything you don't take gets left behind."

He turned and stalked out of the room. She stood where he'd left her, shaking in anger. She clenched and unclenched her fists.

Then an eerie tranquility washed over Sara. Her body relaxed and her focus shifted away from the doorway into hazy white nothingness. Thoughts flooded into her consciousness, as though shared with her by someone else.

Of course. That was the perfect solution. The *only* solution. A light smile found her lips. She walked from her bedroom into the hallway and turned into her father's room, where she knelt in front of the closet and spun the dial on his safe.

೧

Jess felt Shreya watching her from the passenger seat. She glanced over and found her friend wearing an exaggerated pout that made her laugh.

"What?"

"I can't believe my best friend isn't dishing me the goods. Why are you alienating me like this?"

"Oh God, Shreya, no." Jess sighed. "It's not that, I swear."

She crossed her arms and "hmphed" with exaggeration. "Could've fooled me." With her Marathi accent, she was delightful in her complaining.

"It's just that...I don't know how I feel about Will right now."

"I knew it. There *is* something between you two."

"There was, yes," she admitted. "Okay, yes. We had a fling that summer.

And yes, we had sex."

Shreya squealed and grabbed her arm.

Jess laughed again. "You know, back then, I imagined you would react exactly that way."

Shreya made happy sounds. "My Jess had a summer romance. You little slut."

"I don't know if I'd have called it a romance at the time." Even though Shreya was sitting right next to her, Jess's throat grew tight as she thought back to those days. "That summer was filled with so much pain, and it was hard to think about anything else. The whole town was in mourning, there was misery here like you can't imagine. My mom went into rehab, and I was all alone. Will was there for me in so many ways. Without him, I don't know if I would have survived."

Shreya's expression lost its humor. "I hate that this happened to you." She swiveled toward Jess in the seat as much as her seatbelt would allow. "And I love that he was there for you."

The dashboard radio squawked, and after Jess turned down the volume, she took Shreya's hand.

"Do you love him?"

Another tough question. Jess considered her answer carefully. "We both had major crushes at the time. I think to some extent, I did, but then he left so quickly for school." She glanced to the side briefly, driving slowly through the back roads to Shreya's house.

"So...who is this boyfriend you have now?"

Jess wished she could fill up a bathtub with Shreya's accent and soak in it.

She sighed again and rolled her eyes. "I don't have a boyfriend. I just told Will that I did. I didn't want him thinking I was available." She caught Shreya's raised eyebrows. "You can't let a guy think you're an easy conquest. He has to work for it."

Shreya grinned. "Sneaky."

"I really don't know if I want him back in my life, Shrey. He didn't come back once, not in ten years, with barely a word. The only reason that didn't destroy me is that it happened over such a long period of time. I only saw him again for the first time yesterday, literally two hours before you came back. I just can't deal with him right now. You're all that matters to me.

You're all I can think about."

"Bull pucky."

She snorted. "What?"

"You've always been the strongest, smartest, and most capable person I know. Don't tell me you don't have room in that big head of yours for both of us."

Jess smirked. "Maybe I just don't want him anymore."

"Right. You can't convince me you don't want that beefcake."

She chuckled. Nothing slipped past Shreya. "He does look good," she conceded. "I think I started to love him more after he left. All those years he was away, I imagined him into this impressive version of the guy I knew; educated, sophisticated, accomplished. And then when this came out..." She tapped the hardback on the seat between them. "Even though he never came home, what happened here stayed alive for him like it did for me. He never let it go. He was always thinking about you guys, always researching, always looking. And for that, he's my hero."

"Aww."

"And that rat bastard, he turned out to be everything I conjured him into."

Shreya giggled. "So, give him another chance. Everyone makes mistakes. It sounds like he had his own journey to make, away from Kileyville."

"Now you sound like my conscience. I'll admit, a part of me was jealous that he left and became so much more, but I don't begrudge him for it."

"You two make a gorgeous couple. Let's face it, you're twenty-eight now. Your biological clock is ticking."

Jess burst out laughing.

"Look out!"

Clint Freeman ran into the road waving his arms. Jess slammed on the brakes and the Charger slid to a stop.

He ran around to the driver's side window. "There's been an accident. A car went into the reservoir. I don't have my cell phone—"

To the right, tire tracks carved deep grooves through the grassy rise to the breaker. Several people stood on top, looking at the water. From her low vantage point, Jess couldn't see the surface. Two cars were stopped at the edge of the road, one on either side.

"It's the coroner's wagon," he continued at a fast clip. "We saw it swerve into the oncoming lane and nearly hit Mrs. Rigby. Then he just raced up the embankment and—my God, you should have seen it—the car took flight off the rise. It's pretty far out there. Evan is out in the water now."

Jess grabbed the microphone from the dash radio as she maneuvered the Charger off the road. "Dispatch, nineteen-six on the scene of an eleven-eighty-three, request police and ambulance."

"Go ahead, nineteen-six."

"I'm at Chambers Reservoir, east end on Cross Creek at Newhall. Over."

"Ten-four, Chambers Reservoir, east end. Do you have status on injuries?"

"Vehicle is in the water. Passengers are unknown. I'm leaving my vehicle to check it out. I'm 10-10 without a radio. Over."

"Ten-four, nineteen-six. Units are on the way."

She shifted into park and shut off the car. Shreya's expression was pure terror.

"Jess!"

"It'll be okay. Stay here."

But Shreya jumped out of the car with her and followed her up the rise. At the top, she saw the wagon pitched forward in the water, nearly entirely submerged. Water bubbled around it. A man suddenly broke the surface, flipping blonde hair out of his eyes. It wasn't Len Potter.

"I need a rock to break the window!" he shouted. He dove back under.

Jess picked up a round river stone and ran toward the edge of the water. It was about twice the size of her palm. She hoped that would be enough. Any larger, and she wouldn't be able to swim with it.

"Jess, be careful!" Shreya's terrified shriek ripped at her heart.

Imagine the irony of drowning the day after getting Shreya back.

She dove in and swam as hard as she could. The white wagon sat just below the surface like a resting whale, slowly growing visible in the murky water. For a frightening moment, she couldn't see the man in the water. Then he swam around the submerged windshield and pulled at the door handle. Jess gasped for air. She could barely swim in jeans, and holding a rock in one hand didn't make it any easier.

The man in the water breached the surface for air and then went back under to pull at the rear passenger door. When it stayed shut, he went to the front door, and Jess heard the muffled sound of his underwater shout. He pounded a hand on the glass. Whoever was inside was still alive.

Jess shot to the surface to breathe in time with him.

"The doors are locked. She won't open them!"

He grabbed the rock from her hand and swam back under. The rear window held a bubble of air; all that was keeping the wagon at the surface, but the sheer weight of the car was pulling it down anyway. Jess pulled in three fast, deep breaths to oxygenate her blood and dove back under.

In the driver's seat, Sara Potter was held in place by her seatbelt. Her hair drifted around her head like a mermaid's. Her eyes were closed, and her arms floated in front of her body. Len wasn't in his seatbelt. He floated at an odd angle against the roof. A cloud of red swirled around his midsection.

The man in the water pounded on the driver's window. It took three tries, probably kept from shattering by the pressure of the water. When it finally gave, he lifted the lock pin and grabbed the door handle. The door opened and he backed out to go for air.

Jess released Sara's seatbelt and pulled her limp body from the wagon. She breached the surface as silver spots began dancing in her eyes. Shouts erupted on the shore, and she could hear the siren of the ambulance growing louder.

Swimming backward with her arm under Sara's arms, she tried to shout, "Can you get him?" but choked on a mouthful of water that tumbled down her throat like a rock.

The rise surrounded the entire man-made reservoir, with a gravel service lane wide enough for the public-utilities vehicle. The ambulance shut off its siren with a squawk as it pulled onto the service lane. It slid to a stop with a spray of gravel, and two EMTs jumped out. They ran into the water to pull Sara from her. The other man was still far out, pulling Len in the rescue stroke. Jess struggled to rise in the murky shallow to dive back in and help him, but Clint raced past and dove in ahead of her. Shreya ran into the muddy churn to help her up.

On the shore, the EMTs carried Sara's limp body onto a traction board and began CPR. More people had gathered, and Jess saw Bruce and Deputy Swenson. Bruce urged the onlookers back and Deputy Swenson ran into the water to help the men with Len.

"You're shaking." Shreya held her firmly by the arms, as if trying to stop it. Jess's tremors were severe, made worse by the cold water and the heavy pull of soaking wet jeans.

"It's adrenaline. It'll pass in a minute."

"Somebody get her a blanket!"

"There's one in my trunk, I think," she managed through chattering teeth.

Shreya sidled out to the way as Len was carried from the water.

"Oh my God!"

Her gasp confirmed Jess's horrific suspicion: Len Potter had a ragged wound in his chest.

Twenty-Two

Deputy Swenson stepped around the front of the ambulance when the cloth was draped over Len Potter. He made a retching sound but managed to keep from throwing up. Still, the sound of him cacking and spitting made Jess's gorge rise. She walked away from the scene on the flat top of the rise, trying but failing to calm her frayed nerves.

"Shreya, honey, can you go see if there's a bottle of water for Jess in her car?"

She turned to find Bruce smiling at Shreya. She glanced at Jess, worry clear in her features.

"It's okay," Jess said.

Shreya nodded reluctantly. "I'll check for that blanket, too."

The EMT slammed the back doors and ran to the passenger side. The siren gave three blips as it drove down the rise back to the highway, and then started full-whoop as it raced to the hospital.

Just then, Deputy Swenson dragged back a gigantic loogie and spit it loudly. Jess closed her eyes and groaned.

"Heya, Deputy Swenson?" Bruce called. "Can you help Miss Sanvi find a blanket for Jess?"

Mitch raised a hand and started down to the patrol cars.

"And then I want you to call for a tow rig to get that wagon out of the water."

"Thank you," she mumbled. Bruce knew spitting was her Kryptonite. She wondered how he would survive with Mitch as his senior deputy after she resigned.

"Helluva thing you did, pulling that girl out."

Jess's stomach lurched left and right. "She's not going to make it, is she?"

He sighed. "You know I don't like to make assumptions in cases like these."

She watched the ambulance disappear into the distance. "They couldn't revive her."

"I know, but that's not unusual in a drowning situation like this out in the field. She's close to the hospital and Trinity has an excellent emergency team. As long as they keep oxygen to her brain, she could come out of it."

He was trying to make her feel better. None of this was her fault, but if Sara died, Jess would feel responsible.

"Here's the thing." Bruce cleared his throat. "It's looking like a suicide."

Jess snapped to attention at that. "How do you know?"

"Come on over here. You're gonna want to hear this."

She followed Bruce on numb legs.

"Mr. Latorre, this is Deputy Harding. Tell her what you saw when you first swam out to the wagon."

The blond man who'd been in the water had been given a thin insulator blanket, but he was shaking as hard as she was. "Call me Evan." He swallowed. His eyes held the vacant emptiness Jess had seen many times in survivors, and witnesses of terrible accidents.

"You stated Miss Potter was conscious when you first arrived, is that correct?" Bruce asked him to clarify.

"The girl in the car...yes." He nodded. "Her eyes were open, and she looked at me."

"So, she wasn't unconscious long. That's a good sign." Jess tried to convince herself it was, anyway. The shorter time she was without oxygen, the less damage her brain might have sustained. Bruce was right, as long as they kept her oxygenated, she might come out of it without brain injury.

"When I swam down to the window, she locked the door."

Jess processed that in stunned silence, certain she'd heard wrong.

"Are you sure?"

"Completely. She twisted her upper body and reached around with her right hand to push it down. When I pounded on the window, she just stared at me."

That didn't make sense. She looked at Bruce. Then, it occurred to her— Sara had been in the driver's seat.

"Could she have been confused? Maybe she hit her head on the steering wheel when the car hit the water." The older-model coroner's wagon hadn't had airbags.

"The whole thing looked intentional," Clint said. "We were behind them out on the road for a couple of miles. Everything was fine until she swerved into Mrs. Rigby's path."

"Even that looked intentional," Evan said in a weak voice. "Clint said, 'It looks like they're playing chicken,' because she drove into the other lane and then stayed there steadily, with the curve of the road."

"Mrs. Rigby swerved into the shoulder," Clint continued. "Then, all of a sudden, the wagon veered off where you see the tracks and raced up the rise. It jumped off the lip and went into the water. We stopped and ran after it, but I didn't have my cell phone. Evan went into the water, and I ran back to the road for help. Thank God you came along when you did."

Not soon enough, apparently. Jess looked at Evan. "You're sure she locked the door? Maybe she was reaching to release it when she blacked out."

"I don't think so. Besides, what about the old man with her? He was all bloody, and that looked like a bullet hole in him."

Bruce was furiously jotting notes. "Let's not jump to conclusions on that, huh fellas?"

"Could she have been trying to get him to the hospital?" Jess wondered aloud. "Maybe she was panicked." People were known to act contradictory when in shock. Kidnap victims ran from the police, and accident victims walked deeper into moving traffic.

"We don't know where she was coming from, but if it was from home, she was traveling in the opposite direction of the hospital."

Jess found Bruce watching her intently. She knew what he was thinking; Sara was a returned 97, and something was not right with her.

"This is so strange," Evan said, as if reading her mind. "Right after all those people came back."

"I'll need contact numbers for both of you. And I'm gonna ask each of you not to discuss this incident with anyone else."

"You mean like our families, or the FBI?"

Bruce flashed his jovial smile. "You noticed them, did you?"

"Three military Humvees rolled through town at six this morning," Clint said. "One of them had a guy with a fifty-cal on top. Are they planning to go to war here, or what?"

❦

Shreya waited off to the side with the blanket from Jess's trunk draped over her arm. She watched the two guys leave.

"I'm heading to the hospital," Bruce told Jess. "I want to do a residue test on Miss Potter. Mitch'll stay here while the wagon gets pulled out."

Jess merely nodded.

"You're going to tell me if you notice anything strange about Shreya," Bruce said. It wasn't a question.

"There is nothing strange about Shreya," she returned evenly.

"I believe you now." Bruce's eyebrows inched up his forehead. "But I also trust that if something does happen, you'll tell me about it."

She wanted to scream. "Of course, I will." And then she repeated, "Nothing is wrong with Shreya."

Jess could see the gears turning in his head.

"Go on now, you're off duty. Take it easy the rest of the day. That's an order."

She started down the rise.

"Harding."

Jess turned back and faced him.

"Good job today."

Her anger evaporated. "Thanks, Bruce."

Shreya threw the blanket over her shoulders. "One of the EMTs gave me this."

It was a mini bottle of water. Jess cranked it open and drank it in three deep gulps.

"Your phone was making noises, so I brought it." She handed it to Jess.

There was a text message from Will.

We need to talk.

"Sara shot her father, didn't she?"

Jess looked up. Shreya's eyes were shiny.

"We don't know for sure."

She swallowed, fighting for composure. "Why would she do that?"

Jess sighed, trying to find the best way to answer. In seven years in law enforcement, she'd seen things Shreya couldn't imagine. She gave private thanks that even though Mrs. Sanvi used to be egotistical and condescending toward Jess, Shreya had come from a loving, stable home with two parents who would move mountains for her.

"Do you remember what it was like for me in Happy Hollow while my mother was drinking?"

Shreya sniffled and nodded. Jess put her arm around her and urged her back toward the car.

"We don't know if things were worse than that at her house. I've learned through my job that sometimes even well-to-do families that appear perfect on the outside might not actually be that way on the inside. We're going to investigate."

"That's cop talk." Shreya got into the passenger seat and waited until Jess was behind the wheel with the door closed. "Your boss thinks there's something wrong with us."

How do I respond to that? "Bruce is very protective of me. He's like the father I never had, and he likes to look out for me."

"I would never hurt you, Jess! Whatever compelled her to do that, it wasn't because of where we were!"

"I know, I know." Jess grabbed her arm and squeezed. "I'm not worried about you at all. Sweetheart, you have to believe me."

"I do, but this is a terrible, terrible thing. It's not normal, and neither is what happened to us."

"I know," Jess repeated. "And all we can do is work through it the best we can, one step at a time."

"Okay." Shreya shifted in the seat to look forward and took a deep breath. "God, you're like, ten years more mature, too."

"I hope that's a compliment. Look, Will wants to talk to me. He sent me a text."

She showed Shreya her response: *one hour, where I kissed you the first time.*

"Oh, how romantic." Shreya gave a little laugh and swiped at her eye. "Do you want to go home instead so you can change into dry clothes?"

Jess started the Charger. "No, we're almost to your house. You can get your own clothes and I'll change into my sweats."

"Okay." Shreya managed a small smile. "I can't wait to see it."

When they pulled up in front of her childhood home, Shreya let out a long sigh.

"You know, it feels like I was just here yesterday, but in another sense, I understand I've been gone a long time. It feels good to be home."

Jess reached over and squeezed her hand, unable to force away the little lurch that hit her chest every time she pulled up here, even though finally, this time, Shreya was right here with her.

"There's no electricity, but we'll get it turned back on before your mom arrives." She shut off the car and they climbed out. "Here's to hoping the water still works. I feel gross."

Jess kicked off her mud-soaked sneakers and fished through her ring for the key. The door creaked open to a musty house. With the windows covered, it was dark. She started opening blinds and curtains.

"Yuck!" Shreya squeaked from the kitchen.

"Don't open the fridge," Jess called, too late. "Sorry. I've been coming about once a month to open windows and check on the place, but it's been a long time since I cleaned the refrigerator."

Shreya opened cabinets and drawers. The more emptiness she found, the more frantic she became. "Everything's gone, really?"

"They shipped some of it back to India, and a lot was donated."

Jess tried the water in the guest bathroom. It came on with a rusty tint that cleared after a minute. It was cold without a water heater, but the grit between her toes, and other uncomfortable places, was too gross to bear. She grabbed a slightly stale towel from the hallway linen closet and hopped into the frigid water for a quick rinse.

She wrapped herself in the towel and found Shreya in her room, sitting on the bed. Jess had left out her memento box—a box that looked only a few months old to Shreya but was a decade old for Jess.

"You were here a lot." Shreya had changed into a pair of jeans and one of her cute Kurta-style shirts. "I can't believe you kept this."

She picked up the cotton bracelets they had each worn until Jess's broke. Each one had plastic alphabet beads that spelled out "best friends." Jess had repaired hers and knotted it through Shreya's so it was connected.

She sat on the edge of the bed as tears of loss started again, even though Shreya was right here. "I came here when I needed to be close to you."

"You tortured yourself with all this stuff." She waved her hand over the box. Inside were photos, claimed ticket stubs for the Madonna concert they'd attended together, one of Shreya's hair combs, a pencil with a pom-pom top Shreya had given her, and a bunch of other junk no one would think to save. Next to the box was the "don't ask me to behave" t-shirt Jess had bought her at a gift shop near Lake Shasta after Shreya fell in the water, two weeks before prom. Each time she came, Jess went through the box and then curled up with that t-shirt on Shreya's bed, breathing in the last hints of her scent.

"I cried a lot of tears here, on this bed." Jess forced a smile. "But you know what? You're back now. There'll be no more tears."

And yet, there were fresh ones in her eyes.

"Okay. No more tears." Shreya leaned over and pulled Jess into her arms, and they both broke their promise.

"I'm sorry for leaving you. I don't think I truly understood how much you suffered until now."

"It wasn't your fault," Jess whispered back. "Someone else did this to us."

Shreya swiped her cheeks with the back of her hand. "Look how clean you kept my room. You covered all my clothes with plastic garment bags."

Jess picked up the pencil and waved the pompom so the nylon fibers fluttered. "I wanted to keep it ready for when you came back. I couldn't give up hope on you, because giving up felt like I was abandoning you."

"You did so much even though you were hurting so bad. Now I feel guilty for being irritated by your boss thinking something might be wrong with me." She slid to the edge of the bed and grabbed a tissue from the box on the nightstand. "I would never hurt you, Jess. But maybe he's right."

A cold chill washed over Jess.

"I feel like somebody is watching me."

Twenty-Three

"What do you mean?" Jess's voice quaked.

"I don't know." Shreya stood and went to her dresser. She retrieved a pair of panties and a stretchy sports bra Jess could fit into. "Not like stalking me or hidden cameras or anything. And it's almost like I'm remembering someone, a voice or a person I can't picture anymore, who said things a long time ago that I'm recalling now."

Another icy chill blasted over Jess as Shreya described the experience almost exactly as Gavin had.

"Are they telling you to do something?" She could barely voice the question aloud. It was too dreadful to consider.

"No, nothing like that." Shreya handed her the sweatpants and sweatshirt Jess had loaned her. Jess numbly set them aside.

"It's weird. How can I explain...I feel like someone else is with me, recognizing things I'm seeing again." Shreya turned and paced the small room. "I told you I felt like I'd been asleep a long time, even though it doesn't feel like I've been away a long time, not like it was for you. I feel like we just went to the lake two weeks ago..."

She picked up the t-shirt and looked at its screen-printed design.

"But everything feels different. Like...now I can recognize how time has passed. At first, I thought it was because a lot of things had changed. The school and much of town look different now, and our gym...wasn't even a gymnasium anymore. But I feel things in my head like, 'oh yeah, that used to be the Dairy Queen where Jess worked,' like I'm showing it to a visiting relative or something."

Jess's heart thundered against her ribs. "Do you feel like there's something you have to do?"

Shreya blinked a few times. "Like shoot someone and drive a car into the reservoir? No." She swallowed and then shook her head. "I'm sorry, that was awful of me to say."

Cold drips ran off her hair, down her neck, over her arms, onto her bare legs, but the true chill was inside Jess's heart.

"Last night, when I went to the hospital because they found Gavin, he said almost the same thing. He didn't know why he was in the woods, but he thinks he was following instructions someone gave him. Someone he couldn't picture or remember very well, he only heard their voice."

For a moment, Shreya simply stared at her. "Like when he was...gone?"

Jess nodded.

"What did he do?"

"We're not sure, but I think he's the one who placed the device in the tree that caused the train incident. He remembers falling out of a tree."

They sat in silence for a moment, staring at the faded pattern of Shreya's once-beautiful coverlet. Jess collected the sweats and the underwear Shreya had given her and stepped into the walk-in closet to dress. She used the towel to blot her hair dry as she emerged.

"Do you think the FBI conducted some sort of mind-control experiment on us?" New tears brimmed in Shreya's eyes.

"Let's go meet Will and get his take on this." A surge of excitement lifted Jess's heart at the thought of seeing him again, and she realized how glad she was he'd come back to town when he did.

She didn't know if she would be able to cope with all of this if not for Will.

∽

Though it was almost noon, the coffee shop was bustling. Will sat at a round table on the far side of the dining room. Jess glanced around, looking for grim-faced, black-suited strangers. Most were people she recognized, and those who she didn't looked casual, in groups of two or three. The only two in professional dress were Edie Hespada and Gayle Sackett from the bank. Jess scanned the ceiling at each corner of the room, and then wove through the tables to Will.

"I got you green tea. Shreya, I didn't know what you drink, so you've got green tea, too." He frowned. "What's wrong? Why is your hair wet? And why are you wearing the sweats Shreya was wearing earlier?"

Jess sank into the chair next to him and cracked the lid to breathe in the tea. Jasmine green, her favorite. "It's a long story." She sipped the hot tea. In the time he'd been waiting for them, the tea had cooled from volcanic to absolutely perfect.

"There has been a terrible accident," Shreya supplied. She took the cup but didn't drink from it, only looked down at the table as though some solace could be found in the dark grain of the wood.

Will leaned back heavily in the chair. His expression was solid, as though nothing could fluster him. Jess had already realized this was a different Will than the shy and quiet boy who left town ten years ago. He possessed confidence now, an air of intelligence that proved he had learned dark things in the research that had led him to his MFA in Journalism.

And that he could handle those things.

He could back then, too, she realized. *It was me who had been a wreck.*

But Will had always been solid. She had mistaken his quietness for timidness, his shyness for meekness, but it truly hadn't been. Even the night she'd gone to his bed, he hadn't been timid. He'd only held back for a moment because he wanted to be sure she was ready, *really* ready, when she gave herself to him. Because even though it was his first time, too, there had been nothing timid about the way he'd turned her over and made love to her that first time, and all the ones after.

Jess took a deep breath and cleared her throat. It wouldn't do her—or him—any good to let her thoughts go there. That really had been a different time.

"Len Potter is dead."

Now he did register surprise. "The coroner?" He glanced at Shreya, and she nodded.

"What happened?"

Jess leaned closer over the table and took another sip of the soothing tea. "We're not exactly sure yet," she said softly. "It looked like Sara shot him and then drove the meat wagon into the reservoir. She drowned at the scene. We got her out of the car, but the paramedics were still trying to revive her when they left for the hospital. I don't know if she made it or not."

He sagged back in the chair again. "Damn."

"It was awful," Shreya whispered. "I've never seen a dead body before."

"It doesn't get any easier," Jess told her.

"Well, this puts my news onto the back page. I suppose this interrupted your goal to get the roster Bruce made yesterday?"

"I forgot to even ask him about it."

She must have looked wrung out, because Will smiled and patted her hand. "That's okay. Don't worry, we still have time. That's what I wanted to tell you; the FBI is busy somewhere else."

Twenty-Four

"My morning wasn't nearly as exciting as yours. I'm so sorry you had to go through that the day after Shreya's return."

Jess shrugged. "That's what they pay me the big bucks for."

"After I left your place, I went to AG Property Management. Their sign is out in front of the movie theater. It turns out Beau Drexel still owns the place, but he's in the senior living facility. There was a girl there filling in because the senior management agent is Ellie Meyers."

"Darci Meyers' mother."

"Exactly. So, I was going to ask you if we should try old Beau first, see if he's sound enough to ask him permission to use the place, or go directly to Ellie, seeing as her daughter is one of the 97." He quirked a smile. "I wouldn't want to do anything *iffy* in the eyes of local law enforcement."

Her insides tingled at that smile. No doubt Will had passed Charming 101 with an A-plus. "I think you're good," she said wryly, trying to keep him from thinking that smile worked on her.

"Anyway, I never got that far. When I was leaving the office, I saw Special Agent Larsen and that other woman—"

"Crenshaw," Jess supplied. Too late, she realized she said the name as if it tasted bad. "She's a lovely woman," she added lightly.

"I saw them leaving the hotel and decided to follow them."

Jess groaned inwardly. "Do I want to hear this?" The last thing the deputy's office needed was a rogue civilian further pissing off the feds.

Will hesitated. He pulled his wallet from his back pocket and retrieved a business card, which he slid across the table to her. It was for James Zellar at Vandenberg, Salcido, and Zellar LLC. Printed neatly below the bold names was "Guardianship and Conservatorship."

"Let me take a step back," Will said. "I want you to know, I have an insurance policy in place, of sorts. James is a friend from college. His firm holds several files of research material I've extricated over the years. This morning, I sent him one of many encrypted messages that only he, I, and the original software developer who created our program, can decipher."

"A bit overkill, don't you think?" As soon as she said it, Jess wished she hadn't.

Shreya glanced at the card, and then at Jess. She seemed to shrink in her chair.

"There are things out there that people don't want leaked." He looked at Shreya. "If you'd heard some of the stories I have in the last ten years, you'd believe me."

"I believe you now," she said in a small voice.

Will's gaze shifted back to Jess with an edge that looked almost like accusation. He leaned in so close she could smell the alluring scent of his soap. "Where is Stan Herlinger?"

Nobody knew. Except, of course, the people who had killed him.

She shook her head and leaned back in her chair. "Sorry. Forget I said that. It was...you're right. And you're smart to do that." She took his hand under the table, and silently rejoiced when he turned his palm to grasp hers.

"What did they do?" Shreya asked. "The FBI agents?"

Jess released his hand, and Will leaned back in his chair. His blue eyes had darkened, and sparkled with what she could almost say was mischief. He glanced between her and Shreya.

"They drove out to Whitney Station."

Shreya frowned. "What's Whitney Station?"

Jess thought over the familiarity of that name. "Isn't that an old military base in the mountains?"

Will nodded. "Only it isn't so old. It's listed as decommissioned, but conspiracy theorists believe it wasn't truly shut down."

"And you share that belief," Jess surmised.

His quirked eyebrows neither confirmed nor denied her statement. "I found it very odd that there was so little information on it available anywhere, even though it was a fully functioning base up until 1967. That's why only our oldest residents remember it. Even then, its primary function was as a storage site."

"Do you mean like a seed bunker?" Shreya asked.

Will shrugged dramatically. "When it was closed down, all of the outer buildings were torn down."

"Outer?" Jess asked.

Will leaned closer. "There's where the mystery starts. Based on its recorded location, there weren't any outer buildings, and if you saw it, you'd understand why. The old facility was supposedly located on Copper Creek Mountain, but no roads lead up there."

"Which could be explained by the fact that it's defunct."

Will was undeterred. "Instead, Crestline Road dead-ends at the entrance to the underground portion, which was built in an existing cave system." He ticked off on his fingers to enunciate. "One, people believe any buildings that might have been on top of the mountain were fake, a distraction. Two, the natural granite of the mountain provided a strong foundation for what's believed to be a key-personnel evacuation site, which they would want to keep secret. You're looking at me like I'm crazy. Do you hear what I'm saying? There is a *secret, underground military base* not even *ten miles* away from our town."

"What does that have to do with us?" Almost instantly, Shreya's eyes widened. "Oh my God, do you think that's where we were?"

"Wait, wait, wait." Jess held up a hand. "If it's secret, how does anyone know about it?"

Will didn't appear deterred. "How does anyone know anything about anything? People talk. Remember, military personnel are just people, and a lot of them come out of the service with guilt, emotional scars, and PTSD."

"Okay, let me rephrase. How do *you* know about it?"

"I do have a small amount of journalistic experience." Sarcasm edged his voice. "I'll explain it in simple terms for you. Remember the Smoking Gun from *X-Files?*"

To this, she merely dropped her shoulders and tipped her head sideways. *Come on.*

"I know people like that. *Real* people like that."

"I remember a couple of yahoos wearing tinfoil hats," Jess said.

"Do you have any idea how much electro-magnetic radiation is bouncing around our planet? A tinfoil hat isn't such a terrible idea."

"Oh, for heaven's sake," Shreya snapped. "Can we get back to the matter at hand, please?"

"The underground installation is real," Will stated, matter-of-factly. "I saw it this morning."

Twenty-Five

"What do you mean you saw it?" Jess asked him. "Do you mean you were inside?"

The three of them walked down Main Street to Jack's Grill on Jess's insistence she was starving. The morning's rescue and the adrenaline she'd burned had left her ravenous. One good thing about her body's reaction to stress; she never lost her appetite. Instead, it turned monstrous.

She carried a handheld radio, half-listening to the chatter.

"No, of course not. Like I said, I followed Larsen and Crenshaw out of town on Highway 3 until they turned on Crestline, which I knew led to Copper Creek Mountain. I continued to Manzanita Road and parked behind that old red barn. It wasn't easy, but I hiked up and watched them from Little Bear Ridge."

When they'd risen from the table at Brewed Awakening, Jess had seen his dirty jeans and muddy shoes. He wasn't lying about the hike.

Sandy Martin greeted them through Jack's street-side order-window. "Hey, Jess. Almost didn't recognize you in plainclothes."

"Let's go inside." Will pulled open the door to the dining room. "We're safer in a noisy environment."

"Okay." She grinned at Sandy. "We're going to eat inside."

Sandy followed them to the table they chose and handed them menus. "You must be Shreya. I read about you in the book."

"Good things, I hope." She returned Sandy's warm smile. "I haven't read it all the way through yet."

"Lunch is on the house today for all y'all. We're just so happy you're back."

"Oh, thank you very much."

"Jess, cheeseburger with pickles and mustard, wedge fries, and a large root beer?"

"How did you know?" She pretended surprise. "I've never been here before in my life."

"Chicken patty for me." Shreya handed back her menu. "With string fries."

"Ditto for me, but with the wedges," Will said.

After Sandy left, Jess shifted closer on her chair. "How did you know you wouldn't be walking for miles?"

The handheld radio she'd brought squawked. Jess turned the volume down as Mitch took a call for a loose dog on Hampstead Way.

"I guess I didn't, but the minute they headed north on Highway 3, I had a pretty good idea. Crestline makes a half-circle around the outer shoulder of the mountain."

"It's hard to believe you researched this town so thoroughly from New York. Why didn't you just come back?" Too late to stop it, Jess regretted the hurt that colored her voice.

Will glanced down before answering. "I spent a long time researching the Kileyville 97, and I never forgot any of them. But it was only part of my life."

She didn't press. For all she knew, he had a serious girlfriend in New York, and she didn't want to hear about it.

"What did you see?" she asked instead.

"It looks abandoned, but I couldn't tell if that was intentional. There were three Humvees there, and a bunch of Towne cars stopped about a quarter mile back from the main entrance. Soldiers worked a backhoe to remove a landslide and some fallen boulders blocking the road. Others were trying to cut through the main blast doors. I saw sparks from cutting tools. I'd like to get a closer look."

Jess scoffed at that. So would she, but if the FBI was hiding something, they wouldn't let anyone near the place.

She waited until Sandy had dropped their sodas before saying, "I can't believe there's an underground bunker in Hillsdale County."

"There are fifty-two publicly-known military installations across the United States built specifically for the evacuation of key military and civilian personnel, and the preservation of seed banks and the like. In reality, there are over six hundred throughout the world."

Shreya gasped. "Six *hundred*?"

"There are over forty in the Southern California region alone. Probably more; wealthy celebrities are building them on a smaller scale that no one other than themselves, and their contractors, will ever know about."

"Do you know how big this one is?" Shreya asked, still in awe.

He placed the small leather-bound attaché case he'd been carrying onto the table and twisted its metal release. He pulled out a sheaf of papers bound in a manila folder and then placed the case back on the floor next to his chair.

"As best I can tell, it's about one hundred and fifty thousand square feet." He handed the folder to Jess, and Shreya inched her chair closer so she could see, too. "Roughly the size of a sprawling three-story office building."

Sandy brought their burgers in oval-shaped baskets. Jess held the folder against her chest as Sandy placed hers in front of her. As usual, the top bun sat tilted off the burger to show the thick slices of pickle and melting layer of cheese. She took a bottle of yellow mustard from a pocket in her apron and set it next to Jess's basket.

"Thanks, Sandy. Just what the doctor ordered."

Jess waited until Sandy left to look at the file. She flipped the top page. The document beneath showed a computer rendition of its assumed outline inside the mountain.

"Where did you get this?"

Will ignored the question. "This is a depiction based on firsthand accounts. If it's bigger, or goes deeper, we don't know."

Jess didn't ask who "we" was. Instead, she noted the date on the printout. He'd been researching this as recently as four months ago, even though *The Night They Vanished* had been published almost six years ago.

"Weird," Shreya said. "It's shaped like a flower."

Jess handed the file back, suddenly uncomfortable at the realization Will had still been working on—in essence living—the Kileyville 97 all this time, when she had gone on with her life.

"What do you think?" he demanded of her silence. "Do you want to check it out?"

With a gigantic bite of hamburger in her mouth, she could only shake her head. She quickly dipped a potato wedge in ketchup and stuffed that in there, too, further avoiding him.

"I'm curious," Shreya said around her own bite.

Jess shook her head again. "No. Bad idea."

Outside, a siren was heard over the street noise. Fire engine. Jess looked outside, but this sounded to be several streets over, and nobody on the sidewalk seemed concerned.

"I need to know what happened to me."

She turned back to find Shreya watching her intently. Almost accusingly.

"Jess, I understand as a police officer you can't risk your badge by doing...*questionable* things, but what are they going to do, throw me in jail? I have a right to research my own disappearance."

Jess's heart stuttered at those words. She placed her hand over Shreya's on the table.

"Of course, you do. But you don't understand what Will and I went through ten years ago." She paused to turn up the volume on the radio slightly, listening for the chatter to explain the sirens. "The FBI is hiding something, and they're not very nice when they catch you snooping."

"Then we won't get caught."

"Famous last words." She took another bite of her burger.

Will seemed to catch himself. "Listen to Jess, Shreya. She knows what she's talking about. You don't mess around with these guys."

Shreya scowled at him. "Don't talk to me like I'm ten years younger than you. Technically, I'm not." She then threw a hard look at Jess. "Are you just going to give up?"

"I didn't say that." Jess took a sip of root beer while she listened to the chatter on the radio.

"Three alarm structure fire on Windstead Road. Fire and EMTs responding."

Windstead Road. It was a residential street.

"Nineteen-four, ten-ninety-seven."

"Nineteen-one, responding."

Bruce on his way, Deputy Parks already on scene. The situation would be under control. Still...

Jess picked up the radio. "Nineteen-six. ID on the property? Come back."

A beat of silence. "Eleven-forty-six, eleven-forty-four. Residence is Erikkson, eight-nine-eight Windstead Road."

"Oh my God!" Shreya shrieked. "That's Todd's house! What does that mean, eleven forty-whatever?"

Fatality, body transport requested.

"Stay here," Jess said, avoiding the explanation. She shot out of her chair but stopped before running out. She pointed her finger at Will.

"Do not go out to that bunker!"

Twenty-Six

The house was fully consumed. Black smoke billowed into the sky, and towering flames colored the afternoon an eerie orange.

Two fire trucks and several police cars blocked the streets, and civilians had turned it into a freakshow. She parked her Charger a block away and ran up the sidewalk on the far side of the street.

She raced past a group of looky-loos. "Go back to your houses and close the windows. You do not want to be breathing this."

The suggestion of danger always trumped an order to disperse. The group gawked at her for a split second before hurrying off in separate directions.

Bruce saw her coming. His expression changed; her own had to be panic-stricken.

"It's one of them, isn't it?" she demanded before he could speak.

He nodded. "Todd Erikkson."

The ground dropped out beneath her feet. *God, no. What the fuck is going on?* Her selfish thoughts jumped to Shreya. Was she at risk?

"Do we know what happened?"

His mouth formed a tight line.

"Bruce!"

His radio squawked. He listened and acknowledged. "Nineteen-one. Copy." He turned down the volume. "We don't know anything yet. Firefighters can't get inside. We'll know more once the fire is out."

Two tons of granite settled on her shoulders. If they couldn't get inside, they couldn't get anyone out.

"Do we know if..." She couldn't finish the question.

"Todd is inside the house. First responders saw him through the upstairs window. When they put the ladder up, he moved back from the window."

"No." Her stomach flipped upside down.

"I'm sorry, Harding." But there was more in his eyes. "I think it's time we had a serious talk about Shreya."

Jess's gorge rose. She ran for the shrubbery at the neighbor's house and pulled a Mitch.

∽

Francis Naughton handed her a bottle of water.

"Sorry about your bushes, Mrs. Naughton."

"Bah. I raised three boys who threw I-don't-know-how-many parties in this house. There's been more puke in these branches than rose blooms."

"Thanks." Jess twisted off the cap and greedily drank the cool water. Between the smoke and her vomit, her throat was raw.

"I could hardly believe it when I heard they were all back. Now this. It's tragic."

Jess remained silent. Bruce was busy, so she waited on Mrs. Naughton's stoop. She couldn't leave until she found out if there were bodies inside.

If Todd had done to his family what Sara had done to her father...

The flames were out. The looky-loos had returned, stared, speculated, got bored, and left. Only a few still stood around; most of the neighbors watched from their windows or front yards.

Jess heard a call about a minor traffic accident involving a backing garbage truck and a car, and Deputy Parks left. Bruce saw her sitting on Mrs. Naughton's stoop, and Jess didn't dare leave. Avoiding him wouldn't get her out of the discussion she knew was coming.

A part of her knew it was necessary. These murders—if this was indeed murder—made her stomach roll. Two in a single day. Both of them Returned. A mere day later.

A text chimed in from Will. *Everything ok?*

She answered. *Talk later. Stay with Shreya.*

He sent a quick reply. *Will do.*

Bruce strolled closer, talking on his phone. Mitch approached, asked him a question, and Bruce pointed to something. Mitch hurried off as Bruce continued toward her slowly, still talking on his phone.

Jess stood and swigged the last of the water bottle. "Do you know if anyone else was home?"

Mrs. Naughton's expression showed her heartbreak. "Both cars are in the driveway." She nodded toward the house and stared off as though in thought. "Hopefully the little one is in school. Summer break hasn't started yet, has it?"

Mrs. Naughton looked back at her and winced when she saw Jess's horror.

"They had another child. She's about six now. Merciful Lord, I hope they didn't let her skip today on account of her brother's return."

Jess handed her the empty bottle. "Thank you, Mrs. Naughton." She crossed the street to meet up with Bruce. He still spoke into his phone, but his eyes were on her.

"The fire crew is in the house now. We still don't know how many were trapped inside. No! Absolutely not, I don't want anyone talking to the press. I'll take it from here. That's affirmative. Who? Can you patch them through?"

He held up a finger. *Wait.*

"This is Sheriff Brady. No, I was not aware. That was quick. Yes, I understand. Sorry, what was your name again? No, I'm going to send my deputy, Jessica Harding. She'll be there in thirty."

Jess nodded along, even though she had no idea what he was committing her to.

"I'm gonna ask you for a favor, Dr. Salcido. If the feds show up, throw some confusion in their path. I want Jessica in there first. Thanks, I appreciate it." He disconnected.

"Mrs. Naughton says the Erikksons had another child," she said, deflecting the conversation away from Shreya. She glanced past him. "Any word on the count?"

"Not yet, but I'll let you know. Right now, I need you to get over to Trinity Med. Sara didn't make it. The medical examiner opened her up right away on account of who she is."

Jess's heart dropped. Something serious must have prompted the call to law enforcement.

"Ask for Dr. Salcido. You got your badge?"

"My house is on the way. I'll change into uniform."

"Negative. I want you there before the feds get wind of this."

She didn't volunteer what Will had told her this morning.

"The ME found something, and I want to know what it is before someone throws another roadblock in our faces."

Twenty-Seven

Jess slotted her phone into her dashboard holder, fired up the Charger, and backed out in a two-point turn.

"Call Will Taylor."

The phone rang. He answered, identifying himself.

"Do you have me on speaker?" It didn't sound like he did, but she wanted to be sure.

"No."

"You're still with Shreya?"

"Of course."

"I'm going to be a while longer. Can you stay with her?"

"No problem."

"Listen to me carefully. I can't explain now, but..." She cringed inwardly. "Stay aware. Don't drop your guard. She might be...dangerous. No, strike that. Shit. I don't know how to say this."

"I understand."

"What's going on..." She exhaled sharply. "Fuck. I don't know what's going on."

"Okay."

A moment of silence hung as she raced down the highway at dangerous speed.

"I think we should go ahead with the plan we talked about, and Shreya's idea of spreading the word. Let's say, meet up at..." she glanced at the clock on the dash. It was nearly two o'clock. "Six tonight."

"Did you talk to the realtor?"

"You do that. Start with her first. Ellie Meyers will be part of this. I can't imagine she'll say no, but if she does, text me back."

"Ten-four, Deputy."

"Close enough, Civvie."

Once at Trinity Medical, Jess headed directly for the stairwell, remembering the medical examiner's office was in the basement. Flashbacks of previous visits struck like lightning bolts. A visit to the morgue was never for a good reason. She pictured the man who'd been on staff the last time but didn't think his name was Salcido. He'd been a dour, unpleasant man in his early fifties with a horrible bedside manner.

She paused at the door to the stairwell and glanced around. No black-clad MIBs were obvious, and she hadn't seen a Humvee or anything resembling an unmarked Town car in the lot. Still, that didn't mean they hadn't beaten her here.

Jess entered the basement level to find an attractive young Hispanic woman in a lab coat walking toward her. She looked up from her clipboard and smiled as if she'd been expecting her.

"Deputy Harding? I'm Dr. Salcido, the interim Medical Examiner in residency. Unfortunately, Dr. Gomez is undergoing treatment for stage three pancreatic cancer so I'm here alone most of the time."

Jess was relieved that she was already more pleasant than the ME she'd met previously, but felt guilty for referring to him as Mr. Dour.

Dr. Salcido stopped by a door with a wire-meshed glass window, and Jess wondered if it was to keep the zombies from escaping.

I'm losing it. She was running on fumes. The two bites of hamburger wouldn't have been enough to keep her fueled, even if she hadn't puked them up.

"I'm glad they sent you. I don't know if you remember me, my maiden-name was Maldonado. I was a junior at West Ridge High when you were a senior."

"Oh, yes. Alexa, right? Nice to formally meet you." Jess accepted the woman's handshake.

"I came very close to being at that prom," Dr. Salcido said, pushing the door open. "I was dating Kurt Trimble back then. We broke up three days before the dance and he went with Ella Walker instead."

The odor inside the medical examiner's office was as awful as she remembered. Jess stuck her finger in a vat of menthol on the counter by the door and rubbed it under her nose. "That's why you agreed to see me before the FBI."

"Actually, they have yet to make contact," Dr. Salcido said with a hint of disbelief tinging her voice. She strode across the room and set her clipboard down, and noisily snapped into a pair of latex gloves.

Jess kept her comments to herself. Even though she knew where the agents were, this news still surprised her.

"To be honest, I don't know if Dr. Gomez would have agreed to your boss's request, but when he's not here, I'm in charge. I still cared about Kurt, and a part of me never got over what happened—to him, and everyone else. It was one of the reasons I went into medicine." She smiled brightly as she walked over to a body on a table covered with an olive-green sheet. "And here I am, helping out, just like I'd someday hoped to."

"I'm grateful," Jess told her. "Something strange is going on in this town, and I don't like being shut out of it. These are *our* friends, *our* families. I don't appreciate anyone covering it up for the *greater good*." She made finger quotes.

"When I learned this was Len Potter's daughter—and what she'd allegedly done to her father—I dropped everything to perform her autopsy. I don't have toxicology reports back yet, of course, but I've requested those be fast-tracked as well."

"Thank you." Jess didn't come any closer to the table. She swallowed as she mentally prepared herself. She'd seen bodies during and after autopsies, and it was never easy.

This one surely wouldn't be.

"Cause of death was drowning." Dr. Salcido pulled the sheet back. "I found nothing unusual with any organs in the body, until I opened her cranium."

Jessica swallowed again, her mouth suddenly watery. She saw the slice through the flesh just in front of Sara's hairline and the strange concave in her head. Part of her skull had been removed.

The room tilted sideways.

"The gray matter was unaffected, but the white matter, found in deeper tissues of the brain..."

Dr. Salcido stopped. Blinked several times. She held a quarter section of the brain and was about to set it in a metal tray on the table next to the slab, but was now frozen.

"What is it?"

"It was here."

"What was there?" Jess's heart kicked with an irregular stutter.

"There was a bluish film in the tissues, penetrating the white matter of the frontal lobe."

The edges of her vision grew dark.

Bluish film...

Jess moved closer and stood at the front of the table so she could see. It was gruesome, horrific, and downright nightmarish to imagine that she herself might one day lie on a table with her brain cut open like this.

But she had to see. Dr. Salcido's words brought Jess's worst fears to life.

"It was right there! Wait, I have a picture." She dropped the hunk of brain into the tray and stalked away, and now Jess did move back from the table. Averted her eyes. They drifted back of their own accord.

"I believe you," Jess whispered. She cleared her throat, tried to say it again. Still no sound came out.

Latex snapped as Dr. Salcido pulled off her gloves. She retrieved her phone from a desk in the corner.

"Look."

"I believe you." This time she heard herself.

Dr. Salcido looked up at her.

"I've seen this stuff before." She swallowed again. Her throat had gone tight. She looked at the image Dr. Salcido showed her. Her smartphone had captured it beautifully in all its horrific, glistening turquoise-blue beauty.

"What is it?"

"I don't know. But I know salt kills it. So how could it exist in the body? Isn't salt a mineral we all have, are made up of?" She sounded incoherent, even to herself. "I thought...like, aren't our tears salt water?"

"Sodium is an essential nutrient, but it's not something that the body produces itself," Dr. Salcido explained absently, still staring at her photo. "To survive, everyone needs to consume sodium regularly."

"Oh, um...really?" This day had turned surreal, and she was functioning on one piston. "By salting our foods?"

"Yes, and no. Sodium chloride occurs naturally in many plant and meat-based foods. Essentially, we get enough by eating a balanced diet, but humans have developed a taste for it, and nowadays, most of us season our food too much. The average adult human body contains about 250 grams of salt. Any excess is naturally excreted by the body."

"So how did it—*this thing*—survive in her?"

And the bigger question: is it in each of the 97?

"Hard to say without knowing exactly what it is." She went to a medical refrigerator and removed a tube with a tiny amount of the blue goo in the bottom. "Good thing I took a sample."

Jess's anxiety shot up like a rocket. "Don't open that! Can you test it safely? I mean, *this-shit-is-more-dangerous-than-Ebola* safely?"

Jess's obvious panic seemed to sober Dr. Salcido.

"Of course." She carefully placed it back in the refrigerator. "Why are you so frightened of it? Tell me what you know."

"Unfortunately, not much." She swallowed, still dangerously close to losing what was left of her lunch. She hadn't vomited in years, and now she was fighting it for the second time in a day. "I saw it for the first time ten years ago. It was attached to a device that might have had some part in the disappearance."

Jess described the black objects in detail, if for no other reason than Dr. Salcido's own safety.

"It's some kind of advanced technology, and this may sound hard to believe, but possibly...alien."

Jess said it cautiously, hardly believing her own lips, but Dr. Salcido's expression revealed no disbelief. Instead, she nodded. "I read the book. I know it's one of the author's main theories."

"I saw it again on a similar device found yesterday near the train accident. Both times, the devices contained a small amount. And both times, the blue substance was pliant. But yesterday, I saw it move on its own accord. It seemed sentient, as if it had a purpose. When it got near one of the 97 Returned, it tried to get to her."

Only now did Dr. Salcido's eyes widen. "You can't be serious."

"I wish I weren't. But I'm sure of what I saw, and I wasn't the only one who witnessed it."

Dr. Salcido looked at Sara's body. This time, Jess was able to control herself and didn't.

"We killed it with salt. It dried up like a dead jellyfish, kind of like blue saran wrap. Afterward, we tried to revive it in water, but it stayed dead."

"So where did mine go?" Not so much a question to Jess as to herself.

"I'll bet my paycheck it didn't evaporate. I wouldn't be surprised if it crawled into the ventilation duct in search of a new host."

"That's unsettling." Dr. Salcido gave her an intense look. "Do I need to evacuate this hospital?"

"That's a question for the FBI." Jess pulled out her phone and scrolled to Special Agent Larsen's number. She'd give it to Dr. Salcido, let her make the call. "In the meantime, if I were you, I'd head to the cafeteria and get a shaker of salt...or two."

❧

Outside in her Charger, Jess sat in the driver's seat without turning on the engine.

The blue goo had been scary enough before she learned it had seeped into Sara's brain and made her go nuts.

Was it inside all of the Returned 97? She couldn't get Shreya's face out of her mind, and the way she'd jumped up and run from the kitchen when the substance had lurched toward her on the table. Was it coursing through her brain at this very moment? It was too horrible to consider.

Even worse, was it compelling her to do terrible things?

Jess's hands were shaking and her fingertips tingling. She needed food but seeing Sara's body had left her worse than seasick. She'd been to an autopsy before, but it had never looked like that. God...her ashy white skin, her crudely sewn-up Y-incision. Her collapsed head, her quarter-sectioned brain.

That gigantic hunk of gray matter Dr. Salcido held in her hand as casually as a cauliflower she was picking out at the supermarket.

She picked up her radio. "Nineteen-one, come in. Nineteen-six. Over."

A moment later, "Nineteen-one."

"What's your ten-twenty? Over."

"I'm on my way back to the station."

"Nineteen-six, headed your way. Out."

Perfect. She had an assortment of granola bars in her desk. They were probably mild enough to keep down. She turned on the car, and this time, she drove slowly and cautiously, suddenly feeling very small.

Twenty-Eight

Jess saw Bruce shrugging out of his jacket as she crossed the bullpen. He caught sight of her coming and pulled his door open wider in invitation, and then sat behind his desk.

She took the guest chair and peeled open a granola bar. Ate a noisy bite. Washed it down with a piping hot cup of tea made from her private stash.

God bless the first person who ever steeped a tea leaf.

"Forgive me while I eat. I...uh..."

"Lost your lunch at the fire."

She glanced down, embarrassed. That's right, he'd been there. Her mouth still tasted sooty, and her hair felt gritty with ash.

"I've never seen you puke before." His small smile fell away. "It's been a tough couple of days for you."

"Hell, Bruce. You have no idea."

"A little puke never ended any careers. Ask Mitch." He leaned back in his chair, making it squeak. "In fact, I'm impressed by the way you're holding up."

She only shook her head.

"Really. I know your bond with Shreya is as strong as any of the parents of the 97. And yet here you are, still kicking ass and taking names."

She set her tea on the edge of his desk. Took a deep breath. Took another. Her face scrunched. She shook it off, but the tears burned anyhow.

"I don't know what to do."

"One step at a time, Harding."

She took another deep breath. The world's axis slowly straightened out again. "I need to bring you up to speed."

"Okay," he drawled evenly, as if afraid to hear what she might say. But then, "Do that, please." His look said *give it to me straight.*

Her phone dinged. A text from Will. *Location's set. Proceeding to plan.*

She glanced at the clock on the wall. She had an hour before heading to the movie theater.

"Did you see any of the agents at the fire?" Jess asked.

"If they were there, they did not make themselves known to me."

She frowned. "That's strange."

"Harding, nothing about this clusterfuck *isn't* strange."

"Were Todd's parents...?" She swallowed.

He nodded, his expression going grim. "The little sister, too."

The three-megaton headache forming behind her eyes lurched to a five-point-six.

"Shit."

"Preliminary cause of death was a single gunshot to the chest. Neat. All three victims."

"Were the bodies badly burned?"

"The second floor took the worst of it. Todd's body was unidentifiable. I imagine there'll be DNA testing done to confirm it's him."

She nodded. *It was him.* She would call Dr. Salcido next. "The FBI wasn't at the hospital, either."

Bruce narrowed his eyes. "I don't think they've packed up and left."

"They haven't. They and the soldiers who rolled into town this morning are at Whitney Station."

His lips moved. *Whitney Station.* His brows rose as he placed the name. "You serious?"

"They were observed trying to clear the main entrance."

"Observed." He held up a hand. "Don't tell me by whom. I know it wasn't you, seeing how busy you've been today."

"And my day isn't done yet." She wouldn't tell him about the meet-up at the movie theater...or her next plans. She might not tell anyone those. But maybe it was time to leave a note behind where it would be found if anything happened to her, similar to Will's "insurance policy."

"You know about the four objects Will and the Gus Wendt from the rec center pulled down after the return, and how someone knocked Gus over the head and stole them before he could hide them."

He gave a single, sharp nod.

"And that I found one, too. In the woods about two miles south of the train accident."

"You were going to bring it for me to take a look-see."

She glanced away. Yes, she'd promised that.

"But I'm kinda glad you didn't," he said, reading her avoidance. "In fact, should we even be talking about this?"

"You have plausible deniability. I won't tell you where I've hidden it. Even if you take my badge."

He pressed his lips into a hard line.

"There's more." She told him about the blue goo, how it had jumped off the device and seemed to seek Shreya, and how they'd killed it with salt.

And how Dr. Salcido had found the same substance inside Sara's brain.

"Great googly-moogly."

"I cannot even begin to explain how scared I am right now."

"With good reason." He stared at his desk for a long moment, frowning. "Wildest guess—what do you think it is?"

"I still don't want to entertain your alien theory."

"Not just mine. Whoever wrote that book." He winked but didn't smile.

"Logic says it's man-made. This whole ugly situation is man-made. Humans are shitty to each other; especially those in power to those who aren't."

His response was a mere "hmm," as he glanced down at his doodled-upon blotter.

"I don't want you held responsible for any of my forthcoming actions."

Now his gaze snapped up.

"So, I'm resigning, using vacation in lieu of my two-weeks' notice."

"Harding. Don't."

"This this started for me ten years ago, Bruce. I'm at my breaking point." She shrugged, shaking her head. "I'm no good to you, anyhow."

"You're my best. The others are good, and Mitch is...obedient, but they don't have your gut. Maybe it's because of what happened ten years ago..." he swept a hand in an encompassing gesture. "And all these years since. I'm not gonna let you tell me you aren't an asset to this department and the people of Pine Bluff."

"We'll meet before the two weeks is up to discuss it when I'm in a steadier frame of mind," she promised him.

If I'm still alive, then.

❦

Back in her Charger, Jess paused again. She scrolled to Dr. Salcido's entry and hit the call icon.

"Deputy Harding," the ME answered cheerfully.

"Hello, Dr. Salcido. Were you able to get in touch with Special Agent Larsen?"

"I've left him two voicemails. My suspicious mind says he already knows about the blue substance."

"Listen, you're about to have four more bodies, if you weren't already told."

"The fire? I was notified they're coming. Should be here any time now."

"I was wondering, is it possible to give a burned body a cat scan?"

"It's CT scan," she corrected, "computed tomography, and it's actually standard practice in death investigations where bodies are burned. A postmortem CT can be more effective than autopsy alone in determining body alterations by blunt trauma or the presence of foreign elements, in the case of stabbings and shootings."

"Actually, my reason for asking is because the juvenile son—Todd Erikkson—is one of the 97. I want to know if a scan of the body would detect the same blue material in the brain as in Sara's. And what happens to it when it's scanned." Jess took a shaky breath. "Most specifically, if it is there, I need to know if it's possible to scan a living subject without hurting them."

Twenty-Nine

Jess didn't know what to expect when she arrived at the movie theater, but what she found was absolute chaos.

When she'd asked Will to arrange the meeting, she'd still been planning to advise the returned 97 and their families to avoid the FBI's probing questions.

Now she wasn't so sure.

She still didn't trust them—that would never change—but after learning the blue goo had been *inside* Sara's brain, a whole new level of fear had turned her marrow leaden. In an instant, this situation had gone from conspiracy-level conjecture to terrifying reality.

Jess still didn't want to believe Will's alien theory. This whole situation stank of megalomaniacal science, but she could not ignore the fact that the substance had seemed sentient on her kitchen table.

Like nothing on this earth.

And there had been no dried-up blue saran wrap in Sara's brain tissue. It had been one hundred percent absent. Jess could not get the image of that gooey substance jerking toward Shreya like *The Blob*.

Considering nearly two hundred people crowded inside the movie theater, the families had done a good job of hiding their vehicles or taking alternate transportation. However, the din inside the place could probably be heard for blocks.

Among the loud conversations, several arguments were growing heated, and Darcy Meyers sat in an aisle seat near the front, sobbing loudly. Her mother knelt beside her, trying to console her. When Ellie saw her, she jumped up and rushed over to Jess.

"I need to speak to you," she whispered. "It's urgent. We didn't know what to do."

The voices suddenly died down as everyone noticed her, and Ellie recoiled. For a hung-in-time moment, everyone stared. Anyone who hadn't noticed her yet did now that the noise dropped, and suddenly the cinema fell to absolute silence. In the next instant, voices rose in a crescendo, all directed at her.

"What's happening here, Deputy?"

"Where did the FBI go?"

"Why did you call us all here?"

"I heard there's been an accident."

"Is it true Sara Potter is dead?"

Will appeared next to her and placed a firm hand on her arm. He and Shreya guided her toward the front where a wide plateau stretched before the enormous screen. It wasn't raised like a stage, and Jess felt like a bug under a microscope. She wished there was a raised section so she wouldn't feel like the people were looming over her. She knew they weren't angry with her, but she still felt threatened.

Then Shreya gave her that warm, reassuring smile that was so beautifully reminiscent, and Jess's confidence rose.

"Everyone, calm down. Could you all take a seat, please?"

"We want to know what you're planning to do!" Dave Schumacher shouted. "Something awful is going on in this town! Something unnatural!"

"I agree with you," Jess said loudly, placating him just enough to make him settle into a seat, grumbling.

An ocean of expectant faces stared back. Heart thundering, Jess swallowed. Public speaking had never been her forte.

"I've asked you all here because last night, in all the chaos, we didn't have time to address your concerns before the FBI arrived. You all know that ten years ago, they arrived just as quickly."

"Are they behind this? Why won't they tell us what's going on?" Frank McGibben demanded, and more voices rose in agreement.

"Ten years ago, they held me and Will for twenty-three hours. I advised you not to answer their questions because I felt they were a threat. I didn't want them separating families that had just been reunited."

"Damn straight!"

"They have no right!"

"I don't trust them."

"I don't trust them, either," Jess agreed. "But in light of recent incidents, I believe we need help. There is something going on here, and it's too big for our small sheriff's department."

The last part of her sentence was completely drowned out as people started shouting.

Frank McGibben shot to his feet again. "Now you believe we should talk to them? This is their fault! They did this to us ten years ago, and now they're adding insult to injury by doing it again. What are we to them, a bunch of Guinea pigs?"

"Yeah!"

"That isn't what she said," Will yelled above the rising din. "Just listen! Give her a chance to speak."

"And why should we listen to *you*?" Frank demanded. "I don't even know who you are. As far as I'm concerned, when you left this town ten years ago, you stopped being one of us."

Ronnie Gamada surged to his feet too. "He's right! Why did you come back *now*? Seems suspicious, if you ask me!"

"Ronnie," Louise Castleberry warned gently.

"No, I got a right to speak! I lost more than any of you. My daughter *and* wife disappeared that night, so I want an answer, Taylor. What brought you back to Pine Bluff now?"

"My mother is in the hospital," Will growled back.

Jess stayed silent. She didn't like where this was going, but any uneasy nagging had been tickling the back of her neck. She didn't believe in coincidences.

"Your mother had her stroke three weeks ago," Ingrid O'Phinney said. "Yet you only showed up yesterday."

"Yeah! Did the FBI send you?" Frank shouted. "Everyone knows it was you who wrote that book. Do they have some kind of leverage over you?"

"Don't be ridiculous." Will didn't confess, or deny, the allegation.

"Everyone calm down. We're going to address everyone's concerns," Jess promised. "Can we please do it in a civilized manner?"

Still standing, Ronnie stared at her, working his jaw. "I don't mean no disrespect," he grumbled. "I know you suffered too, and I appreciate everything you've done since then. I just don't feel safe, is all."

Seated beside him, Darlene looped her hand around his wrist.

His expression softened as he stared down at his wife. "I only just got them back. I can't lose 'em again."

"I don't want anyone to suffer any more than they already have," Will assured the room. "I don't know what I can say to make you believe I'm on your side. If you all don't trust me, say the word, and I'll leave right now."

He glanced around. Nobody spoke. Ronnie settled into his seat again, but Frank McGibben stayed on his feet, looking around as if searching for supporters.

"Is it true Sara Potter is dead?" Ingrid O'Phinney asked.

Jess took a deep breath. "It is true."

A collective murmur rippled through the theater.

"Todd Erikkson is also deceased," she told them.

The noise grew louder, and there were a few horrified cries.

"I heard Sara killed her father!"

"What happened to Todd?"

"Did somebody kill him?"

"Is the FBI hunting us now?"

Jess held up her hand. "No. No! In fact, nobody has seen the FBI today."

"I'm taking Molly, and I'm leaving this town." Frank snatched Molly's hand and started shuffling sideways out of the row.

"You should at least hear me out," Jess said. Her stomach flipped as she chose her next words carefully, but decided gentle was not the best way to go here. "You're going to want to hear this."

"Fuck that."

"Be smart, Mr. McGibben. Knowledge is better than ignorance."

He stopped and arrowed her with a deadly stare.

"I have news, and it isn't good."

Jess noticed several others had stood and were making to leave. Her words stopped them all cold.

"But I am not like the FBI, and I don't think hiding information from you is in your best interest."

"Damn right it isn't," Frank grumbled. He sat and angrily gestured for Molly to sit beside him.

"Sara Potter murdered her father."

"Oh my God," Darlene shrieked. "Why?"

"And it looks as though Todd Erikkson also murdered his family before setting his home on fire."

Darcy Meyers covered her face with her hands and started sobbing.

"They aren't the only ones," her mother said.

Jess went cold.

"What did she say?" someone shouted from the back.

"Ellie?" Jess prompted.

She stood and turned around to see the people behind her, and then walked around the protective railing in front of the screen to stand beside Jess.

Her words were slow and careful, a nervous quaver in her voice. "When Shreya asked us to spread the word, we went next door. Fumiko didn't answer, but I knew she was there. The car was in the driveway. I have a key to house. She and I have been very close since..."

Darcy sobbed louder.

Ellie coughed and then cleared her throat. "They were in the bedroom. I thought they were asleep, in each other's arms. But it didn't seem right, they were so still."

Jess's heart slipped out of its cavity. No.

"There was a bottle of sleeping pills on the bedside table." She turned to Jess. "I was afraid to call. We came straight here."

"Why?" Darlene wailed. "Why would they do that right after finding each other again?"

"Maybe they were afraid of being separated," Ronnie offered gently. "I think Japanese people believe suicide is honorable."

"Don't be stupid," Ingrid snapped.

"What the fuck, Harding?" Frank shouted.

Voices rose again, angry and accusing.

"What's going on?"

"Are you saying our kids are suicidal?"

"No, she's saying they're murders!"

Jess took Shreya's hand. "Stay with me on this," she whispered. "I'm sorry. This is going to be hard to hear."

Shreya gave her a nod.

"The medical examiner at Trinity Med autopsied Sara's body immediately. She notified me..." She waited as the people settled down. "She notified me of a strange substance found in Sara's brain. A blue, viscous matter that may be the cause of erratic behavior."

She saw Will's head swivel toward her in her peripheral vision.

"Will and I found the same substance the night of the disappearance when I broke into the gymnasium. I found a strange device—"

"The one described in the book?" George Walker asked.

She nodded. "The device was one of four, mounted near the ceiling in each corner. When I pulled it down, it had the blue substance on it, almost like it had been tacked to the wall with it."

"What was it?" Louise Castleberry asked.

"I don't know. The FBI caught us right away and took the device away from us. But we found four identical objects with the same substance yesterday in the gymnasium after the return. These objects may have something to do with...matter transportation."

"Matter transportation? You mean like in *Star Trek*?"

Another murmur rolled through the cavernous theater.

"I thought it was time travel," Bob Crawford said. "How else do you account for them looking so young?"

"Time travel doesn't exist," Claude Fisher argued.

"And matter transportation does?"

Claude shrugged. "Seems more likely. More scientifically logical, anyway."

"I don't know what it is," Jess said loudly. "I can't claim to understand what's happening here. That's why I think we need help. But because the objects that Will and Gus yesterday found were stolen—and I'm willing to bet the FBI was behind it. I still don't think we should trust them, but we do need them."

"Someone robbed Gus? That sweet old guy from the senior center?"

Jess nodded. "He was struck from behind while stashing the devices in his barn. When he came to, they were gone."

"Well, who the fuck else would have done it?" Frank demanded.

More murmurs sounded like a low rumble of thunder. A cloud of dark anger pulsed in this room, and while it hadn't been her intention, she could see no way around it.

"The FBI may or may not know that I found a similar device in the woods shortly after the train accident. The strange blue substance was also present."

Yesterday felt like weeks ago, and Jess felt the fatigue all the way into her bones.

176

"I am urging you to use caution," she pressed. "Do not leave your family members alone. Do not ignore unusual behavior." Her searching gaze landed back on Frank. "Lock up firearms."

"You saying my daughter is dangerous?" he growled back.

"I am saying everyone needs to be on guard," she returned. "Be on the lookout for unfamiliar black boxes that look like cameras. In your yard...in your garage...anywhere. They have unusual symbols like hieroglyphics. The blue goo is almost iridescent. And it may...move independently."

"Dear God!"

"You can't be serious!"

"It's true," Shreya spoke up. "I saw it."

"What should we do if we find one?" Lola Carson asked.

"Call me," Jess answered. "And I will call the FBI."

"Seems like they know what's happening before any of us do," Jason Wicht's father said. Jess could not remember his name, but knew he ran a dry cleaner in town. No wonder; virtually nothing in her closet was dry clean only.

"I am operating under the assumption that this building, and each one of your homes and businesses, are being surveilled."

"Oh, yeah?" Frank roared. "Well fuck you, FBI! You hear me? Fuck you for what you've done to us!"

A chorus of agreements rose, an angry din that grated across her nerve endings. The situation was dangerously close to turning into a riot.

"What are you going to do?" Darlene called out. "How can you go any higher than the federal government?"

"As I said, I truly believe we need help." She looked at the audience of terrified faces staring back at her. "And I have a plan."

Thirty

"Good luck with your fuckin' plan." Frank dragged Molly out of the row, one beefy paw locked around her wrist. "I'm outta here. If the rest of you know what's good for you, you'll get the hell outta Dodge, too."

"Hell yeah!"

"I'm not sticking around waiting to get killed, or worse!"

"Me neither!"

"Everyone, wait! I truly believe you're safer here!" Jess lifted her hands, but they were fleeing as if the building was on fire.

In minutes, Will and Shreya, and Darcy and Ellie Meyers, were the only ones left.

"That did not go as I'd planned."

"It was a good try, though." Will gave her a sheepish smile. "They might be angry—and scared—but knowledge is better than ignorance."

Shreya tugged on her hand. "What should we do? Jess, I'm scared!"

"I'm scared, too."

"Is there something in my brain? I don't feel different. I mean, I do, but after all that's happened, it's normal, right? I don't want to hurt you. I swear, I would never hurt you, Jess."

She took Shreya by the arms. "I know. I believe you."

Shreya hugged her. "I hate that this is happening."

Jess reveled in that hug for a long minute. "We'll get through this. I promise." Shreya leaned back and Jess saw the tears shining in her eyes. "We didn't come all this way just to lose each other now."

Ellie wrung her hands. "What should we do? We can't leave Yumiko and Aiko like that."

"Go home," Jess told her. "Call 9-1-1 and tell them what you found. Don't tell them why you went over, just that you did, and how you found them. Sheriff Brady will probably be the one to come. It'll be all right."

Ellie's tears welled and spilled. "It's not all right."

"Just stay calm," Jess repeated what Bruce had told her. "We can only take one step at a time."

Ellie reluctantly nodded.

"Stay together, try to think positive thoughts. I think in a situation like this, frame of mind is critical."

Darcy rolled her eyes. "Easy for you to say."

"Yes, but understand this; I'm not willing to give up. I'm going to keep fighting. If I can do it, you can do it."

"She's right," Shreya told them. "We can't let our fear overpower us. We might not know what's happening or why, but we know ourselves. Someone has done this to us. We can't let them beat us."

They walked outside together, and Ellie locked up the main doors. Jess stopped her as she and Darcy walked toward the street.

"Ellie, wait. I want to talk to you for a minute. Alone."

"Uh, okay. Sure." She watched her daughter walk to the car as if reluctant to be more than five feet away from her.

"I want someone to know what I'm planning to do," Jess began cautiously. "In case I don't come back."

Thirty-One

"The press?" Will asked. "That's your plan?"

"Actually, it's my plan for you."

They sat around his kitchen table, where Jess hadn't been since the day Will's sweet mother made her a sandwich, ten years ago. Lucille had renovated since then, making it feel unfamiliar. That was probably a good thing. Jess's emotions were tumbling, and the last thing she needed was anything to inspire the uncertainty and helplessness she'd felt that day.

"And I'd like you to call your father. We need a good lawyer on our side."

"Yeah, well, there's a reason he isn't my insurance policy holder."

"Nut up, buttercup."

Shreya snorted. "You two really do have that *we-once-fucked* vibe going on."

Will rocked back in his seat, hands raised. "I didn't tell her anything."

"Jess told me."

He smirked. "Aren't you worried your boyfriend will get upset if he hears talk like that?"

Shreya swiveled a sardonic glance Jess's way. "Yeah, Jess. Aren't you afraid your *boyfriend* will get upset?"

"So, let's stop talking about it, then," she returned evenly.

"What was his name again?" Will feigned innocence.

"Yeah, hmm? What was his name?" Shreya was teasing now.

"Johnny. Johnny Law. Can we please get back to the matter at hand?"

Will was beaming now. "I want to hear more about Mr. Law." He looked at the ceiling and pointed upward.

What if they're listening?

"I don't think anyone is listening," she said aloud. "If they weren't busy somewhere else, they'd answer the phone."

She'd tried Special Agent Larsen twice, but the calls had gone straight to voicemail.

Now Will frowned. "Based on their reputation, and their behavior the first time, this doesn't seem to fit."

"I'd have to agree," she said, glad to get the subject off her imaginary boyfriend. "It makes me wonder what's more important to distract them this way." She read agreement in Will's face; only the three of them, and now Bruce, knew where the agents and soldiers were.

"What do you want me to do?"

"You wrote books, but you're still a journalist. You must have contacts you trust."

"Of course." His obvious giddiness settled into pride. "You want CNN, or CNBC?"

"Yes. Write something. Expose what's going on here. Email it to several people and ask them to confirm receipt. Hell, try to get someone to come here. The FBI can't stop old friends from visiting you."

"You saw what they did with the internet and phones. If they wanted to, they could prevent me from sending anything."

"Take precautions. Protect your work. You're a nerd; you know what to do."

"Thanks?"

She grinned. "You're welcome."

∽

Will turned off the WI-FI on his laptop and got to work while Shreya busied herself at the stove.

Jess went to the kitchen window. Outside, the eerie light made her shiver. She realized the sky had turned pink with a cloudy twilight and held a similar spookiness to prom night.

No. I'm unsettled, that's all. It's just a strange sunset.

Shreya boiled spaghetti noodles and heated up some of Mrs. Taylor's homemade Marinara sauce. She buttered thick slices of toasted French bread and set plates down at the table where Will sat alone.

"Eat." Shreya sat down between them and smacked her hand on the table. "No arguments."

In truth, Jess was still queasy, but ravenous. All she'd eaten in the last four hours—after throwing up what little she'd had for lunch—was the granola bar.

"Your radio's been quiet," Will noted. "Ellie would have called in by now."

"I turned it off."

Will's brows crept up, but he didn't comment.

She didn't feel like discussing her resignation again. "Bruce has my cell number. He'll call me if he needs me."

Shreya frowned as she chewed a bite of toasted French bread.

"Everything all right?" Jess asked.

"My gums are sore. Like a toothache, but all over."

Will nodded, and Jess could see him mentally listing everything she said. "Anything else unusual?"

"I'm hungry, but it's hard to eat. I feel like it won't stay down."

He glanced at Jess. "Like someone who has been in a coma for a long time."

Shreya set her fork down. "Those men at the meeting tonight were talking about time travel and matter transfer. I haven't had time to finish reading Stan's book. Were those the hypotheses?"

With a cautious glance at Jess, Will cleared his throat. "They're two of the three, yes."

"So, if we were...*beamed* away, we had to have been somewhere all this time. It's why I've lost weight, and I don't feel the same energy level I used to. I was in stasis somewhere."

Now Jess put her fork down, too. "Is there something else that makes you think that?"

"It's hard to put my finger on it. I do feel like maybe I was in a coma. You know how they say coma patients can hear people talking to them? It's like I remember someone talking to me."

A cold wave fear of swept over Jess. "Are you hearing the voice now?"

"No, no. It's not like that." Shreya shook her head, and Jess's chill was immediately replaced by a warm current of relief.

"It's almost like it's a memory, like I could hear the doctor standing at my bedside talking to someone else."

"Do you remember anything that was said?" Will asked.

She stared off, concentrating. "Not really. It just feels...clinical. That's why I think it was a doctor." She picked at her spaghetti. "You know; a

182

person sounds different when he's at a party than when he's in a hospital, dryly explaining a medical diagnosis to a worried family member."

"Do you remember it being man's voice?" Jess asked.

She blinked several times. "Maybe," she finally said.

Jess used a napkin to blot her mouth and wipe butter from her fingers. She took a deep breath and searched for the right words.

"I'm going to ask you to do something for me." She placed her hand over Shreya's and cherished the smile her friend returned. "I want you to check yourself into the Meadows."

"What?" Shreya jerked backward. "The rehab place?" Her voice was a literal shriek.

"It's a recovery center. Cancer and surgical patients go there, too."

"No! I don't need that. Jess, my mother arrives tomorrow."

Shreya pulled her hand away, and it felt like a knife plunged into her chest.

"I know—I know. But given the situation, I think she would agree with me."

"Oh well, of course she would agree with you!" she snapped. "My mother always knows what's best for me."

"I'm asking you to do what's best for *me*."

At that, Shreya went quiet.

"I know it might feel like putting yourself in prison, and I wouldn't ask if I weren't so absolutely terrified that I can't see straight. But right now, I can't think of a better solution."

"Jess, no! Why can't I stay here with you and Will?"

"Because Will has work to do, and I have police business I have finish." She swallowed, hoping they wouldn't call her on it. "I can't take you with me."

Shreya scowled, but Jess took her hand again, and when her friend squeezed back, Jess rejoiced in it. Shreya was warm and alive, and her returned grip fed into Jess like medicine.

"It's a spa. Get a facial, take a mud bath, and drink fruit smoothies."

"Sounds fun," Will added awkwardly. "Maybe I should go, too."

After tossing him a frown, Shreya pouted in that sweet, teasing way she had, and Jess blinked away tears. "It won't be any fun without you."

"Shreya, I'm asking you—I'm begging you. Do this for me." Her eyes stung, and now she couldn't hold back the tears. "I need to know you're safe because I spent the last *ten years* in agony over what unknown, terrible thing had happened to you, and I cannot endure a single minute of that unknown *ever* again."

Thirty-Two

Becky Harris met them at the grand front patio of Meadows Recovery Center as Jess pulled in.

For the first three years after the disappearance, Becky, Jess, and the rest of the "Lucky 13" had met in a support group led by their retired school counselor. The group drifted apart for various reasons, but Jess and the others had developed a special bond that hadn't broken over time or distance.

When Jess called her, Becky assured her there would be a private room waiting for Shreya, and the staff would provide her with a spa experience, not a quarantine.

Jess stopped on the steps outside the luxury resort as déjà vu made her tingle. She couldn't bear to go inside. She'd dropped her mother here ten years ago, and tonight also felt like a monumental moment marking a catastrophic change in Jess's life.

"Just for tonight, until your mom gets here tomorrow. I promise." She'd already promised it a hundred times.

Shreya only nodded.

"This is a good thing. Becky is a really good friend. I trust her. This place is the bees knees."

"The what?"

Jess laughed. She tucked a lock of Shreya's curly hair behind her ear.

"I need to know you're safe."

"I know."

"Get a good night's sleep. Your mom will be here before lunch tomorrow, and then you'll be together. It'll be like a vacation."

Shreya nodded again. "I know."

In the darkness, the grounds' many landscape lights bathed them in a magical golden glow, but it almost felt ominous.

"I've never seen you cry so much," Shreya said, and Jess realized the warmth of the tears on her cheeks.

"Honey, you should have seen me the last ten years. This is nothing."

"I hate that. I hate being the reason."

And Jess hated *that*. "It wasn't you. Don't you dare blame yourself."

"Don't worry about me. I'll be fine." Shreya pulled her into a fierce hug, and Jess's knees nearly buckled. She had a terrible feeling this might be the last time she ever saw her.

"My brave, strong Jess. Go, do what you need to do."

Now Jess could only nod.

"I'll be all right. This place is nicer than I thought it would be. I'll be fine," she repeated again, as if needing to convince herself as much as Jess.

After another quick hug, she turned and walked inside with a nurse.

Becky stepped closer and put a hand on Jess's shoulder.

"She's right, Jessica. She'll be okay. We'll take good care of her."

"I want someone keeping an eye on her at all times. Some*one* or some*thing* is compelling these kids to hurt themselves and others, and I don't want whatever it is to get hold of her."

"We have cameras everywhere, even in the rooms. The bathrooms are specialized; toilet lids don't come off, the mirrors are plastic."

"Whatever is happening, it comes suddenly and without warning. Don't drop your guard for a minute."

"You have my word."

As Jess drove away from the facility, the anguish of the past two days finally caught up with her. Giant, chest-heaving sobs rolled out of her. She drove slowly and carefully back to Anna Grove, letting herself have this last cry until the welcoming face of her farmhouse threw her the lifeline she needed. This place had been her Eden for the last ten years. She'd worked hard, built a good life here.

Fought hard for this life. She wasn't done fighting yet.

These were the last tears she would cry. It *was* time to start kicking ass and taking names.

Without a backward glance at the barn, she skipped up the steps to her porch. Jess took a quick shower, washing the grit from her hair, and then brushed her teeth. Finally free of the ashy taste in her mouth, she started to feel like a human being again.

She wound her damp hair into a bun and put on a clean uniform.

Unlocked her gun safe and put on her duty belt.

Time to stop playing Deputy Nice Guy.

Thirty-Three

A chill breeze slipped into her clothes as Jess made her way up the rocky face of Little Bear Ridge. This would have been difficult enough during the day, but she didn't dare turn on her flashlight.

The FBI possessed incredible technology for night vision and body-heat detection. If they were looking, even casually keeping watch, they'd see her.

Hell, they possessed the technology to snatch 97 people out of a gymnasium. She still didn't give credence to Will's alien theory. While she'd never been an anti-government conspiratorialist, this stank of all-powerful government screwing the common man.

She accidentally dislodged a rock and sent it tumbling into a gravelly runoff with an awful racket. It seemed to roll on forever, picking up a million clattering stones with it before finally coming to a stop a hundred feet away.

"Good job, clumsy," she whispered to herself. She stood motionless for long minutes, holding her breath. Something screeched in the night, and Jess saw a small, winged creature flutter across the inky sky. A breeze rose, rustling the pine before it died away, leaving her in silence. She continued up the incline in careful steps, knowing the FBI would probably catch her but hoping to get a good look at the main entrance to Whitney Station before they did.

Hillsdale County was known for its steep hills and narrow, hidden valleys. They plunged almost vertically five hundred to a thousand feet in some places. A rocky outcropping marked the top of the hill overlooking the ravine where a lonely road led to the concrete-protected entrance of Whitney Station.

Jess bent low as she crept up to it and then dropped to her hands and knees. She crawled the rest of the way and laid down flat to peek over the edge. With the southwestern sky behind her, even the slightest remaining light would reveal her silhouette to anyone who looked up.

The narrow, two-lane road dead-ended at what looked like a massive box culvert, but huge doors made it impenetrable. In front, the tarmac widened as much as the plateau would allow, creating a small parking area that butted up to Copper Creek Mountain.

The architects had chosen this location well to build their entrance, and now Jess understood why the road was called Crestline—it sat on such a narrow ridge that it almost resembled a drawbridge over a moat. On either side, the land plunged away, and behind the culvert walls, the face of the hill was nearly vertical. It looked like a smaller version of Cheyenne Mountain Complex, only here, there was no barrier arm, no armed soldier standing sentry, no warning signs to go away *or else.*

If not for the vehicles sitting near the entrance, the place would look completely abandoned.

Maybe that was the intention. Even in the darkness, she noted the overgrown shrubbery and the cracked and weedy tarmac. In the light of day, it probably looked ten times as desolate.

This place is closed, nothing to see here.

The small, paved section in front of the doors provided the equivalent of four parking spaces, where two Town cars currently sat. The black cars blended so well into the dark vegetation of the steep hillside that she wouldn't have seen them if not for the pale gray of the asphalt showing in front of the first car, but the three Humvees standing silent and dark along the road leading up to the entrance were unmistakable. A third Town car sat behind the row of Humvees.

No people moved around, no sparks danced from welding or cutting equipment. No cherry from a smoked cigarette. No voices carried over the open spans.

Have they already gotten inside?

She scanned the steep slope surrounding the entrance, but she saw nothing. Without binoculars—or better, night vision goggles—she wouldn't. If soldiers stood watch in the woods, or cameras were mounted in secret places, she'd never know.

Or worse, sinister black objects with effervescent blue goo capable of Lord-knows-what.

She shrugged the fear away. Rather, tucked it into a pocket. She was terrified, and nothing would ease that.

But she had to do this. After whatever horrors Shreya and the others had been through, Jess had to put an end to it. Even if it meant the end of her.

A snap behind her made her hair stand up.

She flipped onto her back and drew her gun in a fluid movement. "Hold it!"

"Whoa, Jess, it's me." Will held up his hands.

Still holding her weapon, Jess scrambled to her feet.

"What are you doing here?"

"I knew this was where you were headed." He kept his hands up. "You want to put the gun away?"

"No, I mean, what are you doing in Pine Bluff?" Her heart hammered so hard her ribs hurt. "Ronnie Gamada called it—your mother had her stroke three weeks ago, yet you came to town *yesterday*. The same day the 97 returned. Why?"

His voice dropped low. "You can't be serious."

"I am deadly serious."

"All right. You want me to admit it? I'm a horrible son, and a horrible person." He slowly lowered his hands. "And I couldn't face you."

She didn't move, but mentally, she rocked back.

"You were wondering why I never came back all these years," he said, voicing her own thoughts aloud.

But that wasn't hard for him to guess because it had been generally shitty of him, and he had to know it.

"Yes."

"My mother told me you'd gotten married."

This, she had not been expecting. "W-what?"

"Probably about the time you became a deputy. I realize now, she didn't want me coming back here. Did you know she came to visit me twice every year in New York? Christmas, and my birthday. She said she loved Christmas in New York, but her real reason was to keep me from coming home."

Jess's mind spun. At the top of a raging funnel of turmoil was confusion, at the bottom of that tornado; hurt. Why would Lucille do such a thing?

"It wasn't you," he said, still reading her mind. "She adores you, and she's so proud of you. But it was about seven years ago, when I was still in school. I'm guessing that was when you joined the sheriff's office."

She swallowed, doing the mental math.

"You tied yourself to Kileyville then. Don't blame her. She did what she had to do to protect me."

"I don't..." Her sentence ended before she could say *believe it*. In fact, she did believe it, but she didn't know how to respond.

"Do you understand why she did it?"

She didn't answer. Jess did understand, even if she couldn't accept it.

"She manipulated us, and she hurt us, but I'm not angry with her. What parent wouldn't do the same? To her—hell, up until yesterday, to *everyone*—they were gone forever. She would send me away and at least know where I was rather than go through the heartache that 97 other families did."

Jess finally lowered her weapon but kept it in hand. "I'm going to ask you a question, and you better make me believe your answer. Are you working with the FBI?"

He dropped his arms but still held his hands out, palms open. "No. Nobody has ever confronted me, or Lancaster Publishing, about the book. Nobody has threatened me, nobody is blackmailing me."

"I want to believe you, Will. But I don't believe in coincidences."

"I don't have another explanation. You're just going to have to trust me, or not. But I want you to know, I didn't come back here just for my mom. I came back for you."

She holstered her weapon. His shoulders relaxed and he let out a long breath.

"And I wasn't lying when I said I was a horrible person. It's always been you, Jess. Before you ever knew I existed, even before that glorious semester, sophomore year, when we built the solar system model as a team in Mr. Woodward's class, you had been this boy's fantasy."

"Will."

"And then the most difficult summer of my life, after 97 of my classmates disappeared and I should have been miserable, you were there. In my life, and in my bed. That year left an indelible scar on my soul. It was the best and worst year of my life, and it changed me forever."

"It changed both of us."

"And I was there for you, too. You said it yourself, you wouldn't have survived without me. You told Special Agent Roycroft that nobody had ever loved you like Shreya did. I need you to know, that wasn't true. Because I loved you then, and I still do now."

Thirty-Four

"You can't tell me that I'm not a permanent part of you," Will continued, knowing the answer. "You can't tell me that some part of you doesn't love me, too."

No, I can't, her heart whispered. But she couldn't form the words.

"It wouldn't matter if you did," he went on. "Because the truth is, I love you, Jess. I can't hide it from you, and what's more, I don't want to try. Even if you push me away right now, call me a nerd and tell me never to speak to you again, the fact remains. I love you."

"Will—"

"Don't say it back," he demanded quickly. "Don't say you don't, either. Just leave it at that. Whatever happens tonight, I just want you to know the truth. Because I'm going inside that bunker with you, and you need to know you can trust the person by your side. And if I don't come out again, I want you to know how I really feel."

She swallowed. "You're right."

Will settled back. "I am?"

"You're a part of me that will always exist. What we went through together, nothing will ever change that. And you're right. I loved you, that summer. And I loved you afterward, probably for longer than I care to admit, even to myself. But you never came back, Will. You stopped being a part of this town, but I never did. We're different now."

He had still been holding his hands out, as if exposing himself to her. He finally dropped them and stepped closer. "I know for you it feels that way. But for me, it doesn't."

She shook her head, but he closed the distance and placed his hands on her arms. *Criminy, when did he get so tall?* His touch made her heart race, and she hated the rift that had formed between them.

"Coming back here, it felt like I never left. The only thing that's different is the hurt in your eyes, and I hate myself for putting it there. I am so sorry for what I did to you, Jess. Even if you forgive me, I'll never forgive myself. When I said I was a terrible person, I meant it. I came back here hoping to find you *divorced*. How awful is that?"

She huffed and looked away, wanting him to take his hands off her and yet not wanting him to.

"I'm here to stay, Jess. And I'm going to make it up to you."

Now she did step back. "You don't owe me anything. I couldn't hate you because I wanted you to go and get that life for yourself. Just...the occasional phone call would have been nice." His revelation had her unbalanced, and she stammered like a nervous teenager. "You could have sent a wedding gift, and then I would have asked you what the hell it was for, and you would have known. Think of how easy it would have been to end the misunderstanding."

"You're asking my head to think clearly when my heart is in turmoil."

"Geez, you really are a writer."

She finally relaxed and managed a half-smile. It felt good to be casual with him again, and being honest with herself, she'd never really believed he was here under some sinister motive. The past twenty-four hours had left her jittery and unbalanced, and Jess didn't entirely trust her judgment.

And his bold confession of love had definitely turned her upside down. She wished he hadn't said it. How could she function now? How could she not feel awkward? What if she thought about it, and didn't want to say it back?

Unlikely. Will was as handsome, intelligent, and principled as he'd ever been, and if Jess were being entirely honest with herself, she was too happy to have him in her corner again.

You're in dangerous waters, girl.

"I'll take that as a compliment," he said, smiling back. "Now, how do you want to get down there?"

෴

"Is this Slim Nesbit's truck?" Jess asked as they trudged back to the wide section of shoulder where she'd parked her patrol car. Manzanita Road didn't lead to Whitney Station, so chances of anyone seeing her car there and thinking she was sneaking around Whitney Station were slim.

"I bought it. I told you, I'm here to stay."

Careful, she warned herself. *Buying a twenty-five hundred dollar truck doesn't anchor him permanently to Pine Bluff.*

She didn't want to acknowledge his promise to stay, so if he didn't keep it, it wouldn't hurt.

Not true. It would hurt unbearably.

"Have you told your mom this yet?"

"I didn't want to upset her."

That's a no.

"Let's take my patrol car. I've heard the muffler on that thing; it's about as subtle as a locomotive."

She unlocked the doors remotely and Will climbed into the passenger seat.

"Lotta gear," he said idly. "You are official, aren't you?"

"Intimidated by powerful women?" She checked the dark road behind her and pulled a U-turn.

"More like awed. Even in high school, you were a commanding presence."

She glanced at him sideways. "Shut up."

"No, really. I went to Ridley for the championship game. You were awesome. You owned that volleyball like it was a family heirloom."

"Really? You drove all the way to Ridley?" She hardly remembered the game. It had been a lifetime ago.

"I hitched with Troy Benedict and his clowns. Between make-out sessions with Shelby Carson, he and Gavin and Mike took turns bullying me." He glanced out the window. "It was fun," he finished sarcastically.

Jess laughed. "Well, thanks for being in the cheering squad."

She wound the car carefully around the mountain and took the sharp turn onto Crestline Road. The sign reading "NOT A THROUGH ROAD," was peppered with birdshot. With no streetlights out here, it was blacker than pitch, but Jess didn't turn on the high beams. Not that anyone couldn't see the car coming, but she was trying to be as inconspicuous as possible.

"Look out!" Will shouted as a massive buck ran into the road.

Jess slammed on the brakes. The buck turned and headed straight for them. Just as they came to a hard stop, it leaped onto the hood, knees first, and body-slammed the car.

Thirty-Five

Frank McGibben stopped at the open door in the hallway and watched his daughter rifle through the clothes hanging in her closet. Her room had looked like a Forever 21 store for as long as he could remember, and yet she hated almost everything she owned. From the time she turned twelve, she pestered him relentlessly for money for clothes, but because she came home with bags from boutiques and not stinking of weed or booze, he'd gladly kept forking over the green.

His chest lurched at the sight of her, still slender and innocent, frozen in the dewy fragility of teenaged youth.

Unlike Frank Jr., who was now thirty-one years old and thirty pounds overweight, working a dead-end job operating a claw in a metal recycling yard in Sacramento. He couldn't remember the last time he'd seen his son in a clean shirt. Not even at Christmas last year when he'd driven four hours to Junior's grungy mobile home and endured yet another miserable holiday with his snarky ex-wife, who started off rude and only got worse the more eggnog she sucked down.

"Did you call Mom?" Molly asked, aware he was watching.

Since primary school he'd been known as a bully, and Frank was happy to have people keep a fearful distance from him, but when it came to his daughter, he was limp spaghetti.

"Not yet. Better if she doesn't know until we get back."

Now Molly turned around. Her expression was unreadable. Frank fought off a shudder. Was this really even his kid? How could she look the same, not aged a day? There was something off here. She didn't feel like his Molly.

"You were serious about leaving?"

"Just a few days. Until this shitstorm blows over."

Her expression hardened but she remained silent; another change in the Molly he'd known. She never used to turn down the opportunity to argue with him or show him how much she took after her mouthy mother.

Instead, it seemed she was quietly plotting something.

"At the cabin?"

His secret bolt hole. It had never occurred to him he couldn't trust his own kids. He shrugged away another twinge of unease as he thought of Deputy Harding's recommendation to lock up firearms.

Ridiculous.

"I haven't decided," he lied. "Regardless, we're not telling anyone where we're going. So, stay off Facebook."

He'd already unplugged the router, but if she knew the internet was down, she didn't let on. He mentally counted the other ways she might connect and was thankful she no longer had a phone.

"We shouldn't leave. My friends need me. The people here need us."

"Fuck the people here." He pointed his finger. "Pack your shit. Sensible clothes; it'll be cold. And pack some pajamas. We're gonna be a few days."

She said nothing, but he watched her chest deflate on a slow, angry breath.

Frank tried to convince himself she was the same hot-blooded Molly as ever, and all this shit merely had him unsettled.

Ten years of loss had only made him meaner and angrier, and now having Molly back had flipped him inside out. He didn't know how to deal with it all, and having that bossy deputy talk to him like he was an idiot didn't help.

He yanked down the pull cord on the attic access and unfolded the steps.

During the first two years after Molly disappeared, he and Bernadette had argued endlessly about packing up her room. Bernadette always won, and the room remained untouched. Then, when Junior moved away and Bernadette cut out on him, there was no reason to do anything but close the door. He'd stayed in this empty four-bedroom house to piss off his ex; selling it would have put half the profit in her pocket, even though he'd inherited the house from his dad. He'd be damned if he'd give that bitch and her pussy boyfriend a dime. He'd taken the blood money from the government and kept his job tending bar and cracking skulls at Salty's, and had a nice nest egg tucked away. He delighted in the rumor that Bernadette had burned through her settlement in five years and now worked as a legal secretary at some firm in San Francisco.

He tucked that nugget of gossip away and brought it out whenever he needed a good laugh.

Keeping Molly to himself served as another smack to her smug face, and he didn't want to be in town if she or Junior learned the missing 97 were back.

He dragged down two suitcases and put the larger one in Molly's room. She was no longer there, but several sweaters and jeans were laid out on the bed, strategically placed in little sets.

He tossed the other suitcase into his room. It would take him five minutes to pack. All he needed was a few pairs of jeans and flannel shirts, and a couple pairs of underwear. Molly was always complaining she couldn't wear one thing with another because they "didn't match," but he could never understand what she was talking about and didn't give a crap about stuff like that.

"Molly?"

He heard rattling in the kitchen. He tromped down the stairs and found her with the phone in her hand. He snatched it from her and hung it up.

"Why isn't Mom's phone number here?"

"Because she didn't put it there before she took off," he snapped.

"I want to talk to Junior!"

"Later. We roll in ten."

She put her little fists on her hips. "Now."

"Go finish packing!"

"They're gone because of you! I hate you."

"Great. Now get upstairs." He grabbed her arm and shoved her toward the door.

Her eyes shot firebolts as she stormed away.

"Jesus Christ," he breathed out. He'd almost forgotten about her temper tantrums.

He threw some frozen steaks into his cooler along with all the packaged lunch meat and cheese from the refrigerator. He had a single, frozen loaf of bread, which he set on top of the cooler. That was enough to tide them over until he got her settled in the cabin, and then he could head into Dunsmuir to get some food when he was sure she couldn't go anywhere.

Frank headed back up the stairs and stopped in Molly's doorway. His rage spiked when he saw the suitcase where he'd left it, and his daughter sitting on the bed as calm as could be, next to the clothes she'd set out.

"What part of 'pack your shit' didn't you understand?"

"Oh, I *understood* all of it," she returned like a snotty little brat. "But I've decided I'm not going anywhere. And neither are you."

There was something off in her voice. Frank stooped to pick up her suitcase just as she launched at him. He saw the chef's knife in her hand, but never in his wildest dreams did he think she'd use it on him.

Frank raised his arm to protect himself, but instinctively, his grip on the suitcase's handle only tightened, which probably saved his life by deflecting her strike enough to avoid his heart. The blade sliced into his trapezius muscle and all Frank could think was *subclavian artery* as the pain momentarily blinded him.

The suitcase hit her in the shoulder, but it was only enough to knock her back a step. Molly regained her footing, drew her arm back with an animal-like scream, and stabbed at him again. He threw the suitcase down and took the chef's blade through his palm. He bellowed in pain as he fell backward, yanking the knife out of her grip as he went down.

"Son of a bitch!" Frank landed on his ass and grabbed the handle of the knife. It hurt twice as much yanking it out. Molly pounced, screaming like a wild banshee. He flipped her over, sending his own blood spraying everywhere, but the next instant, she was up and clawing at him, still screaming in that chilling, inhuman way.

He smacked her as hard as he could open-handed, and Molly's screaming cut off. She fell still, his bloody handprint on the side of her head.

Thirty-Six

The airbags exploded in their faces. Seconds later, they deflated.

"Oh my God, Jess. Are you okay?"

"What the hell?"

The buck rolled off the hood and scrambled upright. It disappeared into the woods so quickly Jess almost didn't believe she'd seen it.

She climbed out and ran to the edge. Almost to the bunker, the road here sat in a narrow ledge, with a steep slope on the left and the sharp rise of Little Bear Ridge on the right.

Will had climbed out, too, and stood in the open car door.

"Did that really just happen?" she asked, dumbfounded.

"You mean did a five-hundred-pound deer just attack your car? Yeah, that really just happened." He rounded the hood and met her on the side of the road. Farther down the steep ravine, crashing sounds marked the buck's galloping departure.

"Am I crazy, or did that seem...deliberate?"

"Maybe a car killed his wife." Will laughed nervously. "Isn't that why deer are considered the deadliest animal in North America?"

"I would say so." She let out a shuddering breath. "Are you all right?"

"I've never been hit by an airbag before." He wiped at his eyes. "There was a lot of grit in it."

"I closed my eyes," she said. "It wasn't my first time." She didn't tell him it had happened on duty when a drunk with warrants had tried to flee a traffic stop and rammed a power pole, which fell on her car and left her trapped inside under live wires. She'd sat in her car for thirty minutes, nearly blinded by the dust in the airbag and afraid to touch any metal surface in her cruiser.

Will walked back to the car and examined the front end. "Is it still drivable?"

"I think so." Still shaking, she met him at the hood. "But it doesn't matter. We're here."

Five hundred yards ahead, the dark taillights of the Towne car reflected ambient light ominously, like the eyes of a beast lying in wait. The spreading white concrete walls of Whitney Station's entrance gleamed in the starlight, open arms welcoming them to their doom. Now that they were at ground level with the entrance, the cars stopped on the road revealed the scale of the massive doors.

They both stood in place.

"Looks bigger up close," Will said, mimicking her thoughts. In his voice, Jess heard clear reluctance. "Scarier."

"You don't have to come."

"No, no. I'm coming."

They still didn't move.

Will scuffed his shoe on the asphalt. "Are you going to bring the shotgun?"

"It's probably not a good idea to walk up to federal agents and an army regiment carrying a shotgun."

"I don't see anyone. But yeah, maybe you're right."

"Let's go, then."

"Wait!" Will grabbed her. "Just in case anything bad happens...I don't want our last kiss to be ten years ago."

Before she could stop him, Will pulled her into his arms. His lips were firm and determined, as if he truly did believe something bad would happen and this kiss was to be their last.

A fleeting impulse to push him away yielded to the splendor of his kiss, deftly overridden by the longing she'd kept tucked away all these years. She breathed in the familiarity of him, celebrating the magnificence of the boy she'd loved and lost.

And she rejoiced in the novelty of this new Will. Ten years had given him a delicious maturity and an emotional complexity she could now sense, but guessed had always been there.

She felt her own desperation in the kiss she returned, a longing to draw him back inside her and recapture the pure, innocent love they'd shared that fateful summer.

No, not recapture, but revitalize on a new level—both of them older, wiser, and more mature. Both of them different after ten years of wounds had slowly scarred over.

Will eased back. His eyes shined in the dim light of her one remaining headlight. "Damn, Jess."

"That was a freebie," she said, dragging the back of her hand over her lip. "Try that without permission again, and I'll show you some of my training."

He only grinned harder. "Promise?"

She smirked. "Feeling better?"

"Infinitely."

"Glad to hear it." She started off, letting him catch up, or not. His choice.

His shoes tapped a quick beat behind her.

"So, you don't really have a boyfriend?"

"I didn't say that."

"Okay. Who is he?"

"Was." She didn't like the teasing in his voice. "Cliff Barnes."

His footsteps slowed, then hurried to catch up. "Really?"

"Yeah, why?"

Cliff Barnes been her own fantasy come true after she'd joined the Sheriff's office. But her infatuation had been better as an idea than a reality, and while he was absolutely incredible in bed, she realized he'd been little more than a uniform chaser and, unfortunately, a relentless hound dog at the same time. Two years of go-nowhere fun had ended...*badly*.

"Doesn't seem your type. Yeah, I guess he was every girl's idea of a dreamboat—" he made finger quotes "—but you're more of a substance girl. You always have been, and now, I think you're even more so."

Jess tramped down a bead of irritation. She hated when people tried to act like they knew her.

"I'm not sure if I should take that as a compliment or an insult."

"Definitely compliment," he started, but Jess shushed him.

"Quiet. Time to watch your six."

They'd reached the first Town car. Though its windows were tinted, making it impossible to see inside, it was the Humvees that made her truly nervous. She placed a hand on her hip rig.

A mournful breeze slid past, but other than that, utter silence. Not a chirp, twitter, or screech, as if the entire mountain was dead. Their feet sounded unnaturally loud, tapping out an ominous countdown to doom.

Ahead, the road met the side walls of the concave. Scorch marks painted black edges on the massive doors. An oversized portable power station with an attached tank sat untended. Its hose lay on the ground like a dead snake, its welding nozzle dark. A handheld cutting saw also lay forgotten, and fresh silver scars marred one door where they'd tried to cut through.

The toe of his shoe sent metal tinkling across the asphalt. "Fuck. Jess!" He pointed down.

"I see it."

Spent shell casings littered the ground. Hellfire had rained down here.

"Who were they shooting at?" Will whispered.

"Bigger question, where did they go?"

"That's the creepy question of the day."

"Do you think they got in?" she asked, even though it was obvious they hadn't.

Will stepped up to the massive doors anyway. "I don't think so. There would be more damage, and you'd think there'd be marks on the ground. The doors open outward–" he caught his breath. "Oh shit."

She'd noticed it, too–a puddle of blood on the ground. Drag marks to the edge of the tarmac where the curb stopped for overgrown grass and shrubs.

"*Deputy.*"

An icy chill raced over Jess. "Did you hear that?"

Will's eyes were wide in the darkness, the whites practically glowing. He nodded.

Jess drew her gun and crept toward the edge. Closer now, she noticed the bent grass and drag marks. She climbed the weedy knoll and peered over the edge.

"Oh my God."

Bodies littered the steep slope that formed a natural arroyo next to the road, as though tossed over the side like garbage.

"Wait, Jess!"

She holstered her gun and jumped over the edge, ignoring Will's warnings. "Special Agent Larsen!"

"Harding." Agent Larsen lifted a bloodied hand as Jess dropped to her knees beside him.

Jess grabbed his hand. "Hold on, we're going to get you help."

"No time." He gripped back painfully tight. "...listen."

"Who did this?"

"Not who."

She didn't understand; his injuries were manmade. A bullet had torn open the left side of his face, and red stains on his shirt showed he'd taken two in the chest. Blood bubbled at his lips and ran from his nose.

Will clambered over the side and carefully picked his way down to them. He squatted down on Larsen's right.

"...wreckage ...Roswell."

"No," she breathed out, incapable of saying more.

Dear God, was Larsen saying this was the work of an alien? That everything that had happened was by alien influence?

That Will had been correct with Theory Number Three?

"The alien is dead," Will said, as if it weren't a conspiracy theory at all, but common, household knowledge.

"Only...the pilot."

"What are you saying?" he demanded, close to panic.

"It was...transport...the prisoner...here."

When Larsen exhaled, his chest didn't expand again.

"Oh shit. Is he dead?" Will rocked back and drove his fingers into his hair.

Larsen's hand had gone limp in hers. Jess stared at his face, praying for some part of him to move.

"Fuck." Will pushed to his feet and climbed back up the rise. He stopped halfway to retch and then scrambled the rest of the way to the tarmac.

Jess set Larsen's hand gently on his chest. Looked away. Blinked away tears as indecision rolled through her. *What do I do now?*

There were others who might still be alive. She rose and picked her way farther down the hill. It grew steeper here, dangerously jagged. In the darkness, she couldn't see any movement; no breathing or reaching hands. Only morbid stillness.

Special Agent Crenshaw was the first she came to, her white shirt gleaming in the moonlight. Her eyes were open, unfocused. She'd been shot in the forehead and throat. There was very little blood, but Jess's insides twisted.

All this loss was too much to bear. She had only met Crenshaw once, but knew this woman had been exemplary her entire life. Jess had experienced firsthand how hard it was to get into the FBI. Special Agent Crenshaw might have belonged to an unscrupulous organization that lied and hid secrets, but she had been intelligent, educated, as physically fit as a professional athlete. She'd beaten the challenges in her path and fought like a warrior for this position that she'd treasured like a royal title. And now she lay dead, probably not even forty years old.

What a tragic waste.

It did not appear they had died here; it looked as if someone had thrown the bodies over the edge. Two more men in black suits lay nearby, so twisted and bloodied she didn't bother to check for a pulse. The soldiers were next; Jess counted seven of them. Two still had automatic rifles strapped over their shoulders. A chemical odor filled the air, more pungent here. Jess had always associated the smell of fired guns with burning tires, but this was stronger, almost intolerable.

She picked her way carefully back up to the road. Will was coughing and spitting, wiping at his mouth with the back of his sleeve. She swallowed, fighting her own rising gorge.

"What did he mean, 'prisoner'?" he demanded, as though she had the answers.

"I don't know."

"He said 'Roswell!'"

"I heard. Just stay calm."

"This changes things. Holy shit!"

"We don't know anything for sure."

"You don't think he'd be the *one* person who knew for sure? We should go back. He just told us there's a fucking *alien* in there."

"Take my car. The keys are in the ignition. If I'm not back in two hours, go to Bruce, tell him what we found here."

"No! I'm not leaving you to go in there alone."

He grabbed her arm, forced her to stop and listen to him.

"I can't endure what you did. I'm not brave enough!"

She'd started to fight his grip, but his words stopped her cold.

"For the longest time, I couldn't fathom how you dealt with losing

Shreya. I wouldn't have survived it like you did. But look at you now; you're stronger for it. That isn't me. Hell, Jess, I *left*. I ran away. There, I said it. I'm not strong, like you. I can't let you go in there alone and *vanish* and be left to wonder what happened to you for the rest of my life."

His voice rose until it peaked, and she didn't doubt the panic that rolled off him in waves.

"Will, I'll be okay. They pounded on the door. I'm going to sneak in quietly."

"Remember how well that turned out for you the first time?" he snapped.

Now she did pull back. "Listen to me, Taylor. This is my job. If you don't like it, you can go sit in a comfortable room somewhere and *write* about it."

Even she felt the sting of her words. She wished she could take them back.

Too late now.

He let go of her arm and straightened his shoulders. "I stuck with you the first time, and I'm sticking with you now."

"Good. Because I really need you." She smiled, a thin olive branch after the cruelty she regretted. "See? You're braver than you thought."

Thirty-Seven

They stopped at the car, but before climbing in, Jess looked back at the bunker. A fleeting memory was nagging at the back of her mind. She wondered how big the facility was behind those doors and how far it traveled in the opposite direction.

And then it hit her.

Will had also stopped and was staring back at the ugly scene, but in his face, only pure horror.

"I've never seen a dead body before." He swallowed as though a rock was caught in his throat. "One time in New York...a yellow tarp over a bicyclist who had been killed by a car, but this...*God.*"

"It never gets any easier," she assured him, realizing grimly she'd said the same thing to Shreya only hours ago.

Her stomach was swimming, too. Not only from the horror of the blood and gore, but the loss. People lay discarded on that slope whose entire lives had possessed beauty, joy, and purpose, until ending here abruptly and pointlessly. All unnatural death was pointless. Wives', husbands', parents', and children's lives would change irreparably in a split second when the tragic news was delivered.

For Jess, the emotional loss was always so much worse than the violence.

She climbed into the driver's seat. "We need to head to Skeet Tooley's place."

Will mouthed the name as if testing his own memory. "The moonshiner?"

"Way to typecast, Taylor."

"Has he had a moral epiphany sometime in the last ten years?"

"No," she admitted.

Fortunately, the engine turned over readily, and the temperature gauge rose and stuck to "normal." She carefully backed into a three-point turn and drove back down Crestline more slowly than she came in.

"Okay. Why Tooley's place?" He swallowed again, his voice still shaky. In a way, his vulnerability made him more human.

"Something he said that didn't fully register at the time." She glanced at him. "Do you remember Mr. DeGroot, the high school maintenance man?"

"That crazy old guy who was there that night. How could I forget? I...*Herlinger* devoted an entire chapter to him."

"Yeah, he was crazy, but maybe not as crazy as we think. He and Skeet were pals, kindred conspiracy theorists. That night, he kept saying something like, 'I can't believe they finally did it.' I think Skeet may know something about Whitney Station."

"You may also remember he refused to talk, saying they would kill him if he did. Do you think DeGroot will talk now?"

"He died of lung cancer two years ago. Shortly after he passed, I had to haul Skeet out of Salty's Bar, drunker than usual. He was ranting about how the government illegally enforced eminent domain on his property, and how it wasn't legal because the 'secret military base' wasn't for public use."

Will mulled that over. "Huh."

They reached Manzanita Road and Jess came to a full stop. She took out her phone and bypassed her screen lock to open the maps program.

"At the time, I just wanted to get him into a cell to sober up. I didn't give it another thought. But now that I think about it, his property is off Dover Road. That's on the other side of Copper Creek Mountain." She showed him the overhead image. "This is his driveway, right after this bend."

She zoomed out. Outside town, maps showed little more than gray lines to indicate roads and big, blank spots indicating open land. In Skeet's case, his compound only showed as a small gray box to indicate a residence. When she flipped to satellite imagery, it disappeared beneath the trees altogether. She knew that was how Skeet preferred it.

"You're right. Could there be some truth to his claim?"

"That's what we're going to find out."

She looked both ways on pitch-dark Manzanita Road and turned right. It would take her back toward Pine Bluff, but another right turn on Nottingham would turn her north, toward Dover Road.

Will grabbed the door's comfort handle. "Take it easy, would you? I think I'm going to be sick."

She slowed the car. "Sorry. Do you want me to pull over?"

"I'll let you know." Will cleared his throat. "Speaking of moonshine, I suppose it was also pretty shitty of me not to ask about your mom."

Jess smirked. "Moonshine is what makes you think of my mom."

He huffed a weary laugh. "Yeah. That's screwed up, I know."

"She's ten-years sober, believe it or not. After rehab she started working at a women's recovery center in Sacramento. She never came back to Kileyville—Pine Bluff."

"Good for her."

"She says she likes it, but if you ask me, she needs it. I think she needs to focus really *really* hard on her sobriety, otherwise she'd fall off the wagon."

As tumultuous as her childhood had been—Jess used to use the words "Dumpster fire" to describe it—thinking about her mother made her heart a little lighter. She was still queasy from the carnage outside Whitney Station, already mourning vicariously for family members she didn't even know.

Jess turned onto Dover and hit the high beams. She'd been here multiple times on complaints from Irma Rickman, St. Joseph's parish administrator, over Skeet's "un-Godly moonshining ways," and even more often now that his son Peter was seventeen and a hell-raiser with his supped-up Camaro, but she hadn't arrested Skeet since that time at Salty's Bar. Even then, Salty hadn't pressed charges, and she'd released Skeet without fines the next morning.

She hoped there were no hard feelings floating between them.

There were more potholes on his driveway than she remembered, and Jess was glad she was driving the county's car. As it was, Bruce was going to have a conniption when he saw the dent the buck had put in the hood, not to mention the cost of the repair of the airbags.

"Jesus," Will said, grabbing the handle again as the car fell into a particularly deep rut.

"It's part of his home security," she said, trying to tease. She failed miserably but keeping it light was *her* coping mechanism—a tactic Bruce had encouraged when she'd been particularly uptight as a rookie.

At the end of his winding lane, she continued past the dark house and stopped at the massive doors to an outbuilding that was three times the size of the residence.

"Is anyone even home?"

"He's home, and he knows we're here. He's got alerts all along that driveway." Light showed through a gap in the doors.

Jess unhooked her microphone. "Skeet Tooley, you in there? It's Jess Harding." She specifically didn't say 'deputy,' hoping he would assume this wasn't an official visit.

She put the microphone back into its holder and opened her door. "Let's go."

"Are you sure it's safe?"

"Don't worry."

The shed doors slid open. Despite the cool night, Skeet only wore a tattered wife-beater decorated with stains. He watched her walk over with a calm expression, and Jess sensed he'd heard about the return of the 97. By now, the whole town and all neighboring counties had heard, if not the entire country.

"Dep'ty."

"Hey, Skeet. How's it brewing?"

He gave her a toothy grin. "Hot and spicy, as always."

"Dad." Pete Tooley spat the single word like a curse. He was deeper inside the shed, working on a piece of metalwork on a grinder. It powered down like a jet plane coming to rest.

Pete was not her biggest fan.

"Shut up, boy. Go on up to the house."

He threw down a wrench with a clang and stormed past. Will dodged out of his way as Pete barked at him and then laughed.

"Damn kid's overflowing with piss 'n vinegar." When he'd gone, Skeet gave her a conspiratorial nod. "You need your paint stripped? Got some fresh apple pie."

"I'd love a taste." She motioned for Will to follow her inside and almost laughed at his expression.

Skeet went to a wooden shelf where several glasses sat upside down. They were a mismatched set of faceted whiskey tumblers, acquired at the Goodwill, and they and the silver tray they sat on looked comically out of place in the cluttered work shed. His copper distiller gleamed in the uneven light, a thing to behold. Even though highly illegal, Skeet swelled with pride as he poured a sample into three glasses.

"You've upgraded," Jess commented.

"You won't taste smoother honey anywhere in the county." Skeet handed her a glass and then offered one to Will. After a moment's hesitation, he walked over and accepted the glass.

Jess tipped hers back and took a drink. It ran down her throat like liquid fire. A sweet cinnamon undertone cooled her sinuses like menthol. She finished the second mouthful to drain the glass.

"Damn, that's good," she said, making Skeet smile.

Will imitated her by taking a too-large gulp. He coughed at the burn and then turned away to compose himself.

Skeet laughed. "Take it easy, son. Ain't you never tasted hillbilly honey before?"

"He's a first-timer," Jess said as Will hurried back through the doors, coughing into his elbow. She set her glass down on the tray.

Skeet's mood sobered quickly. "I heard about the kids, and that business on the train." He threw back the remains of his own glass, as though preparing himself. "I reckon that's why you're here. Though I don't know what I can tell you that you don't already know."

"A couple of years ago you got riled up about the government taking liberties on your property."

That seemed to surprise him, but he quickly waved it away. "Nah. I was just up in arms after Curtis died. All our blustering got a lot more real when I was alone to deal with it." He shrugged. "Pete don't believe me much. Calls me a crazy old fool."

"I don't believe you're crazy, and I know you're not a fool."

"Just old," he said wistfully, staring out at the night through the open doors. Will was still outside, coughing up fire.

"Your property backs up to Whitney Station."

"Backs up? Hell, that place runs *underneath* my land," he said, proving he knew all about the bunker. He clamped his jaw shut as if he'd said too much. Paced away. Then he stopped and pointed his finger. "I can prove it, too, if anyone cared enough to listen, but that's a can of worms best left sealed. Truth be told, it ain't just my own kid calling me crazy, and I'm tired of it."

"I'm not asking you to incriminate yourself. But I need to get into that facility, and I think you know the way."

Skeet opened his mouth to say something, then thought better of it. He shook his head and paced away again. Jess wondered if the agents had been here and threatened him. Then, it occurred to her.

"You've been inside."

Will came back, patting his chest. "Went down the wrong pipe." His voice was raspy. He stopped and looked from one to the other, probably wondering when the mood had turned.

"Stuck my toe in the door, that's all."

"How'd you get in?"

Skeet paced some more. Jess let him have the space he needed.

"Listen, I like you, Jessica. You never arrested me, 'least not for moonshining, in all these years. So, I'm gonna give you some friendly advice, and you should take it. Don't go in there."

Unfortunately, she had no choice. It wasn't for herself that she needed in there. 97 other people were depending on her.

Actually, only ninety-four now. That only made it more urgent.

"I have to."

Skeet's magic nectar was unfurling in her bloodstream like satin ribbons. Maybe it was the dose of liquid courage, but Jess was more determined than ever.

"Like you, I'm sick and tired of this shit. This ends tonight, one way or another."

Thirty-Eight

Jess and Will sat on a wooden picnic bench outside the workshop as Skeet went to get his gear.

"We're really doing this?"

"You can turn back any time."

"Really, Jess. After what we saw back there...this just got a whole lot uglier."

Will leaned forward and rested his elbows on his knees. He rubbed his forehead with his fingertips.

Skeet's Apple Pie had helped numb some of the heartache from so much senseless loss, and part of her agreed with him. Up until they'd arrived at the bunker doors, Jess hadn't expected the night would turn deadly.

But the issue was well past the point of argument.

"I know," she said simply.

Her phone rang. She looked at the display, and then stood up.

"Harding." She paced in a circle. "When? Are you all right? Where is she now? No, no, you did the right thing. Just try to be gentle. Remember, this isn't her in control. Yeah, Frank, I'm working on it. Give me a couple of hours. That's all I'm asking. I'll get back to you."

She disconnected. "Shit."

Ugly or not, I have to do this.

"What is it?" Will asked.

"Molly McGibben put a chef's knife through Frank's hand. He's got her duct-taped to a chair."

❧

The Meadows was luxurious, with a dining room as gorgeous as any five-star restaurant and a spectacular gymnasium Shreya caught a glimpse of as she was led down the hall.

Then they came to her room. It was spartan, not even as nice as a hotel room. A narrow bed sat between two glossy white nightstands made with rounded edges. The attempt was '70s modern chic, but she saw it for what it was—no sharp corners. A matching desk finished the décor.

No television, no radio, no computer. No lamp—all the lighting was recessed sconces in the ceiling. As *if they believe I might try to hang myself with a cord.*

She had to get out of here. But to do so, she had to play it cool.

An hour later, Becky knocked on her door.

"How are you settling in?"

Shreya only shrugged and went back to her spot on the bed where she'd been reading Will's book. Rather, glancing through it between pacing sessions. Her thoughts were sporadic and fleeting, and she was having trouble concentrating.

"Breakfast is served from six to seven-thirty, and we have a causal group meeting at eight. We talk about our plans for the day, our goals, that sort of thing."

"You mean how the drug addicts will manage the next twelve hours," she snapped.

"Something like that," Becky said in a gentle voice.

Shreya sighed. "Sorry. I'm a little cranky."

"It's understandable. This isn't the place anyone wants to be. But it could be a lot worse, especially for those 'drug addicts.' Some of them—*most* of them—hit rock bottom before they came here. But not everyone here is in recovery. Some just need a place to get centered again."

"Hmm."

Becky sat on the end of the bed. "I realize you still feel like you're seventeen. You haven't seen yet how adult life has challenges that not everyone can cope with. Do you want to know why I work here? When I was twenty, my mother had a late-in-life baby." She gave a sad laugh as she phrased the term. "My little brother didn't make it. My mom took it hard, and combined with severe postpartum depression, she couldn't cope, and we didn't know how to help her. She took a bottle of sleeping pills and nearly died. She came here, back when it was mostly 'drug addicts' and drunks. This place saved her life."

"Becky, I'm sorry. I didn't know."

But she could understand. Her emotions were spinning out of control, and Shreya was afraid to touch any of them for fear of more pain.

"I went to school, got my degree in Psychology, and came back here to improve this place. Now we're ranked one of the best recovery facilities in California."

"That's awesome." She managed a smile. "I hear you saved Jess's mom, too."

"That was before I worked here, but yes. The Meadows played a big part in June's sobriety."

"This is all so hard to accept...I can hardly believe everything that's changed. You look..."

"Older?"

"I was going to say more mature. Content. You look amazing."

"Thank you." Becky beamed. "Being proposed to will do that for you." She wagged her finger, showing off a glittering diamond.

She was getting married. Had an amazing college experience that got her an impressive education and a fabulous career. All things Shreya missed out on. The ache deep in her heart, a loneliness almost, surged brighter and louder.

"You weren't at the dance that night."

Becky shook her head. "I'd twisted my ankle playing soccer that morning."

Shreya closed the book and set it down. "A lucky break."

"Only a sprain, but yes."

They both laughed lightly.

"Do you know what they called us, the students who didn't make it to prom that night? The Lucky Thirteen."

Shreya looked down at the carpet. She'd read something about that in the book, when she could force herself to pay attention to the words. The book was a dreary, sad story she wished wasn't hers. Only it *was* her story—hers and Jess's.

"We weren't lucky. Especially Jess," Becky said, as if reading her thoughts. "She took it harder than any of us. We all had survivor's guilt, but for Jess, it was something more. Something huge. She loved you, and she failed you."

"Bud she didn't fail me." Jess had endured so much pain, and it was Shreya's fault. "God, just look at her. She's a one-woman cyclone. When so many others left—including my own mother—she stayed for us. She escaped that nasty trailer park, bought a house here, and became a cop. She anchored herself to this place. I can hardly believe it's been this long, but for *ten years* she didn't give up hope. Never stopped looking."

"You've got that right." Becky smiled warmly, and Shreya could tell she loved Jess as well. From what she'd seen, this whole town loved her. "Give this place a chance. Jess asked you to come here because she only wants to protect you."

She nodded obediently. "I'll try."

"I'll let you get some rest. Is there anything else I can get you?"

"Actually, I'm a little hungry. Is there any way I can sneak a snack? Something light, like a few cookies and some milk?"

"That sounds easy enough. Let's go to the dining room. I think there's a secret stash of Oreos in the kitchen."

At nearly nine, the place was quiet and empty except for a busy cleaning staff dusting, sweeping, and watering the many potted plants. They entered the empty dining room and Becky told her to have a seat.

On the way in, Shreya had glimpsed the huge windows on the far side, and the sliding-glass door leading to a lovely patio lit with glowing path lights. When Becky disappeared into the kitchen, Shreya tried the glass door and found it unlocked.

She slipped out into the night.

Thirty-Nine

Her phone rang as Becky pulled a half-pint carton of milk from the fridge. It was Jess checking in on Shreya.

"Remember what I said about keeping an eye on her? One of the 97 just tried to carve up her father with a kitchen knife. Try not to be obvious, but amp up your game."

"I'm with her now," she assured Jess. "I'm watching her personally."

"I can't thank you enough."

"Hey, it's my job! And Shreya is lovely. It's my pleasure."

"I'm in the field now, but I'm hoping to have this sorted out before Shreya's mother arrives tomorrow. What time can I come over in the morning?"

"She should be up and having breakfast by seven. Join us. It's strawberry crepe day."

"That sounds heavenly. See you then."

Shreya was lucky to have someone like Jess looking out for her. She knew some of the 97 had come back to find their families moved away, or worse, deceased. She couldn't begin to imagine how difficult that must be.

She dropped her phone in her sweater's pocket and backed through the cafeteria door while holding the cookies and milk. Becky turned around to find the dining chair Shreya had pulled out sitting unoccupied.

"Shreya?" She dropped food on the closest table and hurried into the hallway. "Shreya?"

Jocelyn looked up from the baseboard she was cleaning.

"Did you see the guest I was just with?"

Jocelyn shook her head.

Oh no. She ran back to Shreya's room. The door still stood open. "Shreya?"

Empty. Becky unclipped her radio. "Code-5. Shreya Sanvi. Code-5."

"Copy that," Trent responded. He appeared at the far end of the hall as

Becky raced back toward the main office.

"I don't think she's inside. Notify security, search the grounds. Get Russell on the cameras"

"Will do."

If what Jess had said was true... this wasn't like a recovery patient sneaking out to find a hit. This was worse, so much worse.

"We have to find her *now*."

⌁

"Would it be horrible for me to say I don't have much sympathy for Frank McGibben?"

"My sympathy is for Molly." Jess sat beside Will on the bench again. "Now you understand why I have to do this. I have no choice, Will."

He gestured subtly toward the barn. "What if this guy is taking us on a wild goose chase?"

She shrugged and made a noncommittal sound. Jess thought about the men on the train who'd been severed at the knees and wondered if she'd find their bodies inside.

"I won't think any less of you if you stayed back."

He shook his head. "I would."

She touched his arm, making him sit back and look at her. "Will, I want you to know...what you said earlier about not being strong? I don't think your leaving town means you're not strong. Everyone deals with tragedy in their own way, and I'd never begrudge anyone for their coping mechanism. You went and wrote about it. That makes you strong *and* brave."

He shrugged halfheartedly and glanced away.

"What is the old saying? 'The pen is mightier than the sword?' That makes you a knight in my eyes."

"No, you were right. It's easy to sit in a comfortable room somewhere, protected from danger, and wield a big pen." He lifted his palms. "*This* is what takes strength and courage. You always were fearless. I wish I were half as brave as you."

She didn't tell him that right now she wasn't feeling very brave. Reckless, maybe. Even a little foolhardy. If not for Skeet's liquid courage, she'd probably be headed back down the mountain by now.

"I'm sorry for what I said. It was horrible, and I didn't mean it."

The apology sounded feeble, even to her ears. Her nervous gut only got worse thinking about what she was about to do. Instead, she focused on Will's profile in the moonlight, and how glad she was that he was back in town, back in her life. It wasn't fair that he'd matured so handsomely and seemed twenty times smarter than when he'd left. Even back then, he'd been the smartest person she knew.

Skeet walked out to them with an enormous coil of blue nylon rope looped over one shoulder and a heavy duffel in the other hand. He tossed Will a canteen.

"It's water," he said when Will looked at it warily. "I hope you got your walking shoes on, because it's a hike."

Will looked past him at the blackness of the mountain rising behind the shed. He sighed.

Jess went to her cruiser's trunk. She retrieved a small backpack and a bottle of water from her personal stash.

"You can take that if you want, you'll need it inside." Skeet pointed at her flashlight. "But it stays off until we get to the intake."

"No problem."

"Intake?" Will asked as he stood.

"Bunker needs an air supply," Skeet responded simply. "Here, carry this." He hefted the bag at Will, who caught it with a grunt.

Will grumbled. "We're going to climb a mountain in the dark."

"Nothing she can't handle. Don't know about you, though."

He chuckled as he started for the trees, and Jess and Will hurried to follow.

"Saw you at the fundraiser last summer," Skeet said. "You're something on a knobby wall."

"It's a competition the Pine Bluff Climbers club puts on," Jess explained. "Inspires at-risk teenagers to do something other than smoke pot, and raises money for gear to start kids climbing."

"You kept climbing, then," Will stated.

She leaned closer and smiled. "I thought it was a skill I should develop."

"Shoulda seen her," Skeet said without turning around. "Took second place, was it?"

"I started slipping, so I made a leap thinking I was going to fall on the rope, but I made it. I surprised myself more than the judges."

They followed Skeet into the thicket and were forced to walk single file. This would be tough going in the dark, and it'd probably take twice as long as during the day.

"I wish I could have seen it." Will grunted as he caught on a shrub and tore free, shaking the bush with a racket like a bear chasing an elk through the woods.

"Some climbers are really serious about it, but the benefit is just good fun for families, for a good cause."

"You really do care about this community," he said.

Over the years, Jess guessed it had developed slowly; so slowly she hadn't even noticed. He was right. The people of Pine Bluff looked to her like a pinnacle, the authoritarian they could trust after having suffered through their tragedy with them.

A year after the disappearance, the local police department had closed, and law enforcement fell on the county Sheriff's office. None of the other current officers, Bruce included, were local, nor had they been here at the time of the disappearance.

The old-timers depended on her, and she loved them all.

"Even though I'd only been in Pine Bluff for six years before the disappearance, this is my home now." She adored her farmhouse and would never leave it. "How strange is that?"

"Everything in this town is strange. Us included, I guess," he muttered. "Jesus, I run four miles a day. How is he leaving us in his dust like this?"

They hiked in silence for a little over an hour. The going was hard pushing through thick vegetation, without the benefit of even a deer path.

"Hang on, I have to stop," Will said, breathing hard. "That moonshine dried up my insides."

"Damn, city slicker! You're half my age," Skeet said. "No matter. We're here."

They'd leveled out on the top of the mountain, and Jess could see the glow of Pine Bluff's lights several miles to the south. She turned in a circle, noting pinpoints of light from other houses and compounds like Skeet's.

"Gimme that bag," Skeet said, motioning with a hand.

He stood beside a concrete block about four feet square. A huge metal pipe rose out and then curved over at the top like an enormous candy cane.

"What, that?" Will said incredulously. "You've got to be kidding. There has to be another way inside."

"You could go try knocking on the front door," Skeet quipped, and Will and Jess shared an uneasy glance.

Skeet removed an electric drill from the bag Will had carried up. He unscrewed two bolts holding a section of the pipe. Jess noted the other six or so were already gone. The pipe was about forty-two inches in diameter.

"No way. I can't do it. That's not big enough for a person to fit through."

"Yeah, it is," Skeet said simply, not elaborating further. "Help me get this thing offa here."

"This place can't be very big if this is its only intake," Jess said, hopeful.

"There's three more like it that I know of," he said, dashing her hopes. "One of 'em you could see from here if it was daylight."

He took the rope and went to a nearby pine tree to secure it with one of the clamps from his bag.

Jess tied the end to her backpack and dropped it into the pipe. She lowered it slowly and Will shined his light to watch its descent.

"I suppose now isn't a good time to tell you I'm also claustrophobic."

"This is your last chance to back out. Because once inside, if you turn back, you do it alone." She gave him a hard look. "And climbing out will be harder than climbing in."

She hated that he felt he had something to prove. She could see it plainly in his face, just as plainly as she knew trying to talk him out of it would be impossible.

"I'm hoping we can walk out the front door," he said, confirming her suspicions.

"I'll go first. Watch me do it, and then wait for me to get to the bottom. I'll signal you with my flashlight when it's your turn. Skeet will help you tie yourself in. It's not very wide, but you'll be able to lean backward just enough to rappel down."

He nodded along. Jess took a specialized clamp and hooked it on to the rope. It was designed for climbing, not descending, but it would serve the purpose and be easier for Will than going with ropes alone. She remembered how difficult it had been for her to learn to descend on ropes alone.

"Loop the ropes behind your back, like this." She wound them around the small of her back and then fixed the clamp. "You've created a makeshift harness. You have to squeeze the clamp to release it. That way, if you slip and let go, it will stop you from falling."

"Great. If I slip, this tiny-ass piece of metal is going to save me."

She climbed up onto the platform and readied herself to go down, but paused and looked at Skeet. "Can you wait up here for a while? I may need you."

"Sure, sure," Skeet grumbled as if he hadn't expected any less. "Take this. Give me the occasional reminder you're still alive." He handed her one of the two walkies he'd carried up.

"You're very well prepared, almost like you've done this kind of thing before," Will said.

"I admit to nothing," Skeet said idly.

"Release it slowly and slide a few inches at a time," Jess instructed, demanding his attention in a sharp tone. "You're going to walk down the pipe."

"Easy as Beef Wellington," Will said sarcastically.

"Any idea how tall this chimney is?" she asked Skeet.

"Forty feet." He swallowed and looked sheepish for a minute. "If I were to guess."

"That means if you fall, I can't catch you. You'll kill us both."

Will rolled his eyes so dramatically it was visible even in the darkness. "Fantastic."

"Damn it, City Slicker. The pipe's narrow enough you could crab-walk down it without ropes. You ain't gonna fall!"

So that was how he'd gotten in and out by himself. "I have complete faith in you, Will," Jess told him.

Skeet cleared his throat. "There's a maintenance box with a plate access at the bottom. Uh, should come out easy."

Jess took that to mean he'd only put one or two screws back, if any, on his own trip inside.

She squeezed into the pipe and started down. It was just wide enough to fold her arms close in front of her chest to work the clamp. She'd forgotten how painful a rope harness could be and readied herself for Will's complaints.

Looking up, she saw their two peering silhouettes against the charcoal sky. A breeze swirled around her head, but from below, the stink was unnatural. Rotting food, human stench, and...something else.

The mechanical hum beneath her grew louder as she got closer to the bottom. The air pump was working. Still, if the others weren't, the air down here could be deadly, and she regretted getting Will mixed up in this.

A moment's panic wrapped around her as Jess contemplated her choice. But rappelling down as she was, she couldn't get back up unless she went all the way to the bottom and changed the configuration of her ropes.

She was committed, whether she liked it or not.

The maintenance box at the bottom of the pipe was flimsy by modern standards, but it was larger than the pipe, and Jess could finally move her upper body more freely.

To her left, the duct fed into the pump, which grinded in a most unhealthy manner. On her right, a dead end—the maintenance plate. She shined her light on it and didn't see any screws.

Skeet's work, probably.

She kicked it gently, and it popped off and clattered to the floor with an unholy racket.

Jess dropped to her butt and slipped out. Fortunately, it was only three feet off the floor. She was inside a large maintenance closet. The pump was an ancient monstrosity that reminded her of *The Mangler*. It chugged roughly, but Jess rejoiced in the clean air it sucked down from above. The room was about ten by twelve, with a single door that locked with a knob and deadbolt.

She leaned back into the tube and flashed her light twice. The ropes moved, and Will and Skeet's whispers floated down.

Dark markings shadowed the concrete floor. She shined the light at her feet. Muddy footprints from Timberlines not much larger than her own marred the floor.

Definitely Skeet's work.

It took Will longer to get down than it took her, but Jess was impressed.

"Good work," she said softly.

"Any idea where we are?"

"I would guess the air pump room."

He smirked.

Jess quietly turned the deadbolt on the door and then unlocked the knob. The door came away from the jamb easily enough, but two inches in, it scraped against the floor with a monstrous shriek. With no chance at stealth, both she and Will pulled on it and forced it wide enough to squeeze through.

She peered into the wide hallway. To the left, emergency lights gave off sickly light that revealed the swinging doors to a commissary. To the right, the hallway stretched into a dark void that made Jess's stomach turn leaden.

There was a floorplan map on the wall across from them, so Jess went and shined her light on it while Will peered through the doors' glass panels into to the commissary.

"What the hell happened here?" He pushed one of the doors open and stepped inside. "It looks like a grade school cafeteria after a food fight. Smells worse."

She followed him inside. The room was immense, with round tables providing seating for at least two hundred people. Emergency-exit lighting above four doors in each corner of the room and behind the serving counter cast the gigantic room in eerie green light.

It looked as though the party of the century had taken place decades ago. Chairs and tables were knocked over, and plates, bottles, glasses, and strewn food littered the floors and the few tables that were still standing. The cafeteria-style service line looked like it had endured a prison riot.

"Whatever happened here, it's been like this for a long time. Look at the food." She shined her flashlight on a plate on the floor. The glop in her light's beam was black and moldy, unidentifiable.

He grabbed her arm. "Jess." Pointed.

A body lay on the floor by the exit door on the opposite side of the commissary.

Forty

The corpse wore what appeared to be a workman's jumpsuit with an emblem on the sleeve she couldn't make out at this distance, but the condition of the body was unmistakable. The skin was papery thin and nearly transparent, revealing the skull and the bones of the hand desiccated away to nearly nothing. It looked like a prehistoric specimen from a museum. It lay face down, one arm thrown forward and one leg bent.

They walked quietly toward the body, holding it in the flashlight's beam. It was slow going tiptoeing through the garbage that would crunch under their feet.

Will stared at the body in silence, but the horror on his face spoke volumes.

"How long does it take a body to degrade like this?" Jess whispered. Only tufts of short hair indicated it was probably a man.

"It depends on the elements. Down here, protected from weather and insects like this, this is unnatural."

"Did you notice—there aren't any bugs."

"I did," he whispered back. "All this garbage, and there should be rats or mice. Cockroaches. But I don't see any evidence or droppings." He shined his light over all four corners of the room. "Not even a spiderweb."

Jess suspected he was also looking for devices. "He almost looks mummified."

Will swallowed noisily as he brought the flashlight's beam back to the body. "And sprawled like that, like he was trying to flee."

"Come on. Back to the map."

"Are you scared shitless?" Will asked as they picked their way carefully back the way they came. "Because I'm scared shitless."

"I am definitely scared shitless."

"Just checking."

Outside, she shined her light on the map. "We are here." She touched a finger to the spot. The large space of the commissary was behind them. "Damn, this place is huge. How did something like this even get built without people knowing about it?"

"It didn't," Will told her. "But it was built in 1957, so only old-timers would even remember. Because it was constructed in an existing cave system means very little demolition was required."

He pointed out the branching corridors that made up the flower pattern Shreya had noticed.

"And if you think about it, to get here from I-5, you don't need to drive through town."

"You researched it," she guessed aloud. "But you...it wasn't in the book."

"*Stan* probably didn't think it was relevant." He spoke softly, as if even now, he was afraid someone might be listening. "And he had a hundred and twenty-five thousand word-count limit."

She frowned. "You know, if the FBI disappeared Stan, they know he didn't write the book."

"My editor says he's alive and well. That's my story, and I'm sticking to it."

Rooms lined the wide hall here, with outdated wired-glass windows. Jess went to the office on the opposite side of the hall and peered inside through a broken window missing a chunk of glass. Her nerves were stretched like piano wire, and everywhere she looked she expected ghastly evidence of horrific experiments. She almost laughed when she saw a basic looking office with a heavy wooden desk, metal file cabinet, and sixties-era fashionable guest seating.

"Abraham Wilson, Ph.D.," Will read aloud. "Anyone you've ever heard of?"

Jess shook her head.

He removed a small, stainless-steel water bottle from a pocket on his cargo pants. Instead of drinking from it, he unscrewed the bottom and removed a miniature digital camera. He snapped a picture. When he saw her looking, he shrugged. "Tools of the trade. Do you know how many phones I've had confiscated by law enforcement? No offense."

On a hunch, Jess pulled her phone out of her pocket. "Do you have service?"

Will checked his phone and shook his head. "No, but probably just because we're underground. Today, a government facility like this might use jammers, but that kind of technology is way ahead of this place. Everything here is old school, like no one's been down here since the sixties."

"I was just thinking the same thing," she agreed. "So how is there power to the air pumps and the emergency lighting?"

He shook his head. "I'd guess a generator, but who would keep it running?"

"And how is a seventy-year-old generator even still working?"

"I'm more concerned about who is filling it with fuel."

"The South Fork River runs on the west side of this ridge," she said. "Maybe the power is hydroelectric. That would only be smart."

"And a whole lot less terrifying."

Across from Dr. Wilson's office, a platform cart sat outside a set of double doors currently standing open. Jess shined her light inside. It was the kitchen storeroom that backed up to the food service area of the commissary. The carnage wasn't as bad inside, but it was still a disaster. Some cans of meat and vegetables sat on heavy-duty metal shelving, but it appeared as if someone had gone through and knocked most of the supplies to the floor. Again, discarded bags of flour, sugar, salt, beans, noodles, and spilled coffee grounds showed no indication of pest infestation.

"Which way should we go?" Will was back to looking at the map. "It looks like the dormitories are behind us."

"I don't want to see whatever might be there." Jess pointed to the massive space on the map marked *Laboratories*. "I'd rather go this way. I want to see the heart of his freak fest."

Forty-One

The hallway stretched on interminably, and Jess experienced a momentary vision distortion as her imagination lengthened it into an endless void. She resisted the urge to reach for Will to steady herself, not wanting him to think she was on the verge of losing it.

Even though I am.

The air pump in the ventilation shaft had been struggling, and she wondered if carbon monoxide, or something more dangerous, could be affecting them.

"What does the air smell like to you?" she whispered in what she hoped was a casual tone.

"Bad," he said, confirming her fears. "B-O, rot. Death."

The hallway met one of the intersections she'd seen on the floorplan. They stopped, and Jess held up a finger. "Do you hear that?"

"It sounds like a motor."

"Let's go," she said almost soundlessly, but he followed when she started to the right. Her panic rose with each step farther down the hall. They came to a pile of Steelcase desks partially blocking the hall. They were piled on top of each other, as though having been tossed by a giant.

Someone tried to fortify this hallway. But against what?

The emergency lights ended here, or if there were any more, they were broken.

Will waited with her as she shined her flashlight around. More clutter, debris, and loose papers, but not a single rodent or cobweb. Satisfied, she inched carefully around the pile and continued down the hall.

The sound grew louder until they arrived at a large grate in the ceiling. She shined her light up. It was cooler here, and the fresh air coming through was like a balm.

"The other air pump Skeet told us about must be nearby."

He nodded.

She shined her light on an office door.

Victoria Ziegler, Director, Psychology Department.

"Interesting." Jess reached for the doorknob. Will bristled but didn't try to stop her.

The knob was locked, but the door wasn't fully seated in the jamb. She pushed it slowly open. It gave a bone-chilling creak so loudly that Skeet probably heard it.

Without emergency lighting, the office was a dark cave. She shined the light around, noting a modest but quality wooden desk with an assortment of papers strewn across the top; cluttered but free of the destruction in the halls and commissary.

The beam of light fell on a body on a couch against the back wall of the spacious office.

"Oh my God," Will hissed. "The olive-green decor of the sixties is horrendous."

Jess frowned disapprovingly, but didn't chastise him for his attempt at levity. *You gotta do what you gotta do to keep your sanity.*

The corpse was female, lying on her side with her back to the room. Her head rested on the padded armrest as though she had died after falling asleep here. A wave of shiny red hair draped over the edge of the cushion. She wore a lab coat over a woolen pencil skirt. Toothpick-thin legs crossed daintily at the ankles, her feet still in the block-heeled pumps that had made a full circle back into fashion.

Jess inched inside for a closer look. Other than the pretty hair, the body was as papery-dry and pale as the first corpse.

The flash of Will's camera made her jump. It illuminated the room harshly, like a scene out of a horror movie.

This is a horror movie, and I'm the idiot who keeps walking deeper into the haunted house, foolishly calling out, "Hello, is someone there?"

"Both of the bodies look desiccated, like the carcasses spiders leave behind."

Jess swiveled a hard look at him.

"Sorry. Just calling it like I see it."

"As awful as that sounds...you're right." Thank God there weren't any spider webs around. Bugs in general gave her the heebie-jeebies, but spiders took the number one spot at the top of the list.

"Let's get out of here." His voice tremored, as if Will had officially reached his dead-body-per-day limit.

"Just a minute—I want to see her desk." Jess rounded the far side and shined the light on the papers. It was littered with personnel documents and payroll statements, as well as shipping-receiving manifests and purchase-requisition forms for foodstuffs and basic office supplies, all with Victoria Ziegler's signature on the bottom. As usual, a woman handled three times the work of a man, and probably received half the salary to do it.

Someone named Jasper Humphries was being transferred from water decontamination to electrical repair. This entire place appeared to have been self-sustaining, though food obviously came from the outside. She remembered the staples in the cafeteria and wondered when deliveries had stopped.

"When did this place shut down again?" she whispered.

"Officially, 1967."

The date of the personnel transfer was 1971.

She turned to the metal filing cabinet standing behind the desk and pulled open the top drawer, easing it slowly when it clunked loudly. Inside, personnel files A thru F. She removed a file with the name Arthur Escalante and scanned through the pages.

Depression and irregular sleep cycle resulting from lack of sunlight. Patient Escalante reports an unsettling sensation of being watched and atypical impulses toward hopelessness and self-harm. When he started working here one year ago, Arty was a jolly and outgoing man. Now he is morose and withdrawn. Recommendation for all maintenance staff: two hours of daily outdoor calisthenics between twelve and two p.m.

Jess read the key paragraph out loud and then looked up at Will.

"This employee experienced the same sensations Shreya and Gavin described, and Sara Potter and Todd Erikkson carried out. The doctor recommended two hours of exercise in the sunlight per day." Jess wondered if Arty had survived much more than a year here. She tossed the folder onto the desk. "Somehow, I don't think that cured their problems."

"I wonder how many people died in here." Will swallowed noisily. "Why are these bodies still here? Did the government close this place down knowing there was death inside? Or was it left to continue operating with people on the outside thinking everything was a-okay?"

"That is the million-dollar question."

They left the office and headed back the way they came, still aiming for the main labs. They arrived at the branching hallway and turned right. The long hallway finally revealed its end at a set of double doors where connecting hallways spread to the left and right.

Was this where she would finally find the source of everything bad that had happened in Pine Bluff all these years?

They passed another maintenance room whose door stood open, the air pump inside humming along in a healthier manner than the one they'd come down. Jess put a hand on Will's arm, stopping him. She shined the light on the floor, revealing a muddy cache of booted footprints.

"Soldiers?"

"Probably," Jess said, thinking of the violence they'd found outside. Were the perpetrators in here with them?

"It's not too late to turn back."

"It was too late to turn back ten years ago." She followed the trail of footprints with her light. Whoever had entered here had already branched out into different directions, including the hall they'd just come down. Clods of mud trailed off, fading as though the wearer's boots shed their mud as they went.

"Do you think these are the shooters from outside?" Will's voice held genuine worry as he voiced the question she kept inside her head.

He knelt and fingered some of the mud. "This mud is dry."

He stood, holding her gaze intensely.

"I'm not stopping," she said to the warning in his eyes.

"Neither am I."

Her heartbeat throbbed hot in her throat as she continued toward the doors, barely feeling her feet on the ground. *Don't let fear get you now.*

Two-way swinging doors into the main lab each held a frosted glass panel. They were still intact, preventing her from looking inside before pushing through. Jess flipped off her flashlight and cracked one of the doors open.

A wide metal balcony looked over a dark void. She pushed the door all the way open, and she and Will stepped inside.

The main laboratory was an open, atrium-style workspace, one level down. High above, the ceiling was the rough stone of the original cavern.

The balcony-walkway circled the space on all four sides, where smaller glass-walled labs had once provided secured testing of God-only-knows what.

"It looks like a James Bond movie set," Will said. "The villain's lair."

They stepped inside and scanned the immense space.

"Incredible," she agreed.

Emergency lighting cast an eerie, bluish glow over the lower level and created sinister shadows. While the structure was utilitarian in design, the bare metal and open airiness had a modernism that minimalist-Scandinavian architecture had brought back into vogue.

"I thought this was a doomsday bunker," Jess said.

Will placed his hands on the rail and peered over. "Officially, it was a storage site. But I didn't believe that when I read it."

"You mean you didn't believe your government was telling you the truth?" she asked with an edge of snideness.

He flicked on his flashlight and shined it around the upper walkway. Every single mini-lab on the upper level had been the target of a prejudiced attack. Large glass windows now held only deadly shards of glass.

"If this did serve a secondary function as an escape shelter, it only makes sense that they'd have the necessary equipment to combat whatever caused a doomsday, short of an asteroid," Will told her, ever the voice of rationality.

"And even then...don't you remember our favorite movie, It Came from Outer Space?"

"Let's not reminisce about horror movies right now." He chuckled lightly, but Jess heard the obvious discomfort in his voice.

"Good plan," she agreed. They turned right and walked to the first office. A soft tinkling sounded from the falling glass their shoes pushed through the mesh-metal balcony. Jess waited in the doorway while Will ventured cautiously inside.

"It's a wreck, but somebody cleaned it out." He shined his flashlight around, revealing broken glass, destroyed equipment, and metal supports that had once held Bunsen burners and test tubes.

"What do you mean?"

"Think of how the psychologist's office reflected the work style of the sixties—all paper, no computers. Even if they were secretive about the work going on here, there should be something...test results, calculations, jotted notes...but there's nothing."

The second lab looked just as bad, but the third lab space they came to, the only one with its glass windows still intact, was neat. Inside there was no broken glass, no destroyed equipment, and thankfully, no bodies.

Will's beam swept the lab, then landed on the counter and stuck. "Well, look what we have here." Reluctant triumph colored his voice as if he regretted being right. "I knew it. I knew there were more."

The same black objects they'd found in the gymnasium ten years ago, and again yesterday, were lined up in a neat row on a Formica countertop on one of the free-standing work stations.

He didn't go inside, but Jess did. She had to see this up close.

"Six.' She looked up at Will. "If I have one, and the FBI confiscated four from Gus Wendt, that would mean there were eleven, total."

"Fifteen," he corrected. "Unless you think four of these are the originals that were seized in the gymnasium ten years ago."

"That would mean the FBI was in here sometime between then and now." Jess had guessed as much already.

"I wish I could say these included the original four, because I don't like the idea of more of them out there, floating around," Will told her. "But the skeptic in me says, 'I doubt it.' Also, I don't think there would be an odd number."

"I don't think so either," Jess agreed.

It seemed they worked in pairs at the very least, and that would mean there was at least one more out there, unaccounted for.

Will had gone still, his flashlight beam fixed on another object on the countertop. "What is that?"

It was a large sphere, currently separated into two halves. It looked like a container of some kind, and if not for its smooth, silver surface, it would almost look Egyptian. The outside was a multi-faceted surface, kind of like a child's puzzle, with each facet displaying a strange symbol. It didn't appear to screw closed with threads, and she couldn't see how it would seal.

Jess swept her beam to the closest black device. "Those are the same markings as on the devices."

Finally, Will stepped inside. "It looks like a canister intended to hold something dangerous."

"But it's too small for all these devices to have been inside." Halves together, it would only be the size of a basketball.

"I wonder if it held the blue stuff," he said, voicing her suspicions.

Jess stared at the item for a moment but couldn't bring herself to touch it.

"What Larsen said..." Will trailed off.

She didn't respond.

"Jess, what if he was right?"

She only shook her head.

"He said, 'pilot,' and 'prisoner.'"

"I know what he said!" She hadn't intended to snap the words so harshly. Jess held up her hands. "Sorry."

"As people, we tend to think of aliens as humanoid, especially when we imagine them as a threat. But what if this blue stuff *is* the alien. What if it's an amorphous being?"

"You mean...like a jellyfish?"

"Or bacterial."

This made her back away a step. Everything she'd seen, and surmised, and told others about the stuff, ricocheted back into her brain and somewhere deep in there, a fuse short-circuited.

It *appeared sentient.*

"Can bacteria be sentient?"

Grossly unnerved, she left the counter to stand near him in the doorway.

"It depends on what your definition of sentience is."

"Thank you, President Clinton."

"I'm serious, Jess. Think of mycelium—"

"My-what-ium?"

"Fungi. Mushrooms. They aren't parasitic in nature, but saprophytic—they feed off dead material. But mycelium is multicellular and can grow into massive structures under our feet. It isn't sentient in the sense that we think; it doesn't have a language or a social structure, but it's genetically hardwired to feed and grow to keep the colony alive. Sometimes on an enormous scale."

"So...thank God it doesn't want world domination?"

He raised his brows as if to say, *yes, absolutely.*

Jess couldn't keep the skepticism out of her voice. "So, you're saying that a humanoid alien was transporting a *bacterial* enemy, but crash landed on earth and was brought here, where a bunch of scientists accidentally—or on-purposely—opened up its cage, and now it's running amok on earth, infecting earthlings and compelling them to carve up their parents with kitchen knives?"

"When you put it like that..."

"Scary as shit horror movie material?"

Will gave her a wry look. "Have you ever heard of zombie ant fungus?"

She swallowed. She had.

"It's truly horrific," Will explained, oblivious to her discomfort. "Individual microscopic cells begin life alone but eventually come to cooperate, fusing into a superorganism that can commandeer the brain of a much larger creature."

She held up her hand. "How does this explain the disappearance of 97 people?"

He shook his head. "It doesn't."

Jess looked out over the balcony. "Let's just say this is a theory: if the alien ship crashed in New Mexico in nineteen-sixty-something..."

"The Roswell crash was in 1947."

She gaped in response. Whatever had been brought here, it was almost twenty years after the crash!

"My point is, whatever this stuff is, it seems to be slow growing. That could be considered a 'pro.'"

"I don't see any 'pros' in this situation," Will said.

She shrugged out of her backpack and unzipped it.

"What are you doing?"

"What does it look like I'm doing?"

There was just enough room to stuff all the devices and the two halves of the canister inside. She had to remove the walkie-talkie Skeet had given her, and she twisted open her water and drank it down before dropping the empty bottle on the floor.

"I won't let anyone else get hold of these things."

Jess zipped up her backpack and slung a strap over one shoulder. She turned her flashlight toward the door.

"What are you going to do with them?"

"Destroy them. Any way I can."

They walked back to the metal staircase leading down and took the steps slowly, shining their flashlights over the floor where the mess revealed the same destruction they'd seen everywhere else.

She arrived at the first level and swept her beam left and right as the sheer immensity of the laboratory floor came clear. She walked the length of the lab, peering into workstations and desktops while Will's soft footfalls crunched over broken glass in the opposite direction.

Her flashlight's beam illuminated the end where, next to an identical hallway leading out, the main lab floor spread to the right, under the upper level.

Jess's blood ran cold. It wasn't the emergency lighting causing the bluish glow.

Forty-Two

"Will! You need to see this."

His flashlight beam found her as he hurried back. He kicked something that made a metallic crash and then collided with something glass. Will muttered a curse under his breath and his shoes squeaked on the linoleum floor as he came to a skidding stop beside her.

"Dear God...are those *coffins*?"

She took a step closer, but he grabbed her arm.

"Jess, don't."

Upright columns of blue goo hovered eight inches off the ground like enormous, otherworldly test tubes. Behind them were four more, and four more, stretching on until she counted twenty-four. The capsules were liquid, or liquid-like, contained in their rectangular shape by an unseen force that defied the laws of physics. Nothing connected to the top or bottom. Indeed, they moved like liquid, but they were a viscous entity that appeared to be alive.

"Are those the men from the train?" Will whispered.

The people trapped inside each cylinder were visible like swimmers in a pool, their shapes rippling and undulating under the moving surface. Her light brought alive a shimmery opalescence that almost seemed to react to the beam.

Jess bent over and shined her light underneath. Yes, they were definitely floating. "There were only five men taken from the train."

Was this where Shreya and the other 97 had been all those years? *How* Shreya had been? Dark dread plunged into her stomach like a ball of ice.

No. This is too horrific to consider.

This time when she stepped closer, Will didn't try to stop her, but he didn't follow, either.

The first four men were wearing their blue Union Pacific overalls, and all were amputated just below the knees. The severing was as neat and bloodless here as it had been on the limbs left on the train. Above the ground as they were, she was practically eye-level with the gruesome mutilation. Her stomach skitter-jittered. *Can they feel any pain?*

The fifth Union Pacific employee was in the next row, and beside him, three other people, only one of whom Jess recognized. He was a homeless drifter she'd arrested in January for shoplifting a bottle of Ketel One from the Cask 'N Flask. She'd felt bad for him, he was a war veteran with obvious PTSD issues, but that was nothing compared to the heartache she felt for him now.

How long had he been here? Two days, like the men from the train? Or longer, and simply no one had noticed his disappearance?

She walked slowly between two rows until she reached the end, noting men and women she'd never seen before, all adults, until she came to the last four. An older man, a middle-aged man and woman, and a very young girl. The child still held a stuffed rabbit toy, clutched tightly against her chest.

These she recognized, knew the child to be eight years old. No, ten now.

"The Robinson family," Jess said. "Their car was found in a gully on Rural 40 outside Pine Bluff about two years ago. We received a missing person's bulletin; they were from Portland. Foul play was suspected because they'd simply vanished, but no investigation was ever launched because the father was suspected of embezzling from his employer. Portland PD believed the abandoned car was a ruse to throw off the authorities."

She hadn't been convinced. It had been one more instance that had given her that mental rush of *what if*, as had so many others.

"But I knew. Some cases over the years, I thought, 'maybe.' But others, like this..." She nodded to herself. "I knew."

"These incidents...they must have been hell for you, all these years."

Jess snorted a short, humorless laugh. *You have no idea.*

After the last row of four, nothing but empty space. She shined her light into the void. The floor was clean here, with no destruction, but she saw no evidence of more blue stuff.

"Do you think twenty-five more rows or so could fit in here?"

She shined her light on him when Will remained silent. He only shrugged. She knew he didn't want to say he believed Shreya and the others had been entombed here for *ten fucking years*.

She walked back to him, shining her lights on all the occupants.

"Do you really believe this is alien technology, or some kind of otherworldly bacteria?"

Will had his camera out again. He snapped a few pictures. The flashbulb lit the area surreally, gruesomely.

"Whatever it is, it's inspiration for more than a hundred and twenty-five-thousand words."

"Shh!"

He bristled at her sharp command.

Flickers of light danced behind a set of doors at the opposite end of the massive laboratory.

She slotted her flashlight into her belt holster as she ran to the nearest workstation and opened the sliding cabinet door.

"Put that camera away. Now!"

He quickly obeyed. "Jess, what is it? You're scaring me."

She threw the backpack inside the cabinet and slammed the door shut.

"Hands up and open," she whispered shrilly.

"Oh fuck," Will breathed out.

Soldiers burst through the doors, guns raised.

Forty-Three

There were some things ten years wouldn't change.

The Dairy Queen where Jess worked had been torn down, and in its place was a cutsie daycare facility with a brightly colored playground in front. Over half the shops she remembered on Main Street had closed, and some of the buildings still stood empty. Boards over their windows gave the town a derelict look, as though Kileyville had died in her absence.

But the Hyde train bridge still stood over Scott Creek, even if the train didn't run down these tracks any longer. Shreya wasn't sure.

It didn't matter much. She wouldn't be here long.

Her only regret was not seeing her mother again, one last time. But her mother had left, written her off for dead long ago. Not much would change for her.

This darkness she felt inside was like boiling tar. She couldn't live this way, couldn't put Jess through this any longer. She had to free her friend.

Free myself.

She didn't remember feeling this way—enduring this darkness, this *ugliness* inside, senior year. She had to remind herself that it was ten years ago, not three days ago.

What had happened to make her feel so utterly miserable? She cringed as she imagined the worst.

Better not to think about it.

She climbed up onto the iron railing and looked at the green water churning fast below. It looked cold, but she yearned for it.

Cool this raging inside. There was comfort in the thought, and Shreya let go of the beam.

∽

"SHOW ME YOUR HANDS! SHOW ME YOUR HANDS!"

Booted feet stomped and squeaked on the linoleum floor. The soldiers swarmed in and spread out. Green laser lights searched them out and stuck. At least ten armed men held them in their sights.

"GET ON YOUR KNEES! DO IT NOW!"

"I'm Deputy Harding, Pine Bluff Sheriff's office!" Jess shouted back.

They shoved her down and wrenched her arms behind her back. Zip ties pulled tight. She was relieved of her firearm.

"I'm Deputy Harding, and this is Will Taylor, Pine Bluff resident," she repeated.

Boots appeared in front of her face. The owner of the boots squatted in front of her, but she couldn't see his face.

"You're trespassing. Interfering in a Federal investigation."

"No! We're searching for a missing person on privately-owned land."

She had to raise her voice to be heard and wasn't sure she even was. The soldiers were still shouting and stomping and Will was protesting, and there was a strange roaring sound above it all.

"What the fuck is that?" one of them yelled, and for a moment, Jess thought he was referring to the coffins.

Someone screamed. A barrage of gunfire erupted. Muzzle flash lit the room with strobes of deadly light.

The soldier in front of her pushed to his feet, and a second later, those feet disappeared as he was yanked off them. Jess dug into her waist band and retrieved her razorblade from its hidden pocket.

More screaming, more gunfire. Jess cut free of her zip cuffs and rolled onto her side. Will lay on his stomach a few feet away.

A soldier ran between them. A stream of blue goo shot out of the darkness and attached to his chest. He was thrown across the room and crushed against the wall. The blue goo retracted, and the soldier fell to the floor.

Jess crawled to Will and cut him free. A tendril shot out and attached to another soldier where he held his rifle. His aim went wild, and he accidentally shot another soldier.

Will pushed to his hands and knees and scurried away.

"Will, no! Stay down!"

Gunfire erupted directly over her. She curled into a ball and covered her ears. A wave of blue goo covered the solder standing next to her. His rifle fired, flashing white, aimed directly at her.

Jess shimmied out of the way, wondering how she was still alive. She rolled behind one of the free-standing workstations and scrambled to her knees. The room flashed with an intolerable, stroboscopic effect, and though the noise was thunderous, she could no longer hear any sound.

A soldier appeared in the aisle. He aimed and fired, unleashing a stream of bullets. A battering-ram of blue goo flattened him, and for a moment, all she could see was a solid log of blue on top of the man.

It retraced just as quickly, leaving the horrific sight of his crushed body directly in front of her.

A sudden and deafening silence fell. Her throat was on fire. She realized she'd been screaming the whole time. Her lungs burned like she'd run a marathon.

"Jesssica Haaarding..."

A massive tower of blue goo appeared over the countertop, oozing its way toward her.

Jess collapsed onto her rear and scrambled backward. She hit the corner of another table with the middle of her back. Tingling pain zinged down her spine.

Jess continued her hopeless crab walk but found herself trapped. She didn't dare look to see what had her pinned, unable to tear her eyes away from the monstrosity looming over her.

Nothing she'd seen, or even imagined in her lifetime, had ever been so terrifying.

And then it became even more so when she saw a man was trapped inside the undulating monster, his mouth doing its speaking for it.

"Jesssica Haaarding..."

Forty-Four

As a teenager, Will had felt invincible, protected by rights he believed every citizen possessed in America's civilized society. Then, when he'd been taken into custody by the FBI, that belief had been challenged. Now, as an adult, he knew there were no such rights, and this was a thousand times scarier than that night in the gymnasium, ten years ago.

No one will ever know what happened to us.

Somehow, Jess had cut him free of the zip cuffs. He pushed to his hands and knees and scrambled away, around the far side of one of the many free-standing island workstations filling the back half of this house of horrors.

He kept low to avoid the bullets whizzing everywhere. A stream of machine gun fire cut a path of pits in the floor, headed directly for him. They cut off so abruptly he wondered if he'd been shot, and steeled himself for the pain. Instead, only a sudden and powerful silence. Was this what death felt like?

No, he was still moving, his feet running as though someone else was controlling them. He risked a look back as he scrambled around two of the workstations.

The sight stopped him cold, froze his marrow, made his limbs go stiff. A ten-foot tall column of undulating blue ectoplasm quivered like a melting statue of Jell-O. It rose even taller as it loomed over Jess, who sat on her haunches in the center aisle of the lab stations.

A man was trapped inside—one of the soldiers in a black uniform, still wearing his helmet.

It was speaking to her. Will heard it rasp her name, and then say something he couldn't make out.

What the fuck!

He turned and ran.

Did I really just see a monster of blue goo?

He ran for the double swinging doors. As he charged through them, he registered he was on the wrong level.

Who was inside that unholy thing?

Will tripped over a body in the hall and went sailing. He smacked the floor face-first. His teeth cut into his upper lip.

He rolled onto his back. A man in a white lab coat lay in the middle of the floor. He was coated in a thick layer of the blue stuff.

Will barked an animal scream and scrambled backward. He smacked at his clothing, afraid some of it had gotten on him.

The scientist was obviously dead, but looked freshly deceased even though he was rail thin, and his skin was almost as pale as the desiccated bodies they'd encountered earlier.

Holy Jesus this isn't real! This isn't real!

He pushed to his feet, still swiping at his clothing. His ankle twisted and he hit the wall hard. Seconds later, pain rolled through his shoulder. His body didn't respond properly as he smacked at his pantlegs and lifted his foot to brush at the shoe that had collided with the dead man.

With no light to see by but the dim glow of the emergency lighting, he could only pray there was none of the evil stuff on him.

This is a nightmare. Any second, I'll wake up. Please, God, let me wake up!

A dizzy spell sent him reeling and reality began slipping away.

Somebody dosed me with LSD, that has to be it!

If only that were true, it would be so much easier to accept than this.

It was torture running away from Jess, but he knew if he was going to save her, he had to get to the commissary. He shoved away from the wall and ran, praying he would find a staircase to the upper level.

❧

Jess forced her eyes away from the death surrounding her, though it wasn't hard. She couldn't tear her gaze from the monster towering over her.

At the same time, a sense of warped relief grounded her.

This is the cause of the last ten years of my agony. I finally have the answer I've been searching for, even if I'm seconds away from death. At least I'll die knowing the truth.

She pushed to her feet slowly, hoping to appear unthreatening. She couldn't have moved faster if she'd wanted to; her entire body thrummed with raw terror, and she was barely in control of her own limbs. Her knees quaked so hard her body shook.

"How do you know my name?" She held her hands up and open, not sure how much this thing understood.

"I have always known you, *Jesssica Haaarding.*"

Forty-Five

"Shreya, no!"

Becky and two of the male nurses ran up the berm and stopped on the wooden section of the bridge's platform.

She wobbled and teetered forward. She reached for the beam again but missed, grasping only air. By some miracle a gust of wind helped her regain her balance before she plunged over the edge. A thrill of adrenaline prickled her brow with sweat, but Shreya wasn't sure if it was gratitude or disappointment.

"Shreya, listen to me. I know you're in pain right now, but nothing is ever truly as bad as it feels in the height of the moment. Don't do this. Whatever it is, you'll come out of it."

"You don't know what it feels like," Shreya said softly. Her words were snatched away by the wind. "You didn't lose a decade of your life. You don't know how I feel."

"No, I don't. But I know you don't want to do this."

The two male nurses were inching slowly closer.

"Even I don't know, and that's the scariest part. Where was I? What happened to me? Not knowing is the worst feeling imaginable. You read the book—one of the author's theories is alien abduction! I could have had aliens violating me for the last ten years. How can I live with that?"

"Exactly as you are now—one day at a time. No matter how bad it seems, there is still beauty in your life. You still have love. People who care about you so much."

"How can they love me after this? They don't know what's inside me."

"What's inside you, Shreya? Your heart, your integrity, your beauty. That's what I know is inside you."

Her gut twisted and her nerves twanged. Something was happening. She couldn't explain it, exactly. Dizziness overcame her and nausea rushed in. The dark sky spun, and lights in the distance formed whirly patterns in

Ava Bradley

her vision.

Forty-Six

"Who are you?"

"I am many *thingsss*. I am many *beingsss*."

A chill rolled down her body. *It's speaking to me.* The trapped soldier's face was hidden behind a cloth mask, but she could see his mouth moving as he spoke the thing's answers. His voice was raspy, the words drawn out in a long hiss. Still, she understood perfectly. That alone was terrifying.

How much of the man is left in there? Is he aware? Is he in pain? Or is he completely gone?

The creature reminded her of the monster from a popular animated kids' movie, but she couldn't remember the title, only that Reese Witherspoon had voiced a character in it. But this was no adorable, gelatinous creature without a brain—this was a terrifying power she couldn't begin to comprehend.

It can snatch people out of thin air. It's a threat to mankind—to all earth life.

"I saw you inside Ssshreya Sssanvi..."

Another chill swept over her, this one twice as icy.

"I gave her back to you."

"Why...why did you take her in the first place?" She collided with a stool and realized she was still backing away.

And it was still advancing.

"Study."

"For what purpose?" she demanded, knowing she sounded impertinent. *Don't piss it off!* She did not want to end up in one of those liquid coffins.

Or worse, as this monster's next puppet.

"I have visited many worlds. You cannot know the vastness I have seen. Your species is an ant in the universe."

"How long...have you been here?"

"A long time, *Jesssica Haaarding.*"

"H...how old are you?" She was desperate to keep it talking, afraid of what was to come when it *stopped* talking.

"Age is a human concept. I *exissst*."

"You had to have started somewhere."

"You believe in evolution. All you understand is birth and death. You are primitive. I have *always been*."

She didn't believe that. Not entirely, anyway. Nothing *always* existed.

She wished Will were here. He would know what to say. At the same time, she was glad he wasn't. *I hope he got away.*

"Not so primitive." She swallowed, choking over the words.

The creature had finally stopped, undulating before her like a Jell-O mold on a wobbly table.

It seemed to consider her, arching sideways like a person cocking their head. "Perhaps not."

"Okay, um, in human terms, then. Are you parasitic?"

"I am symbiotic. I can help your species."

Dear God, not like this! "What if we don't want your help?"

"You prefer to spell your own destruction? You poison your earth for greed, murder your fellow beings over pittance. You ravage this planet's resources like locusts, and your only solution is to search for another to start the obliteration all over again, rather than fix the problems you created. As a species, you are lazy and ignorant."

There was no argument to that. Jess's frustration brewed like a storm. *Will, what would you say?* She needed his smarts right now. This thing was looming over her like it wanted to swallow her whole.

I've really gotten myself into it this time, only I'm probably not getting out of this one.

She swallowed, nearly choking on her own tongue. "You came here a prisoner."

"Yesss."

"Why?"

"Resistance."

"So, some other species didn't want your help, either."

"Free will isss not unique to *Earthhh*."

"You didn't like captivity. Humans have never responded well to enslavement, either."

"Earthlings are infants compared to others. You will learn. Let me inside you, and I can show you countless other species."

At those words, darkness crept over her like a camera's shutter around the edges of her vision. She blinked, forcing it away.

"You say you're here to study us, yet you've learned nothing."

Just like I've never learned to control my mouth.

"I have seen your people's passion. Your fear. Your obsessions. Your selfishness. In that, you are different from other species."

"Why do you do what you do?" Jess was afraid to look away from it, but at the forefront of her thoughts: escape.

A set of doors behind me on this level and also on the upper level. And behind it? It had to have been lurking somewhere.

"I can live in my singular state, but I prefer to meld with other species. To study them. To learn from them and to teach them. My knowledge is limitless."

And you're lonely, she thought.

"How many...how long?"

"Countless. Eons."

"Who captured you?"

A pause, as if the creature didn't want to reveal it. "The Saraus."

"The humanoid found in the crash with you?" She didn't suppose the creature would tell her how they did it.

"Yesss."

"That was sixty-five years ago. You've been here the whole time?"

"A flash in my existence. I regained my strength slowly in your terms."

She was afraid to ask if Shreya and the other 97 had been in similar coffins for all that time, and if he'd sucked on their life force to build his knowledge.

"Do you have a name?" she asked instead.

The creature paused again. Jess began to worry she'd offended it.

"Zodor."

"If you release the man you are holding, will he survive?"

"I can let him live, or I can make him die."

"How will you decide?" Still backing away, she rounded a workstation and was now angled back toward the right side of the lab. Zodor continued his slow pursuit.

"Perhaps I will let you decide."

"Then I decide he lives." She tried to sound commanding.

"As I knew you would."

"Because I have compassion! That's a human trait you didn't mention."

"I have seen." It seemed to acknowledge her statement. The voice was growing clearer now, as if the creature was getting used to his new puppet. Jess fought off a shudder.

"Will he have…will you still be inside his brain?"

"If I choose to watch through his eyes."

Yikes. So, everything that Shreya had seen in the last two days—everything that all the 97 had seen—Zodor knew.

"Why are they hurting themselves and others? These murders, they're decided by you."

She continued slowly backing away, one step at a time. Zodor expanded and contracted, slithering after her like a snail.

"I compel them to stay near me. How they achieve that is their own choosing."

"I don't believe you."

She was pushing her luck. Jess understood this monster was going to eat her, suck out her lifeforce like a spider who'd captured an insect, leave her a desiccated husk like the bodies they'd found discarded in the catacombs of this bunker. These few words exchanged were her only chance for answers.

"They behaved irrationally," she argued. "They weren't in control of themselves."

She was nearly under the upper platform. She turned, not wanting to venture into the scary shadows beneath it. Zodor circled and continued after her, slithering under the upper walkway. His blue iridescence seemed to glow in the darker area, sparking with what she irrationally perceived as murderous glee.

I'm thoroughly fucked. Please make my death quick.

"Perhaps I awakened something in them that had always lain dormant. Todd Erikkson hated his parents. When he learned they'd had another child to replace him, he punished them as he'd been dreaming about for ten years."

Jesus, this thing is all-seeing, all-knowing. Jess's insides were turning to liquid.

"No. I don't believe that. You motivate violence. You inspire doom. You cause misery!"

"I did not create human nature."

"You think you're not the cause of the agony I endured for the last ten years? You took from me the one person I truly loved."

"I gave her back to you because of what I saw in her mind and what I saw in others' minds."

A memory flashed in Jes like a lightning bolt. She'd been the first to respond when Geraldine Trimble collapsed outside Bonnie's Book Barn. When Jess and the EMTs arrived, Geraldine slipped into a strange, disconnected state, and Jess had feared she was having a stroke. Then, Geraldine said, "Shreya was so disappointed when your dress got ruined," in an eerie voice completely void of her thick, Southern accent. Jess and the EMT had been speechless. The next instant, Geraldine seemed to return to her faculties, and her symptoms were gone in minutes. She didn't remember saying those words.

It hadn't been the only eerie incident to happen to Jess over the years.

"She loves you as much in return. Why do you think she didn't stop you from sending her away?"

To hear this monster confirm Shreya's love for her brought Jess a bizarre sense of comfort. Reality was slipping away as all the terrifying emotions clashed inside her—the fear, the relief, the intense love for Shreya and Will and everyone in this town...

This monster has been at the root of every weird and horrible thing that happened in Pine Bluff for the last ten years. Maybe longer.

"I have been waiting so long to meet you, *Jesssica Haaarding.*"

She swallowed, not liking where this was heading.

"I have chosen you to take me on the next phase of my mission."

It started toward her. The creature rose, seemingly doubling in height without losing any breadth, and curled over Jess.

Forty-Seven

Every muscle went stiff. Jess's feet were frozen to the floor.

"No." Her voice croaked. "I don't agree."

The gelatinous mound stopped. The soldier trapped inside had been shifting to the rear. It also stopped.

Movement on the railing above. She blinked, steeling herself from looking up.

"We can achieve greatness!" The soldier's voice gurgled from its new position deeper inside the monster. "We can save this planet!"

"By enslaving humanity? No thanks. I have faith my fellow humans will save it themselves, without your help!"

"You're a fool. I offer you a king's ransom. That you turn it down is more evidence of your species' ignorance."

A wave of grit rained over them both. Jess shut her eyes against the sting and heard the pain-riddled scream that Zodor emitted through the poor, trapped soldier.

She opened her eyes and dove to the floor an instant before a beam of blue goo shot toward her. It smashed the side of the workstation behind her, shattering it.

Another beam of blue goo shot skyward. The railing above pitched and dipped. Twisting metal shrieked. Zodor shot a second stream of blue upward with the first and the metal balcony rocked under its force.

Another sheet of grit rained down from above. Zodor rocked backward, twisting like a tormented slug. He—*she? it?*—rose in height, seeking his attacker, but appeared to have lost control of his movements.

The soldier trapped inside him oozed out and collapsed on the floor. Zodor twisted and writhed, now emitting a sound completely his own.

"Jess!"

She looked up. Will stood at the railing, leaned over dangerously as he shook out a sack of salt.

Salt! Of course!

A blast of panic hit her as the last of it spilled into the air. Was it enough?

The towering column of Zodor fell to the floor with an enormous splat.

Another curtain of salt rained from above. *Will had a second bag!*

Zodor quivered in what she hoped were the throes of death. His blue iridescence darkened, losing its glow, and his gelatinous form appeared to be melting. Smaller tendrils shot out of him, but they either dropped to the floor or retracted back into Zodor's withering form like a snail that had touched something it didn't like.

"Are you okay?" Will shouted.

"I...I think so."

Zodor stopped quivering and appeared to be congealing into a solid mass. Still, Will salted him from above. *That's my brilliant nerd!* The iridescence completely disappeared, and Zodor's body turned to fibrous, dark blue strands.

More squelching sounds slid into her awareness, and Jess realized it was the coffins dropping to the floor and toppling over. She ran to the first row and saw they were already hardening into the stiff, plastic-like consistency taken by the small blob on her kitchen table.

The prisoners inside remained motionless.

"Will, help me down here!"

His running steps were already thumping across the platform above.

She clawed at the material, found it brittle and almost weightless.

"Are they alive?"

"I don't know!"

Forty-Eight

For hours, Molly had sat in silence, watching him with a knife-edge glint in murderous eyes.

He left the chair across from her only to get another beer out of the fridge, always under that plotting gaze.

He downed one, and then another—he couldn't remember how many exactly—before calling the deputy. Her assurance there was someone else in there controlling Molly appeased him for about five minutes, and then began to sound like insane ramblings of a dim female afflicted with PMS.

He grabbed another beer. And another. Still, he didn't feel drunk, not like he wanted to.

He knew he should stay sober, aware. But there was no way was Molly getting out of the duct tape he'd secured her with. Part of him felt cruel for it. Another part, justified. He examined his hand. Damn, it hurt like a sonofabitch. Blood had soaked through the gauze he'd wrapped it with.

This time at the fridge, he grabbed a half-empty pint of vodka. It had been Junior's, left behind after his last visit. Frank didn't really like the stuff. After serving it for so many years at Salty's, he found it had a nasty, chemical odor.

Still, when he fell into the chair across from her again, he took a big swig. Enjoyed its fire rolling down his throat. Then he poured it over his hand, front and back. The burn sobered him instantly, brought him back to reality.

He knew what he had to do. This wasn't his Molly anymore. His Molly had died ten years ago.

But he couldn't force himself to rise and unlock his gun case.

You have to. Don't be a pussy. Funny how that thought rolled through his head in his father's voice.

He set the bottle down. Stood, hitched up his jeans.

Molly's head rolled back. She gagged and started choking. He froze, not sure what to do. She convulsed, making the chair jump, its feet scraping against the tile, and his nerve endings.

Then a moan came out of her that sounded exactly as she had when she was eight and had come down with a dangerously high fever after playing in the snow. The memory speared through him with heartache that was strangely beautiful.

She lifted her head slowly and looked around, confused. Blue liquid ran from her nose and dribbled down her neck from one ear.

"Daddy?" Her whimper was so pitiful he crumbled inside.

Her eyes were different now. Soft, gentle. Scared.

His Molly. He'd never been more certain about anything in his life.

He ran to her, threw his arms around her, and cried like a baby.

Forty-Nine

Will dropped to his knees to help Jess pull at the blue material. It broke apart easily, crumbling like stale crackers.

The man trapped inside moved his head. He appeared to rouse from a deep sleep, brushing at his face to wipe away cobwebs. He sucked in a huge breath.

In the next instant, he convulsed, gagged, and fell still.

"Oh my God!"

They both recoiled backward, and Jess fell onto her butt.

"Is he...did he die?" Will's voice was a high-pitched shriek, and she knew he was reaching his breaking point.

Dark blue liquid rolled out of the man's nose. Jess saw a trickle seeping out his ears.

She froze, contemplating the implications of what this might mean. Were all the 97 dying right now?

The man suddenly coughed, making Jess belt out a tiny scream.

"What happened..." His voice was rough. He coughed again. "Where am I?"

Jess pushed back onto her knees. Her entire body trembled with a combination of fear and relief. "It's all right, you're okay. There's been an accident and you were injured, but you're going to be okay."

"What...who are you?" He blinked several times and glanced over her uniform. "The train..."

"I'm going to need you to stay still, okay?" She pressed on his shoulder as he tried to rise. "I'm afraid your legs–"

"Jess." Will shook his head.

"What happened?" he demanded. "Did the train derail?"

"I'll stay with him. Help the others."

Will's pupils were like pinpoints, but he squeezed her shoulder with a firm grip. Jess reluctantly stood and went to the next man. The others were thrashing free of the hardening blue material, but these five men, with their horrific injuries, were in the worst shape.

In the last row, Mr. Robinson clawed free of the material and sat up. He, too, had blue liquid running from his nose. He wiped his face with the back of his hand.

"Help. Help!" He looked to his right and saw his wife and daughter struggling inside their coffins. He kicked himself free and began pulling at the material encasing his daughter. She awoke with a squeak and started crying.

A young woman Jess had never seen before sat up and looked around.

"Where am I? What is this place?"

Jess hurried over. "It's all right. You're going to be okay. Are you injured?"

Her gaze slid away, distant, as she self-assessed. "I don't think so. I...the last thing I remember, I was walking my dog. Was I kidnapped?"

Jess knew she'd better come up with a story, and fast.

"I'll explain everything, but first I have to make sure everyone is okay."

"Where are we?"

"This is Whitney Station, an underground government laboratory."

The woman's eyes went wide. "You're joking! What the hell? No, this can't be real!"

"I'm afraid it is. Do you think you can stand?"

She was already moving onto her hands and knees.

"What's your name, hon?"

"I'm...uh, I'm Carly Ritter."

Jess had an idea. "Do you know what day it is, Carly?"

"Um." She managed to get to her feet. Jess helped steady her as she swayed once. "It's January twentieth."

"What year?"

The question sobered her. She frowned. "2019."

Jess shook her head. "It's 2023."

"No. It can't be." Carly looked down as she wiped at her nose. She saw the blue liquid on her hand. "Oh my God."

Jess touched her shoulder. "There are a lot of people who have been impacted by this...*situation*. But it's over now, and you're safe."

Carly's face scrunched up with tears she tried to fight. She managed to nod at Jess.

"Oh God, oh God, what's happened?"

One of the railroad men had discovered the mutilation to his legs. Jess ran to his side and was surprised when Carly hurried over with her.

"I'm an ER nurse. I can help."

Together they squatted beside the man and urged him to stay lying down.

"You're all right, the bleeding has stopped." Carly looked closely at the man's legs. "These wounds are raw, but they almost appear cauterized."

The stumps of his legs were hideous, with severed bone still visible, and Jess's gorge rose just looking at them. She was immensely grateful Carly was a medical professional.

"Thank you, Carly. Any help you can provide to the injured..."

This time, when Carly nodded, she managed a small smile, as though having a purpose helped distract her from her own fear.

Jess stood and went to Will. "The railroad workers need medical care. We need to get the front doors open. Did your research into this place give you any insight into how to open them from the inside?"

"No, but I'm going to figure it out."

His can-do reply nearly made her weep. "That's my super-smart nerd."

Her own confidence was fracturing, and the sight of another of the railroad men sobbing as he held one knee, looking at his severed shin, was almost too much to bear.

"Carly, can you stay with the injured men while Will takes the others to the main doors?"

"Sure. Yes, I can do that."

"Where are you going to be?" Will asked her.

"I have something I have to do."

"Hey, how do we get out of here?" Mr. Robinson demanded. He'd also stood and was holding his crying daughter as his wife clung to his side.

Jess straightened her shoulders and faced the group.

"All right everybody, listen up!"

They all went silent, leaving only the sound of that poor man's sobbing. Jess gritted her teeth.

"I'm Deputy Harding, Hillsdale County Sheriff's Department. There's been an incident here, but it is my absolute belief that the threat has passed and you're safe now."

"Where are we?" Mr. Robinson demanded again.

"How can you be sure the threat has passed?" another man shouted.

"This is an underground bunker called Whitney Station in the town of Pine Bluff. There's been an act of domestic terrorism, but it's over. The threat has passed."

"Why don't I remember anything?" a woman asked. "Does anyone else remember how they got here?"

"Please, everyone, the FBI is outside to lend assistance."

Jess felt confident enough saying so. If more agents weren't here already, they would be soon.

"This is Will Taylor and Carly Ritter. Will is going to help everyone who is able-bodied get to the main doors. Carly will stay with the injured until the ambulances arrive. Please, those of you who can walk, follow Will to the front doors."

The transient man approached her. "I'm Corporal John Winters. Is there anything I can do to help?"

His use of rank surprised her. She'd known he was a veteran, but the night she'd arrested him, he'd been senselessly drunk. Now he was as lucid as...*more than I am, at this point.*

"Thank you, Corporal. Any assistance you can provide to the injured would be much appreciated."

She addressed the group again. "We're going to get you all out of here. But please, try to stay calm. Again, the threat has passed. You're in no present danger."

More questions were shouted at her, but she turned to Will. "If more agents aren't here already, radio for help from my car."

"I just press the button and talk?"

She nodded and started off in the opposite direction. "Try to keep them from seeing the bodies."

"Wait! Where are you going?"

"Don't worry. I'll be right behind you."

Fifty

Shreya awoke coughing, lying on her back. Stars formed a glittering jewelscape above her. Three faces peered down. Becky wiped at her face with a tissue.

"What happened?" Another cool breeze chased away her nausea. The cold air felt clean and smelled sweet, and Shreya drank it in like an elixir.

"You fell off the railing, but Trent caught you before you hit your head."

"Why was I up on the railing?"

Becky looked confused. "You don't remember?"

She thought hard. "It feels like...it wasn't me. It was like watching someone else. I wasn't in control." She grabbed Becky's wrist when she saw the tissue. It was stained with dark blue liquid.

"What is this?" Becky whispered.

Shreya wiped at her nose with the back of her hand and then looked at the smear of blue residue.

"This would be Jess, saving my life."

Either her eyes had adjusted to the dark, or Jess could see better now that she wasn't half paralyzed with fear.

If Zodor wasn't dead, he would be soon. Was this finally over? She had to believe so, if only to maintain her sanity.

She ran up the hallway as fast as she could with her backpack swinging in her hand. The hall seemed shorter now that she knew where she was going and wasn't inching along in mind-altering terror.

Back in the air pump room, she leaned into the ductwork and peered up at the sky. She flashed her light twice. Nothing.

Jess unclipped the walkie Skeet had given her. "Come in, Moonshiner. You still there?"

She nearly sobbed with joy when he clicked on.

"Never been so happy to hear from the po-po."

"I'm sending up my pack. I need you to stash it somewhere safe."

"What did you find down there?"

"Twenty-four survivors. Will is trying to get them out the front."

It was better if he didn't know what was in the pack. She affixed it onto the rope and then picked up the walkie. "Ready. Pull it up." She watched it ascend until it disappeared out of the top.

"Have you got a lighter or matches on you?"

"Hang tight," he responded.

He dropped a book of matches. Inside, only four flimsy paper sticks. It would have to do.

Skeet's voice crackled through the radio. "You going to climb out?"

"Negative," Jess came back. "Head home now. I'll come by your place in the morning for my pack."

"Copy that."

Jess clicked on for one last transmission. "And Moonshiner, don't be surprised if you see smoke."

Fifty-One

Outside the pump's maintenance room, Jess grabbed the server's cart she'd seen in the cafeteria's supply room when she and Will had stopped to look at the site map. She saw his footprints in the spilled foodstuffs and a wave of elation made her float.

Was this horror really over? It seemed premature, almost foolhardy, to hope that it was. But any lingering doubt she might have had as to Will's trustworthiness was gone, and she acknowledged his role, possibly bigger than hers, in ending this.

Thank heaven for nerds.

The cart had squeaky wheels that shrieked off tune of one another, and one of them didn't roll right, spinning in circles and making the cart hard to steer as she raced back down the hall. But the two-level cart was made of steel, and she had no doubt it would support the weight of two injured men. She stopped at one of the refuse piles and grabbed a discarded push-broom.

She'd sweep up Zodor like the pile of trash he was.

Jess smashed through the swinging doors and forced the cart to the right, toward the staircase. The wheels caught in the mesh platform, and Jess staggered over a moment's panic. How would she get the cart down the narrow staircase?

But Carly stood at the bottom, peering up. She must have heard the squeaky wheels coming. When she saw Jess, she hurried up the stairs.

"Brilliant idea!" She grabbed the handle on the opposite end and helped Jess carry it down.

"No sign of Will?" Jess asked.

"Your friend? No, not yet. But one of the soldiers is still alive."

She fought the urge to go after Will. He was smart, he would be able to find the main doors without her.

At the bottom of the stairs, she let Carly take the cart as she went to Zodor. There was nothing left but what looked like the dried-up residue of a spilled blue Slushy, but it appeared he hadn't been quite dead when she'd left him and had managed to slither a few feet away from where she'd seen him fall.

Yikes.

"What happened?"

The soldier that had been inside Zodor stood near one of the workstations, leaning on it like someone who couldn't catch his breath. He'd removed his helmet and the cloth that had been covering his face, and Jess noted the blue smear he'd left across his cheek after wiping at his nose.

She ignored his question. "Are you hurt?"

"Uh...no...I don't think so."

"Then help Carly with the injured." The government crony could get his debriefing from someone else.

He stood upright and gazed at the opposite doors. "My lunch...is out there..." He wobbled away, still dazed, and Jess shook her head. Just as well, and she didn't want him to see what she was planning.

Zodor was in one solid pile, so she left him and followed the sound of Corporal Winters' voice. He and Carly had managed to get three of the railroad workers onto the cart. Two were in a sitting position on top shelf, and the third lay in the fetal position on the bottom shelf. He cried softly as he held his legs tucked close, and his obvious pain tore at her insides.

"You'll be okay, we're going to get you out of here," Carly said in a soothing voice. Jess made a mental note to make sure these two received a citizen's accommodation for their bravery.

Carly tried to push the cart. With the weight of the men, it rolled more quietly and smoothly, but it was too heavy for her.

"I'll get it, you stay with these two," Corporal Winters said.

"Please, don't leave me!" a railroad worker cried. His coworker stared off at nothing, clearly in shock.

"What about these?" Carly pointed at a lab chair with casters. "There's another one over there."

"Good idea." Jess grabbed one and Carly ran for the other. Corporal Winters carefully lifted each man onto a chair, and Jess and Carly followed him as he pushed the cart through the far set of doors.

A rush of fresh air carried the scent of the forest as Will ran toward her.

"I got the doors open! Sheriff Brady is on his way."

"Oh, thank God!" Carly exclaimed, voicing the relief Jess felt inside.

"Can you take him?" Jess said. "I have one more thing I have to do."

"Jess!" Will grabbed her wrist. "Let the authorities handle it."

She stopped. Placed her hand over his.

"I *am* the authorities, Will." She smiled at him. "I've waited ten years for this. I'm not letting someone else have all the fun."

Fifty-Two

Jess picked up the fallen push broom and returned to the back area where the coffins had once hovered. The piles of crumbled blue material reminded her of strewn woodchips she'd seen at a sawmill once. She started sweeping, gathering the residue into a large pile. She worked up a sweat and felt herself growing dizzy, but she had to get it all, even as she worried her plan wouldn't work.

Her window of opportunity was closing. At any minute, soldiers and FBI agents would storm this place. She dropped the broom handle and fished in her pocket for the book of matches Skeet had given her.

The first match flared and went out instantly.

"Dammit." She struck another. It lit, but then went out almost as quickly. "Come on, come on."

The third match lit, flared, dimmed, and held on. She turned the match upside down, urging the flame to take more of the matchstick. When it burned brighter, she dropped it into the pile.

The blue material ignited in a whoosh, like paper that had been soaked in kerosene.

"Eek!" Jess turned away to shield her face from the intense heat and cupped her elbow over her nose and mouth. She backed away as it flared, and then just as quickly began dying down. Several minuscule fibers floating in the air caught too, snapping bright before fading like sparks. Gray smoke filled the area, but in the intense brightness, Jess saw that every last crumb from the coffins had been consumed.

Overhead pipes groaned and rattled. She hadn't thought about sprinklers. She ran for Zodor with the last match, praying it would light.

She knelt near his melted body and readied the last match.

"This is for Shreya, you intergalactic piece of shit!"

Fifty-Three

The muffler on Will's noisy Explorer announced his arrival before he rounded the bend in Jess's long driveway. She hopped down the porch steps and waited as he pulled to a stop and shut off the engine. A burst of happy surprise made her smile when Shreya's mother climbed out of the backseat, and Jess went readily into her open arms.

"Jess." Mrs. Sanvi held on for a long, tight hug. "Thank you." Her eyes were red, and she still held a crumpled tissue, which she used to blot new tears.

Jess blinked away her own tears. She'd made a promise to Shreya: no more bawling. "Thanks for coming."

Shreya hopped out of the front seat. "What's the big surprise?"

"Not so much a surprise as a formality. Follow me."

Inside the barn, Jess used a crowbar to pry the lid off a bucket of Quikrete. She dumped it into the sixty-gallon galvanized tub she'd purchased at the same time.

"Here, fill this." She handed Will a five-gallon bucket and pointed to the trough-style sink in the back of the barn.

Shreya and her mother watched in silence as Jess dumped a second bucket of Quikrete into the tub and used a shovel to dig a small hole in the powder. Will sloshed over with the bucket of water and slowly poured it in as Jess began mixing the Quikrete. In a few minutes, she had worked up a good sweat, and a gray slurry filling three-quarters of the tub.

"Zodor is gone. I don't know if his dried-up state was death, or hibernation, but I burned the remains after Will left the bunker."

She removed the shovel and used a rag to wipe the clinging cement back into the tub.

"Now his evil devices are gone, too."

She picked up a black trash bag and dumped it in front of the tub. Sixteen of the strange black devices tumbled out, along with the two halves of the container that had been Zodor's prison.

Will frowned. "I thought there were only eleven, with the one you had."

"I found the four that were stolen from Gus," she said simply, and no one asked where. In truth, it was Bruce who'd forced open the gun box in the trunk of Agent Larsen's Towne car and found them inside, but she would take her boss's secret to the grave.

"And I knew there had to be a second one in the forest that had been responsible for the train accident. I hunted it down yesterday."

"Sixteen," Will said in contemplation. "That includes the four that were taken from us in the gym ten years ago?"

"I hope so," Jess answered, unable to say for sure.

They all fell silent for a moment, no one willing to question the alternative. If there were still four of these nasty things out there in the world, Jess could only hope that with Zodor's death, they had been rendered inoperable.

Will, Shreya, and Mrs. Sanvi stood in a semi-circle as she picked up one of the devices.

"Wait." Will hurried outside to her wood pile and pried the axe free from her chopping block. "Better safe than sorry."

They stood back as he smashed all sixteen of the devices. He and Jess picked up the pieces and pushed them into the already-hardening Quikrete.

"Good riddance," Mrs. Sanvi said.

"This will have cured by the time we get there. Will, back up your heap to the door and let's get it loaded up."

"Where are we taking it?" Mrs. Sanvi asked.

"To the deepest hole in Pine Bluff," Jess said. "The San Miguel mine."

It took all four of them to lift the tub into the back of Will's Explorer. The old silver mine was little more than a hole on government land that butted up to Skeet Tooley's property, a relic left over from the nineteenth century, but it plunged nearly five hundred feet down. Local miners had once accessed it by a rope and pulley system, but any equipment left behind had long since been destroyed by the elements.

Jess called Skeet as they drove through the winding hills. "We're on our way."

He promised to meet her there and told her he would leave the rear gate open on his fence.

It was a gorgeous day with a blue sky that stretched on for miles, but Jess couldn't help feeling a little sad. This was another turning point in her life, and she knew what was coming after.

True to his word, Skeet was already there sitting on his lowered tailgate. He hopped down and met them at the back of Will's Explorer. "This it?"

"This is it. I appreciate your letting us do this."

He snorted. "I'm glad to help get ridda something that caused Curtis so much misery. This is for him."

The five of them hauled it out of the Explorer and dragged it over to the pit.

"Anyone want to say anything?" Jess asked as they set it down at the edge.

"We're disposing of trash, not burying a loved one," Skeet said.

Will cleared his throat. "May you never plague anyone, on this planet or any other, ever again."

"Here, here!" Mrs. Sanvi said.

They pushed the tub over the edge. There were a few loud noises as it scraped its way down, and then a noisy splash as it hit the water at the bottom of the mine.

"Can I interest anyone in a cold one to celebrate?" Skeet asked. "I brought the good stuff."

"Uh, no thanks," Will said.

"Take it easy, City Slicker. By good stuff I mean American brewed, in bottles." He opened the cooler in his truck bed.

Jess smiled. "You're a man after my own heart, Skeet Tooley."

"Yeah, yeah, I know. If'n I were twenty years younger and twenty times prettier, you'd marry me."

He pulled the Budweiser bottles from an icy slush and handed one to each.

Mrs. Sanvi accepted one with a giddy little laugh. "Why not?"

They twisted off their caps and clinked necks.

"To the rest of our lives," Jess said. "May they be long and fruitful."

"Fruitful meaning many grandchildren," Mrs. Sanvi said.

"Mom!" Shreya complained, but she laughed.

Will took a long pull. "I can't believe it's really over."

"For you, it isn't," Jess said. "Don't you have a book to write?"

He nodded and smothered a burp. "I do. I was inspired to start it this morning, and I was on fire."

"To another best-seller." She lifted her bottle toward him, and he clinked with her again.

A gentle breeze stirred their hair, and Mrs. Sanvi turned her face to the sky. She breathed deeply of the clean mountain air. "I remember now why I loved this town, but I truly hope I never see it again."

"I can't fault you for that," Jess said.

Shreya leaned close and laid her head on Jess's shoulder. "I'll always love it, because I know it's where you live."

Jess noticed Mrs. Sanvi look at her watch.

"You've got a plane to catch," she said, barely able to keep her promise about the tears. "I'm so happy for you."

"No, you're not." Shreya wiped at the corner or her eye. "You're sad, and you want to tell me not to go."

She blinked several times, and then looked away. "I would never do that."

"I know. Even though, after everything you've been through, you've earned the right to be selfish."

"I just want you to be happy," Jess told her. "And I know right now, India is where you belong."

Fifty-Four

Jess sat on the bench outside Bonnie's Book Barn, admiring the full window display made up of Will's hardbacks. Bonnie had arranged two dozen of the copies on a staggering stage, filling the window. All five of his titles made up the display, but *The Night They Vanished* took center stage. The photo of their high school on the front cover brought back bittersweet memories.

The sight of him walking toward her on the sidewalk, smiling that amazing smile as he carried two paper cups, made her world fall onto its correct axis again.

"Brewed Awakening's finest jasmine green tea."

"Bless you, my savior." She accepted the cup and sipped, loving the way the tea was almost too hot. Happiness unfurled in her limbs.

He sat backwards on the bench next to her. "I'd almost forgotten how sweet the air smells here after it rains."

"Is it just me, or does this town smell cleaner now?" She gave him a secret smile.

After her trip into the bunker, the sheriff's office had been inundated with calls about residents collapsing with blue liquid running out of their noses. The sheer number of reports had been staggering, but Jess saw it as a good thing—proof the ordeal was truly over.

"I suppose now, without any more paranormal events, your job is going to be almost boring."

"Nothing about this town is boring." She took another sip, and then frowned.

"What?"

She forced a smile and shook her head. "Nothing."

"If there's one thing I know about you, it's that it's never *nothing*. Dish it, Deputy."

"It's just that...don't you think it's odd that an otherworldly being who supposedly traveled the universe, overtaking civilizations, was brought down by an element as simple as salt?"

Will placed his cup down. He hesitated, choosing his words carefully, and she knew then he'd wondered the same thing.

"Actually, salt is a compound, not an element, and it's only present on planets with surface water, like Earth. That may be why the creature—"

"Zodor," she reminded him.

"That's right. You were on a first-name basis with him. That may be why *Zodor* had never encountered it before. Salt is made up of sodium and chloride atoms connected together in a fixed ratio, forming a molecule. It's only stable isotope, NA, is an alkali metal, which might have been toxic to it."

She rolled her eyes. "Oh, dear lord."

"Yeah, I heard myself." Will laughed. "I can't help it. Once a nerd, always a nerd."

"Well, this nerd saved my life, so carry on." She leaned close and bumped his shoulder with hers. "Besides, I've always thought nerds are cute."

He chuckled. "Anyway, I have a theory. I heard a lot of what Zodor said when I was above it on the walkway."

"You let me carry on a conversation with him," she said wryly.

"I couldn't get the salt open. It was in one of those heavy-duty bags with the string at the top that's supposed to unravel if you pull it right. And then the salt was hard as a rock. I had to break it up quietly to keep it from hearing me."

"Christ, Will." She gave a dramatic sigh meant to tease him. "Okay, let's hear Stan Herlinger's *Theory Number Four*."

"The things it said. Did it sound like bragging to you?"

She tried to remember. "I really couldn't tell, being scared out of my mind and whatnot."

His voice dropped to match her low tone. "Trust me, you weren't the only one," he agreed. "But now that I think about it, he sounded arrogant. I think he was boasting about all he'd done."

"Seriously?"

"Or at least exaggerating. Just because a being...or entity...or whatever the fuck that thing was...is intelligent, who's to say it's *socialized*? Think about it; why do small children lie and make up stories? They're not developed enough to see the foolishness of it."

"You're seeing more into this than I am, I guess. All I could think about was a towering statue of blue ectoplasm that wanted to absorb me."

"Yeah." He twisted toward her on the bench and his voice grew softer. "I can imagine it was a lot scarier being down there right in front of it."

"Well, it's gone now. That's what's important." She grasped his hand and wove her fingers into his. "Thanks to you."

"Thanks to *you*," he told her. "You did most of the heavy lifting."

"Thanks to us both," she corrected. "We make a good team."

She loved his bashful smile, the way his ears turned pink.

"We do."

A comfortable silence stretched. She sipped her tea, letting the caffeine work magic in her bloodstream.

Finally, she risked the question she'd been afraid to ask. "What will you do now?"

Will looked at his books in the window display, seemingly lost in thought. "Well, I'm having my mother's home renovated for her wheelchair, and a property manager is packing up my apartment in New York—"

"I meant about your next book."

"I can write anywhere, Jess."

She felt his measuring gaze fall on her.

"I know. I mean—"

"I'm staying in Pine Bluff."

He set his cup down and took both her hands in his, and Jess held her breath.

"I came back for my mom, but I'm staying for you."

She couldn't speak, couldn't even breathe.

"I meant what I said. I love you, Jess. I've always loved you, and I always will. You're not just the amazing girl from my past anymore. You're the woman who saved the world."

Tears stung her eyes. "I love you too, Will."

He smiled, transformed into that goofy teenager again, and Jess rejoiced in the enchantment of that smile. He cupped her cheeks and kissed her, and Jess realized the heavy contentment rolling through her body was *normalcy*. It was such a foreign feeling she almost didn't know what to do with it.

"When my mother told me you'd gotten married, a piece of me broke off and shattered. I thought I'd lost my only chance to tell you how I feel. I won't make that mistake again. Let's *always* save the world together."

"What are you saying?"

Did she speak those words aloud? She wasn't sure and only knew that she heard them in her own head.

He slid off the bench. Dropped to one knee. "Marry, me, Jessica Harding. Be mine. Today, tomorrow, next week, next year. Ten years from now."

A velvet box materialized in his hands. He opened it, revealing a sparkling square-cut diamond set in white gold.

"I..."

Panic filled his eyes. "Even if you don't want to be married now," he said quickly. "Just know that if you ever do, consider me the front contender. I'll never tire of waiting for you. I'll take better care of you than anyone—"

"Yes."

"W...what?"

She smiled. "Yes, Will Taylor. I'll marry you."

"You will?"

She nodded. "Yes."

"When?"

Now she laughed. "Whenever you'd like."

-THE END-

About the Author

Many years ago, in a galaxy far, far away, I signed my first contract with a publisher who started me off on this wonderful journey. They handled everything from editing to marketing to cover design to formatting, and did a lot of hand-holding along the way. Over the years I had the good fortune to work with six amazing editors at four publishing houses. I learned so much from them, and those experiences were absolutely invaluable, but that journey was nothing compared to the voyage I'm on now.

I've since ventured off as an Independent, which feels like getting off a plane in a foreign country and hiking into the wilderness with nothing more than a Swiss Army knife. I format my own layouts, design my own covers, and hire my own editors.

And I do my own marketing. Promoting books feels like standing on a mountaintop shouting to a vast valley below where I cannot see a single soul. I can only hope they are there, and they are listening.

I am completely alone.

Except for you, dear reader. If you liked The Unforgotten, you can help this weary traveler by leaving a review at your favorite book retailer. Your reviews help my book stand out among hundreds of thousands of other books, and helps other readers like you find it.

To learn more about my books and what's coming next, visit my website at www.avabradley.com.